PRAISE FOR *THE G* ... *S*

A brilliantly drawn, cruel world, where a violent war from the air threatens two sisters with separation and corruption. But love and devotion – and a way to harness wings – *might* save them all! Anna writes powerfully and passionately about the struggles of love, sisterhood and the supernatural. With echoes of classical mythology, this is a very modern story of choices – and truth that transcends rules and boundaries. And it's one of the most exciting flights I've ever been on!

BARRY CUNNINGHAM
Publisher
Chicken House

THE GIRL WHO GREW WINGS

ANNA WATERWORTH

2 PALMER STREET, FROME,
SOMERSET BA11 1DS

Text © Anna Waterworth 2023

First published in Great Britain in 2023
Chicken House
2 Palmer Street
Frome, Somerset BA11 1DS
United Kingdom
www.chickenhousebooks.com

Chicken House/Scholastic Ireland, 89E Lagan Road, Dublin Industrial Estate,
Glasnevin, Dublin D11 HP5F, Republic of Ireland

Cover and interior design by Andrew Davis
Typeset by Dorchester Typesetting Group Ltd
Printed in Great Britain by Clays, Elcograf S.p.A

FSC
www.fsc.org
MIX
Paper | Supporting
responsible forestry
FSC® C018072

1 3 5 7 9 10 8 6 4 2

British Library Cataloguing in Publication data available.

PB ISBN 978-1-912626-54-0
eISBN 978-1-915026-69-9

For Simon
You hold the hand inside me

ℙROLOGUE

First there was nothing. Then there were three: the Moon Goddess, the Sun God and his Divine Shadow. Both the Sun God and his Divine Shadow loved the Moon and craved her affection, but she could love only one. She chose the Sun. And from their union came children. Mankind.

What of the Divine Shadow? Filled with jealousy, he slithered beneath the Earth and created a land of eternal ice — cold enough to numb the most broken of hearts. And every year, from this Underworld, he snatches a peek over the horizon to spy upon his love, gripping the Earth in his wintry claws.

1

ICARI

Demons of the Underworld do not deserve their wings, we mortals do. Not to fly, but to flee, for even a pinch of powder ground from their milk-white feathers allows us to escape our earthly pains. Mama and I are Healers, so we're permitted to possess and administer the silver dust known as devil wing for medicinal purposes only. We are not, under any circumstance, allowed to trade or sell it; this privilege is reserved for the High Priest and noblemen, for whilst devil wing numbs pain, it soon makes slaves of those who ingest it, and he who controls the drug, controls the addict.

Power begets power.

So it's no surprise that my limbs shake as Mama and I trek through the oasis to the marketplace, one vial each of devil wing hidden in our apron pockets. Mama said we only needed one vial, but we brought another just in case – sometimes traders can get greedy. The vials themselves are no bigger than amulets, yet the closer we get to the village, the heavier they grow. Soon they'll be boulders that bend our spines.

Mama and I are not criminals. We are in the business of helping the sick, not nurturing addiction. Yet our sanatorium is unusually full, draining the shelves of ointments and linen wraps, and devil wing is the only thing we have to trade of any worth. I inhale deeply, trying to still my nerves, a nest of vipers in my belly.

'It will be fine, Icari,' Mama whispers as we wind our way through the huddle of mud huts towards the village agora. 'Nothing I haven't done before. Try not to fidget so. You are ten years and six, practically an adult.' Yet despite her words, her knuckles protrude from her fists like polished stones as she grips her medical satchel, a telltale sign she's as anxious as me.

The scent of moist earth and jasmine blossom makes way for that of plaited breads and flower oils as the agora comes into view, a large clearing in the mud huts and sycamores. Normally, I love the agora – the clamour of people, the children playing with stacking stones, the air thick and moist with river dew. Normally, I don't have a vial of devil wing stashed in my apron, weighted with the possibility of twenty public lashings.

Today is market day, and the expanse of sunbaked mud hides beneath the usual selection of higgledy-piggledy stalls, set out in a crescent shape reaching from the marble temple of Father Sun, Guardian of Life, at one end, to the stone monument of Mother Moon, Guardian of Death, at the other. Locals and traders from nearby villages gather to sell clay pots and woven papyrus baskets, spools of bright fabrics, and hampers filled with barley or salted meats. A boy turns a desert hog on a giant spit whilst the flames hiss their objection beneath; the smell of roasted flesh taints the air, causing my mouth to fill with saliva.

The appearance of the city guard is unusual – they generally don't care what goes on beyond the city walls – yet still I'm relieved when I note their absence. As if reading my thoughts, Mama squeezes my arm and smiles her soft smile.

'We will be quick,' she says. 'Father Sun will keep us safe. And I know the trader, remember? He's expecting us.'

As we cross the agora, she glances to the Sun Temple, a thin needle of grey barely able to contain one tenth of the villagers in worship. The symbol of the Sun God gazes down at us, the face of the temple: a gold disc with doleful eyes and a sheath of barley slung across its middle. He is the God of the Healer, so naturally, I glance at him and kiss my fist, a sign of respect. But my eyes, ever curious, drift without permission towards the monument of Mother Moon – Goddess of the Embalmer – at the opposite end of the agora.

'Icari,' Mama whispers, following my line of sight. 'Remember your Calling.'

'Surely there is no harm in looking, Mama.'

She breathes out slowly through her teeth.

Only a lucky few are born with the Calling, meaning they are able to call on one of the Celestial Trio: Father Sun, Mother Moon or the Divine Shadow. I am a Healer, which means I have the Sun God in my veins, enhancing my ability to treat disease and injury, just like Mama. Embalmers, however, call on the Moon Goddess, preserving the dead with such skill, their bodies never decay, never returning to the dirt from whence they came. And the Alchemists, the rarest and most feared of all the gifted, summon the power of the Divine Shadow, enabling them to transmute bad into good, be that rust-coated metal to gold, damaged crops into fields that grow tall and thrive, or the wildest of storms into the calmest of skies.

It is only permitted to practise one Calling in the Sunlands – indeed, it is only permitted to *possess* one – so when Mama discovered she had two in her blood, Healer and Alchemist, a target was painted upon her head, splashed in colours of fear and envy. She only practises as a Healer now, and so far, she has escaped all punishment but for idle gossip and the occasional jibe, for Healers are well-loved.

'Come, Icari,' Mama says, pulling me from my thoughts.

I follow her towards a stall slightly removed from the others; a misplaced tooth in a perfect smile. I have never seen a stall like this before, magical and disturbing in equal measure. Row upon row of glass bottles glisten in the heat, some containing jewel-bright liquids flecked with golds or fragments of petals, others stuffed with coiled snakes submerged in vinegar, or animal paws preserved in vivid powders. On either side of the stall's wooden frame, sheets of starched linen are displayed like flags, pinned with sun-dried scorpions and lizards. One such sheet holds an array of butterflies, their wings fanned out and tacked in position. A small whimper escapes my mouth.

Mama's arm is around my shoulder in a heartbeat. 'Worry not, they are free now.'

I know what she means: free to fly to Mother Moon and rest for eternity with the stars, free from the hardship of life. But my eyes still smart at the thought of their pretty, flightless wings forever frozen in this outstretched position, as if death plays a cruel joke, or the Divine Shadow himself mocks them.

A trader steps from behind the stall. He wears the simple linen tunic of a male villager, yet the knowing, sun-wrinkled look of a traveller. When he sees Mama, recognition flashes on his face, though he covers it swiftly with a neutral bow of his head.

Mama's hand slips from my back. 'We need bone dust and the tips of the eucalyptus leaf, if you have them.' She pauses. 'And mint-infused linen wraps.'

'Come, won't you see for yourself, Healer?' His voice brims with warmth.

Mama slips inside the stall, and I let my eyes wander, the anxiety finally dissipating in my gut. Soon, the deal will be done.

Beyond the mud huts, across the oasis, the city Appollis climbs up the great mountain of the same name, and crowing from the peak is the citadel, home to the High Priest of the Sunlands, with palaces and temples of marble and gold. This is where Mama trained as an Alchemist over twenty years ago, though she rarely talks of it now. Poorer folk like us live outside the city walls in the oasis that rings the foot of the mountain. The oasis is as bountiful as it is beautiful and lies between Appollis and the Redland desert, providing the city a buffer from sand clouds, desert beasts and the fire-viper-haired witches of the Farlands, who are said to steal women and turn men to stone with only a glance.

Away from Appollis, the Nubi river peeks between the trees, a ribbon of blue that feeds the oasis. The heat in the agora is unbearable, stripped of any shade, yet hemmed in by trees and buildings that block the river breeze, and I gaze at the waters, longing to throw off my tunic and cool my skin in its icy depths, allowing it to revive me as it does the whole oasis.

On the edge of the agora, something strange catches my eye. A pile of dried grass and wood, of loose desert weeds and twists of old bark; a pile made strange by the fact it has clearly been gathered in the Redlands where the ground grows cracked and arid, and brought to the oasis in preparation for a bonfire.

'Why would they build a bonfire there?' I call to Mama.

'What's that, dear-heart?' She moves towards me, temporarily abandoning the deal.

I point. 'Look. Someone's built a bonfire on the treeline.' I glance at Mama. 'Don't they normally have bonfires in the middle of the agora, away from the huts and the plants?'

Fear tremors beneath her features. 'Yes, and not on market day.' Her voice is hollow, removed. She looks at the trader, her face hardening, then moves towards me, stretching out her palm in a gesture that is both pleading and demanding. 'Give me the devil wing, Icari.'

Glancing about me, I shake my head, alarmed she would talk of it so openly. 'But ... people might see.'

'Now is not the time to argue – just give it to me.' Her voice is all spikes and angles, completely unfamiliar, and I recoil as if slapped.

'Mama? What's the matter?'

'If they catch you with it ...'

'If *who* catches me?' I close my fist firmly around the vial in my apron.

Her eyes slide away from me, her expression pulling between fear and affection. The name of the High Priest leaves her lips in a whisper. 'Uriel.'

Following her gaze, I find him part hidden in the treeline, his robes of silver and gold sparkling amidst the shadows. Despite the arrogant tilt of his chin, he is alarmingly hand-some, with a regal jaw and a shock of charcoal hair spilling on to light brown skin. On his head sits an ornate headdress of gold-and-silver vines that hold the symbol of the Alchemist to his forehead – a wisp of shadow, snaking upwards like a plume of smoke, made all the darker by the backdrop of a golden sun.

The High Priest is the most powerful man and Alchemist in the Sunlands. Mama once told me that she trained with him at the citadel, though it is hard to imagine their paths merging; everything about him shouts of wealth and import-ance, whereas Mama remains humble and poor.

Beside him stands a tall lady, whose black gown and silver headdress tell me she's Madame Embalmer, tutor to the embalming students at the citadel. Indeed, her silver-streaked hair and milk-pale skin suggest she's so dedicated to Mother Moon, she's modelled her look on the goddess herself. Madame's eyes lock on to Mama, and she clasps Uriel's arm as if holding him at bay. Her lips move, a frantic blur, and whilst I'm unable to hear what she's saying, I can tell from the panic in her expression that she's trying to talk the High Priest out of something.

'Mama? What's happening?' My voice trembles. What could Uriel want with our little village?

He holds Mama's gaze for a moment, then raises a hand.

Two burly guards appear beside Madame Embalmer and guide her away, even as her desperation rises.

Madame's voice peaks and I catch her words on the breeze. 'Don't do this, Uriel, I beg of you. There must be another way.'

I'm about to ask Mama what Madame means, when more guards emerge, stepping from behind trees and huts, filtering through the crowds and converging like a swarm of locusts before descending upon us. Terror unfurls through my body and I reach towards Mama, whose face holds the reflection of my own – features pulled wide by panic. For a moment, our fingers connect, then the gruff hands of the soldiers are upon us, wrenching us apart.

The guards' tunics are slashed diagonally down the middle, one half gold and boasting the symbol of Father Sun, and the other, silver, with Mother Moon holding court. If it weren't for the long spears clutched in their hands and the crossbows slung across their backs, I would appreciate gazing upon their splendour.

Two guards hold me steady, expecting me to fight, their fingers digging into the exposed flesh of my upper arm. They needn't have bothered. Mama once told me that fear divides us into three groups: the fighters, the runners and the statues. Sephie, my twin sister, is without doubt a fighter. I'd always assumed I'd be a runner, but current circumstances suggest I am a statue. So as well as being completely paralysed, unable to snatch a breath, I'm crushed by disappointment.

A broad guard shoves Mama's arm behind her back, ignoring her yelp of pain. Even this isn't enough to awaken my courage. My ears ring, my heart slams against my ribs, and the vial inside my apron is now heavier than a hundred stones, so the guards have to drag me to the centre of the agora behind my mama.

The punishment for the illicit sale of devil wing is twenty public lashings.

An explosion of adrenaline floods my system and the world tilts.

A crowd begins to form, watching us with sad, helpless eyes. Despite the whispers of witchcraft, Mama is well-loved by the villagers – our whole family is, for it is to us they come when they are at their most vulnerable, and we never turn them away.

A man wearing a sneer and a headband of leaves dipped in gold, denoting his status as a general, steps towards us. His face reminds me of the pickled snake in the jar, with its pale, lifeless skin, black wide-set eyes, and a broad mouth with lips so thin it's as if they've been removed. He leans towards Mama and in one fluid motion plucks the vial from her apron. The silver powder sparkles within, a dusting of frost, and he holds it to the sun as if examining a jewel, clicking his tongue against the roof of his mouth.

'Devil wing?' Even his voice is a snake – fanged and quick – and when he looks at Mama, violence simmers in his eyes.

I would do anything to help Mama, for she is my best friend, my mentor, my world, and I know that not having reached my eighteenth birthday yet, any judgement of me will be far softer than any of her. So why can't I say that the devil wing is mine? Fear has turned my words into leaden balls, which clank around my belly, too heavy to rise up my throat, let alone burst from my mouth.

Whatever happens to Mama now, it will be my fault.

2

ICARI

'I am the village Healer,' Mama says, still restrained by the guard. Her hair, a dark veil, falls before her face, yet she refuses to look away or lower her voice. 'My possession of devil wing is permitted by order of the citadel.'

Approving murmurs swell from the villagers, yet the guards silence them, collectively slamming the wooden butts of their spears into the earth and sending a mighty *thwack* vibrating through the surrounding mud huts. A reminder of how strong they are, and thereby how weak we are.

Mama looks to the High Priest, who continues to hover, watchful and sombre in the treeline. 'Uriel,' she shouts. 'What have I done to deserve such treatment?'

The High Priest simply lowers his gaze.

Whip-like, the General grips Mama's cheeks, squeezing so hard her lips pucker and she whines in pain. 'As Healer, you are permitted to use devil wing to ease your patients' suffering. You are *not* permitted to sell it.' He throws her away from him.

'I don't intend to sell it,' Mama replies, her deception curdling the air.

The trader points an accusatory finger at Mama, and the

voice that moments ago held only warmth now holds only disdain. 'The sorceress lies, my lord. She just offered me a trade – devil wing in exchange for medical supplies.'

The General feigns shock, then glances at the crowd in a show more befitting of a grand open-air theatre than our little village; he actually looks disappointed when the villagers, rather than outraged, simply look afraid and confused. He must know that nobody cares if we trade devil wing for supplies, so long as we can treat them when they fall ill. Indeed, the guards don't usually bother themselves with such transactions, yet here they are, a small army, having hidden in the surrounding oasis.

The trader backs away, but not so far that I can't see the flash of coin deposited into his palm by a nearby soldier. The realization lands like a fist against my cheek. It was a set-up.

As confirmation of my theory, Mama spits at him and hisses the word, 'Traitor.'

Even as the injustice builds inside me, it shocks me deeply to see Mama act this way when she's usually so soft-hearted.

Leon, my parents' closest friend, pushes through the crowd with strong, confident arms. Just the sight of his kind face, his warm brown skin, dappled with sweat, and long black hair sends relief filtering through my body. Leon will make everything OK; he always does. He is the Embalmer of the village, and as such, demands respect, for the souls of the dead may only journey to the afterlife if their bodies are preserved by hands blessed with the Calling of the Moon Goddess. The guards will listen to him.

Ruari, his seven-year-old son, hovers at his side. He is a smaller version of his papa, all warmth and spark, so it is unusual to see his expression so pained – then I realize it's because he's seen the guards.

Leon stoops so he can whisper in Ruari's ear. I read his lips. 'Quick, run to the sanatorium and fetch Giorgos.'

Ruari catches my eye, controls the quiver of his bottom lip, and then slips back into the crowd. I suddenly feel very foolish that I never thought to send for Papa.

Straightening up, Leon uses his height to its full advantage. 'What is the meaning of this?' His voice is as strong as his face, and the fingers tapping against his Mother Moon brooch, telling of his role as Embalmer, hold not even a shiver of an apology. Leon is clearly a fighter, I tell myself with a pang of shame.

The General weighs up his opponent, then selects a more appeasing tone. 'This woman has been caught trading devil wing.'

The tendons in Leon's neck stand out like dried river reeds. '*This woman* is the village Healer, blessed with the Calling of Father Sun and trained at the citadel. She demands your respect, your praise, yet you treat her like a common criminal.'

The crowd begins to stir, only to be silenced by another thump of spears against dried clay.

'She trained in alchemy,' the General fires back. 'Yet now she is a Healer. It is not natural or permitted to have more than one Calling.'

Leon exhales with anger. 'See her brooch?' He jabs a finger at the tiny pin on Mama's tunic. 'The citadel accepted Daeda's chosen path years ago.' He spies the High Priest Alchemist and his scrunched face opens with hope. 'Uriel, you must stop this madness.' Yet as he moves towards the figure in the trees, the guards block his way with a cross of spears.

'Her brooch does not render her exempt from the law,' the General says, his tone quickly shifting to something more dangerous. 'And the trading of devil wing is a serious matter.'

Leon falls silent for a moment, his eyes swinging between the soldiers. No matter how strong he is, how well respected, or how true the light of Mother Moon flows in his veins, he does not have at his disposal a small army clutching weapons.

The reaction of the crowd — snatched whispers and a flurry of gasps — alerts me that something significant is occurring near the treeline. A group of guards have begun to move the dried vegetation at the edge of the agora to the centre, their faces as devoid of life as the firewood in their arms. Instinctively, the stall owners move away, dragging their wares with them. Leon follows my line of sight and all of the bravado falls from his face.

I know what's happening — of course I know — yet my brain is as frozen as my body, and I simply can't accept it. Even as they bring the stake from the treeline and plunge it in the centre of the pyre, the earth submitting to the filed point with a resentful sigh; even as they slop the oil drained from the trunk of a firetree upon the mound, transforming it to a glistening rainbow beneath the sun, and the pungent scent assaults my nostrils; even when the villagers scream and Leon starts throwing his fists and feet at the guards only to be overwhelmed with a downpour of wooden spears wielded like clubs, I still can't accept it.

'You cannot do this,' Leon roars, his nose and chin

bloodied, his left eye closed. 'The punishment for trading devil wing is the whip, not execution.' His words sound slushy and I notice his bottom lip is puffed and bleeding. 'And burning?' he shouts. 'Her body will never journey to the heavens if it cannot be embalmed. She has a family. Please, for the love of Mother Moon.' He looks to Uriel once again. 'Uriel, my lord, *please.*'

The High Priest blinks slowly, then circles his hand in the air, gesturing for his men to proceed. As he shares one last look with Mama, I swear a solitary tear glistens on his lashline.

The guards lead Mama towards the stake, only just pulling her back as she darts towards me and whispers, 'Tell Sephie and Papa that I love them.'

Numb, paralysed, somehow I manage a stilted nod.

She holds my gaze with wide, tear-filled eyes. 'And I love you too, Icari, with all my heart.'

And only now do I truly accept what is about to happen.

They are going to burn Mama.

My knees buckle, the bones pulled from my body, and the earthy colours of the agora taper into black; if it weren't for the soldiers holding me up, I would smack the ground like a sack of skin. When I rally, Leon is by my side, and the guards, perhaps realizing I am little threat, allow him to wrap an arm around my waist. He becomes an anchor and I begin to weep, great waves of anguish pushing through me. Surely my entire body will shake to pieces, come apart at the joints, if I cry any harder.

Not only am I to lose Mama in life, I will lose her in death. For an incomplete corpse means an incomplete soul, unable to journey to the afterlife. She will simply cease to be.

Mama is lifted on to the pyre and lashed to the stake with crude leather strips. Her black hair hangs around her face, and her olive skin gleams in the sun. I've never seen her look so proud, so beautiful. And I want to wail and scream, to throw my fists with the force of the Divine Shadow himself, even though I remain immobilized by fear, pinned like a flightless butterfly, only able to sob and sob and sob.

The General stands before the pyre. His face glints with pleasure and sweat as he addresses Mama. 'Do you, Daeda, confess to dealing devil wing without regard to the citadel and, as such, worshipping the Divine Shadow?'

Mama shakes her head, raising her voice above the thick air of the agora. 'I was trading devil wing for medical supplies so I could treat the wounded and sick.'

The General drops his voice, a low hiss that I only just pull from the buzz of terror. 'Perhaps we should search your daughter? I wonder if she carries devil wing also.'

Of course – the vial in my pocket. All I need to do is lift it into the sunshine, screaming the words, *I asked Mama to carry a vial for me – both vials are mine!* Yet it is as if I am a corpse in the grip of rigor mortis, and I choke on the words.

'No, please, not Icari,' Mama whispers, her face slack, like the skin is no longer attached to her skull. It is the first time I have seen her look truly afraid.

He nods, his voice lifting. 'Then I ask again – do you, Daeda, confess to worshipping the Divine Shadow?'

Silence.

Then, Mama croaks a resentful, 'Yes.'

He grins. 'Pardon?'

'YES!' she screams, her voice tearing at the edges. 'I confess to worshipping the Divine Shadow.'

A giant crevasse opens inside of me, splitting my body down the middle so that I can't breathe or think or even cry. Mama has confessed to witchcraft. Even her name shall be destroyed by this man. I collapse against Leon, my limbs trembling, and gaze at my glorious mama through a haze of tears.

Without another word, the General grabs a stick topped with an oil-soaked rag and plunges it into the firepit beneath the roasted desert hog. A wave of nausea slams into me as I realize Mama faces the same fate as the charred animal. Some villagers begin to cry, whilst others appear horrified by the unfolding scene. All the while, the General sidles towards the pyre, leaving a trail of smoke in his wake.

I hold Mama's gaze, wishing I could rip her from the flames, or throw myself upon her and cradle her whilst she burns. But I'm simply too scared.

The General holds the flame above the pyre, pausing only to glance at the High Priest.

For the first time since arriving, Uriel speaks, each word a carefully aimed weapon. 'By order of the citadel, the sorceress must burn.'

'No,' I whisper.

I suddenly feel like I'm far away, watching the scene through an upended glass, or perhaps trapped in the space between waking and sleep, unable to emerge from a cloying nightmare. The world slows and the General touches the flaming stick to the pyre. The fire accelerates with painful speed as the flames grow around Mama's feet, and what started as a ring of golden shoots crawling up the kindling quickly transforms into an angry blaze – a flock of red and orange birds, flapping their wings in a roar of smoke.

Yet Mama does not scream. Not once. She barely even winces.

She is using her powers to numb her pain. For the Alchemist inside her did not die when she chose the path of Healer. Indeed, she could call upon the Divine Shadow and quell the flames in a heartbeat if she chose to. But if she does, they will burn me instead.

Her final act is to protect me.

Through the film of shock, I keep holding her gaze, ignoring the flames as they climb higher and higher, clawing their way up her body.

I'm here, Mama.

I love you, Mama.

And just before she disappears behind a wall of fire, her beautiful face gone for ever, the crowd begins to whisper. Within moments, people are pointing upwards, jumping on the spot, shrieks of wonder filling the air.

The smoke forms a column of grey, only to break apart above the village into a million flakes – pieces of soot or the blackest of snow. And as the flakes disperse, they gain form, clarity, weight. They become butterflies. At first, ghost-like and fragmented, but gradually transmuting into real creatures. Black, shining, perfectly formed, and moving up, up, up towards the sun until they are no more than tiny dots, journeying to the heavens in spite of it all.

You are free, Mama. You are finally free.

3

ICARI

Leon supports me as I stumble down the mud path towards the sanatorium. Anyone would think it was me who took the beating, my movements juddering, my body broken, for it is loss that has pulled me apart at the seams as if I were no more than a paddle doll.

Sephie and Papa run towards us, dried earth flying from their feet as they kick up the mud trail. Ruari struggles to keep up, his cheeks two splodges of pink beneath a film of sweat.

'Icari, what has happened?' Papa shouts. He scoops me into his arms and I crumple against him, wishing I was once again a babe and he could make everything OK with soft words. 'Where is Mama?' The fear in his voice makes me cry even harder.

'They burnt her,' Leon says.

Such simple words, yet they pull the earth from beneath my feet.

Sephie's scream hits my ear like the cry of a wounded animal. We are twins, our connection strong, and I feel her pain like a horse's kick to my gut. She sinks to her knees, her face all twisted up so she doesn't look like my sister any more. And suddenly, the desire to heal, to soothe, knits me back together, at least enough so my limbs become my own again and I'm able to untangle myself from Papa's embrace and rush to her side. She clings to me, her sobs mingling with her screams.

'I'm so sorry,' I whisper. 'I tried to stop them, I tried, but I couldn't move.' Guilt is the hammer that cracks my voice, causing it to disintegrate into tiny pieces like a smashed pot.

Either Sephie doesn't hear me or she simply doesn't reply, too consumed by her own grief to tend to mine. I squeeze her against me, wishing I could somehow absorb her pain, save her the way that I could not save Mama. Then Papa, Ruari and Leon surround us, leaning into us with their warmth and tears, and there we stay, slumped on the mud trail and cradled by the oasis, just weeping and weeping until we are no more than dried-up husks.

That night, Sephie is inconsolable – she cannot eat, drink or muster any words. All she can do is sit on our papyrus sleep mat, her knees gathered up as if she were a babe yet to be birthed, rocking and wailing into the darkness of our single-roomed mud hut. I wrap my arms around her, yet am unable to hold her still. A breeze wafts through the window – a crude square cut into the clay walls – and stirs the painted veil that separates our sleeping area from the rest of the hut. I inhale deeply so I can savour the perfume of the roses, Mama's favourite, and let the agony of grief wind through me.

Sephie's breathing, however, is laboured, her lungs flutter-ing with no concern for their usual rhythm and saliva rattling at the back of her throat. I have never before known anyone react this way, and working at the sanatorium, I have seen my share of grief. Then Mama always said that whereas I was a peach, soft and sweet with a hidden core of strength, Sephie was a pomegranate, her hard shell built from fight, yet her heart as fragile and ready to come apart as one hundred glassy seeds. I finally see what Mama meant.

'Sephie, dear-heart, you should try to sleep,' I say. Nursing her distracts me from my own grief, my own guilt, and allows Mama to live through my actions – she was a Healer, after all. 'Shall I tell you about the butterflies again? About how she felt no pain and she journeyed to the heavens in spite of the flames?'

A guttural sound dragged from the Underworld itself fills the hut, and Sephie begins pulling at her own hair.

'Sephie, stop!' I grab at her hands, but she smacks me away.

Dark clumps settle around us, dusting our sleep mat like black ribbons. Desperate, I kneel before her, gripping her wrists as tight as I'm able, ducking low and forcing her to meet my eye.

'Oh, my darling, what can I do? Please tell me?' I say.

'Make the hurt go away.' Her breath is tart, her lips cracked, yet they are the first words she's spoken since hearing the news of Mama's death.

My eyes immediately click to the place Mama hides the devil wing. No. I mustn't even consider it. Because of its addictive qualities, only those enduring unimaginable pain caused by the likes of amputation or childbirth are permitted to ingest devil wing. I couldn't bear it if Sephie became enslaved in its frosty claws. And my sister is special, the

Calling of the Alchemist so strong that her blood runs thick with shadow. Who knows the impact of consuming devil wing on one already so entwined with the Underworld. Perhaps a tincture of hazel root and bone dust will help instead.

Tenderly, I release her, then pin back the privacy veil so I can ghost across the clay floor to the water pot on the wooden table. A few medical jars glint on the shelves by the door, and I begin gathering my ingredients, careful not to wake Papa, who whimpers from behind his own cloth wall, his sleep plagued with nightmares.

The light of Mother Moon streams through the doorway, dusting everything in its path silver and guiding my hand as I ladle some water into a small wooden cup. The Calling rises inside me – the warmth of Father Sun flowing through my veins like heated oils or melted wax – steadying my resolve for the first time in hours, and I'm able to unscrew the pots and mix my tinctures and powders without any spillage. My finger leaves a golden trail of light in the potion as I slowly stir. Usually, the light of the Healer makes me smile as it is a link not just to the Sun God, but to Mama, yet today it makes my heart implode with loss.

'Icari!' Sephie calls to me in a voice beyond fragile, reminding me of those pinned-out butterfly wings.

I pause. 'Yes, dear-heart.'

She lays her hand on her stomach, directly over her navel, where we were bound to Mama for nine moon cycles, and through Mama, bound to each other. It is a gesture that only we know, for that is where we feel each other's joy and pain, regardless of our distance from one another. Normally, it feels like a hook pulling beneath my navel, yet right now, my stomach is filled with magma. What kind of Healer would I be if I didn't oblige? What kind of sister would I be?

Quickly, I unhook the veil so that it drifts back in place, obscuring Sephie's view, for Mama always insisted Sephie should not discover her hiding place. Then, crossing to the firepit, I slip my fingers behind the soot-stained rocks and remove the loosened clay brick at the base of the wall. The pyramid of glass vials catches in the light of Mother Moon, and I grab the topmost, which only hours ago rested in my pocket.

'Forgive me, Father Sun,' I whisper to the reed ceiling, grateful he cannot see what I'm about to do.

Removing the cork, I allow myself to stare at the powder for a moment. It always seems strange to hold the actual ground-up wings of demons, and I never fail to try to envision the beasts, even though I have never seen a winged demon in real life. Nobody has. Yet tales of their beauty and cruelty have endured for centuries.

Legend says that in the beginning, the souls of the embalmed would rest with Mother Moon, whereas the souls of those left to rot would simply cease to be. There was no river of lost souls. Not yet. But when the Divine Shadow slithered to the Underworld and created his land of eternal winter, he grew lonely. So to spite the goddess he created an underground river to trap the souls of the embalmed; if he couldn't have her love, he would have her souls. But much to his annoyance, he was only able to attract the souls of those who'd lived a wicked, ungodly life, leaving Mother Moon with the souls of the kind and the good. And so the fate of the dead was rewritten. A soul could go three ways now: to the Underworld, to the heavens, or straight to oblivion.

Yet this still wasn't enough. The souls of the damned didn't provide the companionship the Divine Shadow desired, so he shed his serpent skin and took the form of a man called Aïdes, and from his discarded skin, he forged an army of demons known as the Samael: men with bodies encrusted with frost and two white wings sprouting from their backs. Centuries ago, they invaded the citadel, and if it weren't for Father Sun sending his own army of gold-winged men known as the Illios, Appollis would have fallen and Aïdes would have wrapped the Earth in cold and shadows for evermore.

It is said that after the great battle in the sky, the streets of Appollis ran silver with the blood of demons. The pile of Samael bodies was so great, it filled the citadel courtyard, and the smoke from their pyre was visible from as far as the ocean. But before they were burnt, their wings were removed, which is how a dwindling store of Samael plumes still remains in the Temple of Mother Moon, safe in the citadel.

It is also how a small vial of devil wing now rests in my palm like a shard of ice.

Three firm taps, and I've deposited a hefty dose into the cup. Then, slipping the vial back in its hiding place, I do my best to obscure the wonky brick with a dusting of cinders and dried grasses.

Sephie jolts when I lay my hand on her back. Even in the dimness, her eyes are two red holes sunk into bruises, her usually strong face scrunched like a piece of parchment. I hold the cup to her lips, and with trembling breaths, she slurps down the liquid. A silver string drizzles down her chin and falls on to my hand, so cold it makes me gasp.

Her appetite sated, she leans back against the clay wall and whispers, 'It tastes of winter.'

I watch with relief as her eyes finally close and she reclines on her sleep mat, a faint smile touching her pretty features. Yet without Sephie to care for, my grief returns tenfold – grief and the need to make sense of why they murdered my darling mama. Because I could have saved her, *should* have saved her, if only I'd been brave enough to take the blame for possessing devil wing.

If only I hadn't frozen.

One unanswered question breeds another until my head is a swirling mass of words and injustice. The cup still trembles in my hands, a drop of liquid sparkling in the bottom, so desperate to find peace, I tip it on to my tongue and swallow. It marks a tingling path down the inside of my throat, an icy finger running from my lips to my sternum. Cool hands run across my skin, coaxing the aches from deep within, dampening the memories and the horror, soothing the heat of trauma like a balm. The chasm inside my chest is still there, the wounds of loss and shame still wide and raw, yet I now look at them with detachment. I curl around my sister so that we lie as we once did inside Mama's womb.

It really does taste of winter.

4

One Year Later

SEPHIE

I've only been out of the shade for a few minutes and Father Sun is making me sweat like a sow in heat. He's also turned my favourite jasmine plant into a tumbleweed, all matted and dried up like our donkey Sabu's tail. Father Sun is, quite frankly, a monumental pain in the arse.

My fingers itch with magic.

'Sephie, don't even think about it.' Icari shoots me a warning look from her perch on the wooden bench, a half-plucked chicken carcass slung over her knee like a strange, gruesome quilt. She may lack the gift of alchemy, but she grasped at birth the gift of face-reading. I imagine we lay in our woven papyrus crib, side by side, and she turned to me and thought, *Well, you're going to be trouble, aren't you, sister.* She was right. She was born right. Well, I say right is dull, so I bury my hands in the earth and send my focus down.

The soil is parched, its thirst running as deep as the cracks criss-crossing its surface. I know how it feels. Sending my awareness deeper, I find a more content, peaceful place, where the earth is as soft as moss and dark as molasses.

'Sephie, stop!' Icari's voice lands sharp as an arrow in my side, but I let it bounce from my skin and clatter to the ground as I urge the earth to change. Transmute. Nature submits to the Divine Shadow, it always does, and I sense the moisture filtering slowly upwards until it cools the tips of my fingers.

It is such a relief to embrace my Calling, the wondrous, forbidden part of me. I begin to laugh, deep and sensual, as if thunder fills my belly.

Icari hauls me back, but it's too late. Ha! I look from Icari's angry face to the jasmine flower before us. Petals unfold, each bloom glowing like a tiny star against the clay walls of the sanatorium. The scent of pollen makes me dizzy.

'Don't upset yourself,' I say, dusting my fingers against my apron. 'The courtyard is entirely enclosed. I doubt the birds will tell my secret to the High Priest, and if they dare, I'll transform them into slugs.' I cackle into the sky, a pristine tableau of blue.

Alchemists can't transmute animals, but Icari doesn't laugh. She doesn't even smile. In fact, I think she may have swallowed a lemon. It seems that being right all the time erodes your humour.

She flicks her head to the nearest opening, her voice a frustrated hiss. 'In case you've forgotten, there are windows and doors. What if one of the patients had seen?'

'They're far too ill to concern themselves with my gardening,' I reply.

She still holds the chicken by the neck with a tight fist, as if she's imagining it's me she's throttling. 'Sephie, it just isn't worth it. We're almost ten years and eight, but a month from our Illumination Ritual. Can't you just wait till then?'

Alchemy is the most feared of the Callings, and as such, we are only allowed to practise it once we begin our training at the citadel, aged eighteen. Once I'm accepted, I'll harness my gift, control it, and the whispers of witchcraft shall die on the lips of the locals.

But just as Icari needs to heal bones and skin, I need to heal the world around me.

'It's all right for you,' I say, brushing a lock of her black hair from her cheek. 'You've been permitted to embrace your Calling since you were a snot-nosed child. Healers and Embalmers have all the luck.' I stick out my tongue. 'Yet the heart of an Alchemist doesn't suddenly appear on their eighteenth birthday.' I mime untying a bow and opening an invisible box. 'Happy birthday, Sephie – here's a box of Divine Shadow. Use it wisely, my dear.'

Icari sighs. 'I know. I know.' Her voice softens and her gaze slips to the renewed jasmine. 'It's just . . . your gift is so strong. Which means your link to the Divine Shadow must be too.' She retreats to pluck the chicken from her bench again.

'Yes, but I transform his power into something good. That's what makes me an Alchemist, not a sorceress.'

Tears sparkle on her eyelashes – so dark, she always looks as though she's outlined her eyes with kohl. She is quite beautiful, my sister. We both share the same olive skin and black hair, typical of the Sunlanders, but Icari has inherited Mama's pretty face and soft curves.

'The Divine Shadow scares people,' she says. '*You* will scare people. And your logic, however sound, could not save Mama.'

No, no, no – don't mention Mama.

My stomach tightens and the knife of sorrow slips between my ribs. It's been a year since Mama was ripped from us. A year since I promised Papa that I would hide my Calling, even when I was alone, even when there was no chance of being caught. Yet it was far easier to suppress Mama's memory, and with it, the pain of her loss. Especially with the aid of devil wing. Icari thought I couldn't see when she removed it from its hiding place that night, but veils are thin, and my vision has always been sharp.

I lower my head, too ashamed to hold Icari's eye. That's the thing with people who are always right: their very existence points out how wrong you are.

'Please, don't tell Papa,' I say. 'He'll only worry, and you know how weak his heart has grown.'

'Then how do we explain *this*?' She gestures towards the flowers.

A small patch of garden has now exploded alongside the jasmine, the threads of my magic spreading far. Shoots of red larkspur, a smattering of blue delphiniums and a small rose with petals of deep pink. The scent is glorious. But something else pricks my nose; something metallic and out of place. Every tiny hair on my arms rises up as though the air is charged with static.

Something bad is approaching.

Don't be silly, Sephie, I scold myself, before turning to Icari with a flippant grin.

'It's where I empty the chamber pots, obviously,' I say. 'Gardens love a bit of manure.'

'*Donkey* manure.'

'It's all shit, isn't it?'

This time Icari does laugh. 'Papa may be old, but he is no fool.' She watches me for a moment. 'Speaking of which, I asked him about the High Priest, Uriel, again last night.'

Oh, heck. 'I need to check on the broth.'

'The broth is fine. Listen to me, sister. Papa knows something he's not telling us – something about Uriel and Mama. Maybe he knows something about why Mama was killed.'

I slap a hand to my forehead, feigning realization. 'Crap, I forgot to feed Sabu this morning.'

She gives me *that* look, like my face is glass and she can see straight through it. 'Sephie, why can't you talk about what happened to Mama?'

'What difference will it make? Knowing why she died won't bring her back.' The need for devil wing flares in my stomach, even fiercer than usual.

'I know that, but it might . . .' Her voice wavers. 'It might . . .' The sight of her tears, now free-falling on to the chicken, makes me rush to her.

'Icari? What is it?' I ask.

She looks at me with a guilt-bitten expression, her face all swollen with shame. 'Then it might not be my fault.'

I laugh, with disbelief rather than cruelty. 'How is any of this your fault?' I genuinely want to know. Icari is an old maid in young maid's clothing, always trying to cure everyone and everything, accepting responsibility that would roll from my back as if it were water and I were wax. How she's twisted Mama's death into her yoke to bear isn't just a mystery; it's bloody fascinating.

But Icari just slips on her usual cheery, efficient persona

and stands. 'Come. We have patients to bathe and a chicken to cook. If you could just refrain from boiling the water with your hands, then I'll forget about the jasmine plant, even if you did call me snot-nosed.'

'Well it's the truth,' I say, relieved we aren't talking about Mama any more. 'For you were born with two green candles shoved up your nose.'

I follow her back into the sanatorium, ducking beneath the doorway and the symbol of Father Sun hung above. He looks as smug as ever, and instead of kissing my fist as Icari does, I roll my eyes.

I know this building well, having worked here with Icari since our breasts began to show and the blood in our bellies turned the moss between our legs every moon cycle a dark, slippery red. It's a low structure built from mud bricks, cool inside on account of it being three bricks thick. In spite of this, it's beginning to crumble at the edges. We desperately need a stone building, but stone is expensive, and wealth is immune to gravity, failing to trickle down from Mount Appollis.

Mama fell in love with Papa, a poor farmer, soon after she graduated as an Alchemist from the citadel. She moved to the oasis, living in a house of clay and straw. The poverty and sickness here roused the Sun God in her veins, and she realized she was a Healer as well as an Alchemist. With Papa's help, she built this place: a sanatorium on the desert's doorstep.

It's hardly surprising they murdered Mama. She stepped over every line in the sand they'd ever drawn – from rich to poor, from Alchemist to Healer.

What's surprising is they waited so long.

Same as always, I push the image of her face away. Those kind eyes fill me with a pain that only devil wing can squash.

Whilst I set about bathing an elderly lady who looks like a prune and is too weak to lift the linen rag to her own skin, Icari moves around the sanatorium, whispering her healing words. She treats wounds with pigskin and ointments of eucalyptus and honey balm, a faint golden glow springing from beneath her fingers. I pray to Mother Moon that she'll be selected to practise as a Healer at our Illumination ceremony. Just imagine, if we both live in the citadel for three whole years, shaping our Calling, learning our craft. The thought thrills and terrifies me in equal measure. I'm desperate to openly practise alchemy, to summon the Divine Shadow and numb the hurt, but I cannot imagine meeting the desert roaches involved in Mama's execution. And will the twin daughters of a condemned sorceress really be welcomed into the citadel?

In just a month, I guess we'll find out.

'We're out of pigskin,' Icari tells me, pulling me from my thoughts.

'That's a shame,' I reply.

'Leon will have some.'

'I am pleased for him.'

Icari raises her brow expectantly.

'You know I hate the embalming house,' I say, moulding my features into my best pleading look.

Her eyebrows almost touch her hairline. She's not backing down.

'Fine,' I say, chucking the rag in a clay pot. 'But you can't hold me responsible when I throw up on your medical supplies.'

The embalming house is a short walk from the sana-torium, which means we don't have to lug dead bodies too far, and when I say 'we', I of course mean Papa and Icari, for I'd rather carry a man-sized turd than a corpse. The path takes me deeper into the oasis, and the shade of the sycamore figs has never felt more welcome. I pause to lift my thick, black braid so that the cooler air reaches my neck.

The embalming house comes into view and my heart sinks. I hate death. An obvious statement you may think, yet in the Sunlands, this doesn't always go without saying. We lavish corpses with the same care as the living, throwing more gold at the crypts than the sanatoriums in the misguided belief that honouring death controls it, which is utter camel bollocks. And since they took Mama from me, I struggle with death even more. They will salt and wrap their noblemen, but burn a mother who dedicated her life to helping the poor.

Do you see my conflict? To embrace my Calling, I must train at the pinnacle of this hypocrisy. At the core of the establishment responsible for Mama's death, and beneath the High Priest Alchemist, no less.

It makes me sick.

I glance at the symbol above the embalming house door: a full moon with heavy eyes and generous arms, cradling a huddle of stars. Mother Moon always looks tired, less because she's trapped in a forever night, and more because of the sheer length of time she's been married to Father Sun. Does she ever regret that she didn't choose the Divine Shadow? A wry smile twists my mouth even as I think these heretic words.

Ruari pulls up carrots in the side garden. Mud is everywhere, dirtying his white tunic and smearing his skin.

He waves, brandishing a carrot like a sword, his face hopeful. He'd love me to linger here and play – the village kids steer clear of the embalming house, so sometimes I'm the closest he has to a friend. But I glance back at the sanatorium, knowing Icari is waiting, and for once I resist.

'I'm here on business, I'm afraid,' I tell him, playfully. 'Now, back to your work!'

He blows a raspberry as if to say, *Boring*, then settles back to his digging.

Inside, the air is cooler, but the scent of the palm wine and ground spices used to wash out the abdomen of the dead leaves me even more light-headed than the heat. Leon is working on the body of a young girl. A soft white glow emanates from beneath his fingertips as they brush against her waxy skin: a sign that Mother Moon runs deep in his veins. Corpses preserved this way don't decay, allowing their souls to exist for ever in the afterlife, whether that be with Mother Moon or Aïdes. Normally, I'd shudder at the thought of the Underworld, but right now, covered in anxiety sweat and hotter than a frog in a stewpot, an eternity wrapped in never-ending cold doesn't sound so bad.

Leon inserts a long metal implement into a hole between the dead girl's nose bridge and right eye. I avert my gaze before pieces of brain appear.

'We're out of pigskin,' I say. I need no introduction, after all.

'It's OK, Sephie – I won't yank out her brains till you've gone. You can look.' He glances up from his task and smiles. 'The pigskin is where it always is. Help yourself. Tell that sister of yours that one day I will charge her.'

'She won't believe you.'

'Probably not.'

'She will say that just because you are in the business of death, does not mean you wish to promote it.'

His hand wavers slightly as he suppresses a chuckle, and the implement bumps against the inside of the girl's skull. 'She clearly does not know me at all.'

'Nonsense.' I dart around the table, careful not to look at the corpse's face or to imagine her lifeless body, stretched out beneath the tree-green cloth, and locate the pile of skins with urgent fingers.

Closing my eyes, I connect with my surroundings and the earth beneath my feet. This usually calms me, but today, something crackles within the air. I sensed it back at the courtyard with Icari, and once again, the hairs on my arms lift with fear.

'Something's coming,' I whisper. 'Something bad.' My eyes click open, and I glance at Leon, embarrassed.

He tilts his head and gives me this look like he's seeing me for the first time. 'Be careful what you say beyond these walls, young Sephie. You are yet to wear the protective cloak of the label "Alchemist", and without it, those words smell of witchcraft.'

'That label did little to protect Mama.' It is one of the only times I've spoken her name, unprompted, since her death, and even though it was no more than a whisper, it feels like I've just roared into the abyss.

'Your mother renounced her Calling, Sephie. She renounced her Calling and became a Healer.'

'Mama *was* a Healer,' I snap. 'And even when she was an Alchemist, she only ever used the Divine Shadow for good. She wasn't a sorceress, and it's not like she had any necromancy powers.'

Leon physically recoils from the word 'necromancy' as though just the sound of it will invite the corpse before him to leap to her feet and do a little dance. Necromancy is the rarest of all the alchemy skills, strictly forbidden and striking fear into even the bravest of Sunlanders. Even the mention of it is frowned upon. Yet I refuse to apologize, instead intensifying my frown.

Leon shows me his palms. They're dappled with blood. 'Look, *I* know your mama wasn't a sorceress, of course I know. But by openly flaunting both Callings, she disrespected the citadel.'

'She wasn't *flaunting* anything. She was helping the poor.'

He sighs, long and slow. 'I know, Sephie, I know. I'm just telling you how it was viewed at the citadel.'

'I figured that out for myself when they burnt her.' Unwanted memories drive a spike into my head: the initial punch in the gut warning me that Icari was distressed or in danger, then Ruari dashing into the sanatorium and summoning us to the agora, the stench of smoke upon the breeze. *Don't think about Mama. Don't think about Mama.*

Why is it when you tell yourself not to think about something, you think of it even more?

My chest begins to burn and the urge to cry overwhelms

me. Sweet Mother Moon, what I wouldn't give for a pinch of devil wing! Or, in its absence, to summon the Divine Shadow, to feel him stir inside my veins and numb the hurt from the inside out. But this sometimes causes things to transmute without my permission, and with Leon so near, I cannot take the risk – he won't tell the guards, but he will tell Papa and Icari. And that, my friends, is arguably worse.

The fight suddenly leaves me and I just feel wretched and wrung out. It isn't Leon's fault I can't think of Mama without wanting to scream; nor is it his fault I crave devil wing so. He's only trying to help. I clutch my pigskins to my chest and shuffle to the door, my reed sandals leaving smudges in the dust.

'I've made broth – shall I bring you a bowl?' I say.

It's a blunt subject change, but Leon accepts it with as much grace as a man elbow-deep in brains is able. 'That would be lovely, thank you.' He pauses. 'You know, Sephie, you can talk to me about your mama any time you want. It's good for you.'

I force a smile before fleeing outside. If it's good for me, then why do I feel as thin as parchment, as brittle as a jar? I guess some shadows will always be black as river silt.

Papa is tending to the land, Icari to the patients – no one will miss me for a few more heartbeats. Besides, I've just been to the embalming house; I've earnt a tiny pinch, surely? I slip inside our mud hut, breath held and heart thumping like I'm no more than a common thief. Which I kind of am.

My body knows these movements well: creep behind the firepit, move the loose chunk of clay, tip a small pile of devil wing on to the back of my hand, lick it all down, and pray I don't go to the Underworld when I die.

In an instant, his cold hands are upon me. Soothing, calming, easing. And I drift back to the sanatorium, a smile upon my face, shedding the burden of loss like a heavy, black cape.

5

SEPHIE

Sand builds in the grey hair of the elderly man I'm spoon-feeding. I seriously doubt he's been for a secret stroll in the Redlands when he's unable to feed himself. Glancing to the nearest windowsill, I spy the dreaded golden grains drifting across the clay ridge. My skin bristles.

'Icari,' I whisper.

She looks over.

'We should cover the windows, sooner rather than later,' I say, trying not to alarm the patients.

She nods as she realizes my meaning. We have not been short of dust clouds this season, but my gift tells me that this one has claws.

Icari completes the linen bandage on her patient's upper arm. 'I'll secure the sanatorium; you fetch Papa. He's in the orchard, gathering figs.'

I release a hiss of air. 'Being two minutes my senior does not make you my master.'

Either she doesn't hear or she pretends not to, and begins unrolling the linen sheets, ready to pin in place around the sills.

Running down the dirt path, I head to the orchard where

the fruit trees glow beneath the sun. The wind has already picked up, driving sand into my skin like ivory needles, causing me to curse beneath my breath. The air crackles with threat.

Papa's strong legs protrude from a fig tree like a couple of wayward branches. The leaves shelter him and he has yet to notice the approaching danger.

'Papa,' I call. 'Papa, come inside. A storm approaches from the Redlands.'

'What's that, dear-heart?' He wobbles down the ladder, basket of fruit balanced on his shoulder. A stern breeze whips the sand into his eyes and he blinks quickly. 'Oh,' he says. 'Did you know there's a sandstorm on its way? I better move the animals.'

'There isn't time.' My voice comes out a little shrill, the devil wing wearing off. *Dammit!* I wish no harm on our chickens or goats, of course I don't, and the thought of Sabu suffering fills me with horror, but not nearly so much as the thought of Papa swallowed whole by a mouth of sand and air. And something about this storm doesn't feel right. The Divine Shadow stitches into my heart, stronger than ever.

Dark recognizes dark.

'Leave the animals,' I say. 'Father Sun will protect them.'

He rolls his eyes. I know that he's thinking the storm is Father Sun's doing, I know this because I think it too. Months of heat has loosened the Redlands, turning them into a bowl of dust.

'There is time to get Sabu, at least,' he says. 'He's getting old and won't like the sand in his ears.'

'He's not the only one,' I say, ripping a strip of cloth from my apron and handing it to him.

Abandoning the basket of figs, Papa ties my linen offering around his face and protects his nose and mouth.

'Tether the goats in their pen,' he says. 'Then shelter inside with the others. I'll be as quick as I can.' He jogs in the direction of Sabu's field.

I don't bother arguing. I get my Calling from Mama and my stubbornness from Papa, so I settle on shouting after him, 'Hurry, Papa. Please.'

I leave the shelter of the orchard, heading towards the Redlands, where the goats while away their hours chewing on the dried grasses. By the time I reach the herd, however, they've flocked together, bleating like babes at a withered tit. The wind has strengthened, grazing my exposed throat and pushing beneath my tunic. The soft skin of my thighs begins to sting.

I stop at the rickety fence, a marker that the land beyond belongs to Father Sun alone. The Redlands stretches before me, a sheet of linen dipped in saffron. It is as beautiful as it is endless. Silly stories about fire-haired witches crossing from the Farlands have caused locals to fear the desert, but the only dangers I've ever known whilst living here are dehydration, dust clouds, and sand in my undergarments.

The goats behind me fall silent and the hum of the oasis drops.

But for the buzz of dust, the world holds its breath.

That's when I hear it: a swarm of mosquitoes, swelling beyond the stark line where gold meets blue.

The entire desert groans and the horizon blurs.

A finger-smudge of charcoal appears in the distance, and

suddenly, the sky slips into darkness. A whip of lightning cracks the slate beyond. It takes a second for the thunder to reach me, reverberating through my body like the loudest of drums.

My hair lashes my face, and my skin itches with sand and something else. Something dark and bewitching. It is the Divine Shadow, growing strong in my belly, awakening my senses and running his frosted hands across me as he whispers my name.

The swarm of mosquitoes crescendoes to a mighty drum-roll as the sand cloud finally comes into view: a dark wall heading towards me, moving, shifting, gathering speed. *It will pass*, I tell myself. *Sandstorms rarely kill.*

Yet I know this cloud is different.

I close my eyes and call on my gift, connecting with the sand in the distance. I've never connected with something so big before. It's astonishing, sucking the life force from me, yet making me feel more alive than I can ever recall. I can feel its heat, its rage. Sense a lifetime of drying beneath Father Sun, of nourishing cacti and the desert rose, of yielding to the patter of the scorpion's feet and the swish of the saw-scaled viper's ribbony form. Yet some of the grains don't belong – they are paler, drier, speaking only of death.

This is bad. This is very bad.

My eyes flick open.

This storm originated in the Bone desert, so named not just because it resembles ground-up bone, but because it sucks the life force from anyone – anything – stupid enough to roam its planes. Indeed, the only thing that survives the Bone desert is hopelessness and drought, and its surface is

said to be littered with shards of driftwood, splintered skeletons and flints of milk-pale stone. And now, my friend, is not
the time to ponder the paradox of how any living person
might know this, for our world is built upon legends.
Besides, even a scrap of truth renders this storm terrifying.
For driftwood, skeletons and stones become weapons when
hurled by the wind. They will puncture shelters and skewer
flesh.

The villages at the edge of the oasis will take the worst of
it. They always do.

Papa. Icari. Leon and Ruari.

I have to stop it.

The city bells begin to clang, ringing from the temples of
the citadel, the watchmen warning of the sandstorm
barrelling towards the oasis and the city beyond. *Hide indoors
whilst it passes through.* The watchmen have the benefit of
height. The whole citadel does. They have climbed the highest mast whilst the paupers flail in an ocean of sharks.
Bastards.

Vaulting the fence, I walk towards the ever-nearing wall
of sand. I begin to cough and my lungs burn, but I fight the
urge to cover my nose and mouth for I don't wish to dull my
senses. I need them for what I'm about to do.

Suddenly, I wish an army of winged gods would appear,
clapping their huge wings together to avert the storm, or
swooping down and cradling us in their golden feathers, as
safe as bugs in cocoons. But the Illios haven't blessed our
skies for hundreds of years.

There is only me.

Me and the Divine Shadow.

This thought should terrify me, should make me piss my sand-filled pants, but instead it brings clarity, a sense of purpose.

And with the decision made, a sense of calm follows.

I kick off my sandals. And with every step forward, the sand shifts beneath my feet, pushing between my toes and the tiny swirls in my skin until I'm not sure where the desert ends and I begin. I stretch my arms out to either side, letting the gale carry the Redlands through my fingers like grains of crude salt. I focus on my feet, my legs, my torso. My stupid tunic is about as much use as a stewpot made from butter, and I long for a shield of bronze-coated wood.

My eyes are mere slits, squinting into the darkness. The cloud will soon be upon me, towering higher and higher until I can barely see the sky. Soon the world will turn orange, the air will vanish, and the storm will hurl its worst at me. Yet still, I continue towards it, facing it head on, letting the Divine Shadow consume me entirely.

I am ice.

'SEPHIE, NO!' A voice rings out behind me.

It is Icari, trying to convince me to hide my gift, to pull down my linen shutters and block out the Divine Shadow as if *he* were the storm to be feared.

'Not now, sister.' My voice sounds focused, unfamiliar even to me.

'Sephie, they've rung the bells!' she screams, though the sand erodes her voice. 'They're watching and they'll know. They'll know.'

She is, unsurprisingly, right. The watchmen will see the storm drop suddenly from the sky and they will smell witchcraft. Yet if I do nothing, if I simply hide away, everyone I love will perish.

'This storm comes from the Bone desert,' I cry, without looking back. 'Go inside.'

'Sephie, it just isn't worth the risk. Please, I cannot lose you too.'

I shut out her cries. The storm is almost upon me and the decision is already made, for the Divine Shadow isn't about to release me. So I send my focus back to the world around me, radiating in all directions like the rays of Father Sun himself. And even though the cloud is near, so near, I'm ready for it this time, summoning all of my strength and the Calling within.

Then, I open my eyes.

The sandstorm looms over me like a mighty wave. This close, the black has transformed into a swirling mass of golds and reds and whites, with flashes of boulders as big as my head and shards of bone as sharp as blades. Without flinching, I send my awareness into the cloud, becoming the deafening drone. I sense every grain of sand, the spaces in between, every collision as the particles knock up against each other.

The Divine Shadow exudes from my every pore and the numbness surrounds me. And I bind the cold to the storm, weaving the glacial flow to every grain of sand and the wind on which it rides. Quickly, the thrum beneath my feet slows, the howling subsides, and my skin finally stops burning. The dust settles around me, smothering my feet and allowing the air to clear as though after a fire.

I can breathe again.

The Divine Shadow leaves me and I slump to the floor, every morsel of energy spent.

'Sephie!' Icari rushes to me and flings her body over mine. She is weeping, her tears gratifyingly cool against the heat of my cheek. 'You brave, brave fool. What if you'd failed? The storm would have ripped you apart.'

My voice has abandoned me along with my grit, so I just stare at the debris spreading before us, a carpet of pale stones and flints, of branches ripped from trees and the occasional desert rat, stunned and pondering just how they ended up so far from home. And all the while, the bells of the citadel continue to ring, reminding us that the watchmen remain true to their name. Soon the city guard will arrive, looking for answers, looking for their sorceress. And what better place to start than the daughters of a murdered witch.

6

SEPHIE

Icari helps me back to our hut, and Papa runs from the sanatorium, deep worry lines carving up his face.

'Praise the Sun God, you're both safe.' Papa takes me from Icari, his arms surprisingly strong. 'Please tell me you didn't stop the storm.'

My silence confirms his suspicion.

'How could you?' Anger breaks through his concern, and I know he's thinking of Mama.

'I had to.' My voice shrinks and falls to the floor, slipping between the cracks in the clay, and I feel like I'm four again and he's caught me drinking all the goat's milk.

'But it was just a sand cloud,' he says. 'It would have passed.'

I let him guide me into our hut. The scent of home – of dried grass, leaven bread and tallow wax – coaxes tears of relief from my eyes, and the urge to sleep overwhelms me. I glance to the place where Icari hides the devil wing, a dislodged brick only half nestled back into place, and my body aches for it.

'The storm carried with it the debris of the Bone desert,' I finally say.

But Papa doesn't hear, distress and sand clogging up his ears. Instead, he sets me down on a wooden chair whilst Icari fetches boiled water to bathe the redness from my skin.

'Don't you remember what they did to Mama?' he says.

I'm not sure if the words or the press of the cloth makes me wince more. 'No, Papa, I forgot. Remind me.'

He sighs. 'We need to hide you. Before the city guards arrive.'

When Icari finally speaks, she looks like a corpse, all stiff and absent, as if her soul is somewhere else.

'Hide her where?' she asks.

It's an innocent enough question. The High Priest's reach is far, and most Sunlanders know my name – the daughter of a slaughtered witch has a reputation, after all. And fleeing to the Redlands isn't an option: even with my gifts, the desert would eventually turn me to dust.

'We will tell them it was a witch from the Farlands,' Icari continues. 'An unknown sorceress with fire-vipers for hair. I will swear that Sephie was with me. The patients will back me up, I know it.'

'They'll know you are lying,' Papa says, panic rising in his voice, the constant dab of the cloth quickening against my sores. 'Why would a sorceress from the Farlands stop a storm? She'd be more likely to send it.'

'Horseshit,' I mutter, at the same time as Icari says, 'Do you have a better idea?'

'Yes – we hide her,' Papa says.

It's like I'm the last piece of bread at the market, bickered over by two old maids.

'Stop.' My voice comes out as a rasp, but it is enough to

still their tongues. Easing the rag from Papa's hands, I squeeze his shoulder and shape my mouth into a stoic smile. 'We will show the city guard the flints and rocks at the door of the oasis. That will be enough for them to know I transmute the Divine Shadow into light, that my allegiance lies with Father Sun and Mother Moon, and not with the Underworld.'

I speak only the truth. Whilst Father Sun is annoyingly righteous, and death turns my stomach, I would never side with the Divine Shadow. For I am an Alchemist, not a witch, and my role is to flirt with the devil rather than lie with him.

'Your mama was the kindest person I've ever known,' Papa whispers. 'And that didn't stop them . . .'

'I am not yet ten years and eight,' I say. 'Perhaps they won't execute a child so freely.'

Icari whimpers and I feel a shard of glass in my gut, an echo of her pain, because Icari and I sense each other's emotions as only twins can. Of course. She once told me she tried to claim Mama's devil wing was her own, as they would not dare execute a child. But she couldn't do it. At the time, I was too wrapped up in my own pain to comfort her, to tell her it wasn't her fault Mama had died.

Don't think of Mama.

I take her hand, wishing I were a better sister.

'Let us keep our calm,' I say. 'The oasis is big, there are many villages . . . and sandstorms *do* abate of their own accord. I think we will be OK.'

Hope surfaces on Papa's worn face, so I smile, ignoring the anxiety roiling in my gut and the aching tiredness in my head.

Icari puts on her Healer head and says, 'Come, Sephie,

you need sustenance and rest.' She is so adept at switching manners, I sometimes fancy she has a selection of heads she can whip on and off, slung in a sack over her shoulder, like she's carrying pumpkins to market.

She lifts the privacy veil and ushers me on to a papyrus mat. Only a trace of distress remains on her face in the form of frown lines. 'Papa can cook the chicken whilst I tend to the patients. I imagine they will all have sand in their wounds now.'

She kisses me on the head, then leaves the room, and I wonder if she simply cannot tolerate my presence whilst we wait for the guards to arrive – as if looking at me will cause her too much pain. Then I remember, it's me who avoids distress, not Icari. She only took devil wing once, the night of Mama's execution. After that, she said she needed the pain, that it was the only thing that kept Mama close to her.

We were formed in the same womb, yet we are so very different. Healer and Alchemist. Softness and fight. The two sides of Mama, embodied.

Sephie, for the last time, stop thinking of Mama.

The sound of Papa chopping turnips at the kitchen table provides a welcome distraction, and I let my eyes flicker shut, the rhythmic sound of the knife calming my nerves. My strength returns, a welcome chill travelling beneath my skin.

After a while, the sound of hoofs against dried mud drifts through the windows. I jump to my feet and duck beneath the veil to see Papa staring at me, his face gripped with fear, knife shaking in his hand.

I hold his gaze. 'It will be OK, Papa.'

If he notices the tremble in my words, he doesn't say

anything; rather, he lays down his knife and crosses to where I stand. 'I am here, my darling girl. I am always here.'

We embrace. It reminds me how tall I have grown.

The firepit draws my eye. A dose of devil wing will ease any punishment, and it will certainly ease the hammering of my heart and the burning in my chest, but the sound of a spear clobbering against the wooden door whisks away the opportunity.

Outside is a small group of the city guard, five in total, all on horseback. They wear the silver-and-gold hue of the citadel, carry curved blades in their leather belts and cross-bows on their backs.

Papa holds my hand like I'm five, and I let him, not only because I feel about five, but because it won't harm to remind the guards that in spite of my height, I am not yet an adult.

The ugliest man wears a headband of leaves cast in gold, and the horse on which he sits huffs damp air from his flared nostrils so I can barely hear the pounding of my own heart. In any other circumstance, I would lay a soothing hand on his velvet nose. But now is not the time.

'There was a mighty sandstorm heading towards the city,' Headband states. He carries a huge spear, which I can only imagine is overcompensation for the size of his sexual organ. Men and their silly insecurities.

'And the villages,' I mutter. 'The storm was heading to the villages too.'

Icari arrives from the sanatorium. Upon seeing Head-band, she stands rigid, held to the ground with tree gum. I don't need to feel her fear in my belly to know that this man terrifies her.

I study his face. Of course. The headband of gold; the thin-lipped mouth. Icari told me about him once when I was held safe in the grip of devil wing. It is the general who slaughtered Mama. Fury swells in my chest, transforming my muscles into coiled springs. Only the sight of the crossbows and Icari's and Papa's unshielded chests stops me from flying at him in a swirl of fists.

One of the horses nearby shifts his hoofs, disrupting the dust.

Headband sniffs. 'The watchmen informed us that the sand cloud was to hit here first, this very village, yet it fell from the sky before penetrating the oasis.' He pauses. When none of us speak, he simply says, 'Sandstorms don't drop from the sky.'

Another man appears from behind the soldiers. He is mounted upon a grey steed and wears the symbol of the Alchemist upon his head. But even without this, his identity would be apparent. The shadows beneath my skin respond to his. Like I said, dark recognizes dark. The High Priest did not light Mama's pyre, but he ordered it. His hands are stained with her blood. And he trained with Mama; he knew how kind she was. The urge to kill him arrives quickly, and I long for a crossbow of my own to aim it straight at his shadowy heart. I settle instead on a killer glare.

'Giorgos.' He speaks Papa's name with an intense quietness.

Papa offers a small bow. 'Uriel.'

Headband steps between them, as if my ageing, weapon-less Papa is somehow a threat, then his eyes widen at Icari in sudden recognition. 'Was this the home of the sorceress

Daeda?' he spits.

Papa squeezes my hand. *Stay calm*, he tells me silently, before meeting Headband's eye. 'Indeed,' Papa says. 'She is my wife . . . *Was* my wife.'

Headband smirks. 'What a coincidence that the dust cloud should fall at your door.'

I realize I'm grinding my teeth.

'Which of you girls is the sorceress?' he barks suddenly. 'Tell us now or we shall beat it from you.'

Papa draws us both close so we become a single being. I can hear his breath quicken, see the terror in Icari's dark eyes. But before we can answer, Uriel urges his horse forward, a hand raised. 'What my comrade means to say is, which of you has the Divine Shadow in their blood?'

I step towards him. 'My lord, if you look beyond, to the Redlands, you will see there was little choice. The wind passed over the Bone desert – there were rocks and flints and pieces of—'

'Enough.' Headband strikes me around the face with the handle of his blade. It is quick and brutal, causing me to sprawl on the floor, my hand clutching the site of pain.

'Son of a dung beetle,' I hiss.

He raises his blade for another strike. 'You address the High Priest without permission, then you *insult* him?'

'I was insulting you, sir.'

'Please, my lord,' Papa garbles, dropping to my side. 'She is still young and without her mama's guidance—'

'That's enough, thank you, General,' Uriel says.

I'm not ashamed to admit that I'm relieved when Headband lowers his blade, for whilst I am filled with fury, I am no masochist. Icari joins Papa, and they help me manoeuvre into a sitting position. The welt rises quickly beneath my fingers and I long to call on the Divine Shadow to extract the worst of the sting, but that would mean to risk buds nearby bursting into bloom, sand moving beneath our feet, or drops of rain pattering from a cloudless sky. Then I would be in even more trouble.

How I ache for some devil wing.

The High Priest stares at Icari. 'Did you stop the sand cloud?'

I wonder if he notices how pretty she is, how she looks like Mama, with her dark, flashing eyes, her sharp cheekbones and sleek jaw, completely at odds with the soft curves of her body. I always resented that I ended up looking more like Papa. On a bad day, more like Sabu.

'Well?' Uriel says, when Icari simply gawps.

'It was me,' I say.

He pauses, then shifts his gaze to me as I squat, toad-like, on the ground. Does he look . . . disappointed? Or does he recognize the shadow within?

He smiles, revealing a perfect set of teeth. 'Of course it was you. I see it now.'

Dismounting from his horse, he stands but an arm's length from me. Our eyes meet and the chill of the Divine Shadow moves within, extinguishing the rage and the incessant desert heat that rolls in from the Redlands. Yet wonderful though it is, I push it away, afraid of what might happen.

I struggle to my feet and stand tall as I am able. 'Yes. I am the Alchemist.'

Headband hovers in my peripheral vision, and I pretend he is an annoying gnat. Unaware he's been demoted to bug status, he raises his weapon for another strike, but before I can even lift my hand in defence, the High Priest has grabbed Headband's arm, saving me from another welt.

Headband lowers his blade, a look of annoyance settling into his small features.

'Have you been to your Calling ceremony yet?' Uriel asks me, his voice low and silky. 'Have you been selected to train for three years at the Temples of Mother Moon and Father Sun?'

I shake my head. 'No, my lord. My Illumination Ritual is next month.'

'Then you are not yet an Alchemist,' he replies, before pausing and adding, 'In a month we shall see if you are one. Until then, you will resist the Divine Shadow, however strong his grip. You are dabbling in things you can't yet control.'

Dabbling. I resist the urge to roll my eyes. I wouldn't call stopping a deadly sandstorm *dabbling.* But I nod regardless, not wanting another smack.

The High Priest looks at Papa. 'Giorgos, you must keep your daughter in check, or she will end up like Daeda. Nothing but a scorch mark on the dried mud of the oasis floor.'

I ball my fists so hard that my palms begin to bleed, and Papa, my darling Papa, simply nods.

The High Priest returns to his steed in a swish of sparkling threads. I wish I could transmute him into a fly, then I would watch him feast on goat turd before stamping him into the ground.

'Wait,' Headband calls, still clutching his blade with intent. 'She has committed sorcery without the blessing of the citadel. She is like her mother, no more than a filthy witch, and should be burnt as one.'

Untamed, the anger bursts from my mouth, surprising even me. 'Isn't it strange how men cannot be killed for witchcraft. Only women. Tell me why, High Priest, tell me. I would really like to know – why are you so afraid of women with powers?'

Icari and Papa tense beside me. Even the sand seems to tense beneath my feet.

Yet the High Priest simply turns his horse and throws over his shoulder, 'Twenty lashes, and that's the end of it.'

'No!' Icari gasps, her horror echoing my own.

I'm about to object, but Papa clamps a hand over my mouth. 'Hush,' he whispers. 'It could be much worse. It could be much, much worse.'

Headband pushes me against the wooden pole in the centre of the agora, exactly where Mama died. The pole is made from the trunk of an almond tree – I can sense something of its spirit lingering beneath its smooth, whittled surface, how it once enjoyed Father Sun upon its leaves and dropping nuts to the floor like tasty gems. I lean my cheek against its sun-warmed side whilst Headband binds my hands around the pole. The villagers watch in silence. Then the sound of something tearing fills my ears and I'm wrenched backwards.

I gasp, only to realize the soldiers have ripped the back from my tunic. Father Sun now assaults my skin and I lean against the wood of the almond tree, embarrassed by my sudden semi-nakedness.

Papa and Icari stand nearby, holding their courage and each other's hands as tightly as they're able. Icari looks more terrified than me, and she's doing her finest impression of a corpse once again. Though I can already smell the soothing ointment she's stashed beneath her apron, ready to apply as soon as I'm released. She won't dare carry devil wing in her tunic, not since the burning last year, but I know she will permit me to have some when I'm back at the sanatorium. A whipped back warrants the strongest anaesthetic.

I dry-swallow.

Headband steps forward and addresses the crowd, his hand clutching a strip of olive bark. It quivers in anticipation and my stomach roils. A fresh onslaught of panic fills my limbs and I struggle against my bindings. I even consider summoning the Divine Shadow and risking further punishment, but Papa's words ricochet around my skull: '*It could be much worse.*'

Headband raises his voice so it sails above the papyrus rooftops and the overhanging sycamore branches. 'By order of the High Priest, Sephie, daughter of Daeda, is to receive twenty lashes for insolence.'

Insolence? Why, that arsehole of a flea-bitten camel! Why does he not proclaim I practised alchemy without the blessing of the citadel? But I am barely able to think this through when I hear the whip, swishing through the air and cracking against my skin.

Holy shit, that hurts!

A branding iron of red-hot pain lands upon my back, quickly spreading to every part of me. I try not to scream.

Crack. Another burst of pain. This time, my scream echoes around the village.

I look at Icari and Papa to draw solace from their presence, even as the world begins to spin.

Swoosh. Crack.

I bite my tongue and my mouth fills with blood.

Swoosh. Crack.

As the pain intensifies, something strange happens. I think of Mama. Of how she burnt, right here, in the centre of the agora, and I let her smiling face and soft voice fill my head. It's as though the physical hurt has paved the way for the emotional, so even though I'm gargling my own blood and weeping into a dead almond tree, for the first time since her death, I feel strangely content.

7

SEPHIE

That night, I lie on my front in our little clay hut, groaning like a wounded dog. My back is ablaze with pain, and I can tell from Icari's face, it looks as bad as it feels. She mixes a strong dose of devil wing into a cup of water whilst Papa checks on the patients.

'I would have taken the lashings for you,' she says, stirring slowly. 'I wanted to, but when I tried to speak . . .' Her words die alongside any hope of receiving pain relief this century.

'I stopped the sand cloud, not you,' I snap. 'Now give me the wretched drug, for my agony is far worse than your guilt, I assure you.'

My friends, I know I sound unkind, but my back is burning like a bitch. Fortunately, she finishes her stirring and hands me the drink.

'Sorry.' She says it again for good measure. 'Sorry.'

I gulp down the liquid, colder than frost. Now I know how a Redland tree feels when the skies finally open. The silver elixir spreads down my trunk and reaches every tip of me, every leaf, every tiny green vein, and the pain blunts almost immediately.

Maybe this is how it feels to be a Samael. To be Aïdes himself.

To live in the Underworld.

Is it really so bad?

By the time our Illumination Ritual arrives, Icari's ointment has worked its magic and my back is covered in no more than a mesh of silvery lines.

Icari traces them with a curious finger as I pause, half dressed, in our hut.

'They will never go entirely,' she says, a note of regret in her voice. 'But they are quite beautiful, like a snowflake.'

I laugh. 'More like an avalanche of pain.'

'They still hurt?'

'No. Just the memory.'

'The only wound I cannot heal,' she says, helping to gather my gown around my chest and secure it around my neck.

Our gowns are simple: a drape of white silk, cinched at the waist with a twist of gold-and-silver ribbons. I have waited so long for this day. I should be excited, but instead I feel sick.

I'm about to come face to face with Uriel and the General once again.

Just the thought of those dung beetles and my stomach is a clenched fist.

Icari smiles. 'It will be OK. *We* will be OK. If we can survive the death of our darling mama and twenty public lashings, then we can survive this.'

I don't correct her when she uses the term 'we' because I

know she felt the lashes as deeply as I did.

She hands me a wooden comb. 'Will you help?'

I braid her hair in silence, enjoying the way it silks through my fingers like water. Then, I pin it up and weave freshly picked jasmine and olive leaves through the plait. The white flowers shimmer against her black hair, creating a nightscape. Not for the first time, I wish my mane were as lush as hers.

'Perfect. Now your turn,' she says, admiring her reflection in a small handheld mirror.

She begins combing my hair with coconut water, bringing out the curl and making sure it covers my scars. When she's finished, she presents me with a coronet of roses, previously hidden beneath her sleep mat. A crown of deep pinks, vibrant reds and a colour so delicate, it matches the uncurled palm of a newborn. She's picked them from our little courtyard, from my secret alchemy spot that my dear, gullible Papa actually believed I cultivated with human shit.

'I made this for you,' she says. I must recoil, because she adds, 'Don't worry. I trimmed the thorns so it won't scratch.'

It isn't the thorns that worry me. Mama's favourite flowers were roses, so the coronet is basically a crown of sorrow, but I force a smile for my sister's sake.

'Oh, Icari, it's quite lovely.' I place it on my head and offer a quick curtsy, tipping my chin like a lady and pulling my most pompous face.

She laughs, a musical trill. 'You look gorgeous.'

'Well, thank goodness for that. I could do with looking my finest when I meet all the pretty boys and girls of the citadel. Our little village hardly has much to offer in the way of romantic adventures.'

'What about Xanthos? He's still sweet on you, has been for years.'

'Oh, please.' I throw her a fleeting wink. 'Xanthos kisses like a fish.'

'A fish?'

'A drunken fish, no less.' I let my tongue flop around my lips whilst fluttering my lashes.

She laughs. 'What about Selene then?'

'Selene smells of frogspawn that's been left out in the sun all week.'

Selene doesn't smell of frogspawn, dried or otherwise. She smells wonderful — of pollen and fresh sweat — but I can't bring myself to admit that Selene hasn't spoken to me since I was accused of insolence and whipped. Worse — that things began to cool immediately following Mama's death. Turns out being the daughter of an executed witch isn't an aphrodisiac. But I've never told Icari this, simply because it would involve talking about Mama. Regardless, distress crosses her face as she puts two and two together. She always was annoyingly astute.

'Oh, I see,' she mutters, her eyes dropping.

'Screw Selene,' I say, taking her hands. 'Screw the lot of them.'

I expect her to laugh, or at least make some feeble pun about how me not screwing Selene was, in fact, the issue, but instead, she simply sighs and says, 'Perhaps when we are at the citadel, we will find some answers.'

'Answers to what?' I drop her hands, knowing fine well what she means.

'To why Mama was executed.'

She's so predictable.

All the same, a terrifying emotion I can't name forces its way up my throat. 'We know why. She was caught trading devil wing. She confessed to witchcraft. I know it was a forced confession, but nobody cares about that.'

'They were going to burn her whether or not she said she was a sorceress. Her confession was simply the honey on the cake.' She pauses. 'No. There's more to it. Why was the High Priest Alchemist present?' She holds my upper arms and pulls me towards her. 'He was crying, Sephie. Uriel was crying when he ordered her death.'

'I know this. How could I not? You go on and on about it like a braying ass.' I snatch myself away, unable to tolerate the pain. My eyes slide to the wonky brick, desperate for devil wing, but I settle instead on summoning the Divine Shadow to numb the hurt.

She doesn't snap back. She never does.

When I've calmed, I say, 'Sorry, you are not an ass, but we've been over this. Mama was caught trading devil wing.'

'I've never heard of anyone being executed for trading devil wing before. And you know she was set up – I told you about the soldier paying off the stall-keeper.'

'You did. Many times.' I fidget with the coronet. I suddenly hate it. *Loathe* it. Why did Icari have to choose Mama's favourite flower?

'Sephie?' she says, frustrated. 'Why do you think they wanted Mama dead? Because of her dual Calling?'

I suppress the urge to hurl the coronet across the room. 'I don't know. Men love to burn witches – it makes their cocks grow. Everyone knows that.'

'Mama wasn't a witch,' she says.

'No woman is a witch, and a small cock is always a small cock, and yet here we are.'

'All bodies are beautiful, sister.'

'You've entirely missed the point, *sister*.'

Ignoring my tone, she chews on her bottom lip. 'Did you know that possessing two Callings was only banned some fifty years ago. Before that, it was revered. Why the sudden change of heart?'

'Because only women have dual gifts. It's just another way of controlling us. Secretly, we scare them.'

She sighs. She often sighs. 'It just makes no sense.'

'It makes about as much sense as witches from the Farlands turning men to stone and stealing God-fearing women from their beds.' I pretend to be a ghoul, swiping at her with my tongue lolling out, hoping laughter will make her forget. 'Just scary stories to keep us down and keep men on top.'

'I still don't understand why Mama was killed.'

I resist the urge to crush a rose in my fist. I'm done talking about this. It's our Illumination Ritual and I want it to be a joyous occasion, not one steeped in trauma and loss, so I squeeze her hands and smile. 'When are the villagers arriving to help at the sanatorium? Papa won't like it, you know – he's become quite set in his ways.'

'Why can't you talk about Mama?'

I open and close my mouth several times, trout-like, Xanthos-like, but no words come.

'You barely mention her,' she says. 'And whenever Papa or

I do, you change the subject. It isn't healthy, dear-heart. If you slam the door on grief, it simply climbs through the window when you least expect it.'

'I don't want to talk about it.'

'I rest my case. If we discover why they murdered her, maybe we can—'

'What?' I snap. 'Get some justice? Send the High Priest to jail? Make you feel less guilty that you just stood there whilst she burnt.'

Her face wells with hurt and I think maybe I've gone too far. Damn my vicious tongue!

'Icari, I'm so sorry.'

But she shakes her head. 'No. You're right.' Her voice is annoyingly level. 'We may never get justice, but don't you want to know? For your own peace of mind?'

'No. I want to forget. For my own peace of mind.'

'You can't erase her, Sephie.'

The shame lands swift, brutal, an axe to the chest. I ban the tears from my eyes and command the cool shadows to run through my veins. 'I just want the pain to stop.'

Without another word, I turn away and roughly adjust the blasted coronet so it sits squarely on my head. I'm as ready as I'll ever be.

On the day of the full moon, every child who turns ten and eight years within that moon cycle must gather in the Court of Ash. Appollis is a large city with a sprawling oasis at its foot, and some months the numbers swell to at least a hundred. There, at half-light, beneath the watchful eyes of the High Priest, the Hopefuls perform the Illumination

Ritual. Only the few blessed with the Calling in their veins stay on at the citadel to complete their training. The rest go home. And whilst there is no shame in failing the Illumination Ritual, there is no shortage of praise for those who succeed.

The city walls come into view, a banner of stone, and the guards immediately raise the gates for our cart to pass through. After all, it is the day of the Illumination Ritual and we're wearing dress robes – even a guard can work that one out. I glare at them as we pass. Did they tie Mama to the pyre? Did they watch on as the skin lifted from my back? They don't even look at me and I silently seethe. When I am an Alchemist, they will look at me, that's for sure.

The cart winds through the city. Both Icari and I sit in silence whilst we take in our surroundings. Trips to the city are as rare as they are exciting. The houses here are mostly built from stone, with neat wooden shutters that close against the bugs in summer and the frost in winter. Some buildings loom several storeys high, with yellow-and-white fronts, painted in honour of the citadel. Others are squat and left plain, their stone roofs awash with moss and curls of violets – these are my favourite. If I were a house, I would cultivate violets on my roof.

I wrinkle my nose against the smell. The stink of unwashed armpits mixes with the pollen of roses and jasmine that spill from pots and climb up the trunks of olive and lemon trees. My stomach growls as I smell the roasted meats and fresh breads wafting from the wooden stalls that edge the streets. It seems every day is market day here in Appollis.

Sabu takes us higher and higher, zigzagging up the

mountain. The air grows cleaner, Father Sun stronger, and the citadel eventually appears, a thatch of gleaming marble. I have only been here once, as a small child with Mama and a very snotty Icari, and even then we simply peered through the gates, our little faces clutched with wonder. The rest of my childhood, it was a sparkling jewel in the distance, the key to my future as an Alchemist. But since Mama's death, the jewel has cracked and dimmed, becoming only a means to an end. The end being my eternal numbness.

I glance at Icari. Her face is taut, her eyes glassy, and I know she's thinking of Mama too. I twine my fingers through hers and she offers a wan smile.

The citadel is walled, just like the city itself. Concentric circles of protection. A guard checks our names and waves us through the gates. I narrow my eyes in his direction and the cockroach winks. The nerve of him.

Up this high, the air smells blue. I inhale deeply, trying to calm my nerves. Then, my legs sore and cramping, I dismount the cart. The journey has taken almost half a day, and evening fast approaches. My mouth is dry and my belly empty, so I'm relieved when the servants bring water for Sabu; his thirst will be double mine after all that pulling.

We walk beneath a huge arch built from marble and decorated with ornate carvings, but it is the sight beyond that robs the breath from my lungs. I wasn't expecting to see it so soon. The Court of Ash. A huge stretch of marble glittering beneath Father Sun like a frozen lake. Noblemen, servants and other Hopefuls mill about, but even the crowd cannot dull its splendour. This is where the Samael were burnt all those centuries ago, their bodies stacked higher than the palace itself. I practically drool at the thought of all the devil wing reaped from their feathers. Somewhere, here in the citadel, is the largest stash of devil wing known to mankind. My veins fizz with anticipation.

The Sun Temple, a huge building of pale marble, sits at one end of the court, and the Night Temple – place of worship for the Embalmers and hallowed house of Mother Moon – sits at the other, and whilst it is smaller than the Sun Temple, its black-as-tar marble renders it an imposing counterpart. When I succeed at the Illumination Ritual, I will be allowed in the Sun Temple at dawn and the Night Temple during the gloaming, because the Divine Shadow does not receive a temple and, as such, the Alchemists must share the other two. We get the best of both worlds, and my heart flutters at the thought of it.

A servant sweeps by, handing us tumblers of ruby-coloured liquid. I assume it's wine, until it hits my lips and I taste the raspberry, sweet and tart all at once.

I drink deeply.

Papa straightens his dress tunic, a clean, white drop of linen, enhanced with gold-and-silver embroidery. Mama made it for him as a gift on their wedding day and it still fits him perfectly. He is approaching fifty years and seven, but he is still a striking man. I see a lot of my own face in his, which today, doesn't seem so bad.

He smiles at me, then Icari. 'I remember my own ritual, four decades gone. I was so nervous.'

We have heard this tale many times. Papa didn't *want* to succeed at the Illumination Ritual. He wanted to be a farmer and work the land, and he felt no Calling inside him at all. A concept that is so alien to Icari and me, it always makes us laugh. Yet now, standing in the Court of Ash, watching the noblemen mill around, a small part of me grasps his desire to simply go home.

It would certainly be easier.

Papa launches into the story of his ritual, and Icari, always the kind-hearted one, listens as though hearing it for the first time. I, however, take the opportunity to gaze towards the palace, perched on the summit of Mount Appollis, a breath-taking structure of marble, with turrets of gold and rooftops of pounded silver. Home to the High Priest. My stomach aches with rage. He does not deserve a palace. He deserves the gallows.

'Greetings.' The voice is soft, feminine, and takes me by surprise, and when I look upon its owner, my surprise only deepens. She is the most striking girl I've ever had the pleas-ure of meeting, with black curls streaked with auburn, and freckles of deep russet brown that dust her fawn skin like the prettiest of paint splatters. A look that I suspect has attracted much attention throughout her life.

Is this a terrifying witch from the Farlands? Wearing not a head of fire-vipers but tendrils of hair touched with the colour of autumn? I knew those rumours of witches stealing women from the oasis and turning men to stone were horse-shit. Women *and* the unknown: the perfect combination for fear and persecution.

She tilts her head and I pause, longing to know the story of how a fire-haired woman of the Farlands has survived, nay, *thrived*, in the Sunlands. But manners eventually trump intrigue, and I simply bow my head. 'Greetings.'

'You are a Hopeful?' she says.

'For my sins.'

'It's not so bad.' Her smile presses dimples to her cheeks and suddenly Selene and Xanthos are wiped from my mind.

'And you are training as an Embalmer?' I ask, trying not to stare. How strange she should worship Mother Moon when her black hair is flecked with sunshine.

Her smile broadens. 'It's OK. You can look. I don't mind.'

I shake my head, pretending not to understand, which makes her laugh. She has a lovely laugh, deep and croaky, completely at odds with the lightness of her voice.

'Everyone stares to begin with. Then they get used to it,' she says, tapping her head.

I interpret her frankness as permission to sate my curiosity. 'Are you from the Farlands?'

'Originally, but I was raised here in the Sunlands.'

'That must have been . . .' I pause. 'Hard for you.'

'I'm a fast runner and I've got a mean right hook.'

I warm to her immediately. Not just her heart-shaped face and dirty laugh, but because she brings hope. If someone with a head of fire-vipers can train at the citadel, then maybe the daughters of a murdered witch can too.

'I'm Talia,' she says, extending her hand.

I accept it with zest. 'Sephie.'

Her dark eyes narrow slightly; they're quite exquisite, flecked with green fresh from the oasis. 'Sephie? Daughter of . . .' Her voice fades as she sees the hurt on my face.

'Yes,' I snap. 'Daughter of Daeda.'

'Oh.' She bites her lip, marking two white crescent moons upon her skin. 'I'm so sorry, I didn't think.' She realizes she still grips my hand and gives it a quick squeeze as if she's known me for years. 'Today must be surreal.'

I nod, pushing back a sudden urge to cry, wishing for a nip of devil wing. 'She should be here. She was *supposed* to be here.'

'I'm sure she watches from above.' Her face falls, her eyes drifting away from mine, as if she's recalling Mama's fate. Quickly, she composes herself, though she toys with a silver locket around her neck, belying her discomfort. 'So what is your preferred path?'

'Alchemy.'

'Oh how exciting. Though you must promise not to look down on me after the Illumination Ritual.'

A smile climbs up my face. 'But I can throw you a crust of bread, yes?'

She rewards my joke with one of her throaty laughs.

The sound of a gong reverberates around the Court of Ash, causing us to jump apart. The crowd gathers before the Sun Temple and a fanfare of horns announces the arrival of the High Priest, who walks from the steps, flanked by two ladies.

'Are you OK?' Talia whispers.

No. I want to burn the desert roach alive, see how he likes it.

'Yes, thank you,' I say.

One of the ladies beside him has greying hair and pale skin, and I know immediately who she is: Madame Embalmer. Icari told me how she tried to stop Uriel from burning Mama, so really, I should be grateful to her, but instead I'm furious she failed, and I'm furious she got to see Mama one last time when I didn't.

Shaking the image of Mama from my head, I study the other lady. She has dark brown skin and wears a flowing white gown and a golden headdress that cannot contain her gorgeous black curls. She must be Principal Healer, tutor to all the student Healers. Her eyes seem to smile and I wish she were the High Priest Alchemist. Heck, I even wish Madame Embalmer was the High Priest. Anyone but Uriel. How will I contain this level of rage for three years? Surely my blood will boil dry.

'Are you ready?' Talia whispers.

I must look alarmed, because she smiles and adds, 'For the Illumination Ritual?'

'So soon?'

She gestures to Father Sun, who has already begun to dip in the sky, heralding the approach of twilight.

Another gong sounds, and Icari and I join the other Hopefuls, standing in a crescent shape between the two temples. Icari is on one side of me, and a boy who looks far older than me is on the other. Now that the crowd gathers around the edges of the courtyard, I see that the marble is opalescent and flecked with gold. I imagine I can see the ashes of the Samael ground into the tiny pores of its surface. Did they feel pain when they burnt? Did Mama?

The thought chokes me, so I force my mind back to the Samael. Back to the cold. Back to the numbness that, as of tomorrow, I will be able to draw upon whenever I please. I am so close – it takes all my energy not to do an excited little jig.

The line is only about twenty long, which both pleases and terrifies me. The ceremony should be quick, which means I'll know my fate sooner rather than later.

You already know your fate, Sephie.

The High Priest disappears into the Sun Temple, and even though I have never witnessed this ceremony before, I know exactly where he is going and what to expect, for our world is built on legend *and* rituals. Right now, he's climbing the stairs to the Tomb of Light, situated at the peak of the temple – the glass chamber where the winged gods who fell in the great battle in the sky are now preserved. Unlike the Samael, their bodies were embalmed, their wings left attached, allowing them to journey to Mother Moon and exist for ever in the afterlife.

Mama was burnt like a Samael when she should have been wrapped like an Illios. The familiar rage simmers in my gut and it takes an enormous effort to slap it down. Icari catches my eye and touches the cloth resting over her tummy button. I smile. She always knows when I'm suffering.

Uriel finally emerges from the temple with a feather as long as a spear. In the gloaming, it has a ghostly luminosity, though it is a deeper shade than I'd imagined, the colour of dried sap. I shiver with a combination of excitement and awe.

He raises his voice. 'Greetings, Hopefuls. Welcome to your Illumination Ritual and congratulations on reaching adulthood. The feather of the Illios will respond to those who have the Calling in their blood, revealing whether you are a Healer, Embalmer or Alchemist.' He pauses. 'It is not permitted to have more than one Calling.'

Does he always say this, or is it for the benefit of Icari and me?

'Let the Illumination commence,' he shouts, stepping forward. The scars on my back tingle and the shadow stirs within. How I long to smash in his skull.

Uriel presents the quill to the first Hopeful in line, a young man with the rough hands of a farmer. If he has the Calling of Father Sun, the feather's weak golden glow will intensify beneath his fingers. If he has Mother Moon in his veins, the light will change to silvery white. And if he has the Divine Shadow in his blood and is destined to be an Alchemist, the feather will blacken and wither. I realize I'm holding my breath. I am mere moments away from being allowed to practise alchemy freely and I have never wanted anything so badly.

The Hopeful runs his finger down the spines of the quill. Nothing happens. The onlookers release a soft sigh of disappointment and the Hopeful looks like he may cry. Uriel whispers something to him that I cannot hear, then moves to the next Hopeful.

The process continues with disappointing results until the feather reaches a tall boy with white, mottled skin and black waves of glossy hair curling around his broad shoulders. He has the look of a warrior, a bloodthirst about his strong jaw, and he reaches towards the plume as if he longs to snatch it for his own. Immediately, the feather darkens and wilts at his touch.

The crowd bursts into applause and the Hopeful runs his finger down the feather, causing the darkness to spread like disease.

'What is your name?' Uriel asks.

'Ziris, my lord,' the young man replies.

Uriel nods. 'The Divine Shadow is strong in you, Ziris. Clearly, you are an Alchemist in the making.'

'Thank you, my lord.'

'Where are your guardians?'

A couple steps forward: a handsome woman, and a man who is clearly the root of the bloodthirsty jaw. I cannot help the jealousy that churns up my heart at the sight of his mama and the pride on her face.

Uriel smiles. 'Do you gift your son to the citadel so he may hone his skill, shape his Calling?'

His papa clears his throat. 'It is an honour, my lord.'

Uriel looks back to Ziris. 'Well then, Ziris, welcome to the House of Alchemy.'

The crowd erupts into applause, and without so much as a smile, Ziris bows.

I do not want to train alongside him. Fun will surely bring him out in hives.

My eyes meet Talia's. In the half-light, her hair has lost its shine and the auburn streaks look less the colour of fire and more the colour of marigolds. She flashes a wicked grin and crosses her fingers by her side. What a shame she is not an Alchemist; I would much rather train with her.

Two more unsuccessful Hopefuls, and it is another boy's turn. When he touches the feather, a white glow springs from beneath his fingertips, which he then drags floorward, causing the whole feather to glow silver. Uriel declares him an Embalmer and welcomes him into the Temple of Mother Moon. He has two mamas, both of whom look ready to burst with pride, and my soul blackens and withers like the Illios feather as I think of my own mama again.

Next, it is Icari's turn, and my heart hammers in my chest for her. I know the feather will glow golden – I have seen the light of the Healer spill from her hands since she was old enough to treat patients – but that doesn't stop the nerves soaking my back and moistening my gown. I will stink like a camel's undercarriage before this day is out.

Uriel holds her gaze for a moment. He must recognize her, but he gives nothing away.

Icari raises a trembling hand.

Still yourself, sister – show not weakness.

As her hand connects with the top of the Illios feather, the yellow light of the feather glows strong and true, illuminating her pretty face. Though it is no surprise, she still gasps with delight, her eyes immediately finding a beaming Papa. She runs her finger downwards, leaving a glittering path.

The crowd begins to clap and Uriel turns to face them. 'Giorgos? Do you gift your daughter to the citadel so she may hone her skill, shape her Calling?'

Papa steps forward, brimming with joy. 'Yes, my lord.'

Uriel offers a curt nod, then turns back to my sister. 'Welcome to the Temple of Father Sun, Icari.'

Icari looks at me, the smile can barely fit on her face. I am so thrilled for her. I can sense the happiness radiating from her as if she were an Illios feather herself. She has wanted this all her life. But an awful, bitter part of me feels a little afraid. What if she is chosen and I am not? *Don't be silly, Sephie. The Calling in you is undeniable. You will cause that feather to curl into a blackened ball.*

Uriel stands before me. The sight of his face makes my skin harden beneath my gown, and I remember the last words he spoke to me: *'Twenty lashes, and that's the end of it.'*

He nods, then presents me with the Illios feather.

When I touch the plume, the Divine Shadow roars inside me, turning my blood to iced water, sending shivers across my skin. His shadowy hands all over me, stroking, caressing, sinking into my flesh, and I can hear his voice in my ear, deep yet glass-clear. *Sephie*, he whispers, *I am waiting*.

The feather darkens and withers beneath my hand as expected. But then something else happens: Uriel grabs the feather at the exact same time silver light begins to sputter in the veins of the plumes. We lock eyes and he wrenches the feather from me.

'My lord—' I begin.

'That is quite enough, Sephie. Thank you.' Uriel's expression resets and he manages a thin, controlled smile as the murmurs of the crowd fade away. I wait for him to call on Papa as he did with Icari and Ziris, but instead he simply announces, 'My apologies, Sunlanders. Sometimes, I struggle to keep the Divine Shadow in check. It will not happen again. Thankfully, this Hopeful was able to call on Mother Moon in spite of my interference.'

What? Bollocks of a donkey. It was *my* hand that caused the feather to blacken and wilt. *Uriel* was the one who transmuted the feather to silver. I feel breathless, sick.

'Wait—' I begin, but he silences me with a glare, danger strengthening the contours of his face. My back tingles with the memory of the whip.

And then, with just a few words, he destroys every hope, every dream I've ever had.

'This girl is an Embalmer.' He holds my gaze, dark recognizing dark. 'Welcome to the Temple of Mother Moon, Sephie.'

8

SEPHIE

My world collapses. Not an Alchemist, free to embrace my gift, free to transmute the natural world and to call on the Divine Shadow to numb my pain whenever I desire, but an Embalmer.

A life of pulling out innards in underground morgues.

I can barely stand as Uriel continues down the line. My ears ring, my vision spots and my throat aches with unspent tears. I have an overwhelming urge to just run and run until the citadel is far behind me. But Papa is smiling, the guards are scowling, and if I proclaim to be an Alchemist, if I accuse the High Priest of interfering with the ritual, I will either be accused of blasphemy, or worse, of possessing two Callings. Mama's face flashes in my head and it takes every effort not to cry, but I bottle my emotions like I'm one of Icari's tincture jars.

Finally, the ritual ends and Icari guides me towards Papa.

'Stay strong, sister,' she whispers.

I just about manage to put one foot in front of the other.

Papa embraces me. 'I'm so sorry, dear-heart.' His voice is low and urgent.

'But, Papa,' I reply. 'It was not Uriel who made the feather blacken and wilt—'

He presses a finger to his lips, then whispers, 'I know.'

But I'm unable to still my tongue. 'Uriel transmuted the feather to silver – I know he did. He *wants* me to be an Embalmer. Or more to the point, he doesn't want me to be an Alchemist.'

Papa glances around with panicked eyes. 'Hush now, Sephie. We are fortunate you are able to train in the citadel at all.'

Anger heats my cheeks. '*Fortunate.* You know how much I hate death.' A swooping sensation in my belly as anger dives into fear. 'I won't be able to call on Mother Moon in the catacombs. What then? Will I be expelled? Disgraced?' I grasp Papa's hands. 'Was this Uriel's plan all along?'

'You are being paranoid,' Icari says, her voice level. 'Why would Uriel do that?'

'Because of the dust cloud? Because they fear my powers? I don't know – for the same reason . . .' The words stick in my throat: *for the same reason they killed Mama.* I shove the thought aside.

Papa leans in, his voice only just audible. 'I do not understand what is going on, but it is best if you go along with it. If we fight it, we know what happens.' A solitary tear filters through his smile lines. 'Please. I have already lost your mama.'

His vulnerability deflates me and I'm left just wiping my tears. 'Can I come home with you, Papa?' I'm embarrassed by how young I sound.

'You know that's not an option,' Icari says, so calmly, so balanced, I suddenly want to slap her. 'Nobody *chooses* to leave the citadel once selected. It wouldn't be allowed.'

'Sweet Mother Moon, why is this happening to me?' I say.

'We shall request an audience with Uriel,' Icari says.

Papa looks unsure. His mouth opens as if to speak, only to snap shut again as if spring-loaded when Talia appears.

She grins her dimpled grin. 'Well I bet you weren't expecting that now, were you?' She laughs, as if being an Embalmer is the best thing in the world rather than the purgatory that it is. 'Come, say your farewells and I will show you and your sister to the Great Hall.'

Icari and I bid Papa goodbye. But for the occasional visit, we won't see him for three years, and when I say 'we', I of course mean Icari, for I will be sent home in a matter of days, tail between my legs.

'You mustn't worry about me,' Papa says. 'I will miss you both, but I will be OK. Besides, I have Leon and Ruari.'

'Don't let Ruari swim on his own,' I say, forcing a smile. 'He thinks he can manage the Nubi river, but he still needs a hand under his tummy. And don't forget to close the shutters so the mosquitoes don't get in, and lay off the figs.'

'And take the tincture for your heart,' Icari says, waving a finger at him.

'I know, I know,' he says, suddenly keen to escape in case his own tears should fall.

After one last hug, we watch him leave, carrying the scent of home on his clothes and hair.

9

ICARI

We take supper in the Great Hall, a grand building with stained-glass windows of every colour and a ceiling so high even the sky covets it. The meal is a lavish spread of fresh meats, oil-soaked breads and honeyed nuts. It would feed our village for a week. Normally, I'd feel angry at the display of wealth, when the poor have so little, but I'm distracted by what's happened to Sephie. I glance at her where she sits next to me, barely eating – I can feel her anger burning in my own stomach. How did the ritual turn out so wrong?

Please, Sephie, don't fall apart.

After the meal is over, I wait with Sephie so we can speak with Uriel in private. Clocking the silver-and-gold robes of the alchemy students, I can't help but think of Mama. I imagine a ghost of her moving around the hall, a ghost I can almost reach out and touch.

The High Priest Alchemist sits at his throne, reading a scroll with his quick eyes.

'My lord,' Sephie says, as bold as I feel nervous. 'May we have a word, please?' When her voice trembles, it is with rage rather than anxiety.

I squeeze her hand, hoping both to calm her and to draw on her strength.

Uriel meets her gaze with no apology. 'Sephie, daughter of Daeda. Last time I saw you, I was ordering your lashing. Isn't that right?'

My sister's face twitches, but she doesn't falter. 'That's right.'

He shrugs off his over-robe so that only his embroidered tunic remains, then, wincing, reaches over his shoulder to massage the base of his neck.

'Are you in pain?' I ask instinctively.

'Just an old war wound.'

'I could look, if you like,' I say. 'I am a good Healer.' The words flow as naturally as my Calling, yet I regret them immediately.

'You would heal me even though I ordered your mama's death and had your sister whipped?'

I avert my eyes, humiliated and unsure.

He studies my face. 'You really are your mama's daughter.' A pause, and when I don't reply, he adds, 'It brought me no pleasure to order her execution. But that is the price one pays for trading devil wing. She knew the risk.'

Desperate to discover more about Mama's death, yet scared of further riling the High Priest, I keep my voice soft and my gaze lowered. 'I thought the punishment for trading devil wing was a public lashing.'

He arranges his face into a neutral expression. 'It used to be. We've hardened our stance in the past few years. Supplies are thinning and we need to keep tighter control on what is left.'

I want to ask him why I saw the trader paid off, why they set Mama up, but I don't want to make things worse for my sister.

Sephie speaks with conviction. 'My lord, you know that I'm an Alchemist.'

His features remain motionless. 'I don't know what you're talking about.'

'Of course you do,' she says. 'You saw how I stopped the sand cloud before it reached the oasis.'

A faint smile taints his indifference. 'I checked on your village following a close call with a sandstorm that *naturally* dispersed before reaching the oasis. What I found was a young woman who disrespected me and the citadel. That's why she received twenty lashings. Ask anyone. The General, the guards. They all heard you dishonour my name.'

'That isn't true,' Sephie says, tears springing to her eyes — she starts to step forward. 'You're lying. Why are you lying? If I try to call Mother Moon, and fail—'

'Then you'll be expelled from the citadel,' Uriel supplies, his expression hard.

I hold Sephie's arm, tug her gently away. 'Sephie, stop. This is a fight we cannot win.'

'Listen to your sister,' Uriel says. 'Because if you darkened and curled the feather *and* turned it silver, then you have two Callings, and we all know how that ends, don't we?'

10

ICARI

Thankfully, Sephie and I are placed in the same bedchamber, alongside Talia, the embalming student who wears her red-streaked hair like a lion's mane rather than an ox's yoke, and two other students: an Embalmer named Zalta, and a Healer, Xenia.

'Is it a coincidence there are no Alchemists here?' I ask, brushing out my hair.

'Oh, they have their own bedchambers,' Xenia replies. 'Because they worship at funny times, it's less disruptive if they stick together. They're up before dawn and don't bed down until late, poor things.' She has shoulder-length black hair, deep brown skin, and a smile that never sleeps. Since we arrived, she's been nothing but warmth and welcome.

'And they're far too special to slum it with the likes of us,' Zalta says, before firing a quick glance at Sephie. 'Is she OK? She's barely said a word.'

'*She's* fine,' Sephie snaps.

Zalta, whose bone-thin body moves as quick as her tongue, is clearly not so forgiving as Xenia and shoots Sephie a frown that could kill.

'She just misses Papa,' I add, hoping my softness will

counteract my sister's edge.

'We all miss someone. No need to be a cockroach about it,' Zalta says, tucking her brown hair behind her ears, revealing a pale pink neck with faintly visible veins.

'What were your own Illumination Rituals like?' I ask in a feeble attempt to distract her.

Xenia sits on her bed and brushes her hair, causing the candles to dance. Shadows scoot across her face, transforming it into something mischievous and pretty, like a tree fairy or a river nymph. 'Well, my parents were both teachers, so I had no experience of healing, but I already knew I had the Sun God in my blood. So it wasn't a surprise when the Illios feather lit up gold. But it was still –' she leans forward and raises her brows – 'wonderful.'

'You said you already knew?' I say.

'The bird,' Zalta replies in a bored tone, indicating she's heard this story many times.

Xenia grins. 'I didn't have experience of healing people, but I found an injured bird when I was only ten years and two, and when I splinted its wing, my fingers glowed. That's how I knew. After that, I healed every injured animal I could find.'

'She still won't eat meat,' Talia says as she combs out her curls.

'And what about you, Zalta?' I ask.

She screws up her face as if digging up a memory from the depths. 'It was a surprise. A nice surprise. I come from a family of farriers, you see. No Callings, just horseshoes, so when the feather glowed silver, I don't know who was more shocked, me or my parents.'

Talia sits on the bed beside Sephie and shoots her a sympathetic look. 'We can't always know Mother Moon's plan, but that doesn't mean she lacks one.'

Sephie's motionless face reminds me of a crocodile lurking in the Nubi waters.

'What about you, Talia?' I ask before Sephie snaps.

'I was not surprised when the feather glowed silver.' A corner of her lips curves upwards. 'I always felt an affinity with Mother Moon.' She glances to the window, to the plump goddess-moon beyond.

Beneath the stars, a ball of soft golden light thrums from the top of the Sun Temple.

'What *is* that?' I ask, pointing.

Xenia joins my side. 'Why, that's the Tomb of Light. The feathers of the Illios glow even in death.'

'Of course,' I say, feeling suddenly foolish.

'Knowing it and seeing it are very different things,' Xenia replies, softly.

Sephie finally stands and prepares for bed, and as she slips from her ceremonial gowns, the scars on her back glisten in the candlelight like a dew-sodden cobweb.

Zalta gasps, her discretion swamped by interest.

Talia tuts. 'Zalta! She is not a sideshow to be gawped at.'

'What happened?' Xenia whispers, sympathetically.

Panic gushes up my throat. 'Desert dogs,' I say, cutting over Sephie, whose mouth is open to reply. 'She was attacked by desert dogs.' Best to avoid the story altogether than tell a half-truth.

'They must have been big desert dogs,' Zalta says, her voice sharp.

'The biggest.' Sephie holds my gaze, an accusatory glint in her eye, and my insides knot with guilt, not just because I lied, but because I get to follow my life's Calling.

Talia crosses to the door, checking it is firmly closed, then looks at us each in turn, her face suddenly fierce, the rusted streaks in her black hair brighter than the candles that illuminate it. 'Code of the dormitory: anything we say, anything we see, within these four walls stays within these four walls. Agreed?'

We exchange awkward glances, yet our hesitation only makes Talia grow taller. 'I mean it. The citadel is a viper's nest. But we should not fear the fangs of our fellow chamber-mates. We should sleep safe.'

Zalta and Xenia nod their agreement and I feel that knot in my stomach loosen. And Sephie . . . Sephie is looking at Talia like she's the goddess herself. I haven't seen her look at anyone like that. Not ever. Not even Selene, and certainly not Xanthos. A slight smile warms my face.

'You can't trust Belum,' Zalta says, flinging on her night-gown. 'He's a second-year Alchemist, and everything he hears gets back to Uriel.'

'And Ziris looks like bad news,' Xenia whispers. 'He ate all the stuffed vine leaves at dinner and didn't once pass the wine around.'

Talia snuffs out the candles, releasing the scent of tallow wax and enveloping the room in darkness. We clamber into our beds. I've never lain on a proper mattress before, filled with lambswool and dried grasses; it's like sinking into broth. I miss the papyrus mattress and clay floor of my mud hut more than I thought possible.

I stare into the dark, listening to the other girls as their breaths grow deep and heavy. Yet another noise falls between their breaths: the stifled mew of a kitten. It takes me a moment to realize it's Sephie. Padding across the boards to her bed, I clamber beneath her quilt and pull her near. Only then, her head buried in my shoulder, does she allow herself to sob properly.

'I'm so sorry, dear-heart,' I whisper. 'I wish I could make it better.'

'Why do they still punish me? Was the whipping not enough?'

'I don't know.'

I hold her until the weeping subsides and her breaths mimic those of the other girls. I'm surprised she fell asleep so easily, without the help of the devil wing she's come to rely on. Regret stabs at my side. If it weren't for me, perhaps Sephie would have dealt with her grief.

Eventually, I climb back into my bed with guilt as my only sleeping partner – guilt that I follow my chosen path whilst Sephie cannot, guilt that a mesh of scars doesn't blight my back, and guilt that I did nothing as Mama burnt.

Then, I notice Sephie's coronet, strewn beside her bed and gleaming in a trickle of moonlight; the blooms have been transmuted – they're as plump and bright as the moment I picked them. So that's how she fell asleep so easily, by calling on the Divine Shadow to numb her pain . . .

Oh, Sephie. Practising her alchemical powers has never been more dangerous.

11

ICARI

After breakfast, I visit the Sun Temple for the first time. Stepping inside is like stepping into the sky. The roof consists mostly of glass, so the morning sun streams on to the pale marble and lights it up like polished river stones. The columns are woven with gold-dipped vines, hummingbirds and dragonflies paused in flight, and clusters of fruit trees and potted flowers spill their scent into the air, transforming the space into a giant orangery.

The beauty offers a grateful distraction from the itchy white frock, buttoned from my ankles to my chin. Earlier, as she fastened her own identical dress, except sewn from black cloth, Sephie said the dresses must've been designed by men. I have to agree. Thank goodness for the apron: though it adds an extra layer to sweat into, it also provides a handy pouch for medical equipment. I glance at the cooler, pocket-gifted outfits of the male students and suppress a jealous sigh.

There are about forty of us gathered in the temple, a mixture of first-, second- and third-years, but I am the newest apprentice by at least one moon cycle. I stick to Xenia, recognizing her kindness and recalling Talia's words from last night: *'The citadel is a viper's nest.'*

Soon, Principal Healer arrives, wearing a white gown similar to my own.

'Greetings, pupils,' she says. 'For those of you who don't yet know me, I am the Principal Healer of the citadel, and I like to be addressed as such.' Her voice fills the temple like a bell and I wonder if she knew Mama, trained with her perhaps, for they look of similar age.

Could she know something about Mama's death?

'Yes, Principal,' we chorus.

'Tomorrow you will resume your duties at the sanatoriums, but today is a day of study in the temple.'

'Yes, Principal.'

We follow her towards the back of the temple, and for my benefit, she points out the pews where we sit and contemplate, and the kneeling stones where we bow in prayer. We walk past a small archway leading to a set of marble steps.

'What's up there?' I whisper to Xenia.

'The Tomb of Light,' she replies.

Of course.

Something draws me to it. Curiosity, wonder and something else. The Calling rises, liquid sunshine running in my veins, and I step towards the archway.

Then, Principal is beside me. 'Icari? Yes?'

I nod, words abandoning me. Suddenly I realize I've left the huddle of students behind. How did I wander so far?

'You cannot enter the Tomb of Light,' she tells me, her voice level. 'Only the High Priest, Madame Embalmer, and myself are permitted. I don't care who your mama was.' Her words linger in the air, a waft of smoke in an otherwise clear atmosphere.

'I'm . . . I'm sorry,' I mumble, bowing my head, desperate to ask her more about Mama, yet not wanting to make things worse.

She smiles. 'No matter. Now you know. Head to the study room, please, students.'

I hang back, keeping near to Principal Healer, waiting for the crowd to thin. Reading my intentions, Xenia offers me a small head shake, then hurries after the others.

Principal Healer raises an eyebrow at me, as if to say, *What now?*

'Please, Principal, did you know my mama?' It's far from the question I want to ask, it doesn't even touch upon her death, but I hope it's innocuous enough to get a response.

'*Everyone* knew your mama.' She sails after the students and I have to hurry to keep up.

'Please, Principal, what do you mean?'

'She was unusually gifted, and unusually kind. The two don't always go together.' She gestures to the classroom door. 'I believe you are here to learn about healing, not your mother.'

Frustrated, I nod and follow the others into the room and join Xenia at a desk. Skeletons dot the stone walls, their joints pinned so they articulate when touched, and filling the spaces between are drapes of linen with charcoal sketches of bodies with muscles and veins exposed. The first-years, myself included, are left to pack our medical satchels and aprons with basic supplies, whilst the second- and third-years practise mixing ointments. I glance over at the ingredients and realize I was mixing these ointments for Mama when I was seven.

Xenia mixes her ointment beside me, her tongue clamped between her teeth in concentration.

'Try adding aloe vera and the scale of a river fish,' I say, without looking up from my pack.

She glances at the Principal, then scuttles to the back of the room, where bottles line the shelves, a little giggle escaping from her mouth. A moment later, and she's stirring her ointment with glowing fingers, a look of wonderment swamping her delicate features.

'Icari, it is fizzing,' she says.

'That's a good thing,' I say.

'It will work better now?'

I nod. 'Stops infection in its tracks. You'll see.'

Principal Healer taps on her desk with the tip of her writing reed, causing the soft chatter and the clink of metal upon glass to drop into silence.

She clears her throat. 'The best way to understand the bodies of the living is to dismantle those of the dead. I know this goes against our way of life, the bodies of our lost ones should be preserved so they can exist for ever either with Mother Moon —' she kisses her fist and points to the ceiling — 'or swim with Aïdes in the river of lost souls —' she gestures to the floor — 'so we only dismember the bodies of criminals who would be burnt anyway. Those who would never get the chance to journey to the afterlife.'

Her words are a needle in my gullet. Xenia reaches beneath the desk and squeezes my hand, an acknowledgement of Mama's fate, and this compassionate act, though small, makes my vision blur with tears.

Principal Healer watches me. 'Icari, it is tradition that the newest recruit fetches the cadaver from the catacombs. Though I believe today we are lucky enough to have a body so fresh, it is still in the dungeons. Xenia will help you.'

Xenia leads me through the temple, yet instead of heading to the courtyard, we reach a door hidden behind a veil of fruit trees and bordered by two lit torches.

'What's this?' I ask.

Her hand hovers over the iron handle. 'The catacombs sit directly below the Night Temple so the goddess can guard the dead. And we're not allowed in the Night Temple.' She waits for me to join the dots.

'Oh, I see. There's a direct route to the catacombs.'

'And the dungeons,' she says, as she heaves open the door. A waft of cool stone-infused air fills my nostrils as I peer down a set of steps carved into the ground. Only blackness awaits.

She passes me a torch; the flames warm my hand and illuminate the staircase so it becomes an endless descent into Mount Appollis.

'The dungeons are grim,' she says. 'Try not to look at the heads.'

The walk is cold and riddled with darting shadows, and by the time we reach the catacombs, I'm itching for fresh air and sunlight, but there is no such luck. Xenia leads me through a warren of stone and darkness beneath the citadel. Anxiety squeezes at my throat as I picture Sephie wrapping a corpse, no silver light blooming from her fingers. Will they expel her straight away? I rest my hand on my stomach, sensing her life force and wishing I were with her to share the burden.

Not soon enough, we reach the door to the dungeon. It's solid wood, reinforced with a metal grate; strong enough to keep in the prisoners, but not the stink.

Xenia knocks with surprising strength, before turning to me and whispering, 'The guards are often asleep, and who can blame them?'

A guard opens the door, spear clutched in anticipation of trouble. He's a broad, oily man, who looks like he enjoys inflicting pain, and even at the sight of two unarmed Healers, he doesn't lower his weapon.

The stench of rotting flesh and human waste hits me with full force, causing me to cough and my eyes to sting. I wrap my arms around my chest, warding off the cold and forming a shield against the air.

He smirks. 'Come for the corpse, have you?'

'Yes,' Xenia says, pressing her palms together in a sign of respect.

The guard looks at her hands and laughs. 'No need for that down 'ere. Death don't do manners.' His eyes swing from me to Xenia, me to Xenia, like we're two puddings he can't quite choose between. 'That uppity Embalmer woman asked to see one of you.'

'Who did she ask for?' Xenia says.

He shrugs. 'I've forgotten now. Funny name, it were.'

'Xenia?' she says, tentatively.

'Aye, that's what I said. Funny name.'

She scowls. 'What does she want?'

He wipes his nose with his thumb. 'Damned if I know. She just said she wanted to see you, no dallying.'

'Oh.' She turns to me and shrugs. 'Sorry, looks like

you're on corpse duty alone.'

'Don't worry,' the guard says. 'I'll help her.'

'Thank you,' I say.

He throws back his head and roars with laughter, revealing his back teeth speckled with plaque and food. 'I'm joking, you prat.'

Xenia squeezes my hand. 'Sorry,' she mumbles again, then vanishes back towards the catacombs, leaving me wishing I were anywhere but here.

The guard leads me down a short corridor towards the main cavern. The walls are built from strange bricks with holes in; I look closer and gasp – they are skulls. Human skulls.

He smiles at my discomfort. 'You just wait.'

Only when we reach the main cavern do I understand his meaning. Human heads at various stages of decomposition are mounted upon wooden spikes around the room. I place my hand over my mouth, allowing the scent of eucalyptus oil to cleanse my nostrils as the breath quickens in my lungs.

A second guard lounges beside a table, a tankard of ale beside him. His skin is chalky, cracked, like he's spent too long underground and has started turning into rock.

'She's here for the hag that croaked in the night,' the oily guard says.

The guard at the table raises his glass. 'Help yourself.' His voice is slurred and he swallows a belch.

The oily guard leads me down another long corridor. One side is lined with cell doors, a food hatch cut into each one – watchful eyes appear at the hatches as we pass. The other side of the corridor is built from skulls and bones, with flickering torches, and spikes displaying fresh heads mounted up high. The Calling stirs in my veins, yet I know there will be no healing down here.

I cannot imagine a deed bad enough to warrant imprisonment in this place.

'These conditions are disgusting,' I say, forgetting myself entirely.

'And?' the guard says.

'How will these prisoners be kept safe from disease?' I ask.

He shrugs. 'They're just criminals.'

They're still humans, I think to myself. 'What are their crimes?' I ask.

'Rape, torture, murder.' He lingers on the words, drawing pleasure from their shape.

'Theft?' I ask.

'Maybe. If they were stupid enough to steal from a nobleman.'

I gather my courage, Mama's face clear in my head. 'What about the trading of devil wing for medical supplies?'

He runs his thick fingers through his greasy hair. 'Never heard of anyone stuck down here for that.'

So Uriel was lying when he said they'd cracked down. Questions fire in my brain, and the need to understand why Mama was treated so unfairly burns in my heart.

We reach the last-but-one cell on the corridor and he jangles a set of rusted keys, smiling like he eagerly anticipates my reaction. The door opens. A woman, about Papa's age, dressed in the brown tunic of the poor, lies dead on the floor. The cause of her death is quickly apparent: an oozing neck wound encircled with blackened veins, like the legs of a spider. A simple infection. This woman needn't have died. Horror winds through me.

'Was this woman offered any treatment?' I ask.

'Course she bloody wasn't. She's a criminal. Nothing more than shit on me shoe. We want the scum to die – that's why they're 'ere, you silly cow.'

I recoil from him. His language, his disrespect, it appals me.

'Are you going to shift this or not?' he says, kicking her side. 'She'll start to smell if you leave her any longer.' He pulls the sandals from her feet and tucks them into his trouser pockets. 'They'll fit me wife nicely.'

I hook my hands under the woman's armpits and drag her from the cell, desperate to save her from this vile man. She's surprisingly light, malnourished I suspect, but my back still objects to the extra weight, so I pause in the corridor to stretch my spine.

The guard looks me up and down, then makes a noise like he hasn't eaten in a long time. Then suddenly he's pushing up against me, shoving me into the wall of skulls, his hands on either side of my face, his nose touching mine. I turn away, pressing my cheek against a skull, for his breath is gritty and foul upon my tongue and I would rather be intimate with the skeletons behind me than this disgusting beast.

'Sir, please,' I say. 'I'm sorry if I have given you the wrong idea in any way—'

I know that none of this is my fault, but I will say anything to appease this man right now. I am terrified.

He forces me to look at him, his nails digging into my face, then clamps his mouth over mine. It is hot and wide, and he mashes his lips up and down, smothering the bottom half of my face and forcing his tongue between my lips. It tastes of decay. I wriggle beneath him, desperate to escape, desperate to breathe, and somehow I manage to shake my face free just long enough to shout, 'Help. Please, help.'

I am drenched in panic, consumed with dread. I want to vomit.

'Who's going to help you?' he says. 'There's nobody else here but the heads.'

The sound of a hatch snapping open pulls his attention from me. It comes from the last cell on the corridor. A pair of grey eyes appear in the rectangular slit.

'I am here.' The voice emerging from the hatch is surprisingly clear. Male and educated. 'Minew, I believe?'

The guard called Minew loosens his grip on my arms. 'How do you know that?'

'How do you think?' The prisoner pauses. 'I listen.' He blinks — his eyelashes are as black as beetle shells. 'It is remarkable what you hear when you just listen.'

If I weren't in such deep shock, I would be surprised by this turn of events, but all I can do is gasp for breath and pray to Father Sun that the other guard will come to my rescue.

'Piss off,' Minew yells. 'Can't you see we're busy?'

'I don't believe the young lady shares in your enthusiasm,' the prisoner replies. 'Indeed, she looks positively repulsed. And who could blame her?'

'You little shit.' His ego damaged, Minew releases me and storms towards the cell. 'I'm going to cave your fucking head in.' He begins fumbling with the keys, desperate to get to the prisoner inside.

I should run, just abandon the corpse and flee from the dungeon, but instead I sink to the ground, watching in horror as he locates the right key.

I simply can't let him kill the man in the cell. 'Wait,' I gasp.

Minew turns to me, and everything I want to say, every threat, every bribe, sinks beneath the fear. My face is still wet with his stink and the decapitated heads are sneering at me and I think I may be close to fainting. Yet, somehow, I manage to say, 'Leave him. Or I'll tell Principal Healer what you've done.'

Minew steps towards me. 'And who would believe *you*, daughter of a condemned sorceress?'

He knew who I was all along. Is that why he thought he could get away with assaulting me? I bet Madame Embalmer never even sent for Xenia. I wish I felt angry, for with anger comes power, action, yet I feel nothing but useless and small. Nothing but foolish.

Grinning, knowing he's won, Minew returns to the door.

The prisoner speaks again, his voice far steadier than it has any right to be. 'I think, Healer, that you should seek out Minew's poor, unsuspecting wife. She can't be too hard to track down. I'm sure she would love to know just how much her husband enjoys the company of a certain orderly – a mutual attraction it seems, for there is no accounting for poor taste. Sometimes they lie together in the empty cells.'

I can tell from the way Minew freezes that the prisoner speaks the truth.

'Oh yes,' says the prisoner. 'It's remarkable what you hear when you just listen.'

Minew glances at me with panicked eyes. 'My wife . . . she'd never believe you.'

'Ask her where her missing jewellery's gone,' the prisoner says. 'For when Larisi passes me food, her wrist is now heavy with jewels.' He pauses. 'Larisi. That's the name of your sweetheart, isn't it, Minew?'

Minew's lack of response is confirmation enough.

The prisoner tuts. 'Giving Larisi your wife's bracelets whilst giving your wife sandals stolen from a corpse. It doesn't look good now, does it?'

The grey eyes in the hatch are smiling, and they lend me strength, for if a prisoner in a dungeon so foul can gain the upper hand, then surely I can utter a few sensible words.

So with my deepest breath, I push past the disgust and fear and say to Minew, 'Larisi – what a pretty name. I'm sure your wife would love to meet her. I wonder if Larisi will cover for you once her guilt gains a human name and a face. Or once you've asked for those bangles back.'

Minew finally moves, and when he faces me, he is a different man entirely. He doesn't look capable of pinning a gecko to the wall, let alone a fully grown woman.

'You wouldn't,' he whispers, a plea rather than a statement or a dare.

'Oh, but I would,' I reply. 'I'd do it in a heartbeat.' Years of honesty have prepared me well for this moment – I need only adopt my usual expression and he baulks.

'Fuck.' He drops his head into his hands, rubbing oily skin against oily skin, then looks at me, eyes full of desperation. 'It were just a misunderstanding, I swear it were. I thought you wanted it. When you stretched your back like that, I thought it were a signal. Don't tell me wife. Oh, please don't. She'll kick me out, and she's got some mean brothers that never liked me much.'

'A misunderstanding,' I repeat, trying to plan my next move, for I don't want to let this worm off the hook. 'We can forget about our little misunderstanding if you leave the prisoner be. I'll come tomorrow to check on him, and if he reports any maltreatment, or if I find him injured in any way, I will track down your wife and her brothers quicker than you can say *Larisi*. Understood?'

'Yes, miss.' He bows, pressing his hands together. 'Thank you, miss. I'll bid you good day.' He pauses, unable to meet my eye. 'Or would you like some help moving the cadaver?'

'I think you've touched her quite enough already, don't you?' I say, gesturing to the shoes tucked into his pocket.

Without a word, he places the sandals back on to her feet, then shuffles down the corridor.

I approach the prisoner's cell. The hatch is now closed, so I tap on the door as gently as I'm able. 'Thank you,' I call. 'If you hadn't intervened, I don't know what—'

'Why did you apologize to him?' The prisoner is still near the door, and the strength of his voice reminds me how close we are in spite of the stone and metal between us.

'I didn't,' I reply, confused.

'You did. You said you were sorry if you gave him the wrong idea.'

'Oh! Yes, you're right. I was acting on instinct, I suppose.'

'Your instinct is to apologize to a rapist?' His voice is calm, not a hint of accusation, yet I feel accused regardless.

'No, no, of course not,' I reply.

'Because it matters not if you stripped down to your undergarments and touched your toes – that man has no right to look at you, let alone touch you.'

Just the idea makes my cheeks heat with embarrassment, yet I know he is right. I knew it then, and I know it now.

'The fault lies entirely with him,' he continues. 'His sense of entitlement and his wicked heart.'

'I don't think he was thinking with his heart.'

He chuckles. 'You have a sense of humour.'

'A little. My sister stole most of it when we were together in the womb.'

'You're a twin?'

I nod, then remember he can't see me, so I say, 'Sir, would you mind opening the hatch, for I wish to thank you, and it is rather difficult to thank a door.' I could open the hatch myself, but I'm reluctant to take this last shred of control from him.

After a pause, he replies, 'You don't want to see me.'

'I have already seen your eyes. They are grey, yes?'

'I think so, though I haven't looked in a mirror for a long time.'

I glance around the corridor, trying to imagine what it must be like for this to be the brighter, more scenic side of the door. The torches spill their light on to the severed heads; one is so close to the flame, half of her face has cooked.

'How long have you been down here?' I ask, swallowing my nausea.

'Time loses meaning after a while. There are no windows, only the comings and goings of the guards to remind me that there's a world outside this cell.' Slowly, the hatch slides open. His heavily lashed eyes appear in the slit.

'Yes, your eyes are definitely grey,' I say, blinking back at him. 'The colour of a storm cloud.'

'And yours are brown.'

I nod. Now that I can meet his gaze, it feels as though I can finally deliver the words with feeling. 'Thank you, sir. I wish I could repay you for your kindness.'

'Just seeing somebody who doesn't stink of ale or steal from the dead is more than enough, I assure you.'

I don't smile, even though it is intended as a joke, for his situation is too sad to jest about. 'I will keep my word and check on you tomorrow,' I say.

'Please, do not risk your safety again.'

This time, I do smile. Oh, the irony that he should think of me, the great statue, as a risk-taker. 'I'm afraid it is not your decision to make.'

I can't make out the rest of his face, yet I can tell he's frowning from the narrowing of his eyes.

'If it happens again,' he says, 'knee him in the testes as hard as you can, then jab your fingers in his eyes. It helps if you keep your index fingernails nice and long, just in case.'

His own fingers curl over the edge of the hatch as if proving his point and fall into the torchlight. I gasp at the sight of them, causing them to slink back like a small animal blinded by the light. Yet I saw them long enough to notice the burns. The skin was blackened and crisped around his nail beds, unnaturally shiny and pink across his knuckles. The Calling strengthens inside me, a flood of warmth in the cold dungeons, and I finally find my anger. Someone has surely dipped this man's hands in burning oil.

'You are hurt,' I say.

His eyes shine in the gloom. 'I am a prisoner. The point of my existence is to be hurt.'

I glance at the dead woman still resting at my feet, the evidence of blood poisoning inked upon her throat in black. I don't want this man to share her fate.

'Let me heal you,' I say.

The hatch snaps shut. 'I am fine.'

'You are not fine. You have received burns, and without treatment, they will become infected, especially down here.' The door stares back at me and I rest a hand on the metal, wondering how close he is. 'Have you seen a Healer?' I eventually ask.

He chuckles. The clarity, the volume, suggests he remains only a finger's-breadth away. 'The dungeons are not the Healers' favourite haunt.'

'I have ointment,' I say, retrieving it from my apron, relieved that I failed to notice the small pot lurking in the folds of material when I left the temple. I slip it under the door — it just fits. The click of the lid drifts towards me, followed closely by the welcome scent of eucalyptus and mint.

After a long pause, the prisoner sighs. 'What is in this ointment of yours? It is astonishing.'

'It is my mother's recipe.'

'Your mama was a sorceress, yes?' His question surprises me, even though there is no disdain or fear in his voice.

'No,' I reply, clipped.

'I mean it as a compliment.'

'Surely no good can come of being a sorceress?'

'Well that depends on who you ask — the sorceress or the man whom she fills with insecurity.'

This sounds like something Sephie might say, and he manages to tease the first smile from my lips since the disgusting guard tried to eat my head.

The pot appears from under the door.

'Keep it,' I say, sliding it back with the toe of my sandals.

'They will find it – then you will be doing slops for a year.'

Slop duty involves emptying the prisoner's waste buckets; it is one of the worst punishments bestowed on students, one step behind whipping and expulsion.

The pot emerges once again, and this time I stash it back in my pocket, making a mental note to wash it thoroughly when I return to the dorms. Some illnesses can be transmitted by touch, after all.

'Thank you,' I say, for he needn't have worried about my fate, not now, nor when the guard attacked me.

It feels like a natural ending to our exchange. I've done enough; I should take the opportunity and flee, especially with Minew so close. Yet my veins are hot with Father Sun, and I cannot deny who I am simply because I'm in a dungeon rather than a sanatorium, so I say, 'You must be in pain.'

'Yes.'

'I will return tonight to bring more ointment and something to ease your suffering. It is not up for discussion.' If I cannot help Sephie, protect her from expulsion, then I can at least protect this poor man.

'Thank you,' he replies. The gratitude in his voice makes me want to cry. It will be such a small act on my part, yet he sounds as if I'm about to break him out of prison.

'It's the least I can do,' I say, tightening my grip on the cadaver. 'Farewell.'

'Farewell.'

And I begin the long journey of single-handedly dragging a corpse to the Sun Temple.

Xenia catches me as I reach the Sun Temple, her sweet face wild with anxiety. 'Icari, are you OK? That guard was playing tricks, I'm sure of it. Madame knew nothing of my seeing her, and I'm afraid my mind has run away with itself. I imagined you trapped and . . . well, nothing decent.'

'Your suspicions were correct, but I am fine – nothing I couldn't handle. We must warn the other students though.'

Her face falls and she grips my hand. 'We must tell Principal . . . the High Priest even.'

As much as I like the idea of bringing the guard to justice, he's terrified of me revealing his affair. And that gives me power. Power to access the prisoner, to provide him with the care I've promised him. If the guard is dismissed, I lose that power. 'Nothing actually happened. I don't want to ruin his life.'

She shakes her head, anger and exasperation turning her face into something fiery. 'You're too compassionate, Icari. People should be punished for . . . Wait –' her expression shifts into one of curiosity and, I hate to say it, disbelief – 'you said you handled it. What did you do?'

I long to tell her of the prisoner with the grey eyes, of his clear voice and educated manner, but something stops me. Secrecy? Fear of the rumour mill? Or simply the desire to keep him all to myself? So instead, I share a piece of his advice, reasoning this is the next best thing. 'Keep the nails on your index fingers long. It hurts them more when you jab them in the eyes.'

Xenia's eyes glow conspiratorially. 'I suppose you could say that awful guard has already been punished?'

I nod.

'Very well. We can keep quiet for now ... but if it happens again ...'

I feel terrible for lying to her – but as we walk away, I know I've done the right thing.

I have to see the prisoner again.

12

SEPHIE

I face my first, and probably only, day in the catacombs trussed up in a black embalming gown with no bloody pockets. At least I look as dour as I feel. Bookended by Talia and Zalta, I pass through the Night Temple. Like me, its exterior reflects its interior, for it's as dark on the inside as it is on the outside, with walls and floor of black marble shot through with indigo and silver. I'm too anxious, too grumpy, to be impressed.

'At night, the view of Mother Moon is exquisite,' Talia says, gesturing to the glass-domed ceiling. 'The stars pick out their painted echoes on the walls and floor so that it feels like you're suspended in the night sky.'

'I didn't know you were a poet,' I say.

She grins, then launches into some dirty old tavern rhyme, making me and Zalta guffaw with laughter. She never fails to ease my nerves.

'That one's Mariam's favourite,' she says, touching her locket absent-mindedly.

'Who's Mariam?' I ask.

'Just a childhood friend,' Talia replies, though she avoids my eye.

We reach a large spiral staircase that plunges into the belly of the catacombs and I suppress a shudder.

'What's that for?' I ask, pointing at the rope harness that dangles down the cylindrical shaft.

'For lowering the dead into the catacombs,' Zalta replies.

'Why not just drop them down?' I say. 'They're already dead, aren't they?'

'Don't let Madame hear you say that,' Talia replies.

I follow them down the stone steps, my stomach shrinking alongside the light. I am moments away from expulsion and shame. And to pour embalming salt in the gaping wound, my audience will be a crowd of corpses.

Talia turns to me. 'Are you OK? You look a little unwell.'

'I don't particularly like dead people,' I reply.

'Then you've come to the wrong place,' Zalta says with a wry smile.

'I couldn't agree more,' I snap.

'You'll grow to love it,' Talia says. 'It's so peaceful down there.'

'Yes, I imagine corpses are a little short on conversation,' I mutter.

By the time we reach the catacombs, a series of underground corridors and caverns spiderwebbing beneath the citadel, I'm ready to lose my breakfast. Nerves and the whiff of decay – quite the combination. Torches and lanterns dot the walls, unable to banish the gloom or the eerie chill, and all I want is to go home.

Perhaps expulsion won't be so bad, after all.

We pass the smaller crypts where the approved Embalmers work. There are many crypts, tombs and embalming houses across the city, even more across the oasis – like I said, the Sunlanders love death – but none so big as the catacombs. They wind through the depths of Mount Appollis like intestines. An underground city of death.

We reach the main embalming chamber known as the Grand Crypt, the main classroom for embalming students, and also used to store corpses at various stages of mummification before they are transported to the giant graveyards outside the city walls. It's circular with a domed ceiling, and so vast it almost matches the temple in size. A ring of stone slabs is laid out for the students to work at, about fifty in total. One corpse per slab; one student per corpse. Delightful.

Half-used candles sprout from every surface like fungi, and carved into the rock are layer upon layer of holes, the temporary graves where the bodies are kept. Talia told me at breakfast that they're called loculi. She said they look like a lotus seed pod. I say they look like maggot-eaten flesh. Ladders climb between the holes, allowing orderlies to slide the corpses in and out, and I imagine there's a high turnover of orderlies. Maybe they mark out their preferred hole before they fall to their death. The thought makes an unwelcome giggle crawl up my throat.

'Close your mouth,' Zalta says. 'You don't want the flies to get in.'

'Or the maggots,' Talia says, with a wicked smile.

I know they mean to be playful, but instead they amplify the bilious feeling in my stomach. 'Go drown in a bog,' I tell them.

Most of the students already stand behind their corpses, facing towards the middle of the circle where Madame Embalmer waits. She is paler-skinned than most Sunlanders, and her hair — a sheet of black — is now streaked with grey. It is said that she is only thirty years and two, but the Moon Goddess runs so strong in her veins that silver leaks from her head and blanches her skin. I think she just needs to get out more.

'There's your corpse,' Talia says, pointing to a slab between hers and Zalta's.

I swallow hard, then cross to the body, almost tripping on my stupid dress. A blue sheet is tucked under my dead girl's chin so only her head is visible. She can't be much older than Icari and me, and I decide to call her Agathi, after my great-aunt. Perhaps it will be easier to dismantle her if I think of her as a mean-spirited hag.

I long for devil wing to knock away the sharp edges of nausea, for I cannot call on the Divine Shadow to ease my discomfort, not with Madame Embalmer so close. Imagine if I caused the linen rags to twitch of their own accord, or the saline solution at my feet to transmute back into salt and water. I would be begging for expulsion instead of the pyre.

My eyes dart around the cavern. The devil wing is no doubt stored somewhere in the Sun Temple, seeing as it is only permitted for use by the Healers. But the Samael feathers from which the powder is ground are somewhere near. That's what Talia said, anyway. The pull of numbness overwhelms me for a moment, and I forget where I am.

I stare at the slab and avoid Agathi's judgemental gaze: *You are no Embalmer, are you?* There's a series of grooves carved into the stone, radiating from a central point to the edge of the table. I have no idea what they're for, but the flecks of dried blood don't fill me with confidence.

Madame Embalmer clears her throat. 'Greetings, pupils, let's begin. Our newest recruits can learn by observation, I'm sure.'

The other students busy themselves, lighting candles, stirring molten wax and stretching out pieces of linen. I just stare at the floor, surveying my equipment, unable to look at Agathi, who isn't Agathi, but someone's daughter. Someone's sister.

Madame crosses to me. Her voice drops so I have to strain to hear her above the clatter of the other students. 'Sephie, I was at the ceremony yesterday. It was unusual the way your Calling manifested.'

That's an understatement.

'Yes, Madame.'

'Do you have any experience of embalming?'

'No, Madame.'

'Is it what you'd hoped for? Being welcomed into the Temple of Mother Moon?'

Absolutely not. But the last thing I need is to get on the wrong side of Madame Embalmer, so I choose my words with care.

'I used to visit the embalming house of my village. Indeed, I am good friends with the Embalmer himself, Leon. I understand what an honour it is to preserve our loved ones so they may journey to Mother Moon.' It isn't a lie.

She nods. 'Ah yes, Leon. A good man.' She presses her lips together, and I wonder if she's recalling Mama's burning. The burning she failed to prevent.

'Have you ever opened up a body so you can remove the innards?' she asks.

I offer a tiny head shake, hoping that the horror doesn't claw from my stomach to my face.

'Very well.' She turns to my chamber-mates, who stand either side of me. 'Talia, Zalta, come, demonstrate how it's done.' Offering me a curt nod, she moves to another slab.

Talia approaches, a bloody scalpel gripped in her hand. 'It's probably best if we just get it over with. You will get used to it, I promise. This is the worst part.'

Zalta flips back the sheet to reveal all of Agathi. Slowly, I let my eyes explore her form. She is entirely naked. Her skin is faintly mottled, her eyes and lips colourless, yet she looks like she enjoyed life, what little she had, the spider silk of her smile lines still evident.

Oh, Agathi, what happened to you?

Thoughts of Mama burst into my mind and it takes all of my strength to button them back down.

Zalta folds up the sheet with precise movements. 'For my first few weeks, I imagined they were goats that I was preparing for a feast.'

'I like goats,' I wail.

She shrugs. 'Well, I'd chopped up many goats before, so it eased the transition. Stopped me spitting up my breakfast in front of Madame.'

Talia selects an ivory-tipped chisel from the wooden tray beside me. 'You used to work in a sanatorium, yes?'

'Yes.'

'OK, so maybe think of her as a patient who needs your help.'

'She's dead,' I reply.

Both girls release a coordinated sigh.

'Look, Sephie,' Talia says, and the way she says my name – almost a whisper – makes me instantly soften. 'If you don't embalm her, she won't reach the afterlife. She'll just . . . stop existing.'

'Surely non-existence is better than the Underworld.' I can't resist biting back, even with Talia. It's in my nature.

She doesn't seem to mind. 'At least she'll stand a chance of resting with Mother Moon.'

'Can we just get on with it?' Zalta says, stifling a yawn.

Talia shoots me a sympathetic look. 'Sometimes anticipation is worse than reality.' She positions the chisel in between Agathi's nose bridge and eye, then whacks it with a mallet. The *thunk* of bone causes my stomach to spasm.

Talia glances at me. 'She can't feel it.'

'No, but I think I can,' I whisper.

Ignoring me, she grabs a long metal hook and inserts it into the hole. 'I'm going to remove her brain, piece by piece.'

'I know – I've seen it done before,' I reply.

But I must look quite queasy, because she says, 'Maybe it will be easier if we use the draining method.'

Draining method. That sounds so much better.

Zalta nods. 'Then you won't see her face. It will be easier to imagine her as a goat.'

'Sweet Mother Moon, will you drop the whole goat analogy,' I say.

Zalta demonstrates her offence with a haughty sniff.

'Look away if it helps,' Talia says, gently, before inserting the hook back into the hole and pumping it back and forth. The effort causes both her and Agathi's cheeks to wobble.

'She's liquefying the brain,' Zalta says, a little too gleefully for my liking.

I reply with a strangled grunt. What I wouldn't give for a pinch of devil wing.

'Help me turn her,' Talia says. 'Dead people are heavy.'

Together, we rotate her so she's face down.

Friends, those grooves I mentioned, the ones carved into the slab, are for guiding the lumpy pink liquid into the clay pots below.

I suppress a belch.

Zalta slits open the abdomen, a small incision on Agathi's side, and begins pulling out glistening ropes of intestine. I finally lose my breakfast. Neatly in the clay pot meant for Agathi's guts.

Zalta releases a high-pitched chortle and Talia kicks her in the shin.

Madame Embalmer is beside me in an instant, handing me a sweet-smelling rag to place over my nose. 'You won't be the last, Sephie – try not to fret. Talia, take her outside for some fresh air and a drink of water. She can continue later.'

I don't wait for any further authorization, dashing down the corridor and up the stairs before any more vomit emerges. Only as I stand gazing at the sky, panting, do I realize Talia is behind me.

'It's no shame,' she says.

'I'm going to the orchard,' I reply, abruptly.

Nature will calm me. The grass beneath my feet, the bark against my palms. Father Sun will no doubt cook me in this wretched gown, but it will be worth it.

'Would you like some company?' she asks.

'Yes.' My voice comes out sharper than intended, so I add a quick, 'Please.'

My heart begins to still as the bent trees bearing oranges, limes and avocados come into view. We sit in comfortable silence on a log and watch the Alchemists in the distance. It seems their first lesson is ripening the fruit by laying their hands on the boughs.

I could do that when I was eight, I think, bitterly.

Some of them are successful, causing leaves to swell and peaches to ripen, but others are not. I watch them with envy in my belly, the taste of bile in my mouth. I should be there, dressed in silver and gold, embracing the Divine Shadow. Not sitting on a log stinking of death, awaiting expulsion.

Talia touches me lightly on the shoulder. 'I know this isn't the life you wanted, Sephie. But it is a good life, a respectable life. You *will* be happy.'

'I wish I had your confidence.'

'It is a form of alchemy. Transmuting death into something beautiful and sacred. If you think of it like that, maybe it isn't so bad.'

I study her face. Her freckles are a constellation of stars across her nose; her lips are small yet perfect, the exact colour of rosebuds.

'That's what Mama used to say about healing,' I eventually reply. 'That it's the transmutation of diseased flesh into healthy flesh.' I wipe my nose against the back of my sleeve, grimacing as a silvery slug-like trail like that of a slug appears.

'Your mama sounds very wise.'

My head hurts with the thought of her.

'What happened to your mama?' I ask. 'Your birth mama?' It's an obvious deflection, but I also want to know. Talia is a puzzle waiting to be solved.

She tucks a strand of black hair into her bun, not bothered that her fingers are lightly speckled with blood. 'I was five when I lost her. Or, more to the point, when she lost me.' She folds her arms as if clutching the memory to her breast. 'We must have been on some sort of journey towards the Sunlands, because I was found alone and half dead, wandering the oasis. My mother was nowhere to be seen. I was adopted by Mama and Papa shortly after.'

'Do you remember anything of her? Your birth mama, I mean.'

She shrugs. 'Bits. She looked like me, and she liked to laugh. She was always singing and grew herbs near the ocean.'

'The ocean?'

'Yes.'

'What was it like?' I can't stop the excitement pulsing through my voice. In my world of deserts, the sea is as much legend as the Illios and Samael.

'Endless. And it smells of salt.' She releases a light laugh. 'Maybe that's why I love embalming so much. All that salt. Perhaps it reminds me of home.'

'And you've never had any bother?'

She understands my meaning immediately, what with the rumours of witches from the Farlands with fire-vipers for hair. But she shakes her head. 'It's unfortunate that whenever girls go missing, witches from the Farlands are blamed. So, yes, I've had some bother.' She rolls her eyes. 'But the citadel felt I was young enough to embrace the way of the Sunlanders, so my adoption was blessed.'

'And you *have* embraced the ways,' I say, enthralled by her story and the way her freckles dance when she speaks.

'Yes I have. And so will you. If a sorceress of the Farlands can accept her Calling as an Embalmer, then anyone can.'

She rests her head on my shoulder, something only Icari does, and the familiarity surprises me. But it also gives me hope. Hope that she feels it too – that fluttery feeling whenever we lock eyes, that hot flash of desire whenever our hands brush against each other. If I listen hard enough, maybe I'll hear the beat of her heart crescendo just like mine. We sit like this for a moment, her head on my shoulder, her curls against my cheek, and I find myself relaxing. I exhale slowly, close my eyes; that tightly woven mesh of defences begins to sag.

'The catacombs make me think of Mama,' I say, without thinking.

She looks at me, blinking into the breeze. 'But your mama wasn't embalmed, was she?'

My lips tighten. 'Exactly.'

'Oh, Sephie. I'm so sorry, I never thought . . .'

I stare at my fingers, envisioning a vial of devil wing poised between them, imagining an end to the pain. I consider asking her about the whereabouts of the Samael feathers, but I fall quiet upon noticing Ziris striding between the trees towards us.

His self-satisfied grin is almost as broad as his shoulders.

'Gonads of a lizard,' I whisper under my breath.

Talia grins. 'Do lizards have gonads?'

'Apparently so,' I reply, gesturing at Ziris, who stops before us and opens his hand to reveal a peach.

'For you,' he tells me. 'It will get rid of the taste of sick.'

'How did you know?' I say, wiping my mouth, suddenly worried I've been talking to Talia with a dribble of part-digested porridge on my chin.

He smirks. 'I bet Belum one coin that you'd spit up in your first week, so the least I can give you is a freshly ripened peach.'

Anger solidifies in my belly, but I take the peach all the same. 'Well I'm glad you made some coin. Perhaps you can purchase some manners with it.'

Talia laughs and I let the peach drop to the floor, grinding it beneath my sandals.

'It's not my fault you have no alchemy skills,' Ziris says, any pretence of warmth abandoned.

'I don't know what you mean,' I snap.

'You think I haven't heard the rumours, about your mama being the most powerful Alchemist to walk the Sunlands, and you, following in her footsteps? Well, looks like they were wrong.'

He doesn't like the fact Mama was more powerful than he'll ever be. Such a cliché. Men and their penis complexes – they're exhausting.

Talia stands suddenly, turning her back to him. 'Come, Sephie, I believe you wanted fresh air, not air tainted with insolence and envy.'

'Oh, fall to the Underworld, you fire-viper-haired witch,' Ziris spits. 'I am not envious of *her*, what with her dead sorceress mama and a destiny in the catacombs stuffing cadavers like olives.'

My stomach spins. The urge to wallop his self-satisfied face is overwhelming. I step forward, my fist raised.

But Uriel stalks towards us, his robes sparkling in the sun, his headdress rendering him almost as tall as the trees. 'Careful, young Embalmer. I would take more care to avoid the whip, especially with your history.'

I lower my fist, trembling through a haze of anger. Talia shoots me a curious glance, but says nothing.

Uriel turns to Ziris. 'Why are you here, talking to Embalmers, rather than over there, ripening peaches?' He jabs a finger towards the back of the orchard.

'I'm just enquiring how Sephie's first day is going,' Ziris replies.

Uriel scowls. 'I would say that was rather obvious, wouldn't you? Considering she's here, rather than down in the catacombs.' He glances at the peach stuck to my sole and his scowl increases. 'Back to lessons, girls.'

Patronizing weasel.

We walk away, but not before Uriel shouts, 'And, Sephie, if your stomach or your talent are too feeble for the art of embalming, may I suggest you take up farming alongside your papa?'

Anger squeezes my body so I feel I might burst, just like Ziris's peach. I don't look back, but I can hear Ziris's laugh chasing me all the way across the Court of Ash.

The Night Temple looms over me, no more than a passageway to the catacombs, to death and brain gloop and my imminent expulsion from the citadel.

'What did Uriel mean?' Talia asks. 'About the whip?'

'The scars on my back.' I try to sound nonchalant, but

the tremble in my voice betrays me. 'Uriel ordered the lashing.'

'Why, that no-good bully—'

'He's done worse,' I say. He's set me up to fail at the citadel, denied me my Calling, and he ordered Mama's burning.

No. Don't think of Mama. Not now.

Holy crap, I need some devil wing.

That's when I get this pain in my stomach, a butcher's hook just above my naval. Something isn't right with Icari. She's scared or in danger. Yet I'm ashamed to say, I shrug it away, telling myself she's probably feeling guilty about Mama's death, same as always.

Quite frankly, I have enough problems of my own without worrying about Icari too.

13

SEPHIE

Back in the Grand Crypt, Madame Embalmer takes pity on me, suggesting I spend the rest of the day watching the other students work on their allotted corpses. Lungs and livers are placed in jars; abdomens rinsed with scented wines; bodies salted and left for the orderlies so they can be carried to their stone beds in the wall. Soon, I've managed a whole hour without vomiting. But my head is spinning by the time I reach Mesa, a second-year student who is mostly beard.

Oh hell, there's a bit of entrail stuck in his facial hair.

He begins packing a withered body with oil-infused lambswool, his hands gleaming with a ghostly white glow. 'I salted this gentleman two moon cycles ago,' he says. 'The lambswool will help give him back a more human shape; then he can be wrapped.'

I swallow. Hard.

'Isn't he beautiful?' Mesa says.

He looks like a giant raisin, but I attempt a smile. 'Yes.'

'Just think, in a short while, he'll be ready to journey to Mother Moon.' He pauses, his hand hidden by the flap of leathery skin that used to be a stomach. 'Would you like to help sew him up?'

I'm about to shake my head, when I catch Madame's eye. She nods at me, an indication I should proceed. Well, I managed two nights in the citadel. Two nights before expulsion. That's more than some.

So I simply say, 'Yes, thank you. It would be a privilege. By the way, you have entrails in your beard.'

I leave Mesa to tidy himself and focus on the needle, cool between my fingers. Madame nips the flaps of skin together so I can make the first stitch. This is the moment where my hands should shimmer with silvery-white light, and they won't. In just a moment, it will all be over.

Praise Mother Moon, let us lance this boil.

No more Agathi, no more brain gloop or intestines in pots, or entrails in beards. Yet there will also be no more Talia. My heart aches and I hate myself for always feeling so torn. And as if life wasn't hard enough, the thought of sewing a corpse is now bringing chunks of porridge to my mouth.

Does it really matter if I'm sick again? I'm about to be expelled anyway. But vomiting on a corpse, that would certainly damn me to the Underworld. My soul would hit that river with such a sploosh, even Aïdes would gasp. So I imagine the corpse is a goat. Or a patient needing help. I even imagine he's Ziris, or Uriel, or the General. Every hateful man who's ever resented me or my mother for being more than them.

Don't think of Mama.

Then I begin to stitch.

That's when something far more unexpected than vomit emerges: a silver light that dances beneath my fingers.

I drop the needle and smother a cry.

I must have been mistaken.

'Sorry,' I mumble, before fumbling for the needle, still dangling from its thread, and beginning to stitch again.

It was no mistake.

Once again, the silvery-white glow springs from beneath my fingertips. There is no brushing it away this time. I am an Alchemist first, and an Embalmer second. I have two Callings. Like Mama.

'Sephie, are you all right?' Madame asks.

'Yes,' I say, grinding out a smile. 'I am just –' I cast around for the right words – 'overwhelmed with the emotion of embalming my first body.'

She nods approvingly. 'Of course. It's perfectly normal, my child. You take all the time you need.'

I continue to stitch with trembling glowing fingers, all the time my brain turning faster and faster. So it wasn't Uriel who turned the feather silver at my Illumination Ritual. It was me. So was Uriel protecting me when he claimed he blackened the feather initially? Was he stopping me from being executed for having two Callings? But why would Uriel protect me? Especially after he burnt Mama and ordered my lashings.

Madame pulls me from my thoughts.

'Well done, Sephie.'

As she plucks two coins from her robes, presumably to rest upon the closed eyes of the corpse, I realize I have completed the sutures. It's like my fingers knew what to do, like they were programmed for this my whole life. I marvel at how neat the stitches are.

Madame lifts the coins to her lips to whisper the words of

the Embalmer. 'Taketh your fare to Mother Moon, not to Aïdes's icy tomb.' Then, she kisses the corpse's forehead.

My stomach roils.

Mesa repeats the process.

Then, they look at me, expectantly.

'It is a truly magical moment,' Madame Embalmer says. 'Knowing that you have allowed a soul to journey to the afterlife.'

I stretch out my hand, allowing Mesa to tip the coins into my palm; then I whisper the words, 'Taketh your fare to Mother Moon, not to Aïdes's icy tomb.'

I lean towards the corpse's withered face, my lips puckered.

But no matter how I resist, all I can think about is Mama, turned to dust, never to be salted and wrapped, never to blink down from the heavens. The pungent scent of wood smoke on the wind as Leon spoke the three words that changed everything: *'They burnt her.'*

The withered flesh is almost beneath my lips. Bile crawls up my throat. My gut moans. And even though I know it is risky, even though I know Madame Embalmer is right beside me, I allow the Divine Shadow to stir in my veins. A welcome surge of ice settles the nausea and I manage to kiss the corpse. Yet as my lips press against his cold skin, something else unexpected happens.

His eyelids spring open to reveal two ghastly eye sockets.

Camel crap. Necromancy is bad.

Necromancy is very, very bad.

Then, everything happens at speed. I gasp, whipping back my head. The clang of metal upon stone from the other end of the cavern causes Madame Embalmer and Mesa to spin away from me. I grasp at the moment, running my hand over the corpse's face, reclosing his eyes.

'What was that?' Madame Embalmer storms in the direction of the noise, where a group of students scrape something that resembles a skinned cat into a bronze dish.

I realize my hands still rest on the corpse's face, which is strange; I usually do everything I can to avoid touching the dead. But it's like my palms are gummed to him, and before I can let go, images begin to unfurl in my mind's eye. Images that belong not to me, but to *him*.

He was a tailor and loved to stitch bright dresses for the wives of noblemen. He'd just finished adding the lace to a particularly pretty gown when an unfamiliar pain gathered in his chest and shot down his left arm. He staggered to the ground, where he lay for a while, watching the sunset from his shop window. His last thought was that he never got to finish the pretty frock.

'Sephie?' Mesa says, lifting me from the dead man's memories. 'Are you OK?'

Blinking back tears, I pull my hands from the tailor's head. 'Yes, I'm fine.'

Mesa smiles and begins unfolding the linen wraps.

But I'm not fine. I'm anything but fine. Not only do I have two Callings, I am a necromancer. Worse, I can read the dead. In a land where gifts are expected to grow like beans – neatly, sticking to their own pole or you'll end up smoking on a pyre – this can only mean one thing: I'm officially screwed.

14

ICARI

After dinner, I slip back to the catacombs, armed with a bucket.

The chalky guard opens the door. 'What d'ya want?'

'Is Minew here?' I ask, as innocently as possible.

'He asked to be moved. Bloody wimp.'

I hadn't bargained on this . . . but perhaps I can work with it. 'Oh, OK, because I told him yesterday that I was on slop duty today.' I rattle the bucket, strengthening my story.

'Why – what d'ya do?'

'I . . . I . . . cheated on a test.'

He sneers. 'Aye, that'll be right. It's always the pretty ones. Come on then. I'll let the orderly know he can have the night off.'

Methodically, I empty the slops, trying not to splash my white gown with waste, trying not to inhale too deeply, yet it is sympathy rather than disgust that grows in my belly, for these poor souls are reduced to defecating in a dish and passing it through their food hatch on a daily basis. I make a point to thank every prisoner, even if they are too scared or numb to hear.

By the time I reach the prisoner with the grey eyes, I'm

shaking so much I have to steady myself by leaning against the wall; disease and misery coat my lungs worse than any stench. The shadows of the severed heads dance in the fire-light above me and I wonder, not for the first time, why I'm risking so much for a prisoner. Of course, because he helped me, yet there's something else I cannot put my finger on. I think perhaps he intrigues me.

I tap on the door. 'It's just me. The Healer.'

I hear shuffling from the other side of the door; then the hatch snaps open and his grey, blinking eyes appear.

'You came back,' he says.

I'd forgotten just how disarming his gaze is, intense and curious all at once.

'Are you hurt?' I ask.

'No more than I was this morning.'

It surprises me how relieved I feel. 'Minew has moved somewhere else, so you needn't worry about him any more.'

'That is good to know, although I am sad his wife's brothers will never catch up with him. I rather liked the idea of Minew awaiting me in the Underworld.'

His gallows humour makes me smile, even though I can't bear the thought of his head on a spike. I slide the ointment under the door. The lid clicks and the scent of eucalyptus wafts through the hatch, followed by a sigh. I imagine him dabbing it on his fingers.

'Who burnt your hands?' I ask.

'The guards.'

'When?'

'Does it matter?' His eyes fill the slit again.

'It will help me decide on a treatment if I know how

recent the burns are.'

'I can't remember. A while ago, I think.'

I reach towards the hatch. 'May I?'

Tentatively, his fingers emerge, black and pink, lacquered with balm.

'It's OK.' I use my calmest voice. 'I won't touch – I know how sore they must be.'

This gives him more confidence, and his whole hand emerges. He rotates it slowly, showing me the damage across his palm. In spite of the burns, his hand is beautiful. Large and strong, with graceful long fingers, perfect for playing the lute or whittling intricate ornaments from wood. His lifeline is deep yet continuous, reminding me of the Nubi river cutting through the oasis.

'The ointment will help,' I eventually say. 'But I would like to add a linen wrap to protect the injury from grime.'

His hand vanishes back into the gloom. 'The guards will find the wrap and you will be punished.'

'OK, some pigskin then. You can hide it in your slops tray and I will collect it tomorrow.'

'I have escaped infection thus far. Just your ointment is enough, thank you.'

I sigh, desperately wanting to do more, yet knowing I need to be careful or I risk making it even worse for this patient. And worse for me.

'Surely they don't let Healers roam the dungeons as they please,' he says.

'I'm on slop duty.'

His eyes smile, slate shifting to pale grey. 'A punishment worse than my own. Whatever did you do?'

I pause, not sure whether I should be honest. 'I . . . I . . .'

'You are gathering slops so you can check on me, aren't you?'

'I didn't know what else to do.'

He must tip his head, for his eyes form two points on a diagonal line. 'Your kindness is ill-deserved.'

'Kindness need not be earnt.'

We stare at each other, and, not for the first time, I wish I could see the rest of his face. I've already imagined hundreds of different versions of him, ranging from the sublime to the grotesque. Right now, I imagine him to be fine-featured, with the more commonplace olive skin and black hair of a Sunlander.

Suddenly, I remember the devil wing, a small pouch that I secreted in my apron earlier in the day. It was easy enough to take – and really, I'm just borrowing it – no more than a quick slip of the hand. I'm surprised by just how calm I am. After all, the last time I smuggled devil wing, my darling mama was burnt.

I hold it to the hatch; it glints through the muslin cloth, casting a glow on to the prisoner's face, though he backs away before I see anything more than a fleeting imprint of features.

'This will stop the pain,' I say.

He allows me to drop it into his palm; then the hatch is just a black rectangle. I suspect he's leaning against the wall, untying the cord, and sprinkling some on to his tongue. He chuckles as the silver powder cools his throat. He will feel much better soon – the devil wing will lift not only the pain, but his mood too.

The pouch reappears, a little smaller and dirtied around the edges, and I suddenly feel foolish for simply assuming he wouldn't overdose. I nestle it back into my apron, intending to return it to the sanatorium at my next chance, whilst simultaneously knowing I will probably keep it for my next visit. Then I listen with satisfaction as his breath grows content and heavy. For a moment, I assume he's fallen asleep, so I rest my head against the door, running through his possible faces once again. I'm just imagining him as a sturdy-looking farming type when he speaks, causing me to jump.

'I feel so much lighter,' he says.

Guilt lodges in my heart as I recall giving the same white powder to Sephie. But this is different. This prisoner has no way of becoming addicted. Besides, who could blame him if he did.

'I brought food,' I say, posting a piece of bread through the hatch, careful to avoid the edges where his slop dish may have touched.

A small, excited laugh drifts through the hatch, followed by a series of chewing noises that remind me of a mouse. Perhaps his face has a rodent quality. I listen until the chewing subsides, glad that I can at least fill his belly.

What with the food and the devil wing, he will soon slip into a deep sleep, and I can only hope his dreams transport him to a happier place. I gather myself and my bucket, preparing to leave.

'Wait.' His eyes appear at the hatch again. 'I have so little company. Won't you stay for a moment?'

I glance up the corridor, fearful the guard may become suspicious if I'm gone too long.

'I miss words,' he says.

'Only for a short while.'

He blinks his thanks, then moves from the hatch.

'Tell me about yourself,' he says. The proximity of his voice tells me he's leaning against the door again.

I pause. What is there to say? 'I am a Healer.'

'Tell me something I don't know already.' His voice is gentle, teasing even.

'I am a twin, but you know that also. Oh, my twin is an embalming student.'

Why am I so dull? I should surely have more to say about myself than my Calling and my sibling. Yet I can't tell him the most important thing about me: Mama's execution, or how the need to solve it consumes me, how guilt drives me every single day.

Deflated, I slump against the door, letting my head flop back so it rests against the metal. A warm surge of Calling rises inside. I am close to him. Very close. I imagine that his head touches the other side of the door so we are separated only by a sheet of metal.

I toy with how old he may be, for his voice is strong, young, yet he speaks with a wisdom and confidence that tends to come with age. He said he'd been in jail for a long time – perhaps he was imprisoned as a child.

'Is there something on your mind?' he asks.

'I was just wondering how old you are.'

'I don't know.' There is no hint of humour in his voice.

'Of course you know how old you are.'

'I told you this morning, time has lost all shape.'

'Ah, but you knew it was morning.'

'Because of the comings and goings of the guards, but I don't keep count of the days.'

'An estimate then.'

'I am old enough to leave home, but young enough to wish I hadn't.'

'You must be about my age then,' I say. This pleases me and I knock the wrinkles and grey streak off my mental image of him.

'May I ask you a question, Healer?'

'You may.'

'Why are you so . . . sad?'

The skin on my arms prickles with annoyance. Am I that transparent? 'I'm not sad. I'm learning to be a Healer. It's my life's dream.'

His breaths reach me through the hatch, followed by a scraping sound as he shifts position. His silence is an accusation.

I sigh. Surely there is no harm in sharing a little of my load. 'My mother died about a year ago.' I'm surprised by how easy it is to form the words.

'No wonder you are sad.' His voice is soft, apologetic.

I consider telling him more when my eyes drift to one of the heads on the wall, mouth locked in a never-ending scream, something both white and brown oozing from a nostril. A reminder of how the grey-eyed prisoner will end up, and certainly no place for my darling mama's memory.

'What's your name?' he asks.

'Surely it is my turn to ask you a question now.' I attempt to sound light, for I have no right to drown in self-pity when his ocean is so much deeper than mine.

He laughs. 'I did not realize we were taking it in turns.'

'It is only fair.'

'If ever there was any doubt you are a twin.'

Now it's my turn to laugh. 'So what's your name?'

'Caszeil.'

I wish I hadn't asked. Knowing this makes him so much more than a voice behind a door, so much more than a pair of watchful eyes. I chastise myself for picturing him once again, this time as an academic type, with a monocle, and dark hair tied back with a ribbon. An attachment to a condemned man is foolhardy at best. Yet I can't help mouthing his name, pausing on the gentle *sz* sound as my tongue meets the back of my teeth. *Caszeil.*

'I have never heard this name before,' I eventually say.

Perhaps he is not a Sunlander, after all. A whole range of possibilities open up, for I have heard rumours of vicious Northerners from beyond the ocean with hair the colour of corn and skin paler than Mother Moon.

'Tears,' he says. 'That's what it means. Tears. My papa chose it because he cried a million tears when Mama was lost to him. Now I wonder if he knew my fate all along.'

'You lost your mama too?' Almost as soon as I ask this question, my hand closes around the slop bucket and I resolve to leave, because the more I bond to this prisoner, the harder he will be to lose.

'It is not the same,' he replies. 'I never knew her. You can't lose someone you never had.'

It's as if he's reading my mind. I stand, determined to end the conversation, determined not to consider him a thing to be lost. 'Caszeil, I'm sorry but—'

He cuts across me. 'Why do you apologize so much?' His eyes appear back at the hatch. His lashes are particularly black, even for him, and I realize he's been crying. A flash of something pale crosses the hatch as he balances back on knees. Pale skin? Pale hair? Or perhaps he wears a white tunic. The not knowing nags at me like an unfinished song or a mosaic with a missing piece.

I stutter on my answer. 'I . . . I didn't know just how much I apologized until I met you. Now, every sorry is a stone in my shoe.'

His eyes smile at me. 'Sorry about that.'

I cannot help but grin. 'You did that on purpose.' I place the bucket down, irritated at my hands for accepting that I don't want to leave just yet.

'I still don't know your name,' he says.

'Icari.'

His eyes move up and down, telling me that he's nodding, and I see that pale flash again.

'That is a very pretty name.' He sounds more tired than before. The devil wing must be working its way through his system. Soon he will fall asleep and I will be able to leave without causing offence.

'Thank you.' Instinctively, I lean towards him, wanting to see more, not caring – or believing – that he could jab me in the eye if he so pleased. 'Why are you in here?'

His eyelids grow heavy and he slumps back behind the door. 'I killed a girl. A child.'

And even though I knew he was a criminal, my breath still pauses in my lungs.

'You killed a girl?' I repeat.

His voice grows soft, far away. 'I think about it often since being locked in here. Every day, every hour — sometimes the memory replaces this cell entirely.'

The devil wing is loosening his tongue, I'm sure of it.

'What happened?' I want to know, of course I do, but I also realize he needs to tell me. A confession of sorts.

'I didn't mean to kill her. She was simply trying to escape, an innocent caught in a battle. I was hurling my spear at the enemy, and when they ducked, it hit her straight in the heart. She was dead before she hit the floor.' His voice grows slurred, yet I can hear the tears in every syllable. 'I deserve to be in here,' he whispers.

I dart to the hatch and peer into the gloom. I want to see him, connect with him, look him in the eyes and tell him that nobody deserves to be in here. Nobody. Yet he isn't near enough to the hatch and it's simply too dark. So, holding down my lunch, I reach between two severed heads and grab a torch.

'Caszeil?' I say, lifting the flames to the hatch. 'Are you awake?'

His gentle, rhythmic breaths inform me that he has fallen asleep. The torch casts a blade of light into the cell. Just as I thought, he is slumped up against the door; I can make out the top of his head, a golden sphere, covered in corn-coloured hair. Every mental image of him with olive skin and dark hair evaporates in that moment. He *is* a North-erner. A savage. I should be terrified, shocked, yet I doubt anything could surprise me about this man, for he is so steeped in mystery I've already considered most scenarios. Besides, he seems anything but vicious.

Before I can ponder this any further, I notice the only other part of him visible through the hatch: two bare legs stretching away from the door. I was wrong when I said nothing could surprise me, for I fear I may never habituate to the cruelty of man. Like his hands, his legs are black and pink, dappled with scabs and blisters. I stifle a gasp and tears spring to my eyes as I imagine the torture, the suffering, Caszeil has endured. It is a miracle he has not died from his injuries.

The Calling beats inside me with a heart of its own. Yet Caszeil is now asleep and the guard will surely seek me out if I dally any longer. Grabbing the slop bucket, I race from the dungeons, vowing to return before the first rays of Father Sun tomorrow. Then, I will treat him properly regardless of the consequence, because I am not fit to call myself a Healer if I turn a blind eye to such suffering.

A thought rises and sits like a thorn in my brain: I don't want him to survive simply because I am a Healer, but because of his grey eyes, his thoughtfulness, his playfulness, the way he needs me. I pluck the thought from my mind like the barb it is, because whilst I am innately honest, I have always been able to lie to myself.

15

SEPHIE

I find Icari in the washroom, wearing her nightgown and a strange expression – a mixture of dreaminess and anxiety. I close the door so our chamber-mates can't hear our conversation.

'Where did you go after dinner?' I ask.

She opens her mouth, pauses, then closes it again.

'Icari? Where were you? I have news, important news.'

'I came for a lie-down,' she replies. 'We dissected a woman.'

I peel off my embalming gown, relieved to rid myself of all the little splashes of brain and blood. Sometimes it feels like I'm wearing someone else's skin entirely.

'I *knew* something was wrong,' I say. 'I felt that hook in my stomach again.'

She doesn't meet my eye. 'Yes, it made me quite queasy. I imagine you sensed it.'

I nod, even though I suspect she's withholding something. Normally, I would resent this, for I consider my sister's business my own, and I am, my friends, naturally nosey. But today I don't have room for Icari's troubles. In honesty, I rarely do.

'I have two Callings,' I whisper, my words tripping over themselves. 'The silver light was so very faint, but it was definitely there. I am an Alchemist first, and an Embalmer second.' I cannot help the excitement that surges in my voice. 'And, sister, there is more. I made a corpse's eyes open when I summoned the Divine Shadow.'

'What?' She grips my hands in panic.

'I had to kiss his head as part of the embalming ritual. He looked like a raisin and I feared I'd vomit in his face.'

'That is *necromancy*.' She speaks as though the word itself will cause us to drop to the Underworld. 'A thing of sorcery and myth – something only the most powerful Alchemists can do.'

I roll my eyes. 'Well I didn't mean to.'

'Perhaps it is the combination of your alchemy and embalming gifts.' She releases my hand to rub some calm into her temples. 'Did anyone see?'

I shake my head.

'You must tell no one of this,' she says. 'No one.'

'Really? I was thinking of announcing it tomorrow at breakfast.'

The sarcasm bounces from her as she bites her lip, deep in thought.

'Icari, there is something else,' I say.

'What, dear-heart?'

'When I touched the corpse's head, I could read him.'

'Read him?'

'Yes. I was able to see, relive, his death. He was a tailor working on a dress when he had a heart attack.'

She laughs with alarm. 'You were probably in shock.

Anxiety is a slippery trickster at best.'

'It wasn't the shock,' I snap. 'It was real.'

She rubs the back of her head with vigour, as though trying to remove some disturbing part of her mind. 'OK. Let's think this through.' She sighs. 'Mama always said that the soul hangs in the corpse after death for anything up to several months, before passing to the afterlife or extinguishing entirely, which is why it's so important to embalm the body swiftly. How old was this corpse?'

'Pretty old. He'd already been scraped and dried. We were stitching wool inside to give him back his shape.'

'So you were unlucky. Most souls would have passed by then. Perhaps if you stick to the older corpses, you won't fall foul.'

'I don't get to choose which corpse I embalm.' My voice rises.

She gazes into the basin, as if answers may appear on the surface of the water. Her lips move, though she makes no sound, and eventually, she says, 'So *you* turned the feather from black to silver, after all.' Another bloody sigh. 'Do you think Uriel was helping when he pretended he'd blackened the feather?'

'Or damning me to a life with corpses,' I reply.

'Better that than damning you to the pyre.'

'He could have let me be an Alchemist.'

She shakes her head. 'No, no. Don't you see? If he let you take credit for the blackened feather, then how would he have explained the silvering? It would mean *he* had two Callings, or like he said after the ritual, that he meddled with the Illumination process by transmuting the feather to silver.

Maybe he wasn't helping you or damning you. Maybe it was simply self-preservation.'

'Maybe.' I knead a handful of oiled grain into my skin, enjoying the temporary distraction.

'Who else other than Uriel knows you have two Callings?' she asks.

'Anyone who knew I stopped the sand cloud. So the General and a few other guards.'

'I don't like this, dear-heart.' She washes her mouth with rose water and spits in the waste pot. 'I am certain now that Mama was burnt because of her dual gifts.'

I want to cry, but I replace the sensation with a forced smile. 'Did I tell you that I've called my corpse Agathi?'

I hoped it would make Icari laugh, but instead her face tenses further. 'Didn't you hear me?' she says.

A finger-snap of anger resounds through my body. 'Mama was killed for trading devil wing – we've been over this again and again.'

'A prison guard said that nobody is ever executed for trading devil wing.'

'What were you doing in the dungeons?' I ask.

'Stop changing the subject. I want to talk about Mama's death.'

I lean forward, gripping the wash-bowl with all my might, not caring when the water starts to vibrate and a small crack appears in the clay. The emotion overwhelms me and my thoughts spiral: Mama on the pyre; the raisin opening his eyes; my life mapped out in the catacombs where I have to relive the death of any corpse I touch. I let the Divine Shadow ease through me, desperate for a moment of calm.

'Sephie!' Icari's voice hauls me back to reality.

The water in the clay pot has started to bubble, steam settling on its surface like fog on the Nubi river. I back away, a small cry pushing from my lips.

A loud knock on the door.

We both freeze, staring at each other.

'Who is it?' I call.

'Just me,' Talia replies. I'd recognize her voice anywhere. 'Can I come in? I need to oil my hands – the embalming salts are drying my skin like Father Sun.'

'Just a minute,' I reply.

Icari tips the hot water into the waste pot, an attempt to hide all evidence of my true self.

'You need to help me,' I whisper. 'When I call on the Divine Shadow, *this* happens.' I gesture to the empty, cracked pot. 'And with my necromancy skills, it's too big a risk.'

Her lips settle into a sad smile. 'Then stop calling on the Divine Shadow.'

'I need it, now that I don't have . . .' I daren't say *devil wing*. Not here. I press my palms together in a desperate prayer. 'Please, Icari, I cannot cope without it. I will vomit on a corpse before tomorrow is done. You are a Healer – surely you could smuggle some from the sanatorium.'

'I cannot get you any, Sephie.' Her features are so huddled together, she looks like her head may turn inside out. Is she so guided by rules she will not help her own sister?

'Hello,' Talia calls, a soft knock landing on the door. 'My hands are withered stumps.'

'One moment,' I call back; then I drop my voice. 'Yes, but it is unlikely you will be caught, whereas my continued vomiting is highly likely.'

'You saw all sorts of gore at the sanatorium. Surely embalming isn't so gruesome?'

'It's different, Icari.'

Embalming reminds me of what Mama didn't get. Of what she *should* have got. It reminds me of her non-existence. I open my mouth to tell her this, but the words stick in my throat like burrs.

'That is enough,' Icari says, tears in her eyes. 'I cannot get you devil wing, I am sorry. Your want may be great, but your need is not.'

'Who made you the bloody judge of what I need?' I hiss.

She pushes past me and unlocks the door, marking the end of our conversation. I hate my sister sometimes.

16

ICARI

I sneak down to the dungeons to see Caszeil before I leave for one of the smaller sanatoriums in the city after breakfast.

The chalky guard is nowhere to be seen; only his tankard of ale remains, fizzing on his abandoned table. My fingers grip the pouch of devil wing in my apron and I listen carefully, until I hear a cell door closing, followed by the sound of his heavy boots upon the flags of a corridor. I have only a moment, and losing all sense of caution, I tip a large dose of devil wing into his drink.

'Praise be to Father Sun,' I whisper, buckling under the strain of my misdoings.

I glance at the circle of heads. 'And you are in no position to judge,' I say.

The guard appears. 'You again?'

I nod, clutching my bucket and ordering my eyes not to click to the ale.

He plonks himself down in his chair and raises his tankard to me. 'Well? What ya waiting for? Shit and piss don't collect themselves now, do they?'

I dash down the corridor, but not before I see him take a thirsty swig.

By the time I've gathered most of the slops, the guard is slumped on to his table and snoring loudly. Stealing his key is easy; convincing myself that my actions are justified is not. Yet Father Sun did not make me a Healer so I could turn a blind eye to suffering, and those burns will not heal with ointment alone.

I tremble with the excitement of finally seeing Caszeil, of knowing his face, his mannerisms, then proceed to reprimand myself for such fanciful notions when heads hang from the walls and prisoners die in stone cages all around me. The dungeons are cold – that is why I tremble. It has nothing to do with Caszeil.

'Caszeil, do not be alarmed. It is just me,' I say as I turn the key.

Of course it has occurred to me that a prisoner, no matter how tame they seem whilst behind bars, could become wild when faced with an open door. Yet the heat of my Calling and my knowledge of biology tells me that Caszeil is in no state to attack anyone, let alone a woman whom he so bravely helped, and who, in return, has done nothing but ease his pain.

Besides, I have my scalpel and my acid, and thanks to Caszeil himself, the foresight to knee him in the testes should the need arise.

So, taking a deep breath, then promptly regretting it, I creak open the door.

'Icari?' A small voice followed by some scuffling. 'No, you mustn't come in.'

It is too late. I am already inside his cell.

'Pardon?' I say, a feeble attempt to inject some humour

into such a strange situation and to lessen my nerves.

The light from the corridor torches forms a thick ribbon of orange upon the cell floor, yet there is only my shadow for interest, for Caszeil has shuffled into the back corner of his cell, crouched low like a scared child. A dark shape in the gloom. The thought he could be dangerous seems so ludicrous now, I almost laugh.

'I will not harm you,' I say.

'I know that . . .' His words fade.

'What is it then?' I approach him like I might a scared horse, steady and slow, my palms raised.

He covers his face in a swirl of shadows. 'I fear that if you see me, you will not want to know me any more.'

'Caszeil, you are not a bloom to be valued by the plumpness of your petals.'

'You don't understand. I'm *hideous*.' His voice catches in his throat.

'You are not hideous. You have burns and you need treatment, that is all.'

As I move closer, my eyes adjust to the dark, and his shape gains clarity. He is muscular, strong, and can't have been imprisoned for as long as he thinks, for the meagre portions of daily gruel could not support an exercise regime of any kind in this godforsaken place.

I slide the ointment across the floor to him, aware he is not yet ready for me to close the final few steps between us. 'Let me treat you,' I say. 'Father Sun is strong in my blood. My touch alone will ease your injuries.'

'I fear that if you heal my burns, we will simply be supplying the guards with a fresh canvas.' He pauses. 'And you will open yourself to punishment.' He applies the ointment, slathering it over his legs and torso with long strokes, releasing the crisp odour into the fug of his cell. 'This ointment is wonderful, yet it doesn't noticeably change the appearance of my injuries. The guards need never know. Speaking of which, how did you persuade them to give you a key?'

I hold up the devil wing. 'He really shouldn't drink so much ale; it deadens his taste buds. Anyone could slip anything into his glass.'

He chuckles. 'I like this new you.'

Grinning, I toss him the pouch, yet he doesn't fall upon it as I expect.

'Did it make me fall asleep last time?' he asks.

'Yes.'

The glow of the silver powder reaches his smile. His teeth are surprisingly white considering he's had no access to washing facilities.

'Then I will wait until you've gone,' he says. 'Make the most of your company.'

I should be flattered, but instead feel only sympathy, for the fact he would rather suffer pain than isolation is testament to his loneliness. Rummaging in my satchel, I pull free a chunk of rosemary bread, wrapped in parchment and stolen from breakfast. When I offer it to him, he hesitates.

'Don't make me roll it across the floor,' I say, glancing at the filth.

Slowly, he reaches towards me, falling into the chink of light from the corridor just long enough for me to see his face, framed by two sheets of golden hair. Beneath the burns lies a bone structure that is quite lovely. He was once hand-some. He is *still* handsome, for the wounds tell me nothing of him, speaking only of the cruelty of others, and those grey eyes are still the colour of a storm cloud.

He resumes his position against the wall, sinking back into the shadow, but not before I realize his entire body is burnt, for he wears only a loincloth to cover his modesty. My brow furrows. How has he escaped infection without medical aid? His scent lingers in the air – sweat and ointment – and it strikes me that a patient with such significant burns should smell foul. Indeed, a patient with such significant burns shouldn't be alive.

Was sorcery involved in Caszeil's injuries? Were they inflicted by a witch . . . or an Alchemist? Uriel strikes me as cruel enough . . .

'Thank you,' Caszeil says, nibbling at the bread. 'I did not think you'd return. Not after I told you what I did.'

I gather my skirt and crouch on the floor, not wanting to dirty my gown, yet wanting less to tower over him.

'I am not here to judge you, Caszeil. If I did, I would be a scorpion calling a snake venomous.'

His eyes meet mine and a shiver moves down my spine. The dungeons are cold, I remind myself. It has nothing to do with his steady gaze.

'You have killed someone too?' he asks.

I exhale slowly, trying desperately to curb my tongue. 'My mama.' Why do I confide in him so? Is it because he's a prisoner, and as such unable to share my secrets with anyone but decapitated heads? Or perhaps it's because a fellow sinner cannot pass criticism.

He tilts his head to the side. 'I find that hard to believe. Why don't you tell me what happened.'

The words slip from my lips far too easily, as if they were waiting there the whole time, which I think perhaps they were. 'Mama was arrested for trading devil wing at the village agora and executed there and then by the city guard.'

'Last time I looked, you weren't a guard.'

I cover my face with my hands, an attempt to protect myself from the onslaught of guilt. 'I could have saved her. If only I'd claimed the devil wing was my own. But instead, I just stood and watched. I watched her burn.'

The only person I've ever said this to before is Sephie, and she either tells me to shut up or dismisses my feelings as stupid. There are only so many times one can be shut down before one comes to expect it, which is why I'm surprised when Caszeil simply waits for me to continue.

'I always do that,' I eventually say. 'Freeze in the face of fear.'

After a long pause, he says, 'No wonder you freeze.'

My hands drop from my face. 'Pardon?'

'If you think everything's your fault, if you accept responsibility for all the bad things that happen, no wonder you're too scared to act.'

I wring my hands together, trying to rid myself of the irritation of being analysed so. 'That makes no sense.'

'Doesn't it?'

'Well, whichever way you shine it –' my words disintegrate with shame – 'I am still a coward.'

He shakes his head, causing his golden hair to swing against his shoulders. 'Are we talking about the same young woman? The woman who endured slop duty and drugged a guard simply to treat a prisoner?'

'Your point being?'

He chuckles with disbelief. 'My point being, perhaps your bravery is not a fanfare, but the pure note of a flute.'

'Now you're just trying to sound clever.'

'Your guilt is a millstone, Icari. That's all I'm saying.'

'As opposed to yours.'

'I put a spear in a girl's heart.'

'By mistake.'

He blinks like a lazy cat. 'If only you forgave yourself as readily as you do others.'

'Stop being so . . . wise.'

Those alarmingly white teeth flash at me again, and I wish he would step into the light one more time so I could see his whole face curved into a smile. 'No one has ever called me wise,' he says. 'Or clever.'

'Well, *smart-arse* seemed a little cutting.' I laugh, a welcome break from the horror of my memories.

'Cutting but fair,' he replies.

Realizing my eyes are leaking, I wipe my face. I'm supposed to be healing him, not seeking absolution. 'Sorry,' I say. Then, anticipating his reply, I raise my hand. 'Don't.'

'I wasn't going to say anything.' He's smiling again; I can hear it in his voice. It makes me smile too.

'Why don't I believe you,' I say, enjoying the back and forth. It feels natural, like our sentences were made to slot together. Silently, I scold myself for this thought, for he is a prisoner, a patient, not a friend. So why do I feel so drawn to him?

'Is it normal for Sunlanders to be executed for trading devil wing?' he asks, sensing my change in mood.

'No.'

'Then tell me about your mother. Perhaps we can unravel the mystery as to why she was executed.'

I am equally touched and unnerved by this. 'You would help me like that?' I slump back on my bottom, suddenly not caring if my gown dirties, for the thought of having someone to share ideas with, to help make sense of Mama's death, transforms his cell floor into a soft mattress.

'As I said,' he replies. 'You've drugged a guard and endured slops to bring me ointment. This is the least I can do.'

After a year of being tightly corked for fear of upsetting Sephie or Papa, all of the conspiracies, all of the loose ends bubble to the surface and spill from my mouth. Barely pausing for breath, I tell him Mama's story. How she trained as an Alchemist only to become a Healer when she met Papa and moved to the oasis. How the trader was paid off by the soldiers, and her pyre was ready and waiting, and how Uriel ordered her execution in spite of his tears.

Caszeil's face twitches when I mention the High Priest's name, and I wonder again if Uriel had something to do with his burns. The only thing I don't tell him is about Sephie – her dual Calling and her necromancy skills – for there is too much at stake.

'So your mama had two Callings,' he eventually says.

'Yes, but Uriel knew for twenty years. Why wait?'

'It sounds like your mama scared some powerful people. Perhaps she learnt something more, or gained more skills, which further threatened them. Or perhaps she began using her existing powers in different ways.'

'Mama wasn't a sorceress. She hadn't practised alchemy in years, and when she did, she transmuted the Divine Shadow solely for good.'

'Sorcery. Alchemy. Surely the difference is in the name alone.'

'Alchemists use the Divine Shadow for good, witches for bad,' I say.

'Yes, but who decides whether it's good or bad?'

Now it's my turn to cock my head at him. He has a way of viewing the world that is enlightening and threatening all at once. 'Go on.'

'Your Alchemists, they transmute metals to gold, yes?'

'Yes.'

'To make rich men richer, yes?'

'I suppose.'

'Hardly the actions of a saint.'

He has a point . . . yet it occurs to me that Caszeil may compare alchemy to sorcery because of his dislike of Uriel. I decide to broach the subject.

'Have you met Uriel?' I keep my voice low, secretive.

'I have.'

'Did he . . . burn you?'

'He did.'

I stiffen with anger. If ever I was in any doubt that Uriel was evil masquerading as a man. 'No wonder you hate Alchemists,' I say.

He smiles again, pushing his fair hair from his eyes so that I notice how cold it is again, my skin all a-shiver.

'I don't hate Alchemists,' he says. 'I just don't see them as any different to witches.'

Why is he so protective of sorcery? The answer causes my breath to stick somewhere between my mouth and lungs. His perfect teeth, muscled body, healthy hair – the fact he still survives in spite of his injuries. Perhaps Caszeil is a sorcerer. Male sorcerers are rare, or at least considered rare, for it is always women who are the accused and burnt on the pyre in the Sunlands. But then Caszeil isn't from the Sunlands. And his use of sorcery would certainly explain why they torture him so.

'Icari? What is it?' he asks.

Something about him draws the truth from me like a splinter. 'Are you a sorcerer? Is that why you're here, in the dungeons?'

He moves towards me, crawling so his face is near to mine. I know I should flinch, yet it's a relief to feel such proximity. There's no door between us, no tense pause or stretch of darkness. Even in the dimness, I can see every fleck of silver in his eyes, every blacker-than-black eyelash, hear his breath and smell the soft animal scent of his hair. His lips are full and free from burns; a soft, dusty pink in the torchlight. He is so much more than my imagination could ever have conjured.

'No.' His voice is both gentle and intense. 'I am not a sorcerer. I'm in here because I put a spear in a girl's chest.'

He rests a hand over my heart, which I realize has accelerated in my chest. I study his graceful fingers, wondering if he can feel how fast my pulse races. Does my skin burn because of my Calling or for a whole other reason?

He pulls his hand away. 'Don't be scared of me,' he

whispers. 'I would never hurt you.'

'Caszeil, you misunderstand. I am not *scared* of you. That is not why my heart beats so.' I stumble on my words. Once said, they cannot be unsaid, and my emotions are so new, so fragile, I am yet to trust them. So I shake my head, trying to gather myself. I am a Healer, not a lovesick maid, yet even as I think this, I find I'm reaching for his face. 'You are the first person I've ever talked to like this, the first person to listen.' My fingers hover near to his cheek as I long to cup his skin and rest my lips on his.

Slowly, I close the gap between us.

He shifts backwards. 'Icari, don't—'

'Sorry,' I say, shocked at myself. I have never shared a romantic kiss with anyone, yet I was about to give this precious gift to a condemned man, someone I could never have a future with, someone who could die tomorrow. I stand quickly. 'I just – I just didn't mean to make things awkward.'

He gazes at me. His eyes are two plates of silver. 'Icari, look at me. I am hideous.'

'We've been over this.'

'I'm a murderer. I am not worthy of your affections.'

I realize how ridiculous I've been, how upsetting this must be for Caszeil as well as me; I'm simply taunting him with a life he can never have.

'You're wrong,' I whisper. 'But I'm sorry, I overstepped a line.' My eyes mark their agreement with a fresh wave of tears.

He stands before me. He is taller than I envisioned, his chest broader. He tilts his head again, then lifts my apron and begins dabbing at my cheeks with movements so gentle, so tender, I can't believe he'd ever hurt anyone, let alone an innocent.

'I'm going away for a few days,' I say. 'To a sanatorium in the city, but I'll come and see you as soon as I can.'

He presses a nip of devil wing to his tongue, then hands me the pouch. I expect him to tell me not to visit again, to say I've breached his trust as my patient, toyed with his emotions, but instead he says, 'Well then, I will cancel all my plans.'

17

SEPHIE

As my second day in embalming hell draws to a close, Talia approaches Madame Embalmer with an eager smile on her pretty face. 'Please, Madame, I am low on salt and wraps.'

'You know where the store is,' she replies.

'I wonder, Madame, shall I take Sephie so she knows where it is also?'

'If you like,' she replies.

Talia leads me from the catacombs, up the spiral staircase and into the Night Temple. The sun is beginning to fade and the building awakens as if it were a nocturnal animal. Soon the Alchemists will arrive to worship in the gloaming, ruining the peace and flaunting their Calling, but for now, the temple is entirely ours.

'It's beautiful, isn't it?' Talia says.

'It really is,' I reply, still looking at her.

But despite her beauty, the hairs on the back of my neck rise. Something bad is coming. *Don't be silly, Sephie*, I tell myself. *You're just anxious about being discovered as a dual-gifted necromancer who can read the dead.*

Talia leads me down a small staircase towards the back of the temple, and into a sloping corridor, where she finds an oil lamp. The store room is small but well equipped. Piles of linen and jars of tinctures neatly line the shelves, whilst embalming tools and pots of salt are stacked on the floor.

I expect Talia to select what she needs, but instead she turns to me.

'Getting some alone time with you is impossible in this place,' she says.

I flush. 'What do you mean?'

'I tried to catch you in the washroom last night, then at luncheon today, but there's always someone else around. I need to talk to you. In *private*.'

My heart flutters in my chest. 'What is it?'

'Yesterday. It was me who dropped the liver jar when you kissed the corpse.'

'Oh,' I say, not quite making sense of her words.

'I was trying to help you.' Her eyebrows almost meet her hairline, becoming one and the same. The oil lamp illuminates every lovely russet freckle on her face so they remind me of glow-worms.

'Oh,' I say as the realization dawns. 'You mean, you saw? The corpse?'

'Batting his eyelashes at you? Yes. I saw.' Setting down the lamp, she grasps my hands in a reassuring gesture. 'Sephie, what's going on? You can tell me. I'm your friend.'

I study her face. Those big green-flecked eyes look so trustworthy, and the truth is a weight pressing down on me, a weight I long to share. 'I have two Callings, Talia. I am an Alchemist first and foremost. That's why my back is a mess – I was lashed for stopping a sand cloud, not for insolence.' Once I start, I simply can't stop. 'I was calling on the Divine

Shadow to numb the nausea and stop me sicking up in the dead man's face, and, I don't know, I must have awoken him somehow.'

She stares at me, mouth agog. Her lips try to form words, but instead they just twitch slightly.

Great. I've stupefied Talia. Good job I didn't mention the whole reading-the-dead trick.

'Say something,' I say.

'An Alchemist and Embalmer who can stop a sand cloud and awaken the dead?' Her voice is thin.

I nod, willing her not to scream and run away.

'Ziris was right,' she says. 'You are more powerful than ... than ... Uriel himself.' She grins. 'Good for you, Sephie.'

Praise be to Mother Moon. 'Thanks.'

She pauses, making the connections. 'So *you* blackened the feather and turned it silver – it had nothing to do with Uriel.'

I nod, impressed by her logic.

She pulls me towards her so that her breath lands hot against my face. 'I heard you last night – that washroom is like an echo chamber.'

'Did Zalta or Xenia hear?'

She shakes her head.

'Tell me what you heard,' I say.

'Just snippets, but enough to grasp that you need devil wing.'

Shit. 'Do you think badly of me?'

'I've seen how you struggle with embalming, and we all cope in different ways. When did you first take it?'

'When Mama died.' A barb snags at my heart.

She nods. 'Let me help you.'

'You've already helped me.'

'Oh, I can do more than lend you my ear,' she says, taking the lamp and leading me from the store back to the corridor. We drop a little further down some steps, past a few more entrances, and then she extracts a hair clip from her bun and picks the lock of an innocuous-looking door.

She's amazing.

The door swings open and in the centre of a small room, tied with silver thread, is a small bale of long white plumes.

I gasp. 'Samael feathers.'

My eyes explore the shelves lining the walls. They are bare but for a couple of large jars filled with devil wing. The shadows hunger in my blood.

She nods. 'If Madame had seen what you did to that corpse, you'd have been in serious trouble.'

I look around, expecting a guard or an orderly to appear. 'Shouldn't this place be protected?'

'It's hidden in plain sight. Nobody knows it is here but for a special few.'

'And you know because?'

She winks. 'As a fire-viper-haired witch, I have grown eyes in the back of my head and ears on every door. It's how I've lasted so long. I overheard Madame and Uriel in here once discussing how supplies were getting low. It didn't take a genius.'

'And you showed me this because?'

'Because you need it.' Her breath lands on my face again, as soft as any feather.

Maybe it is the thought of getting more devil wing, maybe it's the closeness to Talia, but I suddenly feel light-headed. Delirious. I'm about to throw my arms around her, an urge I've fought since the moment we met, when she moves towards the shelves.

The sparkling powder illuminates her face as she lifts down a jar and holds it towards me as if making a toast. 'There isn't much left, but I doubt they'll miss a vial.'

I relieve her hands of the glass pot. I'm but moments away from the sweet numbness of devil wing. My veins jitter with excitement and I'm barely able to unscrew the top.

Licking my finger, I dip it in the powder, then suck at it. Ice travels down my throat and the cold wraps its arms around me, far stronger than my Calling.

'Better?' Talia asks, her voice smiling.

'Better.'

She produces a small vial from her apron and winks. Her expression is one of mischief and – dare I say it – flirtation. The lamplight catches the red in her hair, the fawn of her skin, and the pink of her lips. Maybe it is the devil wing making me bold – I lift a lock of her hair from her shoulder and let it silk through my fingers.

'I really like you, Talia,' I say. '*Really* like you.'

Several emotions cross her face, quick as silver-fish, until she settles on regret. 'I like you too, Sephie.' She touches the locket around her neck. 'As a friend.'

I back away, shaking my head and forcing a smile. 'Sorry, I thought . . .' I stumble over my words. 'I got it wrong, that's all.'

She brushes my hand with hers. 'No. You didn't get it wrong. It's just –' she avoids my gaze whilst holding out the charm on her necklace – 'Mariam gave me this before I left for the citadel.'

'Mariam? Your childhood friend?'

'Yes. But she's more than that.' She takes a deep breath and finally meets my eye. 'We're betrothed.'

'Oh.' I suddenly wish I could slip between the gaps in the stone flags and vanish for ever, but I settle for fidgeting with my gown and shifting my weight between my feet. 'Oh, OK. Well, congratulations.'

'I should have told you.'

'No, no, it's fine.'

It isn't fine. It feels like someone's booted me in the chest and I just want the pain of rejection to stop. My eyes settle on the jar of devil wing. I reckon I could swallow the contents in one gulp if I tried.

'Sephie?' she says, her voice heavy with concern.

I reply by attempting to scoop a pile of silver dust into the vial, but I find I'm shaking, and my hand slips. Devil wing streaks my black dress.

'Shit,' I mutter, brushing it down and inhaling the mist so it makes the inside of my nose tingle and my eyes blink.

'Don't fret,' she says. 'The temple is still empty – we can mop it down at the fountain.'

I follow her back to the Night Temple in silence, humiliation and rejection heating my cheeks. How could I get it so wrong? Not only is she unavailable; she's bloody *betrothed*.

The fountain is a blessed distraction, and I let her splash water on to my dress at its edge. Her hands are quick, nimble, and I imagine them running over a girl called Mariam's skin. Jealousy is a pig that grunts and squeals, and I doubt that vial of devil wing will last long.

Just then, an Alchemist drifts through the main entrance,

indicating the start of the gloaming. It is Belum, and behind him is Ziris.

'Curses,' I whisper as we duck behind the fountain.

More Alchemists trickle through the entrance, heads held high like the sanctimonious arses that they are.

The air crackles.

Once again, I get that feeling like something bad is about to happen.

The bells of the citadel confirm my suspicion, awakening from their slumber with a godawful gong.

Talia's brows pull together. 'A sandstorm?' she says.

A large crash replies from above.

'That doesn't sound much like a sandstorm,' I mutter.

The bells hurt my ears, and my skin fizzes with urgency. What in Aïdes's name is going on? Clinging to the edge of the fountain, Talia and I peer around the side. The Alchemists are pointing upwards, towards the high ceiling of domed glass.

Silhouetted against the twilight, a man crawls across the glass, a long cloak trailing behind him. His arms and legs are splayed, bug-like, and his silver cape flutters in the wind.

'Sweet Mother Moon,' Talia whispers. 'Who is that?'

Another caped man appears, then another, until the roof is swarming with men and the sky becomes no more than the grey between them.

No amount of devil wing could still my heart right now.

'Quickly,' I whisper. 'It isn't safe here.'

But before we can move, the ceiling caves in.

18

ICARI

I finish treating a snakebite on a young lady's ankle, removing the now dead river leech and slathering the puncture wound with ointment.

'Thank you,' she says.

I let my fingers linger on the injury, noting how my golden light now wanes, a sign that my Calling is no longer needed here. She will be fine.

'Try and rest,' I tell her. 'Tomorrow, you should be able to walk home.' Judging from her clothes, she does have a home, even if she shares it with several types of mould.

Whilst sealing the wound with pigskin, my mind returns to Caszeil, to his clear voice, pale hair and grey eyes. Why do I want him so? Is it because he intrigues me, with his clever musings and his different view of the world? Or because he sees me as I long to be: brave? Perhaps he makes me brave. I shake the idea away. I am simply confusing pity with affection, the heat of my Calling with the flush of attraction.

I can't believe I nearly kissed him.

The patient closes her eyes and I begin gathering up my tools. Today was my first day on placement. Most Healers choose to train at the citadel sanatorium, but I chose one in a poorer area near to the city wall – a combination of altruism and homesickness. If I close my eyes, I can smell the Nubi river on the breeze, hear the rustling of the sycamores and the song of the munia bird.

Xenia decided she'd come too, and I'm glad for her company – her friendly chatter calms my worries about both Sephie and Caszeil. For in between every thought of my grey-eyed prisoner, I've thought of my sister. Perhaps I *should* sneak her some devil wing; if she attempts to get it herself, who knows what will happen. It is my fault she's addicted, after all.

The main physician, a tall, olive-skinned gentleman called Erastus, sits beside me and observes my work. I warmed to him as soon as I met him, for he reminds me a little of Sephie, the way he jests, the flippancy in his tone.

'Why the pigskin?' he asks.

'To keep infection out and the ointment in,' I reply.

'And the river leech?'

'To suck out the venom.'

He raises a dark eyebrow. 'A controversial method, I believe.'

'The bite was recent. The poison had not had time to circulate.'

He checks the dead leech, fat with toxins. 'This is quite excellent work, Icari. Where did you say you learnt?'

I tell him about home, about the sanatorium on the desert's doorstep.

Erastus, to the point, simply says, 'Well? Are you going to tell me your mama's name, or do I have to guess?'

I falter, never sure how Mama's name will be received.

'Daeda.' My voice emerges a little loud, overcompensating for my nerves.

He looks as though I've pulled a spear from his side. 'Daeda?'

'Yes, that's right.'

Scooping up my hands, an urgency presents in his features. 'Oh, my child, I knew your mama. I *loved* your mama.' He chuckles. 'Not like that, obviously.' I know what he means, for Erastus has a husband named Yiannis, a handsome man whom Xenia and I met when we first arrived.

'Besides,' Erastus says. 'Your mama's heart firmly belonged to another when we trained together.'

I frown, gathering up my utensils. 'Mama met Papa *after* she trained.'

'Yes. But she and Uriel were a couple before then.'

I nearly drop my scalpel. 'Mama and Uriel?'

A million questions sour my mouth. Why did Mama or Papa never mention this? Does it have something to do with Mama's death? Could something as simple as a broken heart really be motive for murder? When Principal Healer said, *'I don't care who your mama was,'* was she referring to Mama's past relationship with the High Priest? I need to tell Caszeil, to watch him chew it over in his sharp mind and help me make sense of it all.

Erastus sighs. 'They were two of the best Alchemists the citadel had seen. We used to joke they would have the most powerful babies ever.'

The thought that Uriel may be my father is a punch to the gut. But I quickly console myself that Sephie is the double of Papa. She doesn't look anything like Uriel. And neither, praise Father Sun, do I.

Erastus looks suddenly concerned. 'Oh my child – you didn't know, did you?'

I shake my head.

'I've upset you,' he says. 'I'm so sorry, I must confess to being a touch overwhelmed. Your mama was a very special lady. When I heard of her fate . . .' He smiles a sad smile. 'Look, why don't you take a break, help Xenia gather fruit for supper. I can finish up here.'

'Thank you,' I say, cleansing my hands in the wash-bowl, relieved to have a moment to breathe.

I pass a pregnant lady, who smiles at me. Her heart rate was elevated when she arrived, but things have settled now. Hopefully, the baby will arrive soon. Erastus has started hinting what a beautiful name Erastus is. Yet for some reason, the sight of her swollen belly saddens me. Perhaps it reminds me of Mama . . . or the fact Caszeil never knew his mother. I chastise myself once again for relating the world back to a prisoner I have only known for two days.

I find Xenia out the back, helping herself to a fig tree.

A loud cry hauls me from the moment – a cry that sounds neither human nor animal.

'Great Father Sun,' Xenia says. 'Was that an oasis bird? It sounded lethal.'

We hear it again, this time louder.

Anxiety slides down my throat. 'That is no oasis bird.' Too loud. Too deep.

Another cry fills the air and a cloud of paper lanterns floats into view, a smudge of light in the gloaming. I blink fiercely. They're moving too fast to be lanterns, and the light is not the warm glow of a candle, but stark and white, like sunshine bouncing from snow. My fingers twine together, even though they are stiff with fear.

The flock of shimmering birds passes overhead, blocking out the sky, the sound of their wings resonating through me like thunder. There are hundreds.

The bells of the citadel awaken, clanging out their warning.

Nearby, citizens begin to scream.

For they are not birds.

They are winged men.

'Icari?' Xenia clutches my arm and her voice wavers.

Terror explodes in my stomach. 'The Samael,' I whisper. 'The demons of Aïdes.'

'It cannot be.' Xenia's features seem to all enlarge at once, eyes widening, her nostrils flaring, a gasp sticking in her open mouth. 'The Samael haven't left the Underworld for centuries.'

She's right, of course. Yet here they are. And they're heading towards the citadel, towards my sister. Towards Caszeil.

Fear nails me to the spot, just like when they burnt Mama and lashed Sephie.

'Look,' Xenia shouts, pointing directly upwards.

Three demons trail behind the flock, perfect crescents cut into the sky and circling above. Quickly, they begin to drop until I can just make out their bodies, silver-skinned and heavily muscled.

Erastus dashes from the sanatorium, his head craned upwards. 'Icari, Xenia. Inside now.'

Xenia streaks up the path, yet I can barely draw breath, let alone move my rock-filled legs.

'Icari, move!' Erastus shouts.

Finally, my feet oblige, yet just as I reach the building, I realize the trailing Samael are, in fact, targeting it. I can just make out the mighty sweep of their wings, each feather extended like a blade, as they drop towards us.

'We need to evacuate the patients,' I say.

'Father Sun, this can't be happening,' Erastus replies.

The hum of anxiety fills my ears as they swoop lower, almost touching the tops of the sycamores. Three bright lights.

'Quickly,' he says, ducking inside. 'We must move the patients to the neighbours' house. It's stone; they'll be safer in there.'

I help the lady with the snakebite to her feet.

Just then, we hear a loud thud on the roof above.

Another thud. Then another.

The point of a spear appears between the reeds above. A child screams. Erastus helps two patients to the door, and Xenia wields a scalpel like a weapon. The flurry of movement sends the flames in the firepit twisting this way and that, scattering shadows across the walls. Yet all I can do is stand, open-mouthed and useless, as the lady with the snakebite hobbles away from me.

Erastus abandons his plan to evacuate. 'Everyone, hide in the back room,' he shouts.

The tops of the trees and the sky are now visible through the ever-increasing holes in the roof, and the spears thrust angrily into the space above the fleeing patients, searching, probing. We are no more than river fish waiting in the depths to be impaled. There are about ten patients in total, and the stronger have already made it to the kitchen at the back. The kitchen is not safe by any means. There are no secret weapons, no concealed armies; hiding is perhaps delaying the inevitable. But prey does not have the luxury of a long-term plan. It snatches at every moment of life.

Xenia grapples an elderly man from immediate danger. There is only one patient left: the pregnant woman over by the firepit. She lies on her side, grunting as though her babe isn't far from this land. I long to follow Xenia and Erastus, but as I watch the lady's belly ripple beneath the stretched linen of her apron, I know that I cannot leave her and her babe alone to die.

The need to heal rises inside me; a familiar, soothing warmth that deadens at least some of the fear. I find I'm able to move again. And as I rush to her, the Samael lower themselves through the roof.

19

ICARI

A pair of ghostly feet dangle mid-air, only a few strides away. I marvel at the talons where his toes should be, like he's strapped knives to his feet. Next come his legs, the skin pale and unearthly like mother-of-pearl, followed by his body. He wears only a loincloth, so I can see each of his muscles, held taut with the promise of violence.

A cool rush of air gushes through the open roof. Or is it from the open door behind me?

The open door. *Escape, Icari. Save yourself.*

But I don't run. And not because I'm frozen. Not this time. But because I am a Healer, and because bravery need not be a fanfare, but the pure note of a flute.

The Samael's talons clack against the mud tiles. The ground trembles with his weight and he spreads his silver wings wide like the hood of a swaying cobra until they seem to fill every space between the walls. A shock of white hair swirls around his face as though he carries the wind inside him. My stomach twists with dread.

He does not lower his wings, and each white feather extends downwards like a long, pointed tooth, creating the serrated edge of a saw. The sight is horrifying. He passes his spear between his taloned hands and my heart leaps into my throat. My own blood burns in my ears. He looks at me with two silver eyes and swivels his head in a precise, jerky motion. Birdlike and unnerving. Two Samael land behind him, their wings vying for space. Their hair is grey, darker than the hair of the Samael directly before me, but their skin is just as moon-pale. They smell of turned milk and carob bark.

The white-haired Samael approaches Xenia and sniffs her neck.

Fear closes my throat, trapping the air in my lungs, yet I realize that this is my chance. Glancing at the pregnant lady, I slip around the edge of the room, moving as quietly as I'm able towards her. If I can just position myself between her and the beast, then maybe she and her unborn babe stand a chance. And if today is the day we both shall journey to the afterlife, at least I will hold her hand.

At least I shall see Mama again.

'Are you the one?' the Samael asks Xenia. His voice is the drone of a mosquito; his silver eyes are the sting.

She shakes her head, a frantic tremble. 'What?'

The Samael before me throws back his head and shrieks, the black cavern of his mouth completely at odds against the shimmer of his exposed throat.

I try to just concentrate on the soles of my reed sandals, gently creaking against the dirt. Yet as I reach the pregnant lady, desperate to lay a soothing palm on her hot brow, I lose my footing, knocking the clay pot from its stand into the fire.

All three Samael spin towards me, talons and spears raised, and my head smacks the wall. My vision clouds, yet I'm still able to see Erastus leaping on to the back of the largest Samael, pulling at his feathers, beating him with his fists.

'Icari!' he screams. 'Run, Icari.'

'Stop her!' the white-haired Samael shrieks.

There is a flurry of wings, of violent bodies, of cobras finally striking.

Erastus is thrown to the ground like a paddle doll. A spear lances clean through his arm. I try to stand, my head filled with the buzz of a thousand flies.

'No,' I yell. 'Erastus!'

The white-haired Samael turns towards me, blood splattered up his arms. He lunges with outstretched talons. I dodge, and my hand reaches into the fire, locating the handle of the clay pot as white-hot pain screams up my arm. I swing the pot with all my strength, yet it misses the demon by a finger's-breadth and smashes against the mud bricks.

The Samael sneers. 'Is that all you've got, Healer?'

Yes. That is all I've got.

'I am so sorry,' I whisper to the pregnant lady. Then I close my eyes, awaiting the incision of each talon against my neck.

20

ICARI

Something falls from the skies and drags me to the floor, and I am cradled by warmth – soft and trembling, like a quilt filled with life. I open my eyes and see only gold, and I briefly wonder if I am dead, already journeying to Mother Moon. I find the pregnant lady's hand, hot and damp and squeezing back. At least we are together. The Samael wails, the sound of something ripping fills my head, and blood spreads across the mud tiles. I am very much alive. Alive and sheltered by a shield of amber feathers.

A man with light brown skin and amber wings has pulled me to the ground and enveloped the pregnant lady and me in his feathers. *An Illios.* Praise Father Sun, for he has sent his army to defend us. The Illios presses his face against mine and his words brush my cheek.

'What is your name?'

'Icari,' I whisper.

'Well, Icari, when I say *run*, you must run outside without a backward glance.' His deep voice is filled with the promise of safety.

'But what about my patient?'

'I will bring her,' he replies. His eyes are large, dark, the colour of oasis coconuts, and I immediately trust him.

I nod.

One moment he is wrapped around me, my ears filled with the sound of his voice and the awful rip of his wings beneath the Samael talons. The next, his body is flipping, twisting through the air, his wings unfolding so that he is a giant auburn moth hovering between us and the demon. I can no longer see his face now that his back is to me, but I hear his voice, loud and clear.

'*RUN.*'

At first, I fear that my limbs will not obey, but the sight of the pregnant lady's terrified face lends me strength. She needs me. So without thinking, I haul her up, push my body beneath her arm and support her towards the exit. She moans with the effort, but fear drives her on, and we move with surprising speed. We reach the path, the gate, and my eyes settle on the sway of the sycamore figs beyond, their leaves whispering of escape.

Erastus's husband, Yiannis, hurtles through the gate, crossbow aimed and ready.

'Where is Erastus?' he shouts. His black hair is plastered to his deep brown skin with sweat, and his muscles are prepped for fighting.

'Still inside,' I manage to gasp.

He rushes to his husband.

The sanatorium is filled with light, both silver and gold. Through the door, I catch a glimpse of the Illios battering the white-haired Samael with his fist. Blood explodes from the demon's face, though it isn't red but silver. Xenia dashes after us and a wave of relief pushes me on. I hear the twang of a crossbow, the zip of an arrow and the thwack of metal on skin, and when I look back, a Samael hits the ground with a blessed thump. The pregnant lady clutches at her belly and I reposition my arm around her back.

We find the door to the neighbours' house left wide open, apparently abandoned in a hurry. The pregnant lady can barely walk; her groaning has stopped and I support most of her weight. I pause to wipe the sweat from my eyes and it's as though the lack of momentum gives her permission to finally give up. She crumples to the ground but a stride from the door. Her face looks pallid, gaunt, as though death has already claimed the flesh from her bones.

'Xenia, help me get her inside,' I say.

She helps me haul the lady into the cottage. 'Hello?' she calls out as we enter.

Only the sound of a faraway scream replies. The neighbours must have fled at the sight of the Samael.

Laying the lady on the ground, I reach beneath her tunic; her breast feels as hot as the Redland sun, but her heart is still. It must have stopped only moments ago.

'Icari?' Xenia whispers.

'She's gone.' Tears spill from my eyes.

'Oh, Icari.' Xenia reaches across the lady's belly to embrace me, and even though I long to sink into the safety of her arms, I shake her off.

'We have work to do,' I say, ripping the tunic from the pregnant lady's belly.

The sight of her naked bump gives me pause. Her light beige skin still glistens with sweat, her navel has popped out as it often does on those with child, and she has a dark line of pigmentation stretching towards her groin. Sadness grips me, squeezing all movement from my body so I'm as still as her heart. She will never see her babe, never kiss its gloopy head. I feel the memory of my own mother pushing at the edges of my grit, threatening to drown me in grief.

Suddenly, a shape moves beneath the skin of the bump, an elbow or knee, maybe even a foot. It lights a spark inside me, and I begin rummaging through the basket on the sideboard with renewed determination. The cottage has everything I need: knives, needles, skeins of thread. I select the sharpest blade I can find, probably used for skinning rabbits.

'How will she push?' Xenia asks.

I poise the blade above the belly with a firm, steady hand. 'She won't.'

And in that moment, the air grows thin, my vision fills with stars, and my ears hum with fear. I can feel Sephie, the hook in my belly pulling so hard I know that something is very, very wrong.

'Icari, what is it?' Xenia asks.

I drop my eyes to the babe inside the woman's swollen belly. Whatever's happening to Sephie, I can't abandon it now.

'Nothing,' I say, and lower the blade.

21

SEPHIE

Sheltering my head from the downpour of glass, I peer through my fingers. A series of silver streaks drop amidst the chaos, thudding against the black marble of the temple and landing on their feet, cat-like. That's when I realize, the caped men aren't caped at all – they have wings. Shining and white and trailing from their blanched bodies.

'Samael,' Talia gasps.

The devil wing combines with the shock and provides a protective haze so I'm able to study the creatures with a strange detachment. 'They're . . . beautiful,' I whisper.

Before Talia can reply, the winged demons begin grabbing the alchemy students by the shoulders, the waists, anywhere they can sink their talons, and rocketing back into the sky.

'They're stealing the students,' I say, dread causing my limbs to tremble.

Belum is attempting to grapple a far bigger opponent, but he is no match, and the demon drives his taloned feet into the boy's shoulders before launching through the broken roof.

'We need to help,' I tell Talia as the shadows surge in my veins.

'Are you mad? They are demons, Sephie. *Actual demons.* We need to hide.'

Her logic gives me permission to swallow down my fight, and we retreat into the catacombs, our frantic footsteps reflecting back at us from the stone tunnels. Together, we burst into the Grand Crypt, our chests heaving, our faces gaunt with terror.

Everyone turns to stare, and I suddenly feel like one of the corpses, naked and splayed upon a stone slab.

Madame Embalmer crosses the floor, a jar containing a heart balanced between her hands. 'Come now, no need to panic. It is simply a sand cloud. Down here is the safest place to be.'

'It's not a sand cloud,' I gasp.

'The Samael are here,' Talia says, her voice spiking with panic.

A light smattering of giggles travels around the cavern, and Madame Embalmer glances down at my dress. A smear of devil wing still remains. Balls. Everything I say will now be dismissed as the ramblings of an addict.

Her eyes narrow. 'That is quite enough, Sephie. Go to your dormitory. I will deal with you later.'

I fold my arms. 'There's no way I'm going back up there.'

A loud clash drifts down the stairs followed by screaming. Madame Embalmer looks towards the door, fear registering on her face. The clack of claws upon steps finds us, followed by the scratch of fingernails trailing against stone. I thought we'd be safe in the catacombs. I was wrong.

'They had wings?' Madame asks. 'Are you absolutely sure?'

'As white as snow,' Talia says.

Something changes in Madame's expression. 'There is an escape hatch.' She pivots on her heel and runs towards the back of the cavern. 'Pupils, leave what you are doing.' She wheels a shelving unit to the side, sending crocks of potions crashing to the floor, and reveals a wooden door sunk into the rock. One of the students helps her heave it open. A thin staircase leads upwards.

Tools and body parts are abandoned, and students flock to the exit like crazed geese.

'Keep going and you will eventually surface outside the citadel,' Madame says. 'Take shelter in the city until all is calm. I'll be right behind you.'

The students are fast, but they are more than fifty, and the tunnel creates a bottleneck. Talia and I are last in line.

A horrific screech sounds from the corridor.

'The Samael,' someone shouts.

The students start pushing and shoving, ignoring Madame's pleas to remain calm.

Talia and I exchange an urgent glance. It is obvious we won't make it to the stairs in time.

'We need to hide,' Talia says.

'Where?' My eyes explore the cave. There are no obvious hiding places – everything is stone, bare.

'The loculi,' she says, dragging me towards the ladders.

'No bloody way.' Just the thought of cosying up with a corpse makes my stomach spin.

'There will be empty ones,' she says. 'We don't have much choice.'

Another ear-splitting screech comes from just beyond the

entrance, and without another word, Talia and I scramble into the nearest loculi and wriggle back inside our respective stone openings. Of course, mine already has a corpse inside – an elderly gentleman who still awaits the embalming process and smells of rotten eggs. Typical. But death is the last thing on my mind right now. Staying alive is all I care about.

From my hiding place, I see at least ten students are yet to squeeze into the escape route. Even Madame Embalmer looks wretched with panic. Zalta appears from the huddle, and I'm about to shout to her, when she makes it to the tunnel. Just in time. Because the shadow of a winged demon falls across the crypt floor like a spike.

There is no door to my loculus, so I stretch out on my stomach, trying to sink into the stone, resting my face in the corpse's armpit and using his arm as a shield. Talons rap against the crypt floor like the claws of a giant rat. Trailing feathers swish upon stone. The skin on the corpse glows as if bathed in moonlight, and the scent of snow fills my nostrils. But above all else, I *feel* them. There's a marked temperature drop in the air and it takes every effort not to shiver.

A strong voice fills the cavern. 'What do you want, demons?'

It is Madame Embalmer. She never made it to the escape tunnel. And even though I'm terrified for her, I can't help feeling a touch relieved that Talia and I are not alone with these beasts.

Tentatively, I peek over the dead man's shoulder. Four Samael stalk the cavern. They move less like humans and more like birds. The wings are immense, dragging behind them like feathered gowns. No wonder I mistook them for capes back at the temple.

Their skin mesmerizes me; in the candlelight, they sparkle like a frozen lake.

Like devil wing.

The largest Samael with a grey, plaited mane approaches Madame. 'Alchemist or Healer?'

'This is the Grand Crypt. You will find only Embalmers.'

He stoops towards her and inhales deeply, smelling her hair and the skin around her neck. Other than the smallest of flinches, she does not move. It is a display of great strength on her part, as she must be about to soil her undergarments.

'Is it her?' another Samael asks.

The Samael with the braid shakes his head. Then, he slashes her chest with a single taloned finger. It takes a moment for my brain to make sense of what is happening. Madame Embalmer is clutching at her breast, blood spurting from beneath her fingers. Then she drops to her knees, slumping into an ever-expanding pool of red.

I long to rush to her, but I know that it will be me next if I do.

The Samael simply points to the escape tunnel. 'Make sure they don't escape.'

Two of the Samael disappear inside the tunnel, their wings plastered against their backs. Within seconds, the screams of my fellow students echo around the cavern. I press my face into the corpse, not caring that his skin feels like damp clay, trying desperately to muffle my sobs and thanking Mother Moon that I have some devil wing left in my blood to numb the terror. How is poor Talia coping? Cooped up in her grave with no anaesthesia at all.

There's a loud thud followed by the crack of bones.

I risk another look.

I wish I hadn't, because there lies Zalta at the base of the escape tunnel, her neck turned at an unnatural angle, her eyes staring into space. Those beasts have snapped her neck as if she were no more than a mangy chicken to be plucked for supper.

The urge to attack, to fight, arrives quickly, but I am no match for the Samael, and I don't want to join Zalta, discarded on the crypt floor.

For a moment, everything falls quiet.

Then, the largest Samael steps over Madame and Zalta, a fox in a henhouse, and opens his wings with a mighty *clack*. His wings are beautiful, each quill shimmering with a silver light that catches the dust in the air and transforms the cavern into a giant snow globe. Wonder entwines with fear and rage until I can barely breathe.

He sniffs the air. 'I know you are near, Alchemist.'

There is only me and Talia left. Does he sense the Divine Shadow in my blood? Dark recognizing dark.

'Show yourself and we promise we will spare you.' He looks beneath the stone slabs.

The smaller Samael jabs his fingernails into the laid-out corpses. Legs, chests, faces – wherever his talons land – testing to see if the dead are in fact faking. These beasts are brutal. The Samael with the plait pauses beside my grave. I hold my breath, my body rigid with fear. This close, I can see the detail of his skin. Iridescent like the wing of a dragonfly, as if he's been dipped in ice or left out on a wintry night to gather the frost.

He sniffs again. His face is angular, his eyes silver. Even his eyelashes are white.

'There you are,' he says.

22

ICARI

I leave Xenia in the cottage, cradling the babe, and dash towards the sanatorium. I've delayed too long – Sephie is in danger.

Yiannis and Erastus have survived, but Erastus is injured, so it's his husband who rides with me across the city on a strong, sleek bay horse almost twice the size of Sabu. As we streak up the cobbled paths, yellow confetti appears above: an army of Illios thatching the skies with wings of golden corn and sleek, muscular bodies. Relief and hope flood my system. *Please, Father Sun, let Sephie and Caszeil be safe. Let the Illios protect them from Aïdes's demons.* Yet the pain in my gut tells me that Sephie is in danger, and I wish I had my own wings so I could fly even faster than the bay.

As the citadel comes into view, a swarm of Samael appears, erupting from the peak of Mount Appollis like silver lava.

'They're leaving,' I shout, unable to stop the hope building.

'But not empty-handed, it would seem,' Yiannis replies, his words landing between the thud of hoofs.

I squint into the distance. Sure enough, dangling beneath

the Samael, like mice gripped in the talons of birds, are people.

My heart folds in on itself. 'They're stealing humans?'

'Alchemists,' Yiannis replies.

Another wave of relief filters through me. He's right. Every single person dangling from talons is dressed in silver-and-gold robes. Could Sephie's black dress have kept her safe?

As we near the citadel, the sound of the battle builds like distant thunder. Shouting and grunting, swords clashing, wings beating. The gate swings open on its hinges and catches in the breeze, as though accepting it can offer no protection when the attackers have wings. Two guards slump against the stone wall, spears protruding from their breasts and blood leaking into the soil.

Yiannis pulls against the reins and leaps from the bay. 'Go, find your sister,' he cries, dashing to the nearest guard and stemming the blood flow.

Terror freezes my legs, for the sounds of the battle are deafening, and the air reeks of blood and rage.

'Icari,' Yiannis cries. 'I didn't ride into danger simply for you to stand there. Go.'

His words are a release, and I run into the Court of Ash.

Yet the sight that greets me only inflates my terror. Samael and Illios are fighting *everywhere*. On the marble of the courtyard, on the rooftops, in the skies. Spears fly, swords clash, gold feathers and silver skin turn the world into a metallic blur. And peppered across the ground, slumped in pools of red, are the city guard.

I can only pray Sephie is safe in the catacombs, that the

twisting of my stomach is my own fear, not hers. But I need to find her. I need to know she's safe. Caszeil too. So I gather all of my courage, pick up a fallen spear and run into the whir of violence.

23

SEPHIE

The Samael reaches not into my grave, but Talia's. Her scream hits my ears as he hauls her from the rock and pulls her against him. My muscles tense like loaded springs. But all I can do is watch as he buries his face in her beautiful hair and inhales.

'You are not the one,' he hisses.

'An Alchemist is close,' says another Samael. 'I sense them.'

The Samael with the braid pushes a taloned finger against Talia's throat. Not enough to kill, but enough to lure ruby beads to the surface of her skin.

He smirks. 'You saw what happened to the moon-haired witch, Alchemist. How much is the fire-viper sorceress worth to you? If you give yourself up, I will spare her. You have my word.'

His word is worth less than pig slop, but I call out all the same. 'Stop!'

'Sephie, don't,' Talia screams. 'He will kill us both.'

I am heavy with fear, but I'll be damned if I let them hurt Talia. I untangle myself from the corpse and clamber from the grave, enraged that these *monsters* dare to threaten the best person I've ever met.

'Is it me that you want?' I ask.

The Samael throws Talia to the ground, where she manages to scrabble beneath a slab. He steps towards me, so close I can smell the cold on him, feel it spooling from his skin like snow in the wind. He moves quickly, breathing in the scent of my hair and neck. His nose brushes my skin. It is so cold, it burns.

'Yes,' he finally says, stepping back. 'It is you that we want.'

Lunging forward, he sinks his fingers into my shoulders. Ten scalpels bury deep into my muscles and I wail in pain. The Samael responds by beating his monstrous wings; the sound hurts my ears and I release another scream as I jerk upwards, my feet flailing beneath me as if I were hanging from a noose and dancing the dead man's jig.

Talia reaches for me, but before I can even say her name, I'm hurtling through the air. The wall of the crypt rushes towards me and I shield my face, mouth open in a silent scream, preparing for an impact that never comes as we drop suddenly, ducking beneath the exit into the corridor. The front of my calves drag against the stone flags and the pain is unspeakable, spreading my flesh upon the floor as if I were no more than butter.

Holy shit, I am going to die.

The demon tucks in his wings and we swoop up the stairway, every step assaulting my trailing legs, catching on my feet and causing me to cry out. Bursting into the Night Temple, we climb higher and higher.

'Stop!' I scream, desperation reducing my voice to a shrill tremor. 'Please stop.'

The marble below is strewn with broken glass, bodies and

blood, a strange mosaic that shrinks beneath me as the Samael beats his wings, causing a rolling rhythm that tears the skin from my shoulders even more. Then, standing below me, no bigger than a doll, is my sister. Her face is racked with fear, yet I have never seen her look so bold. She scans the temple, searching for me, a spear clutched in her hands.

'Icari!' I scream. 'Icari!'

She looks up and her face transforms with horror. Dropping the spear, she extends both hands towards me as if she can somehow close the gap and heave me back down. 'Sephie. No, no, no.'

I wriggle and twist, but before I know it, the wind is upon my face and I'm sailing from the open, jagged jaws of the Night Temple.

24

ICARI

I race from the Night Temple, watching my sister disappear until she is no more than a dandelion seed bobbing in the breeze. A deep crevasse forged from pain and despair opens inside me, and it's like I'm gummed to the floor watching Mama burn all over again. Sucking in lungfuls of metal-tainted air, I long to drop to my knees, to lose myself to grief and to wail and beat my chest, but I have no time for such self-indulgence, for the Samael and Illios have nearly all vanished now, leaving the injured and dying in a tableau of fallen weaponry and spilt blood.

The bodies belong mostly to mortals and the Samael, though the occasional Illios lies broken, their golden wings sparkling beneath the emerging stars. And even though I know I should join the Healers as they rush from the sana-torium, carrying medical aid and stretchers of linen and bamboo, there is something else I must do first.

I need to see Caszeil. I need to know I haven't lost him too.

I dash back inside the Night Temple, the quickest route to the dungeons, for I doubt in the current circumstances anyone will care if a Healer enters the house of Mother

Moon. Nobody even notices me as I stream through the catacombs, and when I reach the dungeons, the main door is already ajar, the keys left dangling from the lock. The guard must have left in a hurry, roused by the shrieks of the Samael.

I grab the keys and creep down the corridor. My heart is a wild animal, for a Samael could easily be lurking in the shadows and I have neither the weapon nor the skill to save myself. Yet the passages are entirely bare, but for the heads, of course. Not a Samael in sight. I release a shuddering breath.

I snap open his hatch. 'Caszeil?'

The sound of his deep, steady breaths find me; the devil wing has cradled him in sleep throughout the entire raid. Thank goodness. With trembling hands, I open the door, desperate to tell him about Sephie and hear his calm voice.

He lies on his side, curled in a ball, and I start to weep again, the relief of finally seeing him combines with the pain of losing my sister so my body feels like it may come apart at the seams. His dark eyelashes quiver as he dances with a dream, and I wish I were in that head with him – anywhere but this reality where Sephie has been stolen by demons.

I know I should let him sleep, yet grief makes me selfish and I drop beside him, resting a palm on his cheek. I anticipate the warm press of his skin, yet he is unspeakably cold – so cold, I whisk my hand away as though bitten. Panic claims me, for only a dead man could mimic winter so. Yet his muscled chest rises and falls, his beetle-black eyelashes continue to tremble, and the corners of his dusty-pink lips twitch as if he's about to say my name.

Of course he is cold. The dungeon chill is inescapable and he has no blanket, no clothes of which to speak.

I touch his cheek again, this time resisting the urge to flinch.

Yet his chill goes beyond the realms of the living.

Has he always felt like this? I wouldn't know, for I've only ever touched him through cloth. My hand lingers on his skin. His burns have the texture of dried leaves, and golden light spills from my fingers as Father Sun floods my veins.

Never before have I seen my glow so bright.

'Impossible,' I say, gasping.

Ever so slowly, his eyelids creak open, revealing the smoke-grey irises beneath.

'Icari,' he whispers.

The way he says my name, hopeful and soft, fills me with more warmth than my Calling ever could. Yet it is only for a moment, because as I lift my fingers from his cheek, a flaw-less palm print of silver remains on his skin. It's as if I'd dipped my hand in molten metal before touching him.

'Father Sun, what is this?' I whisper, leaning closer.

He scrambles into a sitting position. 'Icari, don't. Please.' His voice is taut, rigid, his features gaunt. He looks like a man who's about to lose everything.

Disbelief swamps my brain and my thoughts become sludgy and dense, for I haven't left behind a silver handprint; I've simply healed where I've touched. Something shifts inside me, the beginnings of an earthquake deep in my very marrow as the puzzle of the grey-eyed prisoner suddenly fits together. That is how, in spite of his maltreatment, Caszeil is so muscled, his teeth so white, and his hair so healthy. That is how he's survived torture that would have killed any ordinary man. The earthquake sweeps through me, gaining strength and malice, rattling my skeleton and tearing at my skin. Because Caszeil isn't an Alchemist or a sorcerer, though his veins flow black with the Divine Shadow.

Caszeil is a demon.

25

ICARI

'You're Samael?' I whisper.

He nods, his eyelashes glistening with tears. 'I'm so sorry, Icari. But I swear, I never lied to you.'

'No.' If I say it firmly enough, perhaps it won't be true. 'No. You can't be . . . You . . . you don't have wings.'

He builds himself into a standing position, carefully, so as not to alarm me, then moves into the light. My heart thwacks against my ribs, my skin slicks with sweat, yet all I can do is watch as he turns away from me to reveal two nubs of bone protruding from his back, joined at their base so they form the shape of a heart.

'My name is Caszeil and I am Samael. I was captured centuries ago during the first great battle in the sky. They removed my wings, tortured me for information, then locked me in the dungeons. I believe I was the only demon spared.' He releases a bitter laugh. '*Spared*. I can think of better words.'

I close my eyes and focus on his clear voice rather than his words, pretending he's still my grey-eyed prisoner and not one of the demons who stole my sister. Wishing I could undo the truth: Caszeil is a *demon*. A son of Aïdes. He is our mortal enemy.

A flash of cold reaches down my cheek and I realize he's touching me. Shock kicks my legs from beneath me and I stumble backwards, hitting the floor with a thud.

'Don't be scared,' he says, offering to pull me up with those graceful, damaged hands.

Panic becomes my puppet master, yanking at my strings, causing my limbs to jerk and flail as I claw myself away from him.

'Get away from me,' I cry.

'Icari, please, you know I would never hurt you. I am the same as I ever was.'

Somehow, I clamber to my feet, my gown catching beneath my shoes, my hair spiralling before my eyes. 'Yes, a demon. A *monster.*'

He steps towards me, hands raised, face full of regret; the silver handprint glints from his cheek like a blade in the dark. 'Please, let me explain. I wanted to tell you the truth—'

'Get away, get away!' I scream.

The urge to escape overwhelms everything – the panic, the hysteria, the sense of betrayal – and I dash from his cell, slamming the door and turning the lock with a terrified sob. Then I race down the corridor, unable to keep my eyes from the severed heads, from their mocking smiles and laughing eyes.

The sound of his hatch snapping open and his desperate voice chases me as I flee. '*Icari, wait. Icari, please. I'm sorry. Icari.*'

But I don't stop running until the dungeons are far behind me.

26

ICARI

The Court of Ash is empty but for a few orderlies sweeping the mess, leaving silver and red smears with their brooms. I stand and weep beneath Mother Moon, not knowing where to go or what to do. Not knowing who I am. It's like the whole world has turned inside out and nothing makes sense any more.

Caszeil is Samael.

Shame and disgust fill my mouth as I recall how close I came to kissing him, to *loving* him.

Yet he was only ever gentle – I would go as far as to say kind . . . Was he manipulating me the whole time? Perhaps it was always his plan that I would fall for him so I would aid his escape. Perhaps I would have done had I not realized his true self.

Forgive me, Father Sun, for I am a gullible fool.

'Are you OK, miss?' A young orderly approaches me, her face soft with concern.

I shake my head. I want to tell her that I am not OK. I will never be OK again. For I have lost everything, *everything* – my sister, my grey-eyed prisoner, a world that makes sense. But instead, I bite my tongue until I taste blood.

She offers me a sympathetic smile. 'It's been a tough day, huh?'

I nod.

'Well, they're in the Great Hall,' she says.

'Pardon?' I reply, barely able to think through the haze of self-loathing.

'The students, anyone who's left. They've gathered in the Great Hall to take stock.'

I open my mouth to thank her, but only a strangled sob emerges.

She tips her head as if to say, *You're welcome,* then returns to her sweeping.

I'm about to let my marionette legs carry me to the Great Hall, when that fish hook snags my stomach. I know the feeling well. It can mean only one thing: Sephie is still alive.

The anger, the shame, the sense of betrayal, it all drains away, leaving only hope and a sense of purpose. Because if Sephie is still alive, there's a chance I can save her. Her name leaves my lips in a frantic whisper, and I dash to the Great Hall and the people who will help me get her back.

An urgent buzz fills the grand chamber as the crowd waits for Uriel to make his address. Only Embalmers and Healers remain: some unscathed but for tears, others streaked with the blood of the fallen and the memory of a battle lost. Then my eyes land on Ziris, one of the only remaining alchemy students. Why did he escape when Sephie could not? Father Sun, why is the world so unfair?

I stumble towards Talia, her red-streaked hair a beacon in the gloom, and as she turns towards me I see that her face looks as ragged as I feel: eyes ringed with red, cracked lips, a look of having been scrunched up like a piece of parchment, yet to return to a state of smoothness. Perhaps we will always bear these creases.

'They took Sephie,' she says, her voice hollow. 'We hid in the loculi, but they found us. It's like they were *looking* for her.' She has a cut on her neck that still oozes blood and she touches a finger to it, as if to remind herself that the horror of which she speaks is true.

'I saw them carry her from the Night Temple,' I say.

Grief is a magnetic force pulling us together and we fall into a firm embrace as she is racked with tears. I wouldn't wish this pain on anyone, but I cannot help but feel relieved that someone else feels Sephie's abduction as deeply as I do. It makes me feel less alone.

'She is alive,' I say. 'I feel it as only a twin can.'

Her body relaxes a little in my arms. 'She said you could feel each other, especially at times of suffering.' She swallows the word *suffering* and muffles a sob.

'Hush now.' I stroke her hair. 'She is alive — let's focus on that.'

Suddenly, she pulls away from me. 'Zalta's dead. They killed her like she was . . . was . . . nothing.'

'Oh, Talia.'

We embrace again and I let the tears overwhelm me.

'And Xenia?' she says. 'Is she safe?'

'I left her in the city.' Now is not the time to tell her about the attack on the sanatorium.

'Praise be to Father Sun,' she whispers.

We hold hands and I savour the warmth of her humanity

against my palms, even though the intimacy reminds me of Sephie and draws more tears to my eyes.

Uriel appears at the front of the hall. The crowd falls quiet but for a few gentle sobs. And even though I hate him, I'm grateful for his authoritative presence; a lost flock needs a shepherd. His gowns are torn, splattered with blood, and he's in dire need of a cold compress due to a swollen eye, yet I imagine he was as fierce as any Illios or Samael in battle.

He surveys the students before him. His face is a mask of stoic calmness.

Clearing his throat, he rolls his shoulder, the battle clearly awakening his old injury. 'Praise be to Father Sun for sending the Illios to defend us.' He kisses his fist and glances upwards, a gesture that ripples across the crowd. 'Many Samael were slaughtered at the hands of the Illios – but it was not enough. Only a few alchemy students were saved. Of course you will have questions about why this happened and where the Alchemists were taken, but I have no answers. Rest assured that we are doing everything we can.'

He presses his palms together, pausing to study the stained-glass windows and grand pillars as though noticing them for the first time. 'As for the rest of us, there are many dead and many more injured. If you are standing before me, I can only assume you are well enough to work. Healers, you will tend to the injured in the citadel sanatorium. Embalming students, you will of course be very busy now. There are guards, orderlies and students to preserve, and this must be done with the utmost care and respect. It is an honour and a burden to embalm your friends, and anyone struggling with this task may seek guidance from me.'

'Is it true Madame is dead?' someone shouts.

'She was attacked by the demons,' Uriel replies. 'But thankfully she survived and is receiving care in the citadel sanatorium.'

'And what of the Illios?' comes another cry.

'Two of the Illios were slaughtered at the hands of the Samael, and they have already been laid in their resting place beside their brothers in the Tomb of Light.' He raises his hands towards the skies. 'Enough questions. There is work to do. Please go about your chores with your head held high. We have survived a Samael attack before, and we will again.'

Slowly, the room empties. Talia squeezes my hand and gestures for the door, but I tell her I'll join her later. For now, Uriel has to know Sephie is alive. He has to do something.

When the hall is nearly empty, I approach the High Priest, my stomach filled with wasps. 'My lord, may I have a moment of your time?'

'If it's quick,' he replies.

Up close, it's apparent his damaged eye needs more than a cold compress. The Calling warms my blood. He studies me with his uninjured eye – a flash of sadness moistens the surface. Do I remind him of Mama, whom I've learnt he once loved? I hesitate, unsure if he can be trusted with news of Sephie; he ordered her lashings and killed Mama, after all. Yet surely when it comes to Aïdes, we are on the same side.

'My lord, I believe my sister is still alive,' I say.

His uninjured eye narrows. 'How could you possibly know that?'

'We are twins.'

He makes a noise halfway between disbelief and exhaustion, then turns to leave. But I cannot simply let him walk away.

'My lord,' I say, stepping before him. 'Is there a plan to find her? Did the Illios follow the Samael?'

'No. The Illios were sent to defend the Sunlands, that is all. Whether or not your sister lives, she is now lost to us. Please, tend to your duties.'

And with that, he walks away.

My hand rests against my stomach as my determination strengthens. With or without his help, I know what I have to do.

I have to save my sister.

27

SEPHIE

I used to think I'd enjoy flying. Turns out I was wrong. But then I'd always imagined I'd be a dove or a brightly coloured butterfly, not dangling from the claws of a demon like a rag in a cat's mouth, my shoulders drenched with blood and pain.

We flew over the oasis many hours ago and now there's nothing but desert, washed pale by the light of Mother Moon. In the distance, other students swing from their captors. I recognize most of them, including Belum, and briefly wonder if I look as miserable as them. Like a floppy corpse waiting to be stuffed.

The wings of the Samael above block out the night sky. Each feather sparkles like an icicle in the black.

Never the shy one, I call to him, 'Where are you taking me?'

He responds by digging his claws deeper, pouring more pain into my body and more blood on to the sands below. A disgusting scraping noise fills my head as talons meet my right collarbone. It annoys me that I'm now marked for ever. That when I die, my remains will have five grooves stretching deep into my clavicle.

I call on the Divine Shadow to ease my discomfort. Surely there's no harm in using my gift now? The cold floods my shoulders and I release a grateful sigh. The irony that Aïdes should soothe the pain his army has inflicted is not lost on me. If I weren't so wrung out, I'd laugh.

At some point, it occurs to me that maybe my power could save me. If I could transmute the air into wind, I could bring a storm, I could raise a dust cloud and choke the life from the feathery bastards. It's worth a try. Turning my focus outwards, I try to connect with the air around me, but I'm moving too fast, whipped away before I can sense the drops of moisture, the dust particles, or the ebb and flow of the breeze.

And then I forget entirely because the screaming starts.

The Samael are releasing my fellow students, sending their bodies streaking towards the ground in a blur of silver-and-gold robes. Small clouds of dust explode beneath me. Bones crunch. Flesh splatters.

'No,' I shout, my voice thick with shock. 'What are you doing?'

'Getting rid of the surplus cargo,' my captor growls.

Terror claims me entirely, scrabbling up my arms and forcing me to cling to the Samael's ankles. I squeeze my eyes shut and anticipate the sudden release, the downward pull as my body hurtles towards its end. My only hope is to remain intact long enough so my soul may journey to Mother Moon. But as the seconds turn into minutes, the screaming stops, and I'm yet to be dropped. I open my eyes then immediately wish I hadn't, because I'm the only student remaining, which either makes me the luckiest son of a dung beetle, or the unluckiest.

'Just drop me,' I scream. 'Just do it. I cannot bear this torment any longer.'

'I'm not going to drop you,' the Samael replies.

I risk asking again, for there is nothing more this demon could do to break me. 'Then where are you taking me?' My voice is barely a drawl and I begin to sob.

'Don't cry, my lady. It won't be long.'

Did a demon just call me *my lady*? I don't think anyone has ever called me 'my lady', let alone a Samael. I must be delirious. Hardly surprising considering the circumstances.

Eventually, we reach the Bone desert; great crags jut from the sand like the fins of a river beast, and lumps of rock sprout upwards like giant mushrooms. Father Sun stirs beneath the horizon. Everyone knows that demons cannot tolerate sunshine, which is no doubt why they attacked the citadel at dusk and now travel at night, so I whisper a silent prayer: *Hurry, Father Sun. Please hurry.* I swear he goes slower. Arsehole.

We reach a rocky outcrop, the same colour as the orange part of a flame, and the demon tugs me upwards and into his arms. The cold of his chest makes me gasp. The proximity of his naked flesh offends me.

'Let go of me, you beast,' I scream.

He responds by flipping upside down so my stomach reels, pulling his wings into his sides and descending so fast that I nearly lose my dinner. I try to scream, but the air floods my mouth, extinguishing my voice like a lamp in the wind. The ground is getting closer, the orange rocks rise up, ready to smash me into a million pieces, and just as I decide that this is how I will die, the earth rips in two and a black ravine with no bottom, no light, no hope or life swallows us whole.

28

SEPHIE

Down I fall, deeper and deeper into the black, until the world becomes nothing but darkness and wind and the sensation that my stomach has disconnected from my body. After what feels like a lifetime, the black turns to grey, the rock comes to life with moving shadows, and the tunnel opens into a monstrous cave. The Samael holding me opens his wings and flips into an upright position, fast losing speed. Multicoloured dots explode before my eyes as all the blood drains from my head. More Samael follow from the rip in the cave's ceiling, silver comets that hurtle towards the ground only to transform in an instant into snowflakes that land without noise.

I'm deposited on the craggy ground and my legs crumple beneath me. But I refuse to cower like a lamb, so I force myself to my feet and try to stop myself from swaying. The cave is huge, bigger than the Grand Crypt or the Night Temple, and carved into sections by monstrous stalactites and stalagmites. The entire structure is coated with frost and littered with small fires that do little to counteract the chill. I have never felt such cold. My breath crystallizes in the air before me.

I know where I am. Of course I do. I've grown up with legends of the earth cracking and inhaling demons and poor, unsuspecting mortals. I just never thought it would be me. I stumble from side to side like a drunkard, eyes searching for an escape route even though I know it's pointless. The Samael surround me, picking at my robes with curious eyes, their skin perfectly matched to the frosted stone. I can smell snow and smoke and blood. It makes me gasp.

'I want to go home.' My voice echoes around the rock. 'Take me home.' Panic and anger turn me into a weapon of flailing limbs and I launch myself at the Samael with the grey plait, beating my fists upon his chest, pulling at his feathers. 'Why are you just standing there, you overgrown chicken.'

As if I were a gnat, he swipes me to one side and I land in a jumble of limbs and indignity. Before I can even think about rallying, a voice as deep as it is familiar rings through the cave.

'Gentle with her. She is a precious jewel.'

The demons part to reveal a man. Initially, he's just a broad-shouldered silhouette in the gloom of the cave, yet as he nears, his features emerge: strong and vulnerable all at once, with the symmetry of a flower. Waves of black hair fall across his shoulders, and he wears the robes of a king: drapes of white, edged with silver and gold.

'Welcome to the Underworld, my lady,' he says.

I know that voice better than I know my own, for it has whispered in my ear whenever I've transmuted flowers, or trees, or calmed the winds, or boiled water. It is the voice of the Divine Shadow.

My skin shrinks around my bones.

'Do you know who I am?' he asks.

I nod.

'That's right,' he says. 'I am the Divine Shadow, though friends call me Aïdes. You may call me Aïdes if you prefer, because we're friends, aren't we, Sephie? Good friends.'

I slump forward, all the strength sapped from my limbs. My collarbone is clearly broken, snapped like a piece of firewood, and my heart beats so loudly, I'm afraid he will hear.

He offers me his hand, and our eyes meet. He has the bluest eyes I've ever seen, and his pale skin is shiny, dappled like morning frost on a pane of glass. The Calling roars in my blood, stronger than ever. Dark recognizing the darkest.

I stand before him, straightening up as best I can even though my shoulders thrum with pain. I will never kneel to the devil.

He smiles. 'It's a pleasure to meet you in the flesh. I trust that my demons weren't too rough?' He glances at my bloodied shoulders and shakes his head with affectionate disapproval, like a parent might bestow upon a naughty child. 'They can get a little carried away if you let them.'

'Why am I here?' I hate how my voice trembles, so I repeat myself, this time stronger. 'Why am I here?'

He reaches forward and, before I can back away, takes my hands in his. There isn't a word for how cold his skin is. It's a thousand frozen lakes whipping up my arms, causing me to wheeze and snatch my hands away.

'Don't touch me,' I say.

'I'm trying to help you, Sephie. Why are you so angry?'

I blink, taken aback. 'Why am I angry?' My voice rises. 'Why am I angry? Because your demons got *a little carried away* and murdered my friend Zalta and my teacher Madame, then they ripped me from my sister, from my home. They let my fellow students fall to their death like they were no more than leftovers being scraped from a plate. I saw them explode beneath me.'

'They did what was necessary to bring you to me, that is all.' He presses his hands together and smiles. 'Demons, please, my lady requires further assistance.'

Cold hands grasp my arms, my hair, my legs, so that no matter how I kick and writhe, I'm locked into position, so I scream and scream until the cave becomes no more than the space that houses my screams.

The Divine Shadow walks towards me, his smile fixed. My body takes over and I'm not sure if I'm trying to attack or run away. It doesn't really matter, for I'm held in place like a wooden post regardless of how I strain.

He reaches towards me and fear nests inside fear until I am built from adrenaline alone.

'Don't you fucking touch me,' I yell. 'Don't you fucking dare.'

His silver hands approach my face and I begin to snap and bite at the air, a wild animal backed into a corner who refuses to whimper. Then something strange happens. The pain twisting through my body subsides.

I look down. Aïdes is resting his hands upon my shoulders.

Funny, I'd grown so accustomed to the hurt, I'd almost stopped noticing it, and it's only now, in its absence, I become aware of every incision, every scrap of shredded flesh, the places where my collarbone snapped. I free-fall into the pain relief, into the shadows pulsing through my body and the lack of suffering. I think I may even sigh. I *hate* that I may have sighed.

'There,' he whispers, so close I can smell his breath – sweet and cold, like berries caught in the first frost. 'That's better, isn't it.'

I roll my shoulder. He's mended my skin and fixed the bone, but I can't bring myself to nod, so I simply glare at his feet. They're bare and yet entirely clean, as though he weren't walking on earth, rock and ash.

His cold finger lifts my chin so I meet his gaze.

'Your anger hides something, doesn't it?' he says.

I could spit at him. I'm a pretty good aim and I could get him right in one of those unthinkably blue eyes, but I'm just too scared.

'Loss.' He speaks the word gently, as if aware of the pain it bears. 'And I know all about loss, Sephie, I do. My world is spun from loss. Loss of the one I love. Sorrow that I cannot be with her. We are not so different, you and I.'

I back away from him, thrown off balance by his gentle manner and his heartfelt words. The Aïdes I have feared all my life is full of wrath and bitterness. And yet it is more terrifying finding him like this. The threat of violence just beneath the surface like a second skin.

'Your mother's death broke you,' he continues. 'Shattered you into a hundred pieces. And yes, you stuck those pieces back together with anger, but it has left you a mosaic of your former self. Most people don't see it, do they? But I do. I'm close enough to see the cobweb of cracks running across your skin.'

His words resonate deep within my soul. How does this man of frost and shadow know me better than I know myself? I want to pull him from my brain like a ribbon and hurl him into the flames.

'You seem surprised,' he says, his voice silky. 'Surely you didn't think that I was a monster? I am the Divine Shadow. I am part of you. The *best* part of you, I like to think.'

That cold finger is back, exerting just enough pressure on my cheek to turn my head towards him without leaving a mark.

'What do you want from me?' Each word is like grit on my tongue.

A smile climbs up one side of his face. 'I don't want anything *from* you, Sephie. I only want you.'

'Me? Why?'

He shrugs, nonchalant. 'I am lonely. I have my world of ice, my army and my broken souls, but I am still lonely.'

Anger and injustice grow in my belly. My fists clench at my sides, and my head rings. And suddenly I don't care if he strikes me down. Kills me, even. I'm already in the Underworld – what's the worst he can do? 'So make another friend from the ice of the Underworld and your own toenails or whatever the hell it is you do. Why take me?'

He laughs. 'Oh, I do like your fighting spirit. I will never be bored with you by my side.'

'Just take me home.' I look up: the gaping hole I fell through only moments ago has already closed, leaving only a fine crack on the ceiling. A scab of stone. So I level my eyes at him and muster every morsel of courage. 'I *demand* you take me home.'

I expect him to flare, to drop the fake facade of calm and show his true self, in all of its screaming, thuggish, hateful ugliness. I *want* him to flare. For at least then I will know what I'm dealing with. At least I will get it over with. But instead he simply smiles, as if I were an infant to be indulged.

'You would disrespect your future husband so?' he says.

At first, his words don't make sense. They're just a series of noises and pauses falling from a moving mouth.

'What?' I whisper.

'That's why you are here, my lady.' He cups my face in his palms. 'I intend to marry you.'

29

ICARI

I spend the rest of the night treating the sick in the citadel sanatorium, thoughts of Sephie and Caszeil all twisted up inside me like a mangled copper wire. I can still feel Sephie's life force, her panic, pulling at my gut, but just before Father Sun erupts in the sky, the sensation changes. My hand immediately flies to my stomach, and I wish I were more adept at interpreting these feelings, for she is still alive, I know she is, yet something is different. Her pull has grown . . . *cold*.

A soft voice tugs me from my thoughts.

'Icari?'

It seems to be coming from behind a privacy veil hanging towards the back.

'Icari?'

The voice floats through the thin fabric, and as I walk towards it, the form of a woman sitting up in bed becomes clearer. Pulling back the veil, I find Madame Embalmer, propped upright on several pillows and attempting to smile.

'Icari, yes?' She beckons me into the fabric cocoon.

'Yes.'

'Sephie's sister?'

'That's right.' My sister's name is both a thorn and a salve.

Madame winces with pain, so I pass her the goblet resting on the cabinet beside her, the shimmer of the liquid suggesting it contains devil wing. *Devil wing.* I envision a scythe arcing through the air, striking at Caszeil's back again and again, sending his wings tumbling to the ground in a spray of silver blood. I blink back the tears, angry at myself for pitying a demon instead of focusing on my patient.

She downs a hungry mouthful and I take a moment to study her. Hair licked with silver tumbles down her night-gown, and her washed-out face is even paler than usual, though a hint of colour returns to her cheeks as she drinks, confirming that her cup indeed contains pain relief. Her wound reaches from one side of her chest to the other, a sutured gash that resembles the stitched mouth of a rag doll. Did Caszeil once have talons so sharp he could inflict such harm? Is that why he told me to grow my fingernails, because he knew of their benefits in combat? The thought makes me shudder.

Setting down the empty goblet, she holds my gaze. 'I was only unconscious for a moment. When I awoke, the beasts had taken Sephie. I'm so sorry.'

'I saw them take her,' I say, straightening her bedding to distract us both from my damp eyes.

Tenderly, she stops my hands with fingers still cold from clutching the glass of devil wing. An image of a silver palm print beneath a slate-grey eye forms, unbidden, in my head. I hate that I cannot carve his memory from my brain.

'There was nothing you could have done, Icari.'

'Thank you, Madame.'

She pauses. 'Were you here? When the demons attacked?'

I shake my head. 'I chose a sanatorium nearer to home.'

'Ah,' she says. 'An unusual choice. Most pupils like the prestige of the citadel sanatorium.'

'I'm not accustomed to prestige.'

She smiles. 'Well, it was a more fortunate choice than you realize, for they were here too.'

'What, here? In this very room?'

'So I'm told.'

'Looking for Alchemists?'

She shrugs, then winces, the motion disturbing her injury.

'Would you like me to tend to you?' I ask.

It isn't just a shameless deflection from discussing the attack; the sutures on her wound are clumsy and need redoing or she'll be left with a notable scar. Not that scars aren't beautiful, but I doubt she wants a visual reminder of her ordeal whenever she undresses.

She nods. 'Principal Healer speaks highly of your gift.'

I'm too tired to feel flattered, so I simply begin the examination. A bronze key dangles from a chain around her neck. The head is engraved with tiny images of Mother Moon and Father Sun.

'It's beautiful, isn't it?' she says.

'Yes,' I reply.

'It's the key to the citadel,' she says. 'It works in every door. A skeleton key. There are only three in existence, and I have one of them.' She chuckles. 'Little old me. If only my mother could see me now.'

I nod and turn my attention to the wound. It's been stitched, but badly – perhaps in haste. Discoloured pus seeps from beneath the thread – an infection – so I let my fingers linger on the stitches, allowing the Calling to spread until my hands sparkle with yellow light and Madame lets out a small moan. Then, I unpick the existing sutures and let my needle dance across her wound in precise motions until it looks less like the mouth of a rag doll and more like the delicate stem of a rose.

She inspects my work with a smile. 'You really do have remarkable powers, Icari. Principal told me about you, but to experience your Calling first-hand.' She chuckles at her pun. 'It's quite something.'

'Thank you.'

'Will you be attending the burning this afternoon?'

The wings of the fallen demons have already been harvested, and later today there will be a huge pyre stacked with dead Samael in the Court of Ash. The knowledge that Caszeil could be thrown on this pyre drives a spelk of wood deep into my heart, but I ignore the pain, embrace it even, for a girl who is foolish enough to fall for a demon deserves everything she gets.

'Yes, Madame,' I say, gathering up my satchel. 'It will give me great pleasure to see the beasts burn.'

'Indeed. Although it is a shame they all died.'

I blink. 'Why do you wish a demon had lived? Surely their deaths are welcome.'

'Why, for information, of course. Only a demon can know what Aïdes intends with the stolen students.'

I almost drop my medical satchel. *Only a demon can know.* And I happen to know where the only living demon in the Sunlands is locked away.

'Icari,' Madame says. 'Are you OK?'

'Yes, Madame. Forgive me. There is something important that I must do.'

30

ICARI

The chalky guard is back, but he's already drunk and doesn't bother me as I dash towards Caszeil's cell. Fresh Samael heads stare at me from their spikes, dripping silver blood on to the floor, filling the air with the stench of skinned rabbits or slaughtered goats. I have never been so aware that my belly is full of unspent vomit. Is Sephie somewhere like this? A dungeon filled with decapitated heads? The thought causes my entire body to thrum with pain, and by the time I reach Caszeil's cell, tears dash my face.

Tentatively, I slide open the hatch.

'Caszeil?' I whisper.

Only the drip of the Samael heads replies.

'Caszeil? It is me, Icari.'

Drip, drip, drip.

Panic hovers in my chest, ready to rise up my throat like a locust swarm as I picture him beheaded and flung on to the pyre with the other monsters. He can't be dead – he just can't be. He's my one hope of finding Sephie. But it's more than that. Shame swirls in my stomach as I admit to myself that I can't bear the thought of losing him, even if he is a monster.

Grabbing a torch, I thrust it towards the open hatch. Yet no man – no demon – lurks in the gloom.

Frustrated, close to tears, I rush to a nearby cell and rap on the door.

'Prisoner,' I call. 'Prisoner, I need to talk to you. Don't be afraid.'

The hatch opens and two bloodshot eyes appear.

'What d'ya want?' The voice is female, weak, and I quickly surmise she's either very old or very ill. Probably both.

'Please, what happened to the man in the end cell?' I ask.

'How should I know?'

My fingers locate the bread meant for Caszeil, and I hold it towards her like I'm coaxing an animal from a lair. 'It is yours if you tell me.'

A hungry gasp spills from the hatch, followed by the swipe of desperate fingers, each as thin and frail as the legs of a hoopoe bird. '*Please*. I'm starvin' in 'ere.'

'Tell me about the prisoner in the end cell.' I wince, for kindness should not come with conditions.

'There weren't one.' Her voice wavers. 'Please, just give it 'ere.'

'Is it possible you didn't see him passing by? Could you have been asleep?'

'Not a chance. I sleep with one eye open or the rats eat me toes. I didn't even know there was an end cell till you started going there.'

'Thank you.' I push the bread into her grime-caked hands, for she's told me all I need to know. There must be another way of accessing Caszeil's cell, a secret one.

I rush past his cell to the end of the corridor and begin exploring the stonework, running my fingers over every nook. When I find a loose brick, I pull on it sharply. Something clicks, and part of the wall slides sideways to reveal a musty earthen tunnel carved into the ground.

The sound of someone screaming drifts towards me.

'Caszeil?' I'm ashamed by how my voice quakes.

I creep along the tunnel, the cold causing my skin to bristle and the scent of clay and blood hanging in my nostrils. Soil coats my hair and falls in my eyes, and I listen with horror as the tortured noises grow louder, praying that the groans belong to Caszeil so I can find my sister, whilst simultaneously willing it to be someone else because the thought of him in such agony chills me more than any shrunken tunnel.

Finally, I reach a small wooden door, and as I push my ear against it, the Calling spikes in my blood.

'Caszeil?'

Only the wretched sound of torment replies.

Before doubt can stop me, I lift the heavy metal latch and pull back the door. Stark morning light assaults my eyes and I blink quickly, trying to make sense of the sight before me. A man yelps and scrabbles like a dog, desperately trying – and failing – to escape the rays of Father Sun. His skin seems to be moving, a living patchwork of crimson, pink and black, smoking and bubbling like a strip of cured pig thrown into a fire.

'Help,' he screams. 'Help me, please.'

He is burnt beyond recognition, his voice is warped and unfamiliar, yet I know it is him from the shape of his body, from the curve of his shoulder muscles and the fan of golden hair as he shakes his head.

'Caszeil,' I cry, hoping to alert him to not only my presence, but the escape route.

Yet the suffering has undone his mind and he doesn't even attempt to shelter in the tunnel, so without thinking, I grab him beneath the arms and haul him into the dark. His body slumps against mine and he jerks and twitches in my arms. I find his weight strangely comforting.

'Caszeil?' I whisper.

After a few moments of whimpering, he shuffles deeper into the tunnel, leaving the stench of cooked meat in his wake.

'Caszeil,' I repeat. 'It's me.'

He notices me for the first time. His face is all contrast — glistening pinks and crusted blacks — yet his eyes remain the colour of a storm cloud.

'Icari? Is it really you?'

'Yes.'

He wraps his arms around his knees like he's trying to disappear. Great sobs disrupt his moans.

'Hush now,' I say. 'You're safe.'

He touches his head, then starts, for his golden hair falls out in clumps, leaving behind a smouldering scalp and the occasional charred lock.

'What have they done to you?' I say, biting back my tears.

'They call it the sun pit.'

Inspecting the source of the brilliant light, I discover that Caszeil was trapped inside a small, cylindrical room with no ceiling; a pit sunk into the earth like a waterless well and lined with mirrors, each cleverly angled so no matter where Father Sun sits in the sky, his rays are magnified and aimed at the prisoner. It must have been left from the last Samael attack, though I imagine the mirrors are newer.

'Father Sun, I cannot believe the cruelty of man,' I say, fumbling for my pouch of devil wing. 'Is this how they burnt you the first time?'

'Yes. There is no worse pain than the rays of Father Sun.'

He looks like he has been thrown in a firepit and left too long. I think of Mama and it's almost unbearable. I will not let another suffer like she did. Pressing a fingerprint of devil wing to his lips, I let the sympathy flood my veins and mix with my Calling so I momentarily forget that he lied to me. I forget he is the enemy.

He swallows and releases a sigh, his eyelids flickering as the drug filters through his system. 'You would help me, even though I'm Samael?'

I reply by cupping his face in my hands and letting my golden light spread across his cheeks. His skin eases back to silver beneath my palms, the searing heat fading to cold. The knot of agony in his brow muscles slowly undoes itself. It astonishes me how quickly he heals at my touch. His dark eyelashes quiver, and I begin sweeping his dried hair from his forehead, soothing the blisters wherever I touch so that his features begin to emerge from beneath the mess.

'Your compassion is endless, Icari,' he whispers.

'I can heal you,' I say, trying desperately not to weep, for nobody wants a Healer who is anything but steady. 'I will take you to your cell and heal every last part of you.'

He cradles my wrists and lowers my hands from his face.

The cold winds up my arms, vine-like, and I hate how much I love the sensation.

'You mustn't,' he says. 'They will know someone helped me and they will hunt you down. There is nothing you can do.'

I hold up the pouch. 'Well then, I will give you more pain relief.'

'Yes, but you have to put me back in the pit.'

The realization binds my throat so it hurts to swallow. And the fact that Caszeil prioritizes my safety above his own, that a demon acts so selflessly, it doesn't just knock a hole in my wall of beliefs – it knocks the entire structure down.

'I can't put you back,' I whisper. 'It will kill you.' The thought dismembers me.

'They will kill me anyway, Icari. They only tortured me to find out why the Samael took the Alchemists. When they finally realize I'm not going to tell them anything about the raid yesterday, they will dispose of me, I'm sure of it.'

I shake my head, trying to dislodge the words from my ears. Not only am I thinking about his impending death again, but there is the crushing news that he knows nothing about the raid.

'The sun pit will not kill me, I promise,' he says, reading my expression like only he can. 'I am made from the skin of the Divine Shadow and the ice of the Underworld.'

'That does not make you immortal.'

'No, but it makes me very hard to kill.'

He resembles a living ember. I'm not even sure there's any skin left on his torso; the thought of inflicting further injury makes me dizzy with horror. Yet he's right: if the guards realize I aided a demon, I will be severely punished, then I will never help Sephie. There is no other way. He must go back into the sun pit.

It takes everything I have to gather my resolve.

'Stick out your tongue,' I say.

When he does, it's surprisingly pink and human-looking, and I can't help wondering if it's as snow-cold as his touch. Quickly, I tip the contents of the pouch on to his tongue so that it forms a sparkling pyramid that he swallows in one grateful gulp. The effects are almost instant and he unfurls in my arms like a fern. His eyelids droop and the rhythm of his breath slows.

'Why so sad?' he mutters, gazing at my face from beneath fluttering eyelashes.

I release a shaky laugh, a little touched that he should notice my emotional state, considering the circumstances.

'Where to start?' I whisper, stroking his forehead, an action designed to soothe me as much as him. 'People have died, *friends* have died, then demons stole my darling sister and carried her away like she was no more than a grub in a bird's claw.'

'The Samael stole your sister?'

I nod. 'I'd hoped you'd know where they took her and why. That's why I came back.'

'Oh, that's why.' Disappointment taints his voice.

'Yes. But I now know you know nothing about the raid.'

His smoke-grey eyes meet mine and the corner of his lip lifts. 'I didn't say that. I just said I didn't tell the guards.'

A sense of urgency, of hope, pins my lungs to my ribs so I can't breathe. 'Do you know where they've taken Sephie?'

He nods.

'Where?' I say. 'Caszeil, you must tell me!'

He exhales slowly through his nose. 'I think you already know.'

I explore the contours of his face, still visible beneath the wounds, the imprint of my hands stamped in silver like two beautiful tattoos. *Of course I already know.* From the moment I saw her catapulting into the air, I knew where they were taking her, yet I buried it as deep as I could, packing it down with earth and denial. It is only now, cradling Caszeil, unable to turn from his silver demon skin, I can finally whisper the truth.

'The Underworld?'

The word doesn't do the horror justice.

He nods.

I envision the dark caves of legends, and I get this feeling like I'm suffocating, like my lungs are no bigger than pockets and my throat is stuffed with soil.

'But I can still feel her.' I rest my hand on my stomach. 'I *know* she isn't dead. How can she be in the Underworld if her heart still beats?' I ask, unable to admit to myself I already know the answer.

'Mortals can enter the Underworld if carried by the Samael.'

The image of Sephie in a festering land of tortured souls fills my brain and tears surge down my cheeks.

'The Underworld,' I whisper, lost. 'How will I reach her if she's in the Underworld?'

A faint smile forms on his lips, and for a brief moment, I catch a glimpse of the old Caszeil. 'I can take you there.'

'What? How?'

'I will fly you.'

I shake my head, confused. 'But . . . but they removed your wings.'

He catches a tendril of my hair with a lazy hand. 'So we build me some new ones.'

'We can't build *wings*.'

'Yes we can, with wax and gum and a boatload of feathers. I've been dreaming of it, Icari. I know it will work.'

A bitter laugh springs from my mouth. 'You have lost your mind.'

'I have lost many things, *most* things, but my mind remains intact.' He brings my hair to his lips as if to kiss it, but releases it at the last second.

I grapple with my words, the frustration building. 'But . . . but they won't be attached to you.' How can he tease me when he knows how my heart aches?

Yet not a glimmer of humour emerges on his face. 'Wings need a master, Icari. They will attach to me. The Samael have been fixing their wings since the dawn of our creation. Trust me.'

I cover my face with my hands, for how can I trust a demon? 'And if I build you wings, how do I know you will fly me to my sister? How do I know you won't simply escape? Once a demon, always a demon.'

His eyelashes flutter and he releases a great sigh, the devil wing attempting to pull him into the depths of sleep.

'Caszeil,' I say.

He resurfaces and gazes at me with dreamy eyes. 'What if I tell you something – something I shouldn't? If it turns out to be true, will you trust me then?' His words smudge together and his vision softens so he's now looking through me. Soon, he will be unconscious.

'What kind of thing?' I say.

'The Samael took many students to hide the fact they only wanted one.'

'How do you know this?'

'Because I know Aïdes. He is the creator of all Samael – he is my father.'

My pulse quickens and my mouth dries. 'Which student did he want?'

'If Sephie is still alive, then she is the one.'

'The one?'

'He intends to wed her.'

His words bounce around my head and the tunnel begins to spin. 'He means to make Sephie his bride?'

'I believe so.'

A tidal wave of horror and bleakness and every awful emotion possible slams into me, and I cling to Caszeil like he's the rock preventing me from being swept away. My darling sister married to the devil.

And why Sephie? I think to myself. *Because of her dual Calling, or perhaps her power to stir the dead, to read the dead?* Another thought bubbles to the surface: *does this have something to do with Mama's death? It can't be a coincidence. Both women unspeakably powerful, both women gone.* I shake my head, trying to reason with myself in spite of the grey mist of hopelessness swamping my brain. *No. Mama was burnt. Sephie was stolen by the Samael. It is entirely different.*

'Icari?' His voice is small, yet interrupts my thoughts like a cannon firing. 'If what I say turns out to be true, will you help me build my wings?'

I blink rapidly, trying to process his words. *'Will you help me build my wings?'* Surely I couldn't really help a demon build wings, or work alongside him and aid his escape. Surely that would mean aligning with Aïdes himself. But the alternative is to let my sister wed the devil.

Wed the devil. The thought is too horrific, too disgusting, to even contemplate.

I simply cannot let it happen.

So just before Caszeil submits to the devil wing, his breath soft and cool against my hands, his eyelashes concealing the slate of his eyes entirely, and just before I haul him back to the sun pit and close the door, the guilt crawling up my throat and dragging a strangled moan from my lips, I whisper my reply.

'Yes, Caszeil. If what you say is true, I will help you build your wings.'

31

ICARI

Later that day, Talia and I attend the burning of the Samael at the Court of Ash. A hotchpotch of limbs and torsos rest upon a pyre, the absence of the Samael heads and wings rendering the vision a giant nest of silver snakes. Father Sun is high in the sky and has already made the corpses at the top of the heap smoulder and blacken. The scent of charred meat combines with that of blood and snow.

I glance at Talia. Her jaw is set in a rigid shelf and her fists are clenched, yet a smile touches her lips and her eyes sparkle with triumph as she surveys the dead Samael. I can't help envying her a little, for vitriolic joy is exactly what I should feel. And yet their silver skin makes me think of Caszeil, the stench of burnt meat reminds me of the sun pit and how he wailed in agony, and instead of rejoicing in these demons' deaths, I just feel hollow.

Could I really help Caszeil build his wings? Even if it works and by some miracle he flies, and the ground momentarily opens like a giant, rocky maw permitting us entrance to the Underworld, the thought of sneaking around an underground labyrinth attempting to locate my sister is simply preposterous. And if by some magic, we manage to find her, I'm then completely reliant on Caszeil – a demon – to fly us back to the surface unharmed. And what if the Samael catch us? What if the Divine Shadow himself catches us?

Images of dank caves filled with taloned demons turn my stomach and I clutch my head in the hope I can prevent it from falling apart.

'Icari? Are you feeling unwell?' Talia asks.

'Just a bit of a headache. I will be fine once the Samael are burnt.' I pause, selecting my words carefully, before giving up and blurting out, 'Where are their wings?'

She raises a curious eyebrow, but answers regardless. 'The orderlies were pushing trolleys stacked high with them past the Grand Crypt this morning. They'd covered them with sheets, but it was fairly obvious. What else could they have been? I swear, they think Embalmers are stupid.'

'Where were they taking them?'

She shrugs. 'Deep into the catacombs so they can be ground into devil wing. I'm not sure where exactly. The catacombs are never-ending. Why do you ask?'

'Curiosity,' I say, a little too quickly.

Uriel walks before the pyre to address the crowd, inadvertently saving me from Talia's suspicious eyes. The audience has grown considerably since we arrived; students and staff cluster on the marble of the courtyard, spill up the steps of both temples, and hang from surrounding windows, their robes catching like bunting in the breeze. A mixture of different expressions hang on their faces: sorrow, anger or gleeful excitement. Yet not a single person fails to fall silent as the High Priest raises his hands, a flock united by respect and fear.

'Sunlanders.' Uriel's voice echoes between the temples.

His gowns catch Father Sun's rays like metal, and he's oiled his skin and combed the blood from his hair. If it weren't for the bandage slanting across his wounded eye, he would have erased all evidence of yesterday's battle. I glance at my own blood-encrusted nails and filthy gown. Not all of us have had the luxury of rest and recuperation.

'Before we burn the demons,' he says, 'I'm afraid I have some grave news.' He pauses. 'It's about the stolen alchemy students — their bodies have been discovered scattered across the Redlands. There are no survivors.' He waits, allowing the distraught outcries to fade to a background moan.

Talia clutches my arm as her legs buckle.

'The guards are currently transporting the deceased back to the catacombs,' Uriel continues. 'They were dropped from a great height, but I am confident that with skill and guidance, the Embalmers will manage their reassemblage, ensuring they live on in the afterlife.' He kisses his fist and looks to the skies, whispering a blessing.

I turn to Talia to offer further reassurance, but her face is an echo of itself, all the fight and love, all the *Talia*, stripped from it.

'She's dead,' she whispers. 'Sephie's dead.'

'No—' I begin. Because I can feel her. I know she's alive.

Shaking her head, Talia turns and runs from the courtyard before I can continue.

'Talia,' I shout after her.

Following her is just the excuse I need not to stay and watch Caszeil's brothers burn, yet as I begin pushing through the crowd, a firm hand lands on my shoulder. I turn to see

Uriel, and it's a physical effort not to flinch.

'Icari,' he says. 'I'm afraid your sister's body was not salvageable.'

The logical part of me knows that this should destroy me, yet as my hand touches my stomach, it feels not an empty, cavernous hole, but the dull, cool ache that indicates her existence.

And I have always been good at reading people. Sephie used to joke that I was born with the ability. Uriel is lying. I'm sure of it. Which means Caszeil was telling the truth – the Samael took all of the alchemy students to hide the fact they wanted only one.

Uriel raises an eyebrow, expecting some sort of reaction.

'Thank you for letting me know, my lord,' I whisper.

He nods. 'You may take the rest of the day off to grieve.'

'Thank you.'

Watching him leave, I stand for a moment, jostled by the throng. My insides are a swirling mess of feelings, but I attempt to rise above them and organize my thoughts.

Why did Uriel just lie? He had to tell me Sephie's body was unsalvageable or I would have queried why her body wasn't collected from the Redland desert, but why doesn't he want me to know she's alive? What is he hiding? I wonder again if Sephie's disappearance is somehow linked to Mama's execution.

Just then, the bonfire bursts into life with a mighty whoosh. Orange and yellow tongues lap against silver bodies and the air fills with flecks of ash. The General stands beside it, flaming torch in his hand, sick grin on his snake-like mouth. The memory of Mama's execution flashes into my head and it's like I'm back in the agora, pinned to the ground, filled with panic and horror. I breathe in the smoke from both fires, present and past converging, then I step firmly back into the current moment. It is too late for Mama. But not for Sephie.

My eyes lock on to the Temple of Mother Moon, a shard of black against the sapphire sky, gatekeeper to the catacombs where the Samael feathers hide; my mind reels back to the bronze key hanging from Madame's neck and I begin to draw up a plan. Father Sun throws rays of hot, stifling judgement upon me, but I don't care any more. I refuse to stand by, helpless, powerless, whilst another precious loved one is taken from me.

32

ICARI

'I've brought refreshments,' I say, setting a papyrus mat bearing chopped, honeyed fruits on the bedside cabinet beside Madame. 'You need to rebuild your strength.'

Of course, I don't tell her that I doused the fruit with devil wing before entering the sanatorium.

'Why, thank you, Icari,' she says, nibbling at a finger of papaya.

The cool flesh of the fruit must hide the tingle of the dust, for she doesn't falter as she chews.

I imagine the silver powder coating her throat and the guilt finally arrives, for administering unnecessary drugs to a patient for personal gain goes against the Healer code, and indeed, basic morality. Yet the need to get the skeleton key outweighs everything else, so I simply smile as she eats a stalk of grapes.

'Thank you, Icari,' she says. 'My wound is much better since you tended to me.'

'I can see.'

The wound on her chest has already started to scab; it won't be long until I can remove the stitches. Then my eyes snag on the key around her throat and I remember I won't be here in a few days.

'Please, won't you have some fruit?' she says, lifting the mat towards me.

My stomach tightens. 'Oh no, I couldn't possibly. It's for you, and you need all the sustenance you can get.'

'And when did you last eat?'

'This morning. I'm fine.' It's a lie. I haven't eaten since yesterday before the raid.

My stomach growls as I watch her eat a fig smothered in chopped hazelnuts.

She offers me the platter. 'You're sure? There's plenty.'

I gaze at the fingers of orange, the bright triangles of watermelon and the slices of apple. The temptation to place one on to my tongue and feel the devil wing soothing my throat is strong, and a stab of guilt lands in my side as I recall berating Sephie for failing to resist.

'I'll get something to eat later,' I say, my voice steady.

She pushes a crescent of apricot into her mouth and her eyes grow sleepy. 'Forgive me, child. I am still very tired.'

'Madame, may I ask you something?' I say, aware that she is more likely to answer with candour in this state.

'Of course.'

'You were there when Mama was burnt.'

'I was.'

'Do you know why she was executed?'

She turns on to her side and lets her eyes close. 'Why, because she was trading devil wing. Everyone knows that.'

'Nobody is executed for trading devil wing. They told me so in the dungeons.'

'She was special, Icari. That's why she died. That's why I

tried to save her.'

'What do you mean?'

Her breathing grows heavy and her mouth twitches. She'll be answering no more questions for a while now. I wait for a few minutes, making sure sleep has claimed her entirely. What did she mean when she said Mama was special? Was she referring to her dual gifts, or simply her kind and brave heart? The familiar frustration rises up my throat as I realize I'm no closer to solving the mystery of Mama's death.

Focus on Sephie, I tell myself.

Reaching out, I lift the key from Madame's head. It spins from the chain, catching in the glow of the oil lamp, whispering of danger and locked underground chambers filled with hundreds of white feathers, and when I loop it over my head, it nestles beneath my gown like it belongs. I doubt Madame will wake up till tomorrow morning, by which time, the wings will be built and I'll be far from here.

33

ICARI

The raid has left the underground tunnels in disarray. Students rush back and forth, pasted with blood and fraught expressions, orderlies carry fresh supplies of linen bandages, lambswool and jars of embalming salts, and the bodies of the dead hem the corridors, wrapped not in embroidered body bags, for they have long been used up, but in sacking bound with rope.

Normally, a wayward Healer would be as out of place as a sunflower in an onion patch, but because of the chaos, I'm able to slip unnoticed down the corridors, glancing through half-opened doors and peeking around corners, praying for a glimpse of white feathers. It doesn't take long to deduce that there are too many corpses for the Grand Crypt alone, and the Embalmers have had little choice but to spill into the smaller crypts and sepulchres that line the tunnels.

I make a careful note of my journey, committing to memory the markings on various doors. I'm at risk of becoming lost down here, for this place is a maze, lit only with flaming torches and scented with spices and wine, blood and earth. The urge to turn back overwhelms me; then I remind myself this is nothing compared to where Sephie is right now.

After a mile or so, there's still no sign of any Samael feathers, and I'm fairly certain I'm about to run out of catacombs. The air has grown increasingly clotted and dense, and all I want is to feel the breeze against my skin. I'm about to give up and flee to the surface, when something catches my eye: a white fleck of down, strewn on the floor like a daisy that's fallen from a basket of flowers. The soft, silvery-white glow tells me that it once belonged to a Samael. My gasp echoes around the empty corridor and I dash to it, snatching at it with greedy fingers and savouring the prickle of cold.

The Samael feathers are near.

Trotting down the corridor, pressure building in my chest, I pause only when I reach a crossroad in the tunnels. I spin slowly, panic rising, unsure which route to take, when I spy another scrap of down, glimmering in the distance and marking my path like a silver breadcrumb.

I persist in this manner, following a trail of fallen feathers deeper and deeper into the catacombs, where the walls are no longer built from rock but skulls and stacks of bones, until an unfamiliar noise hits my ears: the rhythmic *clip* of metal against stone combined with a strange grinding sound. A hefty wooden door bearing the symbol of the Celestial Trio comes into view and the noise crescendoes, spilling from beneath the door like the brightest of lights. Heart in mouth, I shove the small feathers I've collected into my medical satchel and creak open the door.

Before me is a huge cave containing a horse-powered mill. The animals loop the outskirts of the chamber with a tired monotony, hoofs dragging, breath laboured, and their leather harnesses rubbing sores beneath their sweat-matted hair. I think of Sabu and click my tongue against my teeth, disapproving, for horses deserve to be locked underground no more than humans. And little wonder they're fatigued when the wooden beams attached to their harnesses could hold up a house, and the stone discs turned by the beams are several times the size of a cartwheel.

A flash of white catches my eye and I look up to see feathers falling from the ceiling like elongated autumn leaves. Orderlies lean from a platform spanning the entire ceiling of the cave and drop monstrous plumes into the mill as if feeding a giant stone beast, who in turn grinds up their offerings and spews them out as devil wing. The air shimmers with glittering dust that cools my tongue as I inhale. Yet no amount of the silver dust could numb the excitement burning inside. I've found what I need.

Piles of white feathers bigger than haystacks peak and trough about the edges of the cave, and a heap of wing bones – plucked clean, paler than the moon and longer than oars – rests near the door, so close that if I reached out, I could touch them. It occurs to me that I could simply come back at night when the orderlies are asleep and steal a complete pair of wings. Granted, they would be heavy and impossible to smuggle without Caszeil's help, but at least we wouldn't have to build them from scratch. We could simply mount them on his back and pray they bind to him. But it seems the citadel has wasted no time dismantling the Samael wings. Not a single pair remains intact.

I consider sneaking into the cave to get a closer look, maybe even swiping the odd feather, when the swirl of

Uriel's dazzling robes and the shape of his headdress catches my eye. He stands at the far end of the cave, talking to some orderlies and pointing to a row of wooden barrels; a ghostly silver glow seeps between the slats, telling me they must contain the milled feathers. I simply cannot risk being seen here. If suspicions are raised, I'll lose all chance of returning in the dead of night to gather what I need. So I pull the key from between my breasts and slot it into the lock, testing to see that it does indeed work in every door like Madame claimed. It turns with ease, the metal bolt protruding and retracting from the edge of the open door like a tongue. Hope and excitement rise in my chest and I slink from the entrance, retracing my steps through the catacombs.

My journey to the dungeons, using the skeleton key and drugging the guard's beer once again, is a blur. I don't even recall the dash through the dungeons – I don't gag at the stench or notice the grisly heads. Right now, all that matters is that I'm standing before Caszeil's cell, keys jumping in my hands as I attempt to unlock the door. Anxiety does strange things to the mind.

Finally, the door swings open and everything seems to stop. My heart. The blood in my veins. Time. Then I see him, stretched out on the floor, charred all over and stinking like a branded ox, and the world snaps back into motion. He's in a worse state than earlier, resembling a heap of bloodied ashes shaped into a man, a single tuft of golden hair splayed across the floor, but he's alive. *He's alive.* Hauling in a huge breath of relief, I rush to his side, the need to heal rising thick and hot like a Redland summer.

'I'm so sorry,' I whisper, hating myself for having left him. Hating myself for caring so.

Tenderly, I smear ointment over his crisped skin. My hands linger – the healing light of Father Sun restores some of his colour. I start with his face, covering his eyes and forehead so that his eyelashes tickle my fingers; then I work my way down to his neck, circling back round to his scalp.

'Amazing,' I whisper, marvelling at his ability to heal.

His eyes creak open as I reach his chest, the heavy muscles rising at my touch. 'Icari?'

I support his head so he can look at me. 'Yes.'

'Your mercy is endless.'

I have no words. It is not endless, or I wouldn't have put him back in that pit. I would have helped him escape. I wouldn't have let the guards torture him like he was a . . . a monster.

But he is a monster, I tell myself.

My head hurts with conflicting thoughts, and my chest is a stretched cloth sack ready to burst, filled with too many emotions. Yet shining through it all is the need to find my sister. So as his eyes close and he dips back into unconsciousness, I try desperately to keep him awake.

'Tell me about yourself,' I say, echoing his words from a few days past. 'About Caszeil the demon.'

'I am servant and son of Aïdes, the Divine Shadow.'

'Tell me something I don't already know.'

He chuckles, before grimacing with pain. 'You would mock me whilst I die?'

'You are not going to die. Now talk. I miss words. Tell me about the Underworld.'

He fixes me in his gaze. 'You humans think that the Underworld is an awful place, a place of cold and despair. You are wrong. Yes, it is cold, but it is also beautiful. Caves grander than any temple, which glitter with frost. Stalactites like upturned mountains.'

I sprinkle eucalyptus oil on to my hands, the fresh scent cutting through the grime, somehow managing to focus on the task at hand rather than dwelling on Sephie's predicament.

'Is your Underworld not *too* cold?' I ask.

He manages the smallest shake of his head. 'Cold is only cold if you are used to warmth. In the Underworld, you feel *nothing*. The cold numbs everything. Not just physical, but emotional too, for I knew not fear, anger or pain until I came to your world. The numbness is bliss.'

'Tell me about Aïdes.' I run the oil across his head, freeing the scorched pieces of skin from his scalp. I want to keep Caszeil awake, but I also want to know the enemy. The man – the devil – who wants to wed my sister.

'Sometimes he is Aïdes. Sometimes he is just shadow. He still mourns for his love. That is why the Underworld is so cold – so he misses her less. It numbs his broken heart.'

'You make him sound—'

'Human?'

'Yes, human, but I wasn't going to say that. I was going to say that you make him sound like Sephie.'

He looks at me from beneath his lashes, curiosity swirling in his grey eyes. 'How so?'

I sigh. He already knows so much, there seems no point withholding things now. 'Mama's death affected her deeply. I mean, it affected us all deeply, but Sephie never really dealt with it. She doesn't talk about her – I don't think she even thinks about her. She just numbs the pain with devil wing. Devil wing or the Divine Shadow.'

Sensing I haven't finished, Caszeil leaves more space for me to fill.

'She asked me to get her some – devil wing, I mean – just before she was taken. I told her it was a want, not a need. I just let her suffer.' I shrink from the memory, the guilt too jagged to bear.

'Sometimes want outweighs everything,' he says, studying my face.

'Sometimes it does.'

Silence stretches between us. I don't think we're talking about Sephie any more.

'Perhaps I was too harsh,' I whisper, bringing the focus back to my sister.

'So much guilt when you are considering rescuing her from hell.'

I smile. 'Stop being right all the time. It is unnerving.'

'Because I am a demon?'

'Yes, because you are a demon. Now stay still whilst I tend to your injuries.'

I begin checking the worst of the burns on his hips, pressing ointment and golden light into every contour. Thankfully, his loincloth protected his private parts from the sun. I am not normally prudish when it comes to such things, but the thought of seeing Caszeil's groin leaves me breathless for reasons I can't articulate.

He sighs as the agony diminishes. 'It must seem strange to you, the idea that Aïdes is almost human. But he really is.

Sometimes he is even kind, though it is a kindness that serves his own needs, never kindness for its own sake, never compassion.'

'That is more human than you think.' I pause. 'Should you be telling me this?'

'Probably not, but I have had a lot of time to think. Since killing the innocent, all I've done is think.'

The muscles on his torso twitch beneath my hands, the skin further healing at my touch.

'How do you heal so well?' I ask, not wanting him to dwell on the death of the girl when he is so unwell.

'I told you, the Samael are tough.'

The burns are particularly bad on his legs, yet by the time I've worked my way down to his feet, his breath is stronger. The knot of anxiety untangles inside. He will be OK.

'You were right.' I pause. 'Again.'

'How so?'

'All of the alchemy students were dropped except for Sephie.'

His face is close to mine, filled with concern, silver skin glistening through the wounds like fragments of a broken mirror. 'So will you help me build my wings?'

I reply by pulling the downy Samael feathers from my satchel. They gleam like a handful of gems and illuminate the cell with their glow. His fingers close around them, his skin touching mine, and the light of the feathers intensifies so I can see every fleck of silver in his eyes.

'I'd forgotten how beautiful they are,' he says.

'I found a cave in the catacombs where they're milling the Samael feathers. There's plumes of every size, wing bones too.'

His lips twitch into a smile. 'Were there any wings left?'

'Not that I could see. I guess they've been dismantled already.'

He presses the feathers against his chest and inhales, long and slow. They must smell of home. 'No matter. We can put them back together again.'

'A key to the citadel,' I say, pulling the key from my gown and letting it dangle between us. 'I'll return to the mill tonight when everyone's asleep and get what we need. There's an abandoned sepulchre nearby that we can work in.'

He grins, his white teeth flashing, his grey eyes shining. 'Oh, to fly, Icari. You will love it.'

'I'm not sure what terrifies me more: the idea of flying over the Sunlands, or the idea of reaching the Underworld.' I pause. 'The Underworld. Yes, definitely the Underworld.'

He studies my face and his smile fades. 'I won't let anyone hurt you – you know that?'

I don't nod or reply, because I don't know this. 'Caszeil . . .' I pause. It's like there's this bottomless well of fear inside me, and the only way I've managed is to block it out.

He rests the tiny feathers on his lap and touches my hand. 'You mustn't worry so. I will leave you at the surface and bring Sephie to you. Nobody will notice another Samael in the Underworld, after all.'

'No.' The word bursts from my mouth before I can think. 'Sephie may be hurt. She may need me right away. I must be with her as soon as possible.' And it's more than that. I feel so much responsibility for my sister, so much guilt, for it's my fault Mama died; it's my fault she's addicted to devil wing. I cannot let her suffer this alone. And if I cannot save her, if she must remain in the Underworld, then at least I shall be with her.

'It is not your fault she was taken,' he says, rubbing his thumb across my palm. 'You have nothing to atone for.'

'It's not that,' I say. 'She's my sister. We belong together.'

His voice grows urgent. 'But you could die. If Aïdes discovers you in the Underworld, you will be entirely at his mercy. I won't be able to protect you.'

'Then I shall die.'

He shakes his head, releasing an exasperated tut.

'What?' I say. 'Will you stop with all your tutting? I feel like an infant who's been caught with an empty jar and jam all over their face.'

He laughs. 'I do not mean to tut at you. It's just –' he sighs, his smile fading – 'I have many brothers. Hundreds. And I would not die for any of them. Not one.'

'Well, that probably says more about your brothers than you.'

'What do you mean?'

'I wouldn't die for a demon either.'

His smile is back, and I get this tingling sensation up my spine. I love that I can make him smile. And his hand still rests on mine. Is it wrong I don't shake it free? I think it is, but instead I savour the fact he touches me with the ease and familiarity of a lover. *A lover? Check yourself, Icari. He is a demon.*

'That is a good point,' he replies. 'Perhaps I am yet to find a worthy soul. Perhaps then I would willingly walk into a dagger.' He pretends to thrust a blade into his chest and sticks out his tongue.

I resist the urge to laugh, fear of what's to come heavy in my mind. 'When we find Sephie, how do I know you'll fly us both to the surface?' It's a difficult question to ask, and it comes out a little loud, a little forceful, but Caszeil doesn't flinch.

'Icari, you have shown me more compassion in a few days than I have known my entire life. I am not going to leave you in the Underworld. Besides, Aïdes knew I was captured, yet he made no attempt to save me.' He gestures to the cell door and beyond, where the heads of his brothers drip from spikes. 'He made no attempt to save any of us. My loyalty towards Aïdes died a long time ago.'

His eyes shimmer and I realize he has a tear, growing in size and weight, teetering on the edge of his lower lashline. Cautiously, he rests a blissfully cool hand on my face. I wish my response were to recoil, yet I find myself leaning into his palm, inhaling his scent.

'I'm sorry I hid my true self from you,' he says. 'Surely you must understand why.'

'Because you wanted ointment?'

'Because I wanted company.'

I nod, a signal that I understand, which is at least a step towards forgiveness.

'I swear that I will never lie to you again,' he whispers.

Silence hangs between us and I study his face, an opal in the pale glow of the feathers. I forbid my eyes from dropping to his chest, for it is wrong to desire a demon. I find myself wishing he weren't born a Samael, that he were simply a man. Yet even as I think this, I know that if he weren't a demon, if he hadn't killed an innocent, lost his wings and been locked away for hundreds of years, he wouldn't be Caszeil. His suffering has shaped him.

I turn my face deeper into his hand, my lips brushing his palm so the heat of my breath reflects back at me. 'You are a demon,' I whisper.

'We have established that.'

This pulls a breathy laugh from my lips, and he smiles at my reaction, his dusty-pink mouth curving at the edges so that he is all cheekbones and flashing eyes. Is my attraction to him deadening my wits? Is my desperation to find Sephie pushing me towards recklessness? Am I nothing more than clay, manipulated by cold, graceful hands? I close my eyes so I can no longer see his face, only feel the cool press of his palm against my mouth.

'I'll return in the night,' I say. 'After I've stolen what I need from the mill room.'

'You must be careful.' He places the feathers back in my satchel. 'If you get caught, you will end up in the dungeon with me.'

I smile. 'I have been careful all of my life, Caszeil. Right now, I need to be a fanfare.'

34

SEPHIE

I did not take the news of my enforced betrothal well, which is why I'm now locked in a small cave with nothing but the dark for company. Apparently, the Samael don't like having their fingers bent back or their arms scratched, and the Divine Shadow absolutely doesn't like obscenities hurled in his face. So they carried me here, twisting and bucking in their arms, then slammed the door. I tried to escape, but unsurprisingly the door was locked. Not that I'd know where to go or what to do if it had opened. Hell doesn't come with a map.

Anyway, I found a ledge to sit on, and I've been here ever since, knees pulled to chin, tears and nose dripping. The cold seeped through my gown long ago like something wicked and insidious. I'd use my Calling to numb the discomfort, but I don't want anything from Aïdes, so instead I distract myself with thoughts of the oasis, of Papa and Icari, of Talia.

Talia.

I whisper her name over and over until it becomes no more than a string of beautiful sounds, like lapping water or the dawn chorus. Until it blends with the *pat-pat* of my heart and replaces the shadows in my veins. I was so upset when I discovered she was betrothed to another – now Aïdes has made a hypocrite of me.

I pick at the rock against my side with broken nails, the anger, the confusion mounting. What I don't understand is why out of all the people in the Sunlands, Aïdes chose me to be his bride. Talk about unlucky. Is it because of my dual Calling, or because I'm a necromancer and can read the dead? Or is it like he said: that we're not so different really.

No. I am nothing like that man. That *devil*.

My stomach growls, my mouth feels tacky and my breath smells sour. I haven't eaten or drunk anything since before the raid. Perhaps I will die of dehydration and Aïdes will have to marry a corpse. A slightly unhinged smile hangs on my lips.

A tap on the door pulls my attention.

'My lady? May I come in?'

It is the Divine Shadow.

'Do I have a choice in the matter?' I reply.

'I bring sustenance from the surface. Fruits, nuts and meats, and a chalice full of pomegranate juice. You may eat and drink, if you promise not to bite me.'

Saliva wells in my mouth and my stomach rumbles like the traitor it is. The scent of roasted duck and honeyed fruits drifts beneath the door, replacing the smell of earth and death. My throat screams for liquid and my belly prays for food, but pride is a heavy boulder that doesn't shift with ease, so I call, 'I'm making no promises.'

The Divine Shadow enters, flanked by two Samael carrying platters of food and a large bronze goblet. Aïdes spreads candles and lamps across the rocks, even though I don't recall him holding anything a moment ago. The flames illuminate the cave so I can see just how small it is – no more than a cell, really – and the Samael spread a fur pelt at my feet, concealing the carpet of frost.

After laying the food on the pelt, the demons leave and there is just me and Aïdes. A date with the devil. Today is the day that just keeps giving.

He sits cross-legged and gestures to the place opposite him. 'Come, join me. You must be ravenous. Father Sun is bedding down on the surface as we speak.' He sinks his whiter-than-white teeth into a leg of roasted goose, causing oil to dribble down his chin, then slurps from the goblet.

I'm repelled by his arrogance whilst drawn by his beauty, just as I'm repelled by the prospect of accepting his offerings whilst drawn by the feast. I'm a seething paradox of emotion and I just want to go home.

Eventually the thirst wins and, tentatively, I slide from the rock on to the fur. It's as warm as if it were still on the back of the animal who grew it, as soft as Talia's hair and Icari's manner, yet I keep my expression stern.

He hands me the cup. 'You must be thirsty.'

The metal is surprisingly warm against my palms, or perhaps I'm so chilled now even an ice block would feel good, and I slurp the sweet crimson liquid with greedy, chattering lips. I falter. Something isn't quite right. Beneath the sugary tones of the pomegranate lies a sharpness, a *coolness*. I'd know that taste anywhere – I'm a connoisseur, after all. Devil wing. Aïdes intends to drug me.

'Is everything OK, my lady?' he asks, studying my face. The candlelight catches on his frosted skin, giving him a reptilian appearance. His hair gleams like onyx.

I nod, my face a blank slate. 'Except for the obvious, yes.'

'The obvious?'

I gesture to the cell, slopping some of the pomegranate juice on to my hands where it beads like blood.

He smiles. 'Let's just enjoy the feast, my lady.'

Everything in my body screams at me to drink. To tip back the goblet and gulp until there is nothing left to gulp and only the scent of fruit remains. Not only does my throat feel like the Redland desert, my tongue rough and my teeth dry, but I know that this fluid offers so much more than hydration. It offers oblivion. No more Talia whispering about her childhood sweetheart, no more exploding students, no more Underworld. No more *this*.

But that is what the Divine Shadow wants. And I am nothing if not stubborn. Besides, how will I escape if I'm drugged? And that is what I want more than anything. To escape. To go home. Back to Icari. Papa and Talia. The decision made, I lift the goblet to my mouth, seal my lips around the metal so no liquid may pass, and pretend to drink.

'Good girl.' He speaks as if I were his pet, which I think perhaps I am. 'Drink it all up and you'll feel much better. Now –' he picks through the platter, fingers hovering over the various meats – 'what would you like to try first?'

Whilst he's focused on the spread, I rest the goblet on the rock behind me and, ever so slowly, begin to tip. The earth drinks the evidence, and when he looks up, a skewer of roughly diced lamb poised between his fingers, my cup is empty.

I take the skewer and bite. Hot oil squirts on to my parched tongue and I resist groaning with pleasure. The meat is heavily flavoured with rosemary and garlic, but I can still taste the silver dust. Even the food is drugged. My head fills with a hundred curse words as I accept that the hole in my stomach will remain gaping and raw for a while longer.

I chew and swallow, he is watching after all, and allow myself the fleeting bliss of a nip of devil wing, but I stop there, licking my lips, then pretending to drink.

'What is your favourite colour?' he asks, gnawing down to the thigh bone of some dead animal. I suppose being a villain is hungry work.

'Why?'

'Must you question everything, my lady?' His voice is indulgent rather than weary or irritated. It makes my skin bristle in the worst possible way. He is a lie wrapped in a neat bow. Danger polished to a high shine. I expect he will smile when he kills me.

I hold his gaze, even as my chest throbs with fear. 'Red.'

My favourite colour is blue: the colour of the Nubi river, the oasis sky, the larkspur and delphiniums sprouting in Mama's courtyard. But there's no way I'm giving the blue-eyed devil the satisfaction of knowing this.

He nods. 'Red. Yes, that makes sense to me.'

'Isn't that a question usually reserved for infants?'

'Do you find me patronizing?'

I nod. The devil wing has made me brave. I've already ingested more than intended. I must be careful.

'Forgive me, my lady. I am not used to human company. At least, not living humans.' He chuckles and places the licked–clean bone on an empty plate.

And whilst he is distracted, I slide several chunks of lamb from the skewer and drop them into my apron pocket.

'Flowers,' he says, plucking a fig from the platter.

I pretend to chew and swallow. 'Pardon?'

'You will need beautiful blooms from the surface on our wedding day – now I know which colour to select.'

I must blanch, because he says, 'You must not fret. I will take good care of you, I promise.' He places the fig on his tongue, then selects a quarter of avocado, the peel removed and the stone replaced with a cluster of hazelnuts. He holds it towards my lips, expecting me to eat from his fingers like a donkey.

I hesitate, partly because the idea of indulging him makes me baulk, but mostly because I cannot pretend to eat when he is putting the food directly into my mouth.

'Is something wrong?' he asks.

'I don't like avocado.' Of course I bloody do. I used to eat them till my belly ached back at the orchard with Papa and Icari. But that memory is dear, so I throw a shield around it.

'You'll like this one.' He moves towards me until the soft flesh presses against my lips and I have no option but to open up.

The devil wing sparkles on my tongue, offering to soothe every woe, every fear, every ache, of which there are many, and it takes every ounce of self-control not to swallow.

'There now,' he says, smiling. 'It is good, is it not?'

I nod and lift the empty chalice to my lips, allowing the contents of my mouth to dribble into the cup.

'Cherry?' he says.

Thankfully, he lets me take my own, which I drop into my apron whilst he's cracking a peanut from its shell.

'How do you feel?' he asks.

'Better,' I say, lying. 'Sleepy.' I let my eyelids flutter and fake rolling my eyes back.

'Why not take a nap, my lady. Everything will feel better in the morning, I promise.'

'Thank you.' It physically hurts to thank my kidnapper and jailer, but the amount of devil wing I supposedly just consumed would make me far more biddable, and I need him to believe I'm anaesthetized. After all, a sleeping prisoner doped with devil wing needs far less supervision than an alert prisoner with all of her wits.

'Why don't you curl up on the pelt,' he says, stroking the fur with seductive fingers. 'And when you awaken, you will be in your chambers where there will be no locks, no cold and no darkness. You will be comfortable and happy, like you should be.'

I yawn and stretch, then lie on the pelt and let my eyes close like a good girl.

'Sleep tight, sweet Sephie,' he whispers.

The door closes, and when I open my eyes, the candles, the feast and even the fur pelt have gone, and I'm all alone on a cold, hard floor.

35

SEPHIE

I don't have time to plot and scheme, only to hide the contents of my apron in a narrow cleft beneath the stone ledge. Then the door opens. I squeeze my eyes shut and lie still as the dead, forcing my breath to slow, even though it longs to quicken and grind, in-out, in-out, like a knife cutting bread.

'I like her better when she's asleep.'

The voice belongs to the Samael who stole me from the citadel and plunged me into the bowels of the earth, the one with the grey plait and white eyelashes. Resisting the urge to scramble backwards, merge into the wall and make myself invisible is as difficult as resisting the urge to knock back the devil wing. But I manage. Cruel hands slip beneath my body, fasten my wrists and ankles with a tourniquet of fingers, then hoist me into the air. I let my body sag as though drugged and heavy with dreams. And then I'm moving, floating, the cold air caressing my face and the rhythm of steps causing me to sway.

'Careful with her. She is a pearl.'

It is the voice of the Divine Shadow.

I ease open a single eye so the world becomes a slit. The

Samael are carrying me through a series of icy caves and tunnels, a maze of glittering rock and eerie silence. At one point, we skirt the edge of a huge underground lake, and I clamp my eyes shut, too afraid to gaze upon the river of lost souls. But I hear them, whispering pleas and prayers from watery lips. A cacophony of regret and fear. Women, children, men. Is it normal to hear the voices of the dead? Or are my powers somehow magnified down here?

I fear I may vomit and give the game away, but somehow I keep it in. The catacombs were *nothing* compared to this. No living person should ever bear witness to this place. There is a line between the before and the after for a reason, and nobody should ever cross it with a heart that still beats.

The whispers fade and I sense we're entering a tunnel as the air grows closer and the breaths of the Samael bounce back at me.

'Close that door,' Aïdes says, his words soft yet laden with malice and rage.

For the first time since arriving, I see a little of the monster beneath the mask.

'Sorry, my lord,' mutter the Samael.

'The girl must never see what lies beyond that door,' Aïdes says. 'Do you understand?'

'Yes, my lord.'

My friends, I am naturally curious, and being stolen by Aïdes does not change this, so I crank open my eyes, just enough so I can see through the dark lines of my lashes.

The demon with the silver plait closes a wooden door that leads off the corridor, but not before I catch a glimpse of what lies beyond. A large cave, not dissimilar from the one I arrived in, wrapped in frost and alight with small, ineffectual fires. But sitting at the far end, rather out of place and forlorn, is a stone building. A temple. It's the first structure that doesn't look naturally occurring and, as such, appears to have been dropped there from the surface.

Very strange.

Why doesn't Aïdes want me to see what lies beyond the door?

Could it possibly be a way out of here?

Sweet Mother Moon, it takes everything I have not to jerk my limbs into a happy dance. It makes perfect sense – a temple, a symbol of devotion and worship, may provide a link to Mother Moon and Father Sun. A link strong enough, *magical* enough, to transport me home. I am of course wildly speculating, but it is all I have right now, so I cling to it as I would a lifeline. And I suddenly feel lighter, for that line is truly the tail of a kite, lifting me higher and higher. I have a purpose.

And just before I'm carried away, I study the closed door through narrowed eyes. It bears the three signs of the Celestial Trio, and what looks like two bands of gold, interlocking to create an infinity sign.

I commit it to memory, suppressing a smile. Because I will return to this door if it's the last thing I do. I will escape this wretched place.

36

ICARI

The bedchamber is eerily empty: where there were five, there are now only two. Zalta is dead, Xenia is with Erastus and Yiannis, and Sephie ... Well, I daren't think about where my darling sister is right now.

I listen for the soft push-pull of Talia's breath – then, quietly, I throw back my blanket, creep to the window and press my forehead against the cold of the glass. The only light comes from the Tomb of Light, Mother Moon and a scattering of stars. Normally the marble of the Court of Ash would reflect the night sky like a shining lake, but the soot from the pyre still dulls its surface. And even though I can't see them, I know there will be guards, dotted across the citadel and hiding in the dark. I'll need to be careful, just like Caszeil said.

I consider my route. The dungeons are attached to the catacombs, so I could go through the Sun Temple, using the tunnel Xenia showed me to fetch the corpse for Principal Healer. But how would I explain my presence in the catacombs themselves?

My gaze falls upon Talia's embalming dress, hanging from a metal rail and nudging up against my healer's gown. Of course. If I wear Talia's black robe as opposed to my white one, not only am I less likely to be seen in the dark when I cross the Court of Ash, but I can pass through the Night Temple, feigning worship, and move through the catacombs without arousing suspicion. Someone would have to recognize me to realize I don't belong, and I haven't been at the citadel long enough for many people to know my face. Besides, I can keep my head down and let my hair obscure my features.

I tiptoe towards the gowns, my eyes never leaving Talia, terrified she'll awaken and thwart my plan. The floorboards creak and groan with every step, and I curse beneath my breath, yet by some miracle, Talia merely stirs as I reach for her dress. It only takes a moment to shrug off my nightgown and pull on the black embalming robe.

When I reach the cold night air, I take a moment to breathe, readying myself for what is to come: creeping into a secret mill, stealing the body parts of demons, and breaking a Samael out of prison so we may build wings and fly to the Underworld. It would be so easy to turn back now . . . But the memory of Sephie's laughter and Caszeil's face, opalescent in the light of the Samael down, impel my feet forward, carrying me away from the safety of the dormitories and all things sensible.

The air tastes of bonfires and burnt meat, and Mother Moon watches me with disapproving eyes. Thankfully, the guards are sparse – the recent massacre has depleted their numbers – and whilst death should never be applauded, I can't help but feel relieved. Indeed, the only guards I can see are standing at either side of the entrance to the Night Temple.

Staying in the shadows, I crouch low and run my fingers along the joint where the marble floor meets the stone wall, gathering a handful of loose pebbles. Then, before I can change my mind, I launch one across the Court of Ash. Years of throwing stones into the Nubi river with Sephie have prepared me for this moment, and the pebble hits the far stone wall with an impressive clatter. The guards spin towards the sound.

'What was that?' one of them says.

The other one shrugs and the grumble of their idle chatter returns. Damn their lazy ways. I hurl another pebble, then another, aiming just beyond the Night Temple, and this time, they take the bait, abandoning their positions and running towards the noise, swords drawn.

Without wasting a moment, I dash up the steps that lead to the Night Temple, grateful my shoes have leather soles and barely make a sound. As soon as I'm inside, I duck behind a pew, expecting the guards to have seen me, or at least to have heard the creak of the giant door as I heaved it open, but as time passes, as their banal chit-chat resumes just beyond the entrance, I realize I've got away with it. A sharp burst of breath leaves my lips and my heart flails in my chest. *Come now, Icari,* I tell myself. *You have only just started. You can't afford to lose yourself to nerves.* I force my attention to the cool length of metal resting against my sternum. Madame's skeleton key. *You can do this.*

The Night Temple is completely abandoned. The glass shards and debris have been swept away, but the roof is still missing, letting the cold and the night sky press down on me as if I were out in the open. I try not to replay the image of Sephie sailing from the jagged hole in the glass ceiling. I try not to hear her screams or smell the blood. Wallowing in memories will not help her. Building wings will. So taking a deep breath, I straighten my embalming dress and continue with the plan, dropping down the spiral staircase into the catacombs.

In the daytime, the dark and oppressive tunnels are an offence to Father Sun, yet in the night, they seem like a natural extension of the world above and I find them strangely peaceful. Only a few torches are left to blaze, and even these have burnt low, cloaking the stone and earth in shadow and swallowing the sharp angles of the tunnels. I feel held, rather than confined, and I wonder if this is how Embalmers feel all the time. Perhaps Sephie would have felt this way in time, had she not been so cruelly snatched from us.

As I retrace my steps to the mill, I pass only the occasional Embalmer working late, who upon seeing my black gown simply nods a sombre greeting. Soon, the light levels dwindle, the stone walls are replaced with stacks of skulls and bones and I realize I haven't passed anyone for a while. Indeed, the tunnels stretching ahead of me are completely black, like staring into the gullet of a beast or the deepest of ravines. I think of the Underworld and shudder. I suppose nobody comes this far at night, so there's little point replenishing the torches. This is a good sign, I tell myself. It means I'll be alone.

Looping back, I lift the nearest torch from its metal wall mounting and wield it before me, illuminating every eye socket of every wall. There is nothing peaceful about the tunnels now, and my mouth dries, my muscles tense.

Pushing down my nerves, I pass the entrance to the mill and choose the door of a sepulchre, marked with an upwards-snaking shadow, the sign of the Alchemist, for it seems fitting we should build demon wings in the presence of the Divine Shadow.

I tap on the door. 'Hello?'

The only response is the fizz of the torch in my hand. Pulling the key from my dress, I unlock the door and peer inside. The chamber is small, carved into the rock like the hollow of a tree. The domed surfaces are painted with silver stars, so it resembles a small Night Temple, and dust swirls excitedly in the torchlight, like it's been held captive for a very long time and can finally see an escape route; it hits the back of my throat, causing me to splutter, which in turn sends the torch flame spiralling. Shadows dance and the entire space transforms into something alive.

At the back of the chamber lies a sarcophagus, a replica of the man inside carved into the lid.

I kiss my fist and whisper, 'I'll be back soon.'

Returning to the door of the mill – my hands shaking, but my head clear – I slot the key into the lock. There's a split second where I pray it won't turn, that I'll be forced to give up on this reckless plan, but the door swings open. I raise the torch before me, gaining strength from its powerful light, and step inside. The cave reveals itself in orange sections as I swing the torch around. Panic escalates; my breath hitches.

'No,' I say. 'It can't be.'

The wooden beams remain, resting on the floor like giant tree roots. The barrels glowing with devil wing still line the side, and the stone mill continues to hold court, dusted silver and supporting abandoned ladders. But the Samael plumes and wing bones have gone. All that is left is a smattering of tiny down feathers glimmering in the dirt.

I spin in a circle, faster and faster, until the flame turns into a streak of gold that splashes light about the cave in a haphazard manner. But no matter how fast I spin, no matter how hard I wish them back into existence, the feathers don't appear. The torch falls to my side, the heat singeing my fingers and the smoke mixing with the scent of snow and horse manure. I had no idea they would mill everything so quickly. How will I rescue Sephie now?

'No,' I tell myself. 'There must be some feathers some-where.' Hearing my own voice is a comfort, as if Mama is speaking to me and telling me what to do. 'Don't give up yet, dear-heart.'

Lifting the torch, I explore the cave more thoroughly, checking beneath the large stone disc, around the edges of the cave and in the empty sacking. The harder I look, the greater my frustration, for the cave has been plucked clean, as if it too were a giant wing bone.

Only when I reach the barrels do I find them: a cluster of long white Samael feathers, bound by a black ribbon and resembling a large spray of barley. Enough for Caszeil's wings. The glow of the devil wing from the barrels must have disguised their light. I set the torch on the ground and slump beside it, cradling the feathers with tears winding down my face. Tears of relief, yet strangely, also of disappointment, for now there is no excuse not to do the unthinkable.

It takes a moment to stand, gathering my muscles and bones into some sort of semblance of a functioning human so I can begin the short journey to the sepulchre, when the door slams shut and a voice that doesn't belong to me rings through the cave.

'What's going on?'

37

ICARI

The voice is female, but seeing as the only torch smoulders at my feet, she is just a black shape stamped on the surrounding darkness. My first instinct is to flee, but she's blocking my escape route, so I just stand, torch sizzling by my feet, feathers cradled in my arms, staring into the nothingness. It's what I do best, after all: freeze in the face of danger.

'Icari?'

This time, I recognize the voice.

'Talia?'

She walks towards me so the light catches the red in her black hair and the furrow of her brow. She's wearing an embalming gown that's several sizes too big and pools around her boots, and the green spokes of her dark eyes flash with curiosity and just a hint of fear.

'What in the name of Mother Moon are you doing?' she says, seizing the torch and pointing to the Samael feathers in my arms.

'Did you come alone?' I ask.

'Of course I bloody did. Who else would be stupid enough to roam around the catacombs when they could be in bed sleeping?'

I release a held breath. 'Thank goodness.'

'I saw you steal my dress and sneak out, so obviously I had to follow. I mean, nobody would opt to wear an embalming robe, and black really isn't your colour.' She gestures to her own gown. 'I had to steal Zalta's spare dress, and it's far too long for me, and probably awful luck to steal from the dead. Anyway, that's beside the point.' She throws her hands in the air as though irritated with herself for babbling. The torch flares. 'What are you doing? Why are you holding Samael feathers?' She revolves in a slow circle. 'And what is this place?'

'It's a mill, probably left over from the great battle all those years ago. They've been using it to grind a fresh supply of devil wing since the raid.'

'And you're stealing feathers because . . . ?'

'I was just looking at them.' The lie causes my voice to waver.

'Bollocks. You were gazing at them like they were gifted by Father Sun himself.' Her eyebrows fire upwards. 'Hang on, that's why you were asking about the Samael feathers at the bonfire this afternoon, isn't it? You were mining me for information.'

'I . . .' What can I say? There's no sensible excuse, and even if there were, my feeble voice would probably alert her to the lie.

'Is this about Sephie?' she asks.

I offer a stilted nod.

'Tell me.' She shoves out her hand as if the truth is something physical I can hand over.

'I can't,' I say.

'Can't or won't?'

'Talia—'

'Tell me or I'll get Madame.' She gestures to the key, still poking from the lock, chain swaying beneath like a wagging tail. 'That's hers, isn't it? I recognize the engravings.'

We stare at each other and silence simmers between us, hotter and angrier than the torch in her hand.

'Fine,' she snaps, before turning to go.

'Wait!' My voice rings throughout the cave. 'Sephie's in the Underworld.'

The words run together, but she must understand, because she pauses and then ever so slowly turns so I can see the horror dawning on her face.

'What did you say?'

'She's alive, like I said, but she's in the Underworld. Aïdes stole all of the alchemy students to hide the fact he wanted only one – that's why her body hasn't been returned to the citadel. She's the only one who wasn't dropped.'

She blinks. She's so close I can see the tears sticking her eyelashes together so they form a series of black spikes.

'In the Grand Crypt, the Samael were looking for Sephie.' Another blink. '*Targeting* her.'

'That makes sense. She was the only one that mattered.'

She shakes her head in disbelief. 'How could you possibly know that?'

'It doesn't matter.' I can't very well tell her about Caszeil. 'What matters is I can reach her – we've got a plan. We can build wings and we—'

'Who's *we*?'

I grip the feathers tighter so they form a shield, and when

I open my mouth, no words emerge. It's like they're wedged in my throat.

'Have it your way,' she says, spinning on her heel and walking purposefully towards the door, leaving a line of smoke in her wake.

'I met someone in the dungeons,' I blurt out. 'A prisoner.'

She slows but this time doesn't turn, which is a relief, for it's easier to utter confessions to someone's back.

'I didn't know at first,' I say. 'I just thought he was a man or maybe even a sorcerer, but after the raid . . .' The sentence peters out.

Until this point, Caszeil has been a secret, locked safe inside. Talking about him not only holds a mirror up to everything I've done and everything I feel – it puts him at risk. And if Talia tells anyone of our plan, it puts Sephie at risk too.

When she finally faces me, all the anger has faded and she just looks lost. Desperate.

'Icari,' she says, her voice soft. 'Just tell me, please.'

It occurs to me that out of everyone in the citadel, Talia is the only person who wants to help Sephie as much as I do. So I take a deep breath and force my voice to remain clear and slow. 'His name is Caszeil and he's a demon. He was captured after the first great battle, when they removed his wings then locked him away. He's promised to fly me to Sephie if I help him rebuild his wings.' I nod towards the bundle in my arms. 'Hence the Samael feathers.'

She opens and closes her mouth a few times, her voice false-starts, and when she laughs, there isn't an ounce of humour in it. 'A *demon* wants you to build him *wings*.'

'Yes.'

'So he can fly you to the Underworld to save Sephie?'

'Yes.' Hearing the plan spoken out loud makes me realize how utterly ridiculous it is; more akin to one of Ruari's stories or the strangest of dreams than a rescue mission.

But Talia isn't laughing any more. Her bottom lip begins to quiver. 'Why take her to the Underworld?'

'Caszeil thinks that Aïdes means to make her his bride.'

She stumbles forward and supports her weight on the barrels, not caring how close the flame gets to the wood. 'The Divine Shadow means to marry her?'

'That's what Caszeil says.'

'And this *Caszeil*. You trust him, even though he's a demon?'

I don't like the way she says his name, turning it into something snake-like and vicious.

'What choice do I have?' I reply.

She peers at me between the curtains of her hair, her expression hovering between disgust and horror, and for a terrible moment, I think she really is going to run to Madame and tell her everything. But instead she fixes me with her dark eyes and says, 'Take me to this demon.'

38

ICARI

Fortunately, the guard remains asleep, so Talia and I are able to slip past undetected. When I pull back the door, Caszeil is curled on the ground, mewing with pain. Something about him looks different – something I can't place. Then it hits me: they've removed two of his fingers. Sliced them off at the lowest knuckle and cauterized the wounds. It must have been agonizing.

'Caszeil.' My first instinct is to scoop him into my arms and comfort him, but I'm painfully aware of Talia's judgement, so I instead press my fingertips to his wounds.

The golden light reaches his face and I see that his eyes are clamped shut and he's covered in a film of sweat; suffering has filed his features to a series of prongs so that I barely recognize him. Anger flares in my chest. They are keeping him alive simply to torture him. I increase the pressure against his wounds and my hands grow warm as the sinews and vessels beneath my fingertips close and seal. It is quite amazing how well Caszeil's flesh responds to my touch.

'Hush,' I say, momentarily forgetting Talia. 'I am here.'

He opens his eyes. 'Icari?'

'Yes,' I say, my words cracking. 'It's me. Are you OK?'

'I'm fine.' He forces a smile, though his eyes are misted with pain. 'It's just a little scratch.'

'You are not fine,' I say, pausing to run a finger beneath his eye and catch a tear, so cold it makes me wince.

'I just need my wings, before they whittle me away to nothing.'

'I know. That's why we're here.'

Talia finally speaks, her voice trembling with rage. 'Icari. Why are you tending to this . . . this . . . ?'

I throw her a quick scowl. 'Do you expect him to help Sephie in this condition?'

She stamps her foot, spraying a mixture of waste and Caszeil's silvery blood on to my face. 'Have you forgotten so quickly? His kind attacked the citadel – then they stole Sephie and murdered Zalta.' The last word dissolves into a strangled hiccup.

'That is unfair,' I say, wiping my face with my apron. 'Caszeil has done nothing to hurt us.'

'Oh, please. They're all the bloody same.'

I sigh and return my attention to my patient. There is little point arguing with Talia right now. Her mind is already made up.

'Do you need devil wing?' I ask Caszeil.

'Yes,' he says.

Talia laughs, a bitter trill. 'Cannibalism. Now I've heard it all.'

'Who is she?' Caszeil asks, nodding towards Talia. 'The witch with fire-vipers in her hair?'

She plonks her hands on her hips. 'Says the *demon*.'

He shrugs and allows me to sprinkle a pinch of devil

wing on his tongue. 'It is no insult. *Witch* is simply a man's word for a woman with power.'

She fidgets with her hair, some of the anger dropping from her voice. 'My name is Talia. I'm Sephie's best friend.'

He studies her face. 'Best friend, you say?'

'I'm here to help,' she replies.

He looks at me, eyebrows raised, and I'm relieved to see his suffering has already eased.

'She knows the catacombs better than me,' I say. 'She'll help us gather the tools we need to build your wings. I already have the feathers.'

'You got the Samael feathers?' His smile reaches his eyes so the flecks of silver spark in the storm-cloud grey.

I nod. 'They'd already milled most of them, but they kept a bundle back, probably for rituals or displays.'

Jumping to his feet, he sweeps me into an embrace. The chill of his flesh pushing through my dress and the scent of his skin leaves me giddy. He smells like the first frost of winter. I sink into his arms, loving the broadness of his chest beneath my cheek, the weight of his chin on my crown.

'I promise I won't let you down,' he whispers into my hair. 'Thank you.'

'Icari,' Talia hisses. 'You are embracing a *demon*.'

The heat of shame rises in my cheeks as I disentangle myself from his arms.

'Are we to endure a running commentary from the witch?' he asks with a side-smile.

'Yes,' she snaps. 'If you want my help, then you shall endure my running commentary, *demon*.'

He opens his mouth to reply, but I silence him with a

frown, then return to his hands, proving that he is my patient and nothing more, both to Talia and myself.

'Do you trust her?' he whispers.

'More than I trust you.' I smile so he knows I'm at least partly joking.

After a long pause, he glances at Talia. 'We will need gum, wax, hammers and lots of nails.'

She scoffs. 'It'll never work.'

'We have been fixing our wings for centuries,' he says. 'Trust me, it will work.'

'*Trust me*,' she says, imitating his voice. '*Now* I've heard it all.'

Yet I can see the hope daring to grow in her eyes; she's just scared of placing her faith in a plan that might fail. I offer her a sympathetic smile, which she shuns with an indignant grunt.

Gently, I remove my hands from Caszeil's wounds. The small plates of flesh have mostly healed, leaving two pink nubs of scar tissue.

Talia gasps. 'Icari, how have you—?'

'The Samael are tough,' I reply, smiling at Caszeil.

'I've seen Healers mend flesh before,' she says. 'But never so quickly.'

I widen my eyes, trying to keep her on task. 'Are all of those things in the crypts? Nails, hammers, wax and gum?'

She nods, still gawping at Caszeil's hand. 'Yes, but how are we going to get the demon to the sepulchre? We can't very well walk him through the catacombs.'

I pull a ball of fabric from my satchel. 'I stole it earlier today.' A quick shake, and the ball opens up to reveal a body sack. I raise an eyebrow at Talia. 'We're just two Embalmers transporting a corpse through the catacombs.'

'Genius,' she whispers.

Just then, footsteps echo down the corridor. 'What's going on?' says a male voice. 'Who's down there?'

A flash of panic in my gut. My hands open as my body slackens with fear, allowing the sack to fall. Another guard must have arrived for a shift change.

'Oi,' he shouts. 'Why's that door open?' The footsteps crescendo to a frantic run.

I only have time to step in front of Caszeil, shielding him from danger, before the guard looms in the doorway. It's Minew, the guard who assaulted me before the raid. Just the sight of him and it's like I'm pushed against the skull wall again, his mouth swallowing mine, his hands everywhere they shouldn't be. My heart throws itself against my ribs.

His eyes fix on me and his hand tightens around his spear. 'Come back for more, have you?' He leers. 'Me wife left me. Turns out she had a bit on the side too.' He steps forward and touches my cheek, his spear glinting in my peripheral vision like a sharpened tooth. 'So why don't we pick up where we left off? We was getting on so well, after all.'

'Don't touch me,' I say, knocking his hand away, refusing to shrink or apologize.

In a blur of movement, Caszeil steps around me, grabs Minew's spear, and swipes his feet from beneath him. The guard lands with a thud on his back. An expression of shock melts into anger and he reaches for the dagger at his hip.

'Why you—'

But he never gets to finish his sentence because Caszeil

has brought the spear down with precision and speed, skewering him through the neck. A grunt of pain, a splatter of blood, and Minew lies motionless.

I open my mouth to scream, but Talia clamps her hand over it.

'Quiet,' she whispers.

Rage simmers in Caszeil's eyes and I feel like I barely recognize him. He reminds me of the General. Proud, arrogant, and alive with the kill. He lets the spear clatter to the ground and his face softens as he absorbs my look of horror. 'There was no other option, Icari.'

I rip Talia's hand from my mouth. 'There's always another option.' But even as I say it, I recall justifying my own actions with the exact same words. Drugging Madame, taking the skeleton key, breaking into the mill and stealing the Samael feathers.

'He saw Talia,' Caszeil says.

'What do you mean?'

'I cannot carry three people. If Talia comes with us to the Underworld, then there will be you, Sephie and Talia to carry home.'

I shake my head, still not understanding.

'Talia has to stay here at the citadel. She isn't leaving like us. If we implicate her in my escape, she will be executed.'

My mouth forms an *O* shape.

'The demon makes a good point,' Talia says.

I gesture to Minew, stuck through like a hog on a spit. 'Well, did you have to do it so . . . so . . . ?'

'So efficiently?' he says. 'Yes. It is kinder that way.'

I glance at Caszeil's hand, at the spaces where his fingers

should be; my people have not gifted him this courtesy. And I must confess, part of me is pleased to see Minew's throat opened and his eyes empty and unblinking. Perhaps that is why I am so upset: not because Caszeil killed him, but because I am glad of it.

Talia gestures at Minew, now framed by a pool of blood. 'Now, let's lock him in the cell and get out of here.'

39

ICARI

Thankfully, the dungeon branches off the catacombs, but our journey is still long and painful and terrifying. My back aches and my arms burn, so I tighten my grip around the body bag, silently cursing Caszeil for maintaining his muscle bulk in spite of hundreds of years in confinement.

The torches on the walls already begin to dwindle, throwing the tunnels into darkness, and I'm not sure how we'll carry Caszeil *and* a torch.

Talia surveys the corridor. 'How will we see?'

A nearby door swings open and a voice pierces the dimness.

'May I carry a torch for you?'

Stepping from a crypt is a young orderly, carrying a broom and a bundle of bloodied rags. 'Or better yet, I can take the head end for you. Bodies get heavy.' He whistles. 'And this one's a beast.'

'You can say that again,' Talia mutters.

The glow coming from an oil lamp behind him spills across the tunnel floor and illuminates every stitch of the woven sacking encasing Caszeil. Suddenly, no amount of material seems sufficient to hide our secret.

The orderly drops the rags and rests the broom against the doorway, ready to assist.

'Well?' he says, arms outstretched so he can take Caszeil from me.

'Er . . .'

'That is so kind, thank you,' Talia says.

She may have saved me from my lack of words, but she's created a far bigger problem, for we can't take the orderly to the mill or the sepulchre. What if the orderly catches a glimpse of the long white feathers? And even if he doesn't, that part of the catacombs is barely used – his suspicions will almost certainly be raised. My stomach clenches with anxiety as I imagine Caszeil leaping from his body sack and murdering the poor boy before us. No. Caszeil would never hurt an innocent. Not again. I'm sure of it.

Talia releases a loud sigh. 'But we are so nearly there, just another couple of turns. And we'd hate to interrupt your work.'

'And he's surprisingly light,' I say, nodding to Caszeil, ignoring my back as it screams in pain. 'Just skin and bones, really. We're fine.'

'Well, if you're sure,' he says, picking up his broom.

We smile and nod, continuing down the corridor, our breath settling only when we hear the sound of the crypt door closing behind him.

'That was close,' I whisper.

'And we still can't bloody see,' Talia replies.

I flip open my satchel. The Samael down I'd gathered earlier exudes its silver light into the tunnel, not enough to see any detail, but enough to stop us tripping or missing a turning.

Finally, we pass the door to the mill, and I count the doors to the sepulchre, my arms entirely numb, my fingers stretched at the joints. One . . . two . . . three. Flinging open the sepulchre door, we heave him the last few paces, falling on the floor beside him as we're sealed inside the chamber. The stack of Samael feathers illuminates the cell far better than the handful of down, so I can at least see to untie the sacking.

'Caszeil, we are here,' I say.

When his head emerges, he is smiling. 'Skin and bones?'

I laugh. 'I had to say something.'

His eyes fall upon the Samael feathers and he stands, shedding the sacking like a serpent skin. 'Sweet Aïdes, you really did find them.' He moves towards them like a father about to be reunited with a lost child and rests his cheek upon their white veins, inhaling deeply.

Talia catches my eye. *Sweet Aïdes?* she mouths.

'It's just a saying,' I whisper.

She exhales sharply. 'I'll get the other things we need and leave you with whatever this is.' She gestures to Caszeil embracing the feathers.

'Talia . . .' I begin, but she leaves the sepulchre before I can thank her.

'I don't think your friend likes me much,' Caszeil says.

'She doesn't know you. She knows only that you're a demon.'

'You know that I'm a demon too,' he replies, shifting the feathers to the centre of the chamber. 'Yet you are able to move beyond contempt.'

'Yes, but when I first met you, you were just a prisoner.'

'True.'

His graceful hands flit between the quills and I track his spine, stretched like a length of beads all the way to the nubs of severed bone where his wings once grew. What will he look like when he has his wings back? Even more powerful? Even more beautiful? I suddenly long to run my hand up the nodules of his back, letting the cold of his skin soothe the heat of mine. And for the first time, I truly understand my sister's addiction, for even though I know Caszeil is a demon, the sworn enemy of my people, I cannot switch off my feelings for him. Is it really so different from Sephie's want for devil wing? After all, they both make us feel better in different ways.

'Come see,' he says, beckoning me over.

I kneel beside him and he lifts the largest feather. 'This is the outer feather. It's the most sensitive of them all. You can feel temperature and pressure changes in the air around you.' He touches the tip, causing the uppermost veins to resist the pressure.

'You must have missed them. Your wings, I mean.'

He grins. 'Like an old friend.' He begins sifting through the plumes, sorting them into piles according to their size, but his movements become more and more frantic, his breath quicker.

'Caszeil? What is it?'

'There aren't enough,' he says.

'What?'

'Feathers,' he says, looking up. 'Are there any more?'

I shake my head. 'They've all been ground up.'

'And where are the wing bones?' He stands, anxiety

causing his silver brow to knit. 'Are they still in the mill?'

'No. They must have ground them into devil wing too. But surely we can build a frame from wood or metal?'

'My wings need to be living things,' he replies, his voice rising with panic. 'Of flesh and blood and bone. Only then will they recognize me as their master. I will not simply mount these wings on my back – I will absorb them so they become an extension of me.'

Part of me must have known he would say this, part of me must have hidden the truth from even myself, for as soon as it's necessary, the solution presents itself in all its blasphemous, sacrilegious ugliness.

'It's OK,' I say, forever damning my soul to an eternity with Aïdes. 'I know where we can get a wing bone and extra feathers.'

40

ICARI

After Talia returns with the tools, I lead her from the sepulchre. The door closes and my chest immediately tightens. Caszeil makes everything and anything seem possible, and in his absence, the uncertainty takes hold and spreads like rot. Talia's intense silence doesn't help. The candle in her hands throws shadows up her face, highlighting every line of disapproval.

We reach the long tunnel that links the catacombs to the Sun Temple and Talia scowls.

'I don't understand,' she says. 'There are no Samael feathers or wing bones in the Sun Temple.'

I raise a single brow. Better not to explain just yet.

Stepping inside, inhaling the scent of damp earth, we begin the journey upwards, ignoring the odd rat as they dart before our feet. Eventually, tree roots begin to punch through the ceiling like fingers, clutching, grabbing at our hair, and the scent of citrus fruit laces the air.

'What are your feelings for that demon?' Talia suddenly asks.

I scowl, the question planting an uncomfortable tremor in my belly. I think I preferred the silence.

'I care for him.' I falter. 'What I mean is, I am caring for him.'

She laughs. 'Sweet Mother Moon, Sephie said you were a soft touch, but this is ridiculous.'

Thankfully, the outline of the door leading to the Sun Temple appears and the fresh air wafts towards us like healing balm.

'We're nearly there,' I say.

When I look over my shoulder, she is watching me with narrowed eyes.

'You cannot keep him, you know that?' she says.

I fight the sudden urge to cover my ears, instead pushing open the door. 'I don't know what you're talking about.'

The sight of the Sun Temple at night silences her, and I allow her a few moments to admire the fruit trees, the pillars and the expanse of gleaming pale marble, the torches reflecting on its surface like lanterns on a lake.

'I still don't understand what we're doing here,' she whispers.

'Patience,' I reply.

Passing behind a screen of fruit trees, I heave open the arched door that leads to a spiral staircase etched into the stone.

'The Tomb of Light?' she whispers. 'There definitely won't be any Samael . . .' She tails off, realization dawning on her face. 'Oh.'

I wind up the staircase, that strange pulling sensation that I felt when I first arrived in the temple strengthening. It's as though something is summoning me. 'Uriel said there were two new dead Illios,' I whisper.

'What about the guards?' Talia says.

'There aren't many left. Besides, they don't think anyone would ever pillage an Illios grave. It's sacrilege of the highest order.' My words echo around the stairwell and I ignore the bayonet of guilt in my side. If this is what it takes to save my sister, I would do it a hundred times over.

The door at the top is wooden, reinforced with iron bars and, of course, a hefty lock. The golden light of the Illios wings seeps from the thin lines around the door, burning a rectangle into the stone. A moment's panic lands inside my chest as I slot Madame's skeleton key inside the lock, but it turns with ease.

'Icari, wait,' Talia says.

When I glance at her, she stands on a lower step, looking up, her eyes wide and teary. She looks ten years younger and I get this sudden urge to hug her.

'I don't think I can do this,' she says.

The disappointment is a fist, but I manage a weak smile. 'That's all right. I can manage alone.'

She takes two steps backwards, dropping further down the stairs, but doesn't turn.

'How will you carry the wing bones without me?' she asks.

'I'll drag them.'

She hovers for a moment, her breath disrupting the flame of her candle and splashing shadows across the curved stone walls; then she starts up the stairs again. 'Let's get it over with.'

'Thank you,' I whisper, as she pushes through the door.

'I'm doing it for Sephie,' she replies.

The sight of the tomb stills everything. It is quite beautiful, built from glass panes that allow the night sky to shine through, with pillars draped in brightly coloured linen and wound with vines and jasmine. A group of dead Illios lie upon bejewelled plinths, their bodies wrapped in embroidered linen, and their wings spread beneath them like yellow, glowing blankets. The more recently slain gods are easy to spot because their wings glow stronger and their bandages remain the brightest of whites, yet to fade in the sun.

'Which one?' I ask, as we approach the dead Illios. 'I think it should be one of the new corpses. The feathers will be fresher.'

'Icari, you sound like you're talking about dead pigeons, not *gods*.'

I recoil. 'I know, I know, and may Father Sun forgive me, but words are the least of our concerns considering what we are about to do.'

She grimaces, then points to the nearest. 'That one.'

I trace my finger across his bandaged features. Was he handsome? Young? Did he know the Illios who saved me at the sanatorium? An even more horrifying thought surfaces in my mind: could he be the Illios who saved me? Remorse gathers in my chest, but I push it down with firm hands. *Sephie needs me.*

We roll him over, grunting with the effort; his body may be empty, but his wings are heavier than a sack of bricks. When he lies on his side, I realize just how difficult this is going to be, for one of his wings is still tucked beneath him.

'Curses,' I mumble.

After much pushing, he finally slips to the ground in the position we need, lying on his side with both wings spread behind him. My hands naturally move down the back of his neck, along his spine, towards the place where his wings attach to his body until I feel a break in the linen strips, a protrusion of something hard and smooth. I lean over him – the faint scent of embalming oil catching in my nostrils – and examine the joins more closely. Two knots of pale bone, each doused in tiny gold feathers, erupt from the linen strips.

A shiver of dread passes through me as I pull the saw from my satchel. My whole life, I've known that dissecting the bodies of the dead is the ultimate sin, for it means they're unable to journey to the afterlife. And yet here I am, about to dissect an Illios. *A god*. There is no greater crime. My hands begin to tremble, my heart quickens beneath my ribs, my mouth dries.

'It's OK,' Talia whispers. 'He's already been embalmed. And he's a god – he'll already be with Mother Moon. Their souls . . . journey faster.'

'You are sure.'

She nods, so hard I fear her head may come loose.

I'm not sure I believe her, yet Sephie's face swims into focus and any fear, any anxiety, hardens into determination. I cut open a lady to save the babe inside her, surely this isn't much different. So, placing my knee on the wings, just shy of the joint, I begin to saw as near to his back as I'm able. White powder explodes around my hands, bits of yellow down spiral into the air like tiny birds breaking free. My body trembles with the effort, vibrations travel up my arms and into my chest, and a terrible grating noise fills the chamber.

A mighty crack and the first wing slumps free.

It's like watching the greatest tree in the forest felled. What was once great is now reduced. Humiliated. For a moment, I'm completely silent, completely still, desperate to mark the momentous act in some way befitting to the gods.

'You really did it,' Talia whispers.

'I really did.'

Then, I repeat the process on the remaining wing. This time, I'm expecting the awful cracking sound, like a neck snapping, but it still makes my stomach turn when it arrives. The final wing falls beside its twin, making me think of Sephie and me, curled around each other in Mama's womb. *At least we are stealing them both*, I think. *At least they will stay together.* It is some consolation.

'Come,' Talia says. 'Now is not the time to contemplate all we've done.'

Swallowing down the shame, I help her lift the wings into the body bag. Yet they are too long for the sack, too lush, and the many feathers simply refuse to stay covered.

'It's not going to work,' I say, surprised by how close my tears are to the surface.

She chews her lips. 'We don't need all the plumes, do we?'

'No.'

We begin plucking feathers from the bone, our movements manic, our logic being that if we do it quick enough, our actions somehow don't count. I imagine death has loosened the quills from the bone, for they come away easier than expected, like teeth from rotten gums. Once they're thinned out, we punch a hole through both ends of the sack so the tips of the feathers and the sawn-off bones can poke through.

I observe the scene before me. A wingless god still slumped on the ground, golden feathers littered around the room as if several magical birds have been slaughtered, and a body bag that barely contains the desecrated wings. Thank goodness Father Sun sleeps right now, for no amount of prayer or good deed will undo what we have done.

'What's the matter?' Talia asks.

I gesture to the wings. 'The wing tips aren't covered, and the feathers are glowing – they'll stand out a mile in the catacombs.'

'We didn't pass anyone on the way here.' Her tone belies the optimism of her words.

'Yes, but we bumped into that orderly when we were carrying Caszeil.'

She thinks for a moment, then rips a few strips from her embalming gown. 'Bandages,' she says, passing me a couple of thick black ribbons.

Loosely, we bind the protruding wing tip and the ends of the feathers, smothering the golden glow as best we can.

'Better?' she says.

'It'll fool nobody up close,' I say, observing the taut sacking, pulled out of shape by something that clearly isn't a corpse, topped and tailed with wodges of black binding. 'We'll move as quickly as we can. That's all we can do.'

By the time we reach the catacombs, we're dizzy with exhaustion, and all that's keeping me going is the image of Caszeil's smile when he sees the wing bones. But we're close now – just a few more turns . . .

'Talia, Icari, what a pleasant surprise.'

I expect it to be the orderly from earlier, for the voice is young and male, yet as he steps from the shadows, a nearby torch illuminates his pallid skin and strong jaw. It's Ziris. A rush of adrenaline overrides the pain in my muscles and joints.

'Ziris,' Talia says, angling her body so he cannot step past her and examine our strange cargo.

'And why are you out of bed?' he asks.

'I could ask you the same question,' Talia replies.

'I'm running an errand for the General.' He folds his arms, turning his broad shoulders into an immovable object. 'Your turn.'

'We're transporting a body,' I say, ignoring the gathering sickness as an image of the thin-lipped General who burnt Mama bursts into my mind's eye.

Ziris scoffs. 'In the middle of the night?' A single, pointed brow shoots upwards so he's all angles and disbelief.

'People die in the night,' I reply. 'This is one of my patients at the citadel sanatorium. She died from an unknown disease, so Principal Healer wanted her carried far from others.'

He takes a step back.

Talia smiles, clearly understanding. 'Oh yes, Principal was quite clear that the dead can be as contagious as the living. She asked us to lock the victim away in a distant crypt until the risk passed.'

Another two steps backwards. 'Oh, well if that's the case, I won't hold you up.'

Relief swells in my chest . . . then Ziris's expression changes from concern to gleeful arrogance.

He was mocking us.

'Do you really think I'm that stupid? What's in the body

bag? Show me. Now.'

My stomach rotates as I block his way, shielding the Illios wings from view. Yet in a single movement, he throws me to the side and sends me careering head first into the tunnel wall. A collection of skulls tumbles into the dirt, and my crown pulses from the blow.

'Icari,' Talia shouts, dashing towards me.

Vulture-like, Ziris bends over the sack and pulls the binding free. The yellow glimmer of holy feathers illuminates his pallid skin and blade-like cheekbones. His face transforms into a wicked smile.

'Is this what I think it is?' He touches the plumes. 'Why, yes. Yes it is. Which begs the question, why are you transporting disembodied Illios wings through the catacombs?'

I open my mouth only to inhale dust. Talia stoops beside me, I think to help me up, but instead her fingers fasten around one of the fallen skulls and she spins in a whir of black robes and rusted black curls. And with a mighty *thunk*, she smashes the skull across Ziris's face, sending him crumpling to the floor.

For a moment, nobody moves.

Talia clings to the skull, her eyes locked on Ziris like she can't quite believe what she's done, whereas I remain slumped against the wall, my head ringing with the assault and my vision misted with shock and dust. And Ziris just lies there, eyes closed, blood oozing from a gash on his forehead, mimicking the dead. Then it occurs to me: maybe he *is* dead. Talia hit him pretty hard.

Scooting across the ground, I check the pulse in his neck.

'He's alive,' I whisper.

'Shame,' Talia says, dropping the skull beside him.

'Quickly.' I shake the grogginess from my head. 'We can lock him in one of the crypts. By the time someone finds him in the morning, you'll be tucked up in bed, then it'll just be his word against yours that you were ever involved.'

'I doubt he'll even admit I knocked him out.' She grabs him unceremoniously under the arms. 'Boys and their fragile egos.' Her eyes flick to the cut on his head. 'Fragile heads too.'

We shift him into the nearest crypt, rolling him on to his side in case he should vomit, then lock the door behind us. The key releases a satisfying click as the metal bolt slides into place.

41

ICARI

As we enter the sepulchre, Caszeil rushes to take the weight of the bundle, and his smile spreads wider than any wings, just as I imagined. Yet as he unwinds the black strips of embalming robe, his movements grow more and more frenetic. And by the time he's pulled back the body sack, allowing the golden light to drown out the silver glow of the Samael feathers, his smile has been replaced by deep worry lines.

'These are Illios feathers,' he says. '*Illios* bones.'

Talia releases a grunt of frustration. 'Feathers are feathers. Bones are bones. You're hardly in the position to be picky, demon.'

Sighing, he runs his hands down the quills. The golden light dims where he touches.

'Perhaps there are enough Samael feathers for the balance to tip in my favour.' He smiles, but I know him well enough to know it is forced.

Together, we spread the wings out on the floor. With half the quills removed, they look like they've been stolen from a drowned goose, not a god. Patches of pale, smooth bone flash through the gaps created where Talia and I ripped away the fluffy down with the larger feathers. Regardless, they remain huge, stretching from one side of the sepulchre to the other. A shiver of excitement pulses through me as I imagine them mounted on Caszeil's back.

'Thank you,' Caszeil says. 'Both of you.' He turns to Talia. 'It is time for you to leave now.'

She glances at me, her uncertainty obvious in the quiver of her lips. 'I think I should stay. You may need—'

'No,' I say, cutting over her. 'Caszeil's right. If you get caught in all of this, you'll be executed.'

'OK.' Her voice wavers and she swallows. 'Good luck. And tell Sephie . . . Tell her . . .' The words die in her mouth and she holds my gaze. 'You know,' she whispers.

'Yes, I know,' I reply. For Talia has more than proved her love for Sephie.

She pulls me into a brief yet firm hug; then her face morphs into a scowl as she looks at Caszeil. 'Just bring Sephie home.'

'That is the plan,' he replies.

Her frown deepens, swamping her freckles. 'You better do as you say, demon.'

He levels his slate eyes at her. 'I will, witch.'

She exhales heavily, squeezes my hands, then slips from the sepulchre, leaving me and Caszeil alone.

We pause for a moment, absorbing her absence. He's already lit several candles, and the amber light combines with that of the Illios wings, turning his eyes the colour of ash. Our relationship has developed in isolation, yet now, I feel strangely awkward without Talia's presence. Is it because I saw him kill the guard without hesitation or remorse? Or is it because he's no longer imprisoned and diminished? Instead of him relying on me, I'm entirely reliant on *him* to save Sephie.

Perhaps sensing my apprehension, he drops his gaze. 'How are you, Icari?' he asks. 'Sawing the wings from an Illios can't have been easy.'

'I fear my soul may never rest with Mother Moon,' I whisper, my throat tightening.

'So you'll end up in the Underworld. It isn't so bad.'

I laugh, some of the tension flaking from my muscles. 'I think that statement only stands for demons.'

He smiles with one half of his mouth, then examines the wings more closely. Focusing on a single wing bone, he curls and stretches it with interest, his head tilted to one side like a curious child. The bone articulates at two points, so it is in fact three smaller bones linked together to form one, and moves like a giant beckoning finger.

Watching the shift in his muscles as he works, the candle-light making a silver kaleidoscope of him, I'm reminded once again of how strong he is, of how he killed Minew, the guard, as though stamping out a fly. I'm used to Caszeil being vulnerable, lying injured at my feet, and the change unnerves me.

'Come look,' he says. 'We'll need to make holes in the spaces to attach the extra Samael plumes.'

I hesitate, the image of Minew's neck pierced as if no more than a pin cushion still formed in my head.

'What's wrong?' he asks.

'I . . . I don't know. I think perhaps I forgot that you're Samael.'

He studies my face. 'Back in the cell, I told you that I'd never known pain before I came to your world.'

'I remember.'

'I'd never known compassion either.'

I don't know what to say, so I just blink away the bone dust.

'It is only by seeing compassion, memorizing its shape and weight, that you are able to work it with your own hands and make a replica.'

'Are you comparing compassion to pottery?'

'I was thinking of an ice sculpture,' he says. 'But yes, pottery works too.'

I begin to laugh in spite of myself. And I can see his point – if Mama and Papa hadn't cared for me, loved me like they did, would I be the person I am today?

He stands and walks towards me. 'My point is, I was made a demon, Icari.'

'I know.'

'I can choose my father, my home, no more than you can yours.'

The loss of my sister crystallizes in my gut. 'But you can choose your actions.' My arms straighten at my side, forming two stiff rods. 'You didn't have to raid the citadel all of those years ago just because Aïdes demanded it.'

All of the breath expels from his body and his proud chest slumps. 'You are right. Of course, you are right. We were born with free will. It's just . . .' Now he is the one who falters.

'What?'

'It's just Mother Moon's rejection of Aïdes, it is the

fabric of our being. Our entire world is forged from his grief. When we wage war on your people, we wage war on her.'

A bitter laugh bursts from my mouth, bouncing off the stone walls so loud, I fear I will wake the nobleman in the sarcophagus. 'So if you loved me and I rejected you, would you spend eternity seeking revenge?'

He blinks quickly. 'No, of course not, but you are not Mother Moon, and I am not the Divine Shadow.'

'So just because he's eternal, he's allowed to behave like a desert dog?'

'Icari, that is blasphemy.'

'Not for me it isn't. If anyone is going to smite me, it will be Father Sun.' The words cause an unexpected tear to topple from my eye.

He tracks it with his gaze. 'Nobody is going to smite you, Icari.'

I point at the wings, degraded on the ground. 'I have done bad things, Caszeil. *Evil* things. Things I can never come back from.'

'For your sister.'

'Evil is still evil.' The tears thicken, the reality of my actions staring at me in the form of the tattered golden wings.

He smudges the tears from my cheeks with his thumbs. 'Good and evil are not night and day. They are a braid. If Father Sun is as wise as you all say, he will know this too.' He smiles. 'When you reach Sephie, this feeling will pass, I promise.'

'Perhaps you are right.'

He nods. 'Unnervingly right, I've been told. Come. Let me show you how to build a pair of demon wings.'

We work steadily, side by side, hammering holes for the feathers, gluing, easing and dripping, exchanging no glances or words the whole time. The scent of burning wick and Caszeil's skin, so close to my own, are the only things keeping me awake. Eventually, in spite of this, my eyelids begin to droop and the room swims in and out of focus. I begin to wish I could lie down in the sarcophagus behind me, cross my arms and never wake up.

I am on the edge of sleep when Caszeil whispers, 'Icari, see what we have made.'

He helps my aching body into an upright position, supporting me beneath my elbows. I look at the ground and gasp. A giant butterfly gleams at our feet, spread across the floor like a lavish rug, yellows and whites woven together so that, at a glance, it appears the palest of golds.

'Oh, Caszeil,' I say, forgetting the anger, the exhaustion, the fear of failure. 'Just look at your wings.'

We stare at each other for a moment, triumph and wonder hovering in the space between us, and I fight the urge to embrace him, to lay my head against his chest.

'Thank you,' he says. 'Thank you for giving me my wings back.'

I reach forward and touch his fingers, enjoying the bite of cold, for it is achingly hot in the sepulchre. 'I did it for Sephie.'

'I know you did.'

Our fingers twine together of their own accord.

'But I am glad you will be whole again,' I say.

'My wings don't make me whole.' He opens his mouth as if more words wait on his tongue, but he swallows them down, breaking away from me and returning his attention to the wings. 'We just need to get them outside. Then we will mount them on my back and they will bind to me. I will fly again.' He laughs.

I cannot help the tremor of distrust in my gut, the nagging voice that keeps repeating he might leave without me.

Once a demon, always a demon.

'We can use the tunnels to reach the Sun Temple,' I say. 'There's a field around the back, hidden by a grove of acacia trees, so the watchmen won't see until it's too late.'

He slings the wings over his shoulders without so much as a grimace. 'Whatever happens, Icari, I want you to know that you have the strongest spirit of anyone I have ever met.'

That familiar, toxic mix of guilt and shame squirms in my chest as I think of Mama burning on a pyre, of Sephie tied to the whipping post, and how I did *nothing*.

'I am a statue.' The words scratch my narrowed throat.

A curious frown disrupts his brow. 'What?'

'Mama said that fear divides us into three groups – fighters, runners and statues. When I'm afraid, I do nothing.'

'Well, you haven't done nothing now – have you?' He brushes a dark frond of hair from my eyes. 'I am so sorry about your mama. I think I would have liked her very much.'

I nod.

Slowly, I rest a hand against his chest. It is like touching snow. 'Do you promise you won't leave me?' I search his eyes.

'When you have your wings, do you promise you will take me to Sephie.'

'I promise.'

Perhaps it is foolish, but I believe him with my whole heart.

'And Icari,' he says.

'Yes.'

'Your mama missed a group.'

'Pardon?'

'Fear divides us into four groups – fighters, runners, statues, and those who meet their demons with compassion. That's what makes you strong, Icari – your trust, your love, your unconditional kindness. They are your bravest qualities.'

'Mama used to say I was a peach, soft on the outside with an unbreakable core.'

He plucks my hand from his chest and plants the softest of kisses on my knuckles. His dusty-pink lips graze my skin and send shivers through my body.

'A peach,' he says. 'I can think of no better word to describe you.'

And with his kiss burnt in ice against my skin, we leave the sepulchre.

42

ICARI

By the time we reach the outline of the door to the Sun Temple, I'm weighed down with fear and barely able to move my legs, so it's a blessed relief when Caszeil turns and rests the cool of his palm against my cheek.

'We are so close.' His face glows in the light of the wings.

'What if we are caught?'

'Then I will say I bewitched you.'

'What about you?'

'I will say you bewitched me.' He smiles. 'It wouldn't be a lie.'

'Don't joke.'

He sighs and his breath chills my cheek. 'I would rather die than be locked in a cell for another hundred years. So long as you are unharmed and free.'

He lowers his head, and instinctively I rest my forehead against his.

'Come,' he says, 'we must hurry. Once dawn arrives, Father Sun will stop me in my tracks.'

Not to mention Uriel and the few remaining alchemy students who will arrive to worship at sunrise, and the orderlies who'll discover Ziris locked in a crypt. Taking a huge gulp of air, I take the lead and push through the door into the temple. The torches swirl in their metal loops and the emerald leaves sway on the fruit trees, but other than that, it is entirely still. Empty. A quick glance through the glass ceiling tells me that we don't have long. Most of the stars have faded and a tapestry of watery greys has already replaced the black.

I lead Caszeil to the line of fruit trees and peer through the boughs, checking the reach of marble, the pews, the various nooks. Once we leave the shelter of the branches, we'll be completely exposed. My skin feels like it's been replaced with the hottest of coals.

Sneaking towards the exit, I leave Caszeil concealed by the trees, and tentatively creak open the door. No guards. They must be changing.

Just a quick dash and we'll be free.

Glancing again at the sky, I whisper my thanks; then, turning, I beckon Caszeil towards me. He runs across the marble expanse, looking strangely at home, his silver skin an extension of the glistening floors, the wings shimmering behind him like another burning torch.

'Follow me,' I say.

And with a final backwards glance at the door to the tunnel, barely visible through the fruit trees, I throw open the door to the Court of Ash.

Racing down the steps, I expect to hear Caszeil's footsteps and the swish of feathers against granite. But there are only my own breaths and the trill of the crickets, and when I turn, I see Caszeil paused in the marble archway, framed by feathers and their ghostly glow. From this angle, the wings could already belong to him and the sight takes my breath away. He is as beautiful, ethereal, as he is terrifying. At first, I assume he's drinking in the mountain air, the infinite sky. Then I notice his expression as he gazes at the remains of yesterday's bonfire: broken.

'Is this where they burnt my brothers?'

'Yes,' I reply, overwhelmed with sympathy, for I couldn't look at the black mark left by Mama's pyre on the agora floor without feeling like I was skinless.

I reach towards him, partly to comfort him, partly to break him from his trance, when a loud thud resounds around the Court of Ash. Caszeil drops to the ground in a blur of silvery skin and pale feathers, blood oozing from his head like liquid metal. It happens so quickly, like a bird shot from the sky with an arrow, I don't even have time to gasp.

Standing in his place is Ziris, holding a torch dripping with silver blood, causing the flame to sizzle like water on hot coals. He must have escaped, then waited to ambush us. That *weasel*.

He raises the torch above Caszeil, preparing for another strike.

'Ziris, no!' I scream.

I wish I could say that I think of Sephie, or Mama, or even myself, as I sprint up the steps and hurl my body through the air towards Ziris, but it would be a lie, for I think only of Caszeil, of preventing that torch from battering the life from him.

I connect with Ziris with a crack of limbs and we land back inside the Sun Temple, thudding against the marble. The torch rolls across the floor and he clambers on top of me, pinning me to the ground by the wrists. He leans forward, his black hair forming a wall so his hateful face is all I can see — so close, I can make out every blade of stubble upon his broad jaw, the beads of saliva gathering in the corners of his mouth.

'She should have hit me harder with that skull,' he says.

I buck and rear beneath him, but he's just too heavy to shift.

He lowers his face so he's close enough to kiss me, or maybe even bite, but instead he whispers, 'The General knew you were up to something, so he had me follow you. Looks like the old git was right. The apple doesn't fall far from the tree — and you're as rotten a piece of fruit as your dead witch of a mother. Your dead sister too.' He barks out a laugh. 'The great and powerful twins from beyond the city walls — just look at you now.'

Hatred as deep as the Nubi river settles into my bones. For Ziris, for the General, for every man who has ever made me feel small.

'*Witch* is simply a man's word for a woman with power,' I hiss. 'And Sephie is not dead.'

It's as if I haven't spoken; his breath fills my face. 'I couldn't work out why you'd steal Illios wings. *Illios* wings. But now it all makes sense. You were doing it to free a . . . a . . .' He gestures to Caszeil with his head, never tearing his eyes from mine. 'A *monster*.'

'You are the only monster around here.' I bring my knee up firmly, a satisfying crunch hitting my ears as I connect with his testes.

Groaning, he rolls from me, clutching himself, and I scrabble into a sitting position. At first, I think he's going to grab the torch and clout me too, but instead he throws back his head and begins to shout.

'Help! Help! A Samael has attacked me.' His voice is alarmingly shrill and threatens to split my eardrums. He will surely rouse every guard in the citadel.

'A Samael didn't attack you,' I say. 'I did.'

Ziris continues to wail, a human alarm bell, yet a gentler noise permeates the blare. It is Caszeil, moaning as he regains consciousness.

There is still time.

Rushing to his side, fuelled by hope, I cradle the wound on the back of his head, setting my fingers aglow with healing light. His blood is so cold it's like cupping a handful of water from the Nubi river in the winter months, and his eyelashes have never looked so dark as they flutter open.

'Are you OK?' I ask.

He nods, and I help him stand, surprised how his body trembles.

That's when we see them. Rushing across the Court of Ash, weapons raised. A group of guards.

'No,' I whisper.

As if in response, the bells from the watchtower ring out and more guards spill on to the marble.

No, no, no.

Our escape route is entirely blocked and there's nowhere to go but back inside the Sun Temple.

'Quickly,' I shout, helping Caszeil gather up the wings.

We move away from the exit, heading further inside the building.

Ziris sneers at me from the floor. 'Where will you go now, Healer?'

My eyes swing around the marbled walls. We have only two options: the catacombs or the dungeons. Neither will provide a launching site. Then, the twinkle of the final few stars catches my eye, and I look towards the glass ceiling.

'Can you punch through?' I ask.

Caszeil nods. 'But the wings need to meld to me – it will take some time.'

The guards run up the steps. In just a few seconds, they'll be inside. I'm about to surrender, just throw up my hands and scream into the gloom, when a surge of warmth spreads through my body and I'm drawn, as always, to the Tomb of Light – the greenhouse in the sky. Of course. Caszeil can punch through the glass panes. And the door is reinforced with metal and bolts; it should give us enough time for the wings to bind to him.

Grabbing Caszeil by the arm, I drag him towards the arched doorway that leads to the Tomb of Light. The guards swarm into the temple just as we reach the spiral staircase. The General muscles his way to the front and his face breaks into a sick, lipless grin as he pulls his crossbow from his back and shouts, 'Take aim.'

The guards follow suit. A sea of crossbows point at me, and my joints lock into place, holding me completely still.

This is how I will die.

Then a cold hand grips my arm and yanks me backwards, causing me to sink into the stone stairwell just as the twang of metal strings reverberates throughout the temple. A wave of arrows thwack into the wall where I stood only moments ago and my head explodes with anxiety.

'Thank you,' I gasp.

A smile flits across Caszeil's face. 'Any time.'

Grabbing a handful of feathers, ignoring the hammer of boots upon marble and the cry of gruff voices, I help Caszeil haul the wings up the steps – gravity has surely filled each quill with river silt, and every bump threatens to pull my spine apart. Boots thud against the bottom step as I fumble with the lock. The sound of darts hitting flesh pulls a scream from my mouth, and I brace myself for a wave of pain, or for Caszeil's pierced body to slump at my feet, yet when I turn, I see that Caszeil has raised the wings so they form a giant shield.

'Hurry, Icari,' he says.

The footsteps approach just as the key slots into place and turns. The door falls open and we burst into the Tomb of Light, heaving the wings behind us. Another twang of strings followed by the patter of arrows against wood. Caszeil holds the door shut whilst I shove the bolts into position. We're just in time, for a mighty thump tells us that the guards have begun throwing their weight against the wood.

The Tomb of Light is as calm and beautiful as I remember, completely oblivious to the chaos beyond the door, yet the evidence of my most shameful moment is everywhere, frozen in time as if in a painting or mosaic. Nearby lies the Illios with the missing wings, looking like a mortal rather than a god, and the feathers Talia and I plucked away in manic handfuls still dust the floor like golden ribbons.

Caszeil touches my shoulder, so gently, at first I assume it is the brush of a feather. 'Try not to look.'

Another dull thud comes from the door, and I imagine the soldiers hurling their bodies against it.

'Can you lift the wings on to my back?' he asks.

I take them from him, yet without Caszeil's help, I'm dragged to the ground. 'They're too heavy.'

He adopts the foetal position on the floor so the two nubs of bone left by his amputated wings protrude like the newly sprouted horns of a billy goat. 'Can you push them against me? It will just be for a short while – the wings will do the rest.'

It takes all of my strength to hoist the wings towards his back and manoeuvre them into the right place. My hands are too small for the task, my arms like strips of parchment, and the base of the wing bones skates across his skin.

Suddenly, an almighty boom causes the panes of glass to shake in their frames. The door bows, raining dust and splinters on the ground. The guards have brought a battering ram.

I grind the bones closer to his spine, worried I'm going to hurt him, feeling like I'm trying to tame two wild animals who want to do the exact opposite to what I ask. Then, by some miracle, the base of the wing bones skid over the lumps on his back. And it's like the nubs are covered in gum, for the wing bones stick to them. The mass of feathers grows instantly lighter, the pain in my arms easing as if a bag of rocks has been plucked from my hands.

'Something's happening,' I say.

The Samael feathers spark in the gloom, their light intensifying like the dial on an oil lamp has been turned up.

Caszeil roars with delight. 'I can feel them! I can feel my wings.'

The door booms again, yet I hardly hear it, too transfixed by what is happening before me. The bones begin to merge into his back, his silver skin growing around them, fastening them in place. Caszeil roars again, only this time it is a scream of pain, and I imagine the wing bones growing, burrowing into his spine and adhering to his skeleton. He screws up his face in agony and reaches out a flailing hand. I grab it and let him squeeze until my fingers crunch, grateful I can share some of his pain.

'It's working,' I say, my voice filled with joy. 'You're getting your wings back.'

He screams in response, drowning out the battering ram and the cries of the guards. The primal depths of his pain remind me of women during childbirth, and I speak to him as I would to a patient in labour, offering words of hope and encouragement.

White down sprouts rapidly from the wing bones, covering all of the bald patches and blending the existing feathers together so nobody would ever know these wings were built rather than born. The transformation looks like it's going to be a success, and I can barely contain my excitement. In just a moment, he will sweep me into his arms and we'll burst through the glass, soaring over the citadel and beyond so we may rescue my sister.

I'm coming, Sephie, I say to myself. *I'm coming.*

Then something changes. Caszeil's cries are no longer racked with pain but sorrow. Desolation. It is the cry of somebody who has lost everything.

'No,' he shouts. 'Please, no.'

'What is it?'

He doesn't need to reply, for I can see the golden Illios feathers upon his back turning dark and wilting. The Samael feathers remain strong and true, their light strong, yet they only serve to show just how black the Illios feathers have grown.

The screaming stops and his voice emerges a ragged whisper. 'I can't feel them any more.'

And just like that, the wings fall from his back.

'What's happening?' I say as I help him into a sitting position.

He reaches for the wings, his face drawn with despair. 'They rejected me. The Divine Shadow in my blood has withered the Illios feathers.' He rests his head in his hands, tears shimmering on his cheeks. 'I'd hoped there would be enough Samael feathers, but I was wrong. I'm so sorry.'

I fold my arms around him and let him weep, listening to the pounding of the battering ram, watching as the metal reinforcements disfigure, savouring the chill of his tears as they land on my shoulder and suck the heat from my skin. Comforting him deflects my own pain, and if these are our last moments together, I want to spend them wrapped in each other's arms.

'We were so close,' he whispers, nuzzling into my neck.

I reach out and touch the feathers. They would have been glorious.

Oh Sephie, my darling Sephie, I'm so sorry.

The sobbing stops and his head lifts from my shoulder. 'Icari, look.' He points to the feathers beneath my hand.

Where I've touched, the blackened Illios plumes have changed, *transmuted*, regaining their colour just as they might in the Illumination Ritual when touched by a Healer.

'Try again,' he says, shuffling on his knees towards the wings.

Another thud. The door bows – time is a knife edge, yet I let him gently guide my hands so they rest upon the dark Illios feathers. Not only do the Illios feathers regenerate, changing back to their former yellow selves, but the inter-mixed Samael feathers glow even stronger beneath my palms.

'How is this possible?' I whisper.

He gazes at me with admiration and tenderness. 'Icari, have you not wondered why you can heal me so? It is not just because the Samael are tough. It is because I am half dead, and you have Father Sun *and* Mother Moon in your blood. My flesh responds to you because you are part Embalmer.'

I look at my hands, shocked. 'What? No, I can't be part Embalmer. I would know.'

'Would you? Have you ever wrapped a corpse?'

I shake my head. 'But at the Illumination Ritual, I didn't see any silvery-white light.'

'So it is not as strong in you yet as Father Sun.'

'Or perhaps . . .' I stumble on the words, recalling the feel of his cool skin beneath my touch, the surge of Calling like I've never felt before. 'Perhaps your presence awoke some-thing in me.'

He looks at me from beneath the feathers of his eyelashes. 'I like that theory more.'

'Is this why the Tomb of Light has always drawn me so? Because the corpses of the Illios were reaching out to me?'

He nods. 'Death and Father Sun combined.'

The hammering on the door breaks our gaze, so I return to the wings. My magic is spreading quickly, the light travelling along the broken plumes. Within moments, the wings are like new again.

'Icari, these wings are yours,' he says.

In spite of the buzzing in my ears and the thump of the battering ram, I laugh. 'What?'

'The wings. They are yours. It is *you* who must wear them.'

I stand, shaking my head, terrified and bemused in equal levels. 'I cannot *grow wings*.'

'Whyever not?' he says, standing to face me.

'Because . . . because . . .' I exhale quickly with disbelief. 'Because I am not a god or a demon.' I gesture to my body. 'I'm just a girl.'

He tilts his head, yet his face remains completely straight. 'A girl who's healed a broken creature for no reason other than kindness. A girl who is willing to enter the Underworld to save her sister.'

I gaze at the feathers on the floor, my back itching with the thought of it. Yet even as I know Caszeil has a point, I know it only in my head and not in my heart. Self-doubt eats me from the inside out; I am a hollow shell, too weak to even attempt such an impossible task. I couldn't save Sephie from the whip. Why on earth did I think I could save her from hell?

Another explosion of wood pulls me from my thoughts. I stare at the door. It is starting to give up – flashes of gold-and-silver uniforms appear through the cracks.

'Icari,' Caszeil says. 'Are you ready?'

I take one final look at Caszeil's face. 'I'm sorry,' I say. 'I just can't.'

'You deserve to fly as much as any god, any demon. Any man.'

I step backwards, shaking my head, the thought just too preposterous to do anything but make me feel horrified and insufficient all at once. 'Caszeil, I—'

And then, I don't have to think about it any more, because the battering ram breaches the door.

43

ICARI

The ram has created a portal into another world, a world made of men and weapons and everything real. A crossbow pings, followed by an arrow whizzing by my ear and impaling a nearby pillar. Fear is no longer a thing that sits inside me. It spills out of my every pore, my mouth, my eyes, cloaking me so all I can see is our impending capture and our imminent deaths.

Another blow to the door. Hinges and bolts buckle like twigs and the wood is reduced to a heap of kindling. Caszeil pushes me behind him as the guards rush into the Tomb of Light and someone begins to scream. It takes a second to realize it's me. Then a hundred grabbing hands fall upon silver skin and Caszeil is wrenched away from me, swallowed by a wave of gold-and-silver uniforms, hate-filled eyes and flashing weapons.

Shouting his name again and again, I grab at the guards and try to dig him free, not caring when I'm kicked and punched, the pain simply spurring me on. Then someone yanks me by the hair. I reel backwards and the General shoves me to the ground, pushing his elbow into my throat so my lungs fail me and my vision fills with stars. My hatred for him is eclipsed only by my fear that Caszeil is already dead.

The guards part and Caszeil lies on the ground, his hands and feet chained. He's been badly beaten, and the Calling swells inside me at the sight of his silver blood. But the rise and fall of his chest tells me he's still alive.

His lips part. Such a small movement that clearly causes him great pain.

'Icari,' he whispers. 'You don't need me – you just need the wings.' There's a wet catch in his voice, forged from tears and blood. 'Fly to the centre of the Bone desert and you will find a crag of brilliant orange—'

The General boots him in the stomach. 'Do I need to cut out your tongue, Samael?'

I'm about to object, to yell and claw, when a familiar voice cuts through my rage.

'Wings?' Uriel sweeps into the room, his robes catching in the light of the feathers. He seems far more interested in the wings than in Caszeil or me, and he kneels beside them with an expression of awe and something else that I can't place. Envy, perhaps?

He looks at Caszeil. 'So you fancied yourself some new wings – is that right, demon?'

Caszeil nods. 'Maybe you should try it.'

Uriel responds with a brutal kick, perfectly aimed at Caszeil's face. His head snaps to the side and an arc of silver blood sprays from his temple; then every taut muscle seems to droop as he falls unconscious.

'No!' I shout.

The General places a blade to my throat and breathes into

my ear. 'That's what you get when you fuck a demon.'

The word 'fuck' is as brutal as a boot, for what Caszeil and I have has only ever been gentle and loving. I begin to cry, great heaving sobs that hurt my body and threaten to split my ribs.

Uriel wipes his boot against the ground, leaving a smear of silver. 'Take the beast to the dungeons.'

'He is not a beast,' I say, my voice ripping as I struggle against the General.

The guards lift Caszeil's slack body and I reach a desperate hand towards him. Pain shoots up my neck, into my head, as the General pushes the blade into my skin. Something warm trickles down my throat. Blood.

'Don't worry,' the General hisses. 'You're coming too.'

'No,' Uriel says. 'Leave the girl with me. I wish to speak with her alone.'

'But—' the General begins.

'Go.'

The General nicks my skin one last time, then follows the guards from the room. I catch one final glimpse of Caszeil's sleeping face, his gleaming skin, before he slips from view. It feels like my insides have been removed.

Lying on the ground, holding my throat and marvelling at how hot my own blood is, I glance around the Tomb of Light. The dead Illios sleep on. Uriel observes the wings on the floor, then reaches behind his neck, rubbing the old injury as I've seen him do many times before. Suddenly, it makes sense why Caszeil taunted him about growing wings, and why Uriel then kicked him into silence: Caszeil knew Uriel's secret.

'You're an Illios?' I say, before I can stop myself.

Uriel smiles a thin smile. 'Well done, Icari.' He turns away from me and pulls down his robe. The nubs have been filed right down, but other than that, they are the same as Caszeil's and still form a heart shape.

'Why?' I ask.

'The Illios needed someone they could trust in the citadel.'

'You're a spy?'

He doesn't answer. Instead, he passes me a kerchief and gestures to the wound on my neck. 'Apply some pressure and you'll be fine.'

I use the kerchief to mop my face and instead press my fingers to the cut, allowing my own Calling to seal my flesh, all the while my head spinning with this new information.

'Did Mama know?'

Is that why he killed her? To keep his identity hidden?

'Of course not,' he said. 'Although our romance helped me to maintain my cover.'

Anger grows in my chest, and I want to shout in his face that my mother was so much more than a cover, yet I'm so shattered by the sight of Caszeil being carried away, so broken by the sight of our beautiful wings, strewn on the ground like a couple of wounded soldiers, that the words don't arrive.

He smirks. 'Speaking of romance, what did the demon promise you to entice you into helping him? Were you lying with him? Or did he offer you riches? An eternal life of opulence in the Underworld?'

I throw the kerchief at his feet, a small act of defiance.

'He said he'd take me to Sephie.'

His eyes narrow. 'What?'

'He said he'd fly me to the Underworld so we could rescue Sephie.'

After a stunned pause, a deep laugh rolls from his lips. 'And you believed him?'

'Yes.'

'How could you be so naive? He was just using you to escape.'

'That isn't true. Just now, he told me how to reach the Underworld without him. He *wants* to help Sephie.' Tears heat my eyes. 'He wants to help me.'

'And what use is knowing the location of the Under-world if there's nobody to fly you there?'

I stare at the wings, Caszeil's words echoing in my head: *'It is you who must wear them.'*

'Caszeil thought . . .' I tail off. I can't bring myself to say it and have the man who ordered my mother's death mock me, so instead I say, 'Can you ask the Illios to fly me there? You're one of them – surely they'll listen to you.'

'Only the Samael can enter the Underworld. That's why we never tried to help. We couldn't.'

It takes a moment to make sense of what he's saying. 'So you *knew* Sephie was in the Underworld all this time?'

'When her body wasn't found, I feared as much, yes.'

'Did you know . . . ?' I don't know how much informa-tion to reveal. I trust Uriel no more than I trust Ziris and the General; the fact he is an Illios does not change this, not any more. Good and evil are not night and day. They are a braid. Yet he is my last chance, my *only* chance to save Sephie and

Caszeil, so I blurt it out regardless. 'Did you know Aïdes intends to marry her?'

Very slowly, he nods.

A wave of fury pushes salt into my eyes and steals my breath. 'All this time, you knew? And you did *nothing*? No wonder Caszeil wanted me to wear the wings – he knew there was no other way.'

His deep laugh rolls around the glass panes of the Tomb of Light. 'The demon wanted *you* to wear the wings?'

'Yes.' My spine straightens with indignation.

'A woman with wings. Never have I heard such nonsense.'

It is one thing for *me* to think this, but for a man who has done nothing but control and punish the very women he should have protected – it makes my skin crawl.

'Why can't a woman grow wings?' I say, my voice firm. 'We can grow actual humans in our bellies – why not wings? We can grow ideas and love and gifts and strength – why not wings?' I think of Mama on the pyre, of Sephie carried away by demons, and the anger shakes my whole body like a tree in a gale. 'You would rather see us whipped and burnt than see us fly. Is that it?'

'Enough!' He exhales slowly and closes his eyes. 'Icari. I didn't want to kill your mama. It was a necessity. And I don't want to kill you. There will be a trial, for what you have done is punishable by death.' He leans towards me, dropping his voice low. 'You must say that the demon enchanted you.'

I glare at him, wishing I had a weapon or the savage nature to strike him down.

'Icari.' He takes me by the shoulders. 'The trial. You must say the demon enchanted you.'

His words gradually filter into my consciousness.

'I will say nothing of the sort,' I reply, even though it's what Caszeil told me to say too.

He sighs. 'Then you will die.'

As he turns to leave, his gaze lands on the wings. The Illios feathers have once again blackened and curled.

'What's happened to the feathers?' he asks.

'The Illios feathers spoilt when they were mounted upon Caszeil's back.'

'But they were gold. When I first arrived, I could have sworn they were gold. Why have they faded so quickly?'

I shrug, too exhausted to make sense of it. 'I healed them when I touched them. I suppose it doesn't last long.'

He doesn't reply for a moment; then, very quietly, he says, 'I really didn't want to kill her, Icari.'

The need to know about Mama surges inside. I'm about to ask him more – why he killed her if he didn't want to. And most importantly, is it somehow linked to what happened to Sephie? But I'm silenced by the beat of the executioner's drum. A relentless, rhythmic thud like that of a heart. A heart soon to stop.

A sad smile touches his mouth. 'Come. It is time to see your demon again.'

44

ICARI

The first rays of dawn slide in from the east as I'm marched across the Court of Ash towards the Sun Temple. The guards have worked fast, for a trial is nothing without an audience, and a crowd has already gathered: students, orderlies, guards. A sea of judging eyes.

Caszeil kneels on the steps of the Sun Temple, surrounded by soldiers. His ankles and wrists are still chained, and the point of a spear forces his head to bow as if in worship. They are mocking him, strong-arming him into revering the sworn enemy of his own father, yet I'm grateful for the wedge of shadow gifted by the tower of marble, for I know how Caszeil would hate to smoulder and writhe before those who draw so much pleasure in his suffering.

I'm forced to my knees beside him. I can feel the coldness from his skin, and the urge to rest my hand on him is overpowering. Yet the way he refrains from acknowledging my presence – not even a flick of his grey eyes in my direction – suggests he's still trying to save me in all this. For a girl who is greeted by a demon is a girl destined to decorate a spike.

'Are you ready to die, Healer?' It is the hiss of a familiar snake.

I turn to see the General. Of course it is he who holds the spear against Caszeil's head. Any excuse to inflict pain.

Uriel strides before us on to the grand steps, Madame Embalmer and Principal Healer close behind. Madame Embalmer looks stronger, and her sympathetic smile suggests she has no knowledge of the devil wing I deposited in her food yesterday. A glimmer of hope lights up the grey. If I explain that Caszeil and I were trying to help Sephie, trying to stop her from being forced to marry Aïdes, then surely Madame will persuade Uriel to show mercy.

'Madame, please listen—' Yet before I can get any more words out, a dirty rag is stuffed in my mouth by a guard.

'First, the demon.' Uriel's tone tells me there will be no mercy.

The General eases back the spear so Caszeil can lift his head, meeting the High Priest's gaze. It is the first time I've seen him in natural light and it is quite magical; pockets of healed skin catch like silver coins – hard to think my hands rested there only hours ago. I try to engrave the image of him on to my brain. His strong profile, the darkness of his lashes, the fuzz of his golden hair, regrowing since I cradled his head with my healing hands.

Uriel addresses Caszeil with a note of grandeur in his voice. 'Demon, your sentencing is at dawn, your execution at sundown. Blessings be to Father Sun and Mother Moon. Now is your chance to tell us how and why Icari, daughter of Giorgos, assisted your escape. The more you tell us, the less painful your death.'

I notice he uses Papa's name instead of Mama's, perhaps attempting to distance me from Daeda, the slaughtered witch. Is he trying to help me?

'Speak now, demon,' he says.

No matter how sharp their spears, the soldiers cannot make Caszeil's voice bow to Uriel, and it fills the courtyard like a rebellious glass bird. 'Principal Healer, you sent Icari to the dungeons on her first day to fetch a cadaver, is this correct?'

'Why, yes, I did,' she replies.

'That was when I first met her, when I bewitched her. It was not hard, for she is young and impressionable.'

I know him well enough to recognize the hidden smile in his words. Even now, he gently teases me.

'Since that day,' he continues, 'I have used the Divine Shadow to control her, forcing her to do my bidding and aid my escape.'

The General sneers. 'She does not seem bewitched.'

Caszeil keeps his gaze upon Uriel. 'The Divine Shadow is artful and cunning, hiding his true self from even experienced Alchemists like yourself, High Priest. And you know all about hiding true selves, don't you?'

'Watch your tone,' Uriel replies. 'For deaths can be quick, or they can be prolonged.'

'For centuries, I believe,' Caszeil says, and I will him to fall silent, not wanting his suffering drawn out.

Uriel's gaze slips to me. 'Can anyone else testify that Icari was indeed bewitched?'

'I can.'

A voice from the crowd.

I turn to see Talia. Father Sun bless that brave fire-viper-haired witch, for she looks more fearsome, more determined, than any god I've ever seen.

Her mouth sets in a courageous line and her nightgown billows in the breeze. 'As you know, I share a bedchamber with Icari. I noticed a change in her after her first day training. She was staring into space a lot, sleeping with her eyes open. Classic signs of bewitchment, I believe.'

'And why did you fail to report these signs?' Uriel says.

Talia does not falter. 'I thought she missed her papa. Then when her sister was taken, well, I just assumed she was in shock, mourning. Now it all makes sense. The Icari I met after the Illumination Ritual would never have aided a demon, I'm sure of it.'

Another voice cuts through the air. 'My lord, nothing this sorceress from the Farlands says can be trusted.'

Ziris.

My heart grinds to a halt in my chest.

He steps from the crowd and narrows his eyes. 'Last night, I discovered the witch helping Icari carry *Illios* wings through the catacombs.'

A collective inhalation of breath fills the courtyard.

'That is untrue,' Talia shouts. She is more adept at lying than me, and her nostrils flare with indignation. 'Ziris hates me. Everyone knows that.'

'Did anyone else witness Talia assisting Icari?' Uriel asks.

'No—' Ziris begins.

'And why didn't you report this immediately?' Uriel says, his brow raised.

'Because . . .' His voice peters out as he considers admitting he spent the night locked in a crypt with a wound inflicted by Talia and a skull. His ego clearly wins and he lowers his eyes. 'I don't know, my lord.'

'Perhaps we focus on Icari for now,' Uriel says, his voice even.

Ziris glares at me. 'Let me tell you about Icari. I saw her with the demon in the Sun Temple. It was I who raised the alarm. Not only was she helping the Samael – she seemed . . . If you please, my lord, I cannot bring myself to say it.'

'You are safe to speak,' Uriel says.

He takes a deep breath, as if he's about to utter something truly profane. 'She didn't seem bewitched. She seemed a little in love with him.'

Caszeil forgets he is not supposed to look at me. His grey eyes meet mine. They are filled with hope and possibilities. And in spite of his impending doom, the corner of his lips – now a deep rose pink in the sunrise – twitch into a smile.

Uriel looks at me. 'It is your chance to speak now, Icari. Were you bewitched by this demon, or were you acting on your own free will?'

The rag is pulled from my mouth and I keep staring at Caszeil, hungry to memorize the exact shade of his eyes in the pale morning light.

His brow furrows, and his eyes widen as he silently wills me to say I was bewitched. And it is tempting, for speaking the truth will lead to beheading and cremation; not only does fear of death consume me, but nobody will save my sister once I am gone. Yet without Caszeil, I cannot reach her anyway, and perhaps life without Caszeil, life without Sephie, is no life at all. Perhaps, for once, I should go down fighting.

I take a deep breath and level my eyes at the crest of Father Sun on the peak of the temple. If it is my last breath, it will at least be an honest breath.

'Caszeil is no monster—'

A strong voice cuts over me. Feminine and self-assured. 'My lord, I can vouch that Icari was bewitched.' Madame Embalmer offers me a reassuring smile. 'Icari has been tending to me, and in hindsight, the signs of enchantment were clear. I believe her own testimony to be worthless, so deep does the Samael's magic run.'

I gawp at her. Is she helping me because I healed her, because she liked Sephie, or simply because she couldn't save Mama?

Uriel nods. 'Very well. A moment, please.'

The High Priest, Principal Healer and Madame Embalmer confer in hushed whispers for a short moment, their gaze moving between me and Caszeil. Then Uriel turns to address the crowd.

'The demon shall be executed at sundown, and, Icari, you will be held in the dungeons until the monster is dead.'

Madame rests a hand on his arm. 'High Priest, if you don't mind me asking – why the dungeons? If she was bewitched, then she is a victim in all of this too.'

'Why doesn't she go home?' Principal Healer says in her usual pragmatic tone. 'I'm happy to return her to the care of her father.'

Madame Embalmer nods. 'Far more appropriate for a young girl who has been toyed with so.'

The urge to tell them I wasn't toyed with, that I knew exactly what I was doing, that Uriel and the General are the monsters, not Caszeil, scrambles up my throat. But I am silenced by Uriel's firm voice.

'Then it is decided. The demon shall be executed at sunset, and Içari shall be returned to the care of her father.'

I should be relieved, grateful even, for I have been spared the sight of another person I care for destroyed on the pyre, but instead I feel trapped. Like I'm stuck in the pause between two consecutive heartbeats, awaiting the inevitable with dread and the knowledge I can do nothing to stop it happening.

Caszeil will die. Sephie will marry the devil. And all I can do is wait.

'The show is over,' the General roars. 'Everyone clear out now.'

'Caszeil,' I whisper.

Arrowheads level at his golden crown, cruel hands grip at his silver-coin skin, but as he's hauled to his feet, he meets my eye. '*A little in love?*' he whispers.

And I don't care who hears, so long as he does, so long as he knows before he dies.

'Just a little,' I say.

And then he is gone.

45

SEPHIE

I wake with a gasp. At some point, whilst pretending to sleep, I must have fallen asleep for real.

I'm lying on a soft mattress stuffed with mosses and wool. A fur pelt is wrapped around my shoulders. Aïdes was right. My chambers are warm and comfortable. Hangings of opulent colours decorate the frosted walls, and woven rugs the colour of rubies cover the hard, cold floor so I can walk without fear of frostbite.

I'm suddenly aware of what woke me: the butcher's hook in my stomach, even stronger than the hunger. Something is wrong with Icari. She's distressed, beyond distressed. She hasn't felt this upset since Mama was burnt. I rub my eyes, anxiety about my sister's welfare and my own situation combining to form a noxious mess. It's not like I can do anything to help her stuck down here. Besides, we left things so badly, I don't know if she'd accept my help even if I could offer it.

I cross to the mirror mounted on the wall and gasp. I barely recognize my reflection. Black marks hang beneath my eyes, my olive skin looks waxy, and my lips are so cracked they would make the Redland desert proud.

I have to get out of here.

I remember the door with the interlocking golden bands. The door that hides the temple and maybe . . . just maybe . . . an escape route. It was only a short distance from my chambers – two straight lines and only one bend. It will be easy to find. All I need to do is slip past the guards.

The door to my chambers opens. I spin around as if caught in the act.

'My lady, you're awake.' The Divine Shadow enters the room. His pristine bare feet barely dent the rugs as he crosses towards me.

I try not to recoil.

'How did you sleep?' he asks, his voice mild. 'You look refreshed, if I may say so.'

I look like crap, we both know this, but instead I say, 'Thank you, my lord.'

You see, the Divine Shadow thinks I ate enough devil wing to knock out a small army last night. If I tell him where to shove his niceties, he'll know I'm faking.

'Breakfast will be served shortly,' he says, stroking a glacial finger down my cheek. 'But I thought first you may wish to dress.' He crosses to the large wooden wardrobe opposite the bed and flings open the door to reveal a row of gowns, each one a different shade of red.

'What do you think?' He beckons me over.

Light-headed, unsteady on my feet, I cross to him. Velvet, silk, gossamer. Each frock trimmed or shot through with gold-and-silver thread. In any other circumstance, I would rejoice, but right now, all I can think about is food. Strawberries, red wine, cherries, undercooked beef. If I could eat these gowns, I would.

'Beautiful,' I mutter.

'Why don't you pick one out?'

Without thought, I grab the nearest dress, the colour of roasted beetroot.

'Perfect,' he says, smiling.

I pause, waiting for him to leave, and when he doesn't, I say, 'A little privacy, please?'

'Really, my lady? We are to be wed. Your body will be mine, and mine yours.'

'We are not wed yet.' It is as outspoken as I dare, considering I'm supposed to be doped.

He seems to consider this, his frosted skin catching in the torchlight, his perfectly symmetrical features creasing slightly. 'As you wish, my lady.'

He leaves me to unpeel my embalmer's gown, caked with blood and grime, and to pull on the beetroot robe. My hands shake and I'm so weak I fear I will simply topple, caught up in the red material like mince in a sausage skin. Yet somehow, I manage to wriggle inside. I feel ridiculous. Dirty, blood-encrusted, consumed by thirst and hunger, yet draped in lavish cloth. I'm a pig with a sceptre. A turd in a tiara.

I slump on the bed and cry without tears. I guess living mummies have no liquid to secrete. Will I really be able to resist Aïdes's offerings again? I visualize that chalice brimming with pomegranate juice and my head reels with longing.

You must resist, Sephie, a voice whispers. But it isn't my voice. It's Icari's, Papa's and Talia's. It may even be Mama's.

Everyone I've ever loved woven together into a lullaby.

You must resist, Sephie. You must.

The Samael arrive shortly after, carrying sweet-smelling platters of honeyed fruits and roasted puddings. I expect my mouth to well with saliva, but of course, there is only sand and grit and a hundred brutal summers. Next, Aïdes enters the room, the bronze chalice gripped between his hands. The scent of squeezed pomegranates turns me into a ravenous wolf who longs to howl and pant and drink and drink until I'm no more than a sleeping lamb.

Stay strong, Sephie.

He looks me up and down. 'My lady, you look quite lovely. Ready for a banquet.'

'Yes.' It is the first honest thing I've said to him since waking.

I run the scenario through my mind. Aïdes will sit and I'll pretend to drink and eat. Then, as soon as he leaves, I'll scurry around the room concealing the evidence. But instead of sitting, the Divine Shadow places the chalice on the wooden dresser, smiles, and moves towards the door.

'You are leaving?' I immediately regret the question. I sound too hopeful, too eager.

Yet he simply smiles. 'I'm afraid so. There are preparations to be made.'

'Preparations?'

'Our wedding, my lady.' He presses his palms together. 'It will be a grand affair.'

Friends, this may sound foolish, but with all the horror and famine and general distress, I hadn't even considered *when* the wedding might occur.

'Is it . . . ?' I stumble on my words, scared of the answer, my lips too wizened to move. 'Is it soon?'

'Why, yes, my lady. If everything goes as planned, we shall be wed first thing tomorrow.'

46

SEPHIE

Tomorrow. The word is a noose. I've got less than a day to find a way out. But my chambers are always guarded by those silver turkeys. I rub my face, suppressing a scream. I need to be smart. Not Sephie-quick, or Sephie-strong, but Icari-smart. I need to watch, observe and learn. Which means absolutely no devil wing. There may be an opportunity when the guards swap shifts, or sleep, or whatever it is they do, to slip from my chambers and find the temple.

I risk dipping my finger in the pomegranate juice and moistening my lips. The dull tingle immediately alerts me to the presence of devil wing. I take a slice of melon and dab it to my tongue. Devil wing.

Curses.

Hiding half the contents of the platter around the room and tipping the juice between the cracks in the stone floor is one of the hardest things I've ever had to do. Then I curl in a ball on the bed and feign sleep, trembling all over from the unquenched need.

After a while, the door opens again and I force my eyes to remain closed.

'She must have been hungry,' says a Samael whose voice

I don't recognize.

'Indeed.' This voice belongs to Aïdes.

'Shall I move her, my lord?' It is the Samael with the plaited mane and white eyelashes.

'If you please,' Aïdes replies.

I expect to be lifted again, but instead cool hands grip my ankles and my wrists, and ever so carefully, I'm stretched out and rolled on to my back. I let my limbs flop, which is easier than it sounds, for I am fast approaching unconsciousness. Maybe even death. Only the adrenaline keeps me awake.

A cold finger presses something to my forehead, a piece of string perhaps, then trails down my throat, between my breasts, over my most intimate parts, right down to my toes. I lie, corpse-like, imagining I am somewhere else entirely. Swimming in the Nubi river with Icari, playing sword-fights with Ruari, sharing stories with Talia. My memories are the only thing that stop me from lashing out and bolting from the room.

Another finger presses against my shoulder and runs all the way down my arm, stopping when it reaches my wrist.

What are they doing to me?

My skirt is lifted, hoisted right up to my navel so that my legs and undergarments are on display. I try not to cry out, focusing on the details of Talia's smile in my mind's eye, pretending she doesn't have a betrothed and the locket she wears around her neck is from me. My legs are parted and I repress a whimper. *No, no, no.* A finger of ice presses against the top of my inner thigh, before moving down my thigh, my calf, my ankle.

That's when I realize what they are doing.

They are measuring me.

'I want the dress to be perfect,' Aïdes says, as frosted hands loop my waist.

'Yes, my lord.'

'White, of course, with gold-and-silver embroidery.'

'Yes, my lord.'

Hands slide beneath my buttocks and the string is wrapped around my hips. I want to slap their hands away and bite at their faces. But I must stay strong. I must convince them I am drugged. Harmless. No need to guard me. No need at all.

'Like the others?' a Samael asks.

'Yes,' the Divine Shadow replies. 'Like the others.'

What others? I try to think through the fog of thirst and fear, but my thoughts fall apart as soon as they come together.

Finally, the Samael leave. I'm about to open my eyes when something cold and soft presses against my forehead.

Somebody's lips.

'Sleep tight, sweet Sephie.'

It's Aïdes.

The door clicks shut, but I don't open my eyes for a very long time.

47

ICARI

Papa is as delighted as he is surprised to see me. We eat bread dipped in oils and drink tea sitting at the same rickety table we used to sit at with Mama and Sephie, and I tell him everything that has happened since the Illumination Ritual. Of course, he already knew Sephie had been stolen by demons, but he knew nothing of Aïdes's intentions, or my plan to rescue her. And I leave out the part where I fell for a demon. Papa's heart is weak, after all.

When I finish, he simply pulls me into his arms and, resting his chin on my head, says, 'My brave, brave girl.' His tears dot my crown.

'Why must I lose everyone I love,' I whisper into his tunic. 'First Mama, then Sephie.' *And Caszeil*, I think to myself.

'I don't know, dear-heart,' he says, his words choked. 'I just don't know.'

After tidying the plates, we head to the courtyard; it was Mama and Sephie's favourite place, so we're naturally drawn to it. Sitting side by side on the bench in the late afternoon sun, we take in the flowers. Jasmine, delphiniums, larkspur and Mama's favourite: roses. They're still plump with Sephie's magic and I recall her transmuting them with a smile.

'Papa?'

'Yes, dear-heart?'

'Why didn't you tell me that Mama and Uriel were romantically involved?'

It seems so foolish to chase this mystery now that Sephie is about to marry the devil and Caszeil is about to die – surely I have bigger things to worry about. And yet, I can't fight the feeling that understanding why Mama was executed will shed some light on Sephie's predicament.

'It was a long time ago,' he replies, a little cagey.

I sigh. 'The guard in the dungeon said that nobody's ever been killed for trading devil wing. So I thought maybe Uriel was threatened by her dual gifts. Then I wondered if he killed her because she rejected him. But then Sephie was stolen, and she is so like Mama, and I –' my voice wavers – 'I can't help thinking it's all connected somehow.'

Papa studies my face. The sounds of the helpers tending to the patients and preparing supper drift through the sanatorium windows, and the sky sits above us like a slick of powder-blue paint.

'Your mother didn't reject Uriel, Icari,' he eventually says. 'Uriel rejected her. She was broken-hearted when we first met. Whatever Uriel's motives, they were not fuelled by revenge.'

This new information both surprises and unnerves me. Uriel rejected Mama.

Papa squeezes my hand. 'Sometimes the simplest explanations are the right explanations.'

'You think it really was about the devil wing?'

He shrugs, though it is one of weariness rather than nonchalance.

He folds me into his arms again and I hold the many words I wish to speak about Caszeil somewhere at the base of my throat, where they swell and hurt and make it hard to breathe. His execution is at sundown, and a quick glance at the sky tells me Father Sun is already sinking. The thought of his death is unbearable and a strange urge to scratch myself creeps up on me. I'm like a dog with fleas, a child rolling in a rosehip shrub; if I can scratch and scratch, perhaps I can reach the anguish that sits just beneath my skin and extract it with my nails. I settle on rubbing my arms. Hard.

'Icari?' Papa says, concerned. 'Are you OK?'

'Yes, Papa. I'm just worried about Sephie.'

If only I'd worn the wings like Caszeil told me to. If only I'd been brave enough to push them to my back and try, maybe now I'd be soaring towards Sephie with Caszeil in my arms, instead of sitting here, itching with invisible ants, knowing that Sephie and Caszeil are lost to me.

Just then, Ruari barrels into the courtyard, knocking the jasmine as he passes with his muddy calves and setting the white buds nodding.

'Icari, Icari, I thought I saw you arriving, but Papa said I had to give you some time with Giorgos.'

I sweep him into a hug. 'Oh, Ruari, you have grown.'

He looks up at me, his nose wrinkled. 'You've only been gone a week.'

'Well, it feels like a lifetime,' I say, wiping my tears with a shaking hand.

Leon follows, the worry evident on his face. 'Am I right in thinking Principal Healer and some city guards brought you home, Icari?'

'You are,' I say.

'Icari is in an unusual situation,' Papa offers, glancing at the windows leading to the sanatorium and the possible eavesdroppers beyond. 'Let's head back to the hut. We've got tea and there's some bread left. It will only spoil in this heat.'

Once I've told my story again, Leon releases a hiss of air. 'And you said it was Madame who saved you?' he asks.

I nod.

'She always had a kind heart.'

Ruari, who's been playing outside, rushes to the door, his face alight with excitement.

'Icari, Icari, there is a man here to see you and he's wearing fancy gowns.'

Confused, nervous, I exit the hut. I see his shadow first, lengthened by the position of Father Sun. His gowns turn him into a shapeless block, but the headdress is unmistakable.

'I think these belong to you,' he says.

Blinking away the dust, I look up.

It's Uriel.

He's standing next to a horse and cart. And beside his feet, stretched out in all their glory, are the wings.

48

ICARI

He's transmuted the blackened Illios feathers back to gold so the wings are a sweep of yellows and whites, far shinier than Uriel's gowns, yet so at home amidst the sand and the shrubs, they resemble an exquisite tropical flower that refused to stop growing. And inside every gold or white vein is my sister – the hope of rescuing her, the promise of a life together. Yet even more present than Sephie is Caszeil, for we forged these wings together – forged them from sweat and determination and, above all else, love. The memory of his form bent beside me, dropping melted wax around quill ends, fills every part of me, and tears course down my cheeks.

I drag my gaze from the wings to Uriel.

'Thank you,' I manage to whisper.

He nods, then, in a clatter of hoofs, vanishes into the undergrowth.

The leaves and boughs and sand eventually settle and the oasis returns to normal. The bleats of the nearby herd mix with the song of the munia bird and the buzz of the dragon-fly. Then I realize Leon, Papa and Ruari are at my side, astonishment plunging even Ruari into silence.

'Icari,' Papa finally says. 'Are these the wings you built

with the demon?' He approaches them like they might fly away of their own accord if startled.

'Yes,' I reply.

Leon rubs his face. 'Why would Uriel bring them to you?'

'Caszeil couldn't wear them because they are part Illios. But he thought maybe I could. I think Uriel wants me to save Sephie.'

'You can't wear wings, silly bean,' Ruari says, skipping around them. 'They're not a cloak. They'd just fall off.'

'Not wear them,' I say. '*Grow them*.' The words sound ridiculous spoken out loud, the entire oasis and Father Sun as my witness.

Leon snorts. 'Grow wings? Surely that's a physical impossibility.' He touches the tip of a golden plume as if it might burn him.

'Caszeil didn't think so,' I reply.

'Caszeil is a demon,' Papa says.

Leon circles the wings, his face filled with awe and disapproval. 'Not only is it impossible, Icari — it is blasphemy.'

Ruari bounces between his feet and takes his father's hand. 'You're wrong, Papa. It isn't naughty to help someone. Father Sun would want Icari to save Sephie.'

Papa squats down and studies the feathers. 'And these came from actual gods?'

I nod. 'Gods and demons.'

He kisses his teeth, before resting the flat of his palm against a golden plume. There's a pause, as if he expects something to happen, and when nothing does, he laughs and looks at me. 'I don't suppose it would hurt to try.'

He reminds me of Sephie so much, it hurts.

'Georgios,' Leon says, part exasperated, part impressed. 'You cannot mean it.'

Papa shrugs. 'Why not. Because she's a woman?'

'Because she's mortal,' Leon replies.

'Demons are mortal, technically,' Papa says.

Leon sighs, his breath whistling between his teeth. 'Human, then.'

'Icari?' Papa says. 'What do you think?'

I think of Mama on the pyre, of Sephie tied to the whipping post, of the river clay that filled my feet and pinned me to the ground so I was powerless and insufficient. Then I think of Caszeil, of his courage to grow in the face of suffering and hate, and the faith he has in me. I replay his words just before he was dragged to his trial: *Icari, these wings are yours.*

'I need to at least try,' I say, my voice surprisingly strong.

Ruari jumps up and down, disturbing the sand. 'You're going to fly, Icari. Like a bug.' He extends his arms so they resemble wings and zooms around the treeline, making a buzzing noise like a bee.

Papa's expression grows serious. 'Well OK then – why wait?' Gently, he turns me so I face away from him. 'I'm going to rip your dress, Icari, just so the wings can rest against your back.'

A combination of excitement and fear turns my tongue into a sheet of papyrus that I'm unable to unpeel from the roof of my mouth.

Papa carefully tears the back of my gown and the humid air hits the skin between my shoulder blades. He then returns to the wings and braces to lift.

Leon rushes to his aid.

My muscles thrum, anticipating the weight of the wings on my back.

The sound of feathers trailing across earth and Papa's and Leon's heavy breaths find me; then the knot of the giant wing joint rests against my spine, cool and hard. My ears ring with excitement and anxiety. Every one of my muscles is tense and coiled.

'Do you feel anything?' Papa asks.

I shake my head, tears of despair and disappointment spilling down my face. 'Nothing, just bone.'

'Oh, Icari, I'm so sorry, dear-heart,' Papa says.

But I never get to reply; a scream bursts from my lungs and a pain shoots through my upper back, as sharp and true as if someone had planted a spear between my shoulder blades. I scream again, arching my body, scrabbling at the air before me. The spear twists, sinking deeper and deeper, slicing downwards and outwards and stretching the wound.

'Make it stop,' I cry as I drop to my knees.

Papa is beside me, his hands on my face. I hear his voice, though it sounds like he shouts through water. 'It is working, Icari.'

I reach behind, pawing desperately at the pain, trying to locate the blade, but my fingers bump against bone and feathers alone.

I drop to all fours, panting and heaving as the pain pulses through me and reaches my spine. The agony builds, travelling both towards my skull and my sternum. Red droplets fall on the ground before me.

My arms can no longer take my weight and I collapse

belly-down on the soil. Pain blazes around my ribcage, a crushing sensation. I can no longer breathe.

Papa attempts to comfort me, but his features smudge together, his voice warps into a high-pitched drone. I am about to pass out. My skin is no longer skin, but a sheen of venom. My limbs have surely been ripped away by an army of demons. And my heart . . . my heart has already fallen to the Underworld, dipped in fear and darkness.

I writhe and twist and scream, praying to Father Sun that I will die.

And then it stops.

Papa's voice sounds in my ear. 'Icari? Icari?'

My skin turns back to skin. I can feel the earth beneath my belly and feathers on my back. My limbs and my heart have returned to me. I am alive. I try to speak but instead simply cough.

Papa scoops me into his arms. 'Icari, I thought we'd lost you.'

The Calling has never felt so strong in my veins. Yet it is both hot and cold, pulsing through me, making me feel more alive than ever before.

Leon laughs the breathy laugh of relief. 'Can you stand?'

'I will try.'

I peer behind me, denial and shock balling in my stomach. The wing bones – no longer visible beneath a fresh layer of golden plumage – arch skywards, hung with a sheet of glowing feathers that trail to the ground. I gasp, tensing a muscle I did not know I had. *The wings move.* They no longer weigh me down – rather, they feel natural, buoyant, as though they are part of me.

'Papa?' I whisper.

His face fills with wonder. 'You have grown wings, Icari.'
He throws his hands to the skies, laughing. 'Praise Father
Sun, you have grown wings.'

With a flick of my upper back, I open my wings like a
glorious, shining bloom.

49

ICARI

Papa runs a hand along my left wing bone as if he's rubbing down Sabu. I feel every indentation on his fingertips, the slightest snag in his nails; it makes me gasp.

'Astonishing,' Papa says as he parts my longest quill from the rest, examining the join, which I created with wax and gum only last night. He laughs in disbelief. 'The wax and gum are no longer needed – the feathers have melded into the wing bone just as the wing bones have melded into you.'

'Caszeil said they would recognize me as their master because I have both Mother Moon and Father Sun in my blood.'

I stretch my wings so they reach high above me, casting a halo of gold-and-silvery light around my form in spite of the evening sun. They are so beautiful. And yet, I am not a god. An invisible hand snatches at my throat, stopping the air in my lungs and filling me with panic. 'Can I take them off?'

Leon touches the place where the wings blend into my skin. 'These are not coming off, not without a sword. They are part of you.'

That invisible hand moves to my chest, squeezing my heart and pushing out tears. Never had I even considered a permanent transformation. I was impulsive, rash, thinking only of Sephie.

'Oh, Papa, what will I do?'

Yet Papa simply smiles, takes me by the hand and pulls me towards the Redland desert.

'Right now, Icari, you need to fly.'

As Papa leads me through the sand, Leon and Ruari close behind, I feel every grain shifting, rolling, brushing against the feather tips. It is as though I have an extra pair of limbs with skin so fine, they can detect the movement of a locust wing.

Soon, we find a dune, and I stand on the crest, my toes instinctively curling in their sandals. I look down the vertical ledge only a finger's-breadth from my feet. My head spins, even as my wings open without my permission, sensing the drop and longing to spread. I can almost hear them whispering, *We can do this, Icari.*

My body slicks with sweat. My heart drums so hard, I fear it will rouse every wild dog asleep beneath their stones, and yet I have never felt this alive.

And without another thought, I launch into the sky.

I leave the ledge far behind, thrusting forward so that the wind hits my face and the desert streams below. I should feel terrified, but my wings know what to do, forming a crescent shape so I can feel the lift of the cold desert air pushing me up, up, up. The evening thunders past my ears and I can hardly catch my breath, but my wings feel like they're on fire, screaming with joy.

'Beat your wings,' Papa shouts.

I do just that. Driving them downwards, the quills

instinctively sealing together and hardening into a shield, then releasing them upwards, the feathers separating, rotating, allowing the passage of air. I immediately gain height. It is as though my body fills with light – I feel weightless, part of the sky. A cry of joy escapes my lips and I angle my body upwards, belting my wings as hard as I'm able. The constant whoosh fills my head like the sound of a heart, and soon I am gliding like an arrow towards the sun.

The world changes: my feathers tingle with moisture and the air on my face dampens. I should feel confused, disorientated, but my wings tell me I've reached the clouds, every drop of water hitting my feathers like a hundred icy needle-ends. Mama told me the clouds were made of water. She was right. I ache with cold.

I hover, transfixed, my wings trilling at my side and cutting through the mist. The glow from my feathers illuminates the nearby water droplets; it looks like I'm cocooned in golden rain. Sure enough, pieces of rainbows curve around me, held by the clouds and moving in time to my wings.

Papa, Leon and Ruari are like ants beneath me, and I suddenly long to share my joy. Sensing this, my wings tuck into my sides of their own accord and streamline my body so I hurtle towards the ground. The wind howls in my ears, my quills tremble – blazing with heat and joy – and my eyes are almost forced shut . . . but I can still see the expanse of sand moving closer and closer.

My feathers soon warn me of the fast-approaching ground, sensing the heat of Father Sun as it rises from the sand. For a terrible moment, I think I'm going to smack into the desert and crumple like a moth. Panic immobilizes me.

My limbs stiffen and my body freezes. I open my mouth to scream, but either no voice emerges or I've left it in the clouds. My wings open just as the dust grazes my chest, lifting me away from the dirt and into the air. My stomach lurches and I begin to whoop, my voice reflected back at me from the sand. Then, I glide as close to the ground as I dare and trace the contour of the land; I watch my own shape, a shadow-bird, tracking the surface of the Redlands.

I stop only as I reach Papa, Leon and Ruari, twisting my body upright and planting my feet into solid ground, grateful I still wear my sandals as the desert grinds against my soles. I'm laughing and crying and filled with the love of Father Sun.

'Oh, Papa. That was the most wonderful feeling.'

He wipes a tear from his cheek, the bow of my wings mirrored in his eyes. 'Go, my brave child. Bring Sephie home.'

'I will,' I say. 'But there is something I need to do first.'

50

ICARI

Agile as a cat, I drop to the roof of the Sun Temple and cling to the spire. Have my wings gifted me more than flight? I am stronger, fleet-footed and spry, which is a blessing, for I will need these new skills for what I'm about to do. Pressing my face against the stone tiles – uncomfortably hot from a day's warming beneath Father Sun – I flatten my wings as much as I'm able; the Tomb of Light is nearby, and I hope the glow from my wings will be credited to the dead Illios as the gloaming fades into night.

Caszeil is nowhere to be seen, so I take a moment to breathe and gather my strength. The sight of the crowd fills me with disgust, for the execution of any soul should not be entertainment for the masses. Perhaps Uriel is gifting me the opportunity to swoop in. He brought me the wings, after all, proving himself to be a braid of good and evil, just as Caszeil said.

The night grows strong and my wings sense the stars blooming in the black above me. And it is this simple detail that really drives home the enormity of what has happened to me. I have grown wings. Wings. I can fly like a bird or a dragonfly or a demon. Like a god.

The creak of wooden wheels demands my attention, and a large splint of wood mounted on a low cart, sharpened to a point at the upper end, is manoeuvred into the centre of the crowd by a couple of guards. An impaling stake. My horror ramps up, for I'd imagined a quick beheading, not this disgusting contraption designed for maximum blood and pain.

A platform is carefully positioned above the impaling stake. It's reached by a ladder, up which the prisoner must climb whilst jabbed from beneath with flaming torches and knives, only to be pushed from the top by the guards once he arrives. There is a substantial fall before flesh meets spike. Vomit rises up my throat and tears pulse down my cheeks. Of course they will drop Caszeil from a platform – it is the final insult. *Why don't you fly, wingless demon? Why don't you save yourself?*

Or maybe Uriel is making it easier for me to reach him, a small voice whispers in my head.

As the drumroll builds, Caszeil finally appears.

The guards lead him from around the back of the Night Temple. His skin is baked beyond recognition, smoke curling from his shoulders and the golden sheen of his head stripped back to coals. *The sun pit.* He can barely open his eyes, yet he stands tall, proud, refusing to let his back droop like a thirsty stem.

My chest aches with sympathy, of course it does, yet above all else, I ache with longing . . . Longing to hear his voice, to stare into those eyes. A longing to heal every part of him and to feel our words slot perfectly together.

The guards lead him through the crowd towards the fang

of wood. People spit and throw insults, yet I notice some remain quiet, perhaps wondering who the monster is in all this.

Tightening my grip on the spire, I plan a flight path that best escapes the arrows, then I throw a quick prayer to Father Sun that I will be strong enough to lift Caszeil skywards. I have no weapons, no battle skills – there's no way I can fight the guards if I get this wrong. All I have is my wings, trembling behind me, pulsing with life and power. *We are enough*, they tell me.

A drumroll sputters into life and Caszeil is shoved up the ladder, a spear piercing his legs and feet, chasing him to the top. The General follows, knife gripped between his teeth, mouth set in a sadistic grin.

The crowd falls silent. The drumroll builds. The sight of Caszeil balanced above that giant thorn fills me with a panic I've felt only once before: when my sister was carried away by taloned fingers . . . Yet now *I* am the bird of prey, poised and ready to swoop.

Without warning, Caszeil whirls through the air, twisting around and clasping at the General, before rolling him over his shoulder. In an instant, the vile man is falling. Screaming. The point pierces his back and emerges through his chest. The drums sputter out and the court is filled with the sound of his wails alone. Blood sprays from his mouth like red wine, and slowly, he slips down the widening spike, screaming in agony.

There is nothing anyone can do.

My gut twists.

The General deserves this. So why do I feel sickened by

what Caszeil has done? I drag a fierce hand across my eyes. Caszeil is Samael. He is the enemy. His brothers stole my sister and killed my friends. And this act of brutality proves it. My wings falter along with my resolve.

My hesitation costs Caszeil dearly.

An arrow hits him in the shoulder, then another, and another. His body jerks with each shot. He wavers on the edge of the platform and cries – the sound of a kestrel – then finally buckles. And strong though he is, he cannot overcome gravity. He falls backwards towards the spike.

Caszeil is Samael. He is the enemy. His brothers stole my sister and killed my friends. But this means nothing – *nothing* – now that he's tumbling towards the stake.

My wings respond before I do, clacking open and cata-pulting me over the Court of Ash like a great bird. In less than a heartbeat, I am above him; his body drops towards that hateful blade of wood and my wings fold against my body, pushing me into a nosedive with such force I fear my muscles will rip clean away from my bones. His face twists with horror, he screams my name, and his beautiful hands flail towards me in a final bid to save himself.

Snatching at his wrists, I swoop upwards, plucking him clear of the stake before it can even puncture his skin. I needn't have worried about lifting him, for he feels no heavier than Ruari.

Caszeil releases a whoop of victory, of life, and every vein on my feathers sings with joy as we power into the dome of grey above.

51

ICARI

As we gain height, the spears and roars of the soldiers fade away. Caszeil wraps his limbs around me as if he were a lizard and I the branch. I loop my arms beneath him, pulling him closer – the press of his hot blistered skin cooling against mine is the best thing I've ever felt. I plant a kiss on his cheek.

'You saved me,' he says, pushing his face into my neck, brushing my ear with his lips.

'I did.'

I rescued a Samael. The entire citadel as my witness. I will never be able to return to the citadel, or the Sunlands, yet this realization fills me with surprisingly little dread.

Caszeil holds my gaze. 'Your mama was wrong. You are not a peach – you are a bird.'

I laugh, letting the exhilaration of flight and holding Caszeil lift me even higher.

His face is beneath mine, his grey eyes steadier than the night, his dusty-pink lips no more than a wisp of colour. We smile as we come together for a kiss, for this moment has long been thwarted, its inevitability never presumed, and as our grateful mouths finally connect – Samael against human, cold against hot – I know with absolute certainty that I am in love with a demon.

52

SEPHIE

I have no perception of time as I lie awake, yet watching through the crescent of my half-closed eye and listening to every tiny sound, I start to notice patterns. At regular intervals, the door to my chamber opens, and two guards enter the room. They glance at my apparently slumbering form and then they leave. Two new guards arrive soon after to take up their posts outside my door.

Between two guards leaving and new ones arriving, there's a small window of time.

That's when I'll escape.

It takes a while to hatch my plan, let alone enact it. My brain is sluggish, my movements slow, but eventually, I muster all my strength and manage to select a similar shade frock to my own. Then, I lay it over a log of cushions and cover it with the pelt, ensuring a few flashes of scarlet material poke from beneath the fur. It's an old yet effective trick, one I used to pull on Mama and Papa when I was sneaking out to meet girls or boys at night.

Once the pelt is in place, I stand beside the closed door, back pressed against the wall, and I wait. I'm swaying like washing on the line, my knees replaced by sponges, my head filled with images of water – clear, refreshing, gorgeous water, bubbling over pebbles in a stream, glistening in bottomless lakes, overflowing from ceramic jugs. I can taste it in my aching, shrivelled mouth. Leaning against the rock steadies me, but there is no wall hanging and the frost melts against my back, causing me to shiver all over. I consider licking the walls, I am *that* desperate. But who knows what poison coats this ungodly place.

Eventually, the guards open the door, sandwiching me between the wood and the rock. I hold my breath, count their steps – one, two, three – then slip out of the room whilst they face away from me. Then I'm stumbling down the corridor, my feet suddenly swollen and clumsy, awaiting their cry as they realize the shape under the pelt isn't me. But there is only silence.

I head for the forbidden door – and whatever escape route might lie beyond it.

53

SEPHIE

After dashing through corridors of glittering rock, I find it – the door with the markings, exactly as I remember. I don't hesitate to push it open.

Instantly I realize what lies beyond isn't a temple, as I'd previously thought, but a large mausoleum with pillars, a flat roof and the symbol of Mother Moon and the Divine Shadow painted on the door – a flash of humanity in an elemental world of stone, ice and fire. Disappointment settles in my stomach, thick as river sediment. How will a mausoleum help me escape? And another question nags at me: why are there dead bodies here? Surely mortal flesh remains on the surface whilst the soul alone enters the Underworld.

Climbing the shallow steps leading to the entrance, I take one of the flaming torches from around the door. It feels unusually heavy due to my weakened state, but the heat is a gift against the side of my face.

Breath held, heart spiralling, I step inside.

The mausoleum smells of forgotten places and, faintly, rotting meat. I shudder and the flame dances in my side vision. Stretching away from me are rows upon rows of sarcophagi, each one mounted upon a stone plinth. The only light radiates from my torch and doesn't quite reach the back of the mausoleum, giving the impression that the graves stretch into infinity. Maybe they do.

And something else strikes me. I can sense the dead lying in their stone coffins. I *feel* them. A hundred little hooks in my belly, similar to the connection I have with Icari. Strange. I never felt anything like this when I was in the catacombs back at the citadel, but then, the Underworld has enhanced my Calling, so perhaps this isn't so surprising. How peculiar to be somewhere so peaceful yet to feel like I'm standing in a crowd.

I walk between the sarcophagi, feeling the pull from the nearby corpses and observing their death masks cut from stone. Their ages vary widely, ranging from only just coming of age to old and creased, and some are smiling beauties, whilst others are frogs that chew on handfuls of bees. The only constant is their sex. Every single mask depicts a woman.

Of course, I think with a sad sigh. *Of course the devil has a mass grave filled with women. Even on the surface, women are treated like disposable commodities. Why should the Underworld be any different?*

I let my fingers brush against the stone tombs. Who are these dead women and why are they here? And more importantly, how are they the key to returning to the surface? I approach the sarcophagus nearest the entrance for no other reason than it seems logical, and in a world that makes no sense, a little order is appealing, even for me. I take a second to rest against the stone box because no amount of intrigue can undo the effects of dehydration. The torch trembles as my arm threatens to snap. Shadows leap about the chamber.

The death mask of a young lady, about my age, looks up at me. She has shoulder-length hair, a sweet face, and she reminds me of Xenia. I envision my chamber-mate trapped in the dark gullet of the sarcophagus and a shiver creeps up my spine. The shadowy symbol of the Alchemist is carved into the side of the tomb, suggesting that the girl had the Divine Shadow in her veins just like me.

I deposit the torch in a holder mounted on a nearby wall – I'm going to need both arms for what comes next – and push back the tomb's lid. It takes all of my strength and my muscles burn. A scraping sound fills the chamber like teeth against bone, and dust falls at my feet.

Inside is a skeleton with a dented skull. Clearly no embalming has taken place and my stomach churns at the sight of her – no embalming means her soul has simply ceased to be. So why can I sense her? Is it possible her soul still lingers, trapped inside her bones?

It's impossible to know how long she's been here. She could be centuries old. My fingers thrum with the Divine Shadow and my connection to her grows. I can almost see the invisible cord reaching from her skull to mine, and before I can stop myself, I'm reaching towards her and cupping her head like a fortune-teller holding a glass orb.

In an instant, I'm inside her, overwhelmed by terror, *her* terror, as I relive the memory of her death just like I did with the tailor back at the Grand Crypt. It's fragmented and blurred, as if recalling a dream or a very old memory, yet clear enough for me to recognize the citadel and the Samael flocking overhead like giant birds.

I release her skull with a gasp. She was snatched from the citadel, just like me. And there's only one other time the Samael attacked the citadel: the first battle in the sky. She really is centuries old.

I replace my hand on the skull, sensing there's more to follow. I'm back in the echoes of her mind – it's as though the memory has broken down like her flesh; only the bones of it remain. After she was stolen, the orange earth opened and drank her down, down, down. There was a haze of small fires and sparkling caves and Aïdes's beautiful face. A gold wedding band placed upon her finger. And then there was nothing.

I stumble backwards. My own horror replaces hers, because her story is *exactly* the same as mine. Snatched from the citadel, carried to the Underworld to wed the Divine Shadow. But why did the memory end there? A scared voice whispers in my head, *Maybe that was when she died.*

I feel sick, splintered, yet consumed by the need to know more. Not bothering to replace the lid, I skip a couple of rows, noting that every one of the sarcophagi bears one of the symbols of the Celestial Trio. Every one of these women had the Calling. I slide back the lid of an Embalmer, unveiling another skeleton with her skull caved in. Another invisible cord seems to pull us together, and again, I lay my hands on the smooth bone of her head.

This memory is a little clearer than the last, and I'm able to glean more details about her life and emotions. She was in the oasis watching a young boy pick flowers when a Samael pulled her into the sky. She was a mother, I think. She journeyed across the Redland desert all the while calling the name of the little boy she left behind. Eventually, she reached the crop of orange rock that opened up and sucked her in.

A handsome man with crystal skin awaited her. *Aides.* Then the horror of being ripped from her child disappeared beneath the taste of pomegranate juice and devil wing. She could no longer see the little boy's face when she closed her eyes; she could barely remember his name. But after the ceremony, something wasn't right. Aïdes grew angry. There was shouting. Cursing and raging. He struck her across the cheek with a hand so cold her face shattered. And then there was nothing.

I release her skull tenderly, knowing I would cry if I had the available fluid. Another woman, stolen and taken to hell. Another woman married to Aïdes, and then bereft of memory. I've only read two of the dead, but it's impossible to ignore the emerging pattern.

Quickly, I move towards the back of the mausoleum, heaving back lids and cupping similarly broken skulls. Each time, the story is the same: a woman – Healer, Embalmer or Alchemist – snatched from the Sunlands, forced to marry the devil, then killed following a fit of his rage. The memories grow crisper as I move further away from the entrance, indicating that these women died more recently. Aïdes has been busy snatching and murdering women for *years.*

My horror hardens into rage. But I try to stay calm: there is a mystery here that I need to solve. I don't only want to escape, now; I want to honour these hundreds of women by figuring out why they died. I feel like I owe it to them.

Think, Sephie, think.

I know that the dead women are here because the Samael brought them here. I know that Aïdes married them and killed them. I know they all had a Calling. What I need to find out is *why?*

And even more terrifyingly, is this to be my fate too?

I expect it is.

Balls.

Grabbing the torch, I hurry to the last row. Perhaps the memories of the recently deceased will provide more detail. The women in these graves have teeth and straw-like hair – pieces of skin that hang from their bones like scruffy clothes. I move between them, touching their battered heads.

I was right: these memories are fresher and I'm even able to catch snippets of conversations. After the wedding ceremonies, Aïdes always asks his Samael the same questions: *Is the plan working? Is this woman the bridge I need?* Then the demons reply, *No, my lord.*

Again and again, I watch Aïdes fly into a rage, his beautiful face growing ribbed and cruel, his mellow voice transforming into an axe.

But what does he mean by *bridge*?

The last tombs are all marked with two symbols, and a chill runs down my spine. It's as if Aïdes figured something out . . . or thought he had. Whatever he was trying to get from these women – the *bridge* – he thought dual Callings were more likely to work.

Dual Callings. Like me. Like Mama.

Don't think about Mama.

My heart pauses. My instinct is to shove the thought of her away like I always do, but I find strength from the women around me. The hundred little hooks in my belly make me feel strangely safe. Held. And for the first time since Mama died, I let myself consider what actually happened the day of the burning and why. Could it be that Icari was right all along? Was Mama killed for having two Callings?

Maybe . . . maybe she wasn't killed because people feared or envied her, or because she traded devil wing, but because it meant she was next.

Is that why having two Callings was suddenly forbidden in the Sunlands?

I swallow and pull back a lid marked with the symbols of both the Healer and the Alchemist: Father Sun and a snake of shadow side by side. The corpse has only recently passed, and the stench is overpowering. I retch, my empty stomach desperate to expel something other than gas and pain.

Somehow, I force myself to touch her head.

This memory is as vivid as if it were my own.

She was tending to cattle in the oasis. She liked the cattle because they didn't laugh at her buck teeth or the way she couldn't say her *R*s; it didn't help that her name was Romi and she'd become known in the school yard as Lomi. Romi wasn't even ten and eight; she didn't yet know about her dual gift. She never would. Because that very day, whilst milking her favourite cow, a white demon descended from the clouds, grabbed her around the waist and hoisted her into the sky. Up she sailed like a flag, bending and flailing all the way.

At first, Romi was scared – so scared, she passed out at Aïdes's feet. But the feasts doused in devil wing made it all better. And soon, she came to love the beautiful man who never told her she was ugly or laughed at the way she spoke.

When she walked down the aisle, she felt like the luckiest girl in the world.

Of course, things went sour after the vows. The Aïdes she'd come to love turned into someone unrecognizable and terrifying.

Have you been to the surface? he barked at the congregation of Samael.

Yes, my lord, they replied.

And you're sure it is the same as ever?

Yes, my lord.

Romi shifted her weight. She'd never known Aïdes's voice anything other than gentle, and she didn't like the spike in his words. Surely this should be a time of celebration.

Aïdes threw his hands in the air and began to pace. *There was no frost, no snow?*

A rather nervous-looking Samael stepped forward. *Father Sun still rules the surface, my lord. It is still summer.*

Summer. The word planted a curious fire in Romi's belly. She'd completely forgotten about summer.

Aïdes's face darkened and he punched the wall, sending great cracks spiderwebbing across the rock.

Romi tried to become smaller, to disappear, but her gown was so big and white, it was impossible to be anything other than visible.

What about the spirits? Aïdes asked, studying his fists as if they might swing again. *I can still hear them whispering from the river of lost souls.*

Yes, my lord, the nervous demon replied. *The lost spirits remain where they always have. In the Underworld.*

The Divine Shadow roared. He was a snarling lion. An

angered bear. And Romi was a mouse. He moved to smash the stone again, but instead turned to his bride.

You were supposed to be the one*!*

He yelled the last two words right in her face so she could feel his breath freezing on her skin.

I'm sorry, she said, even though she had no idea what she was apologizing for. *I'll do better, my lord, I promise. Just tell me what you need.*

His nose touched hers, but there was no affection in the action, only violence and hate.

Our marriage, he hissed. *Divine flesh and divine shadow brought together in holy union. It was supposed to bridge the gap.*

What gap? Strangely, she found she was smiling. A fixed grin forged from desperation. Maybe if she was nice enough, *good* enough, she could fix this.

The gap between this world and yours, he said.

What?

Romi saw the fist coming towards her; she felt the air ripple against her cheek just before his clenched hand ploughed through her skull. She knew she was about to die.

And then she did.

I sit on the floor, not even bothering to wipe the slime from my palms.

'I'm so sorry, Romi,' I whisper. 'I'm so sorry this happened to you.' I gaze around the mausoleum. 'To *all* of you.'

The hooks in my belly grow stronger and I sense the echo of their rage. These women know they were wronged.

I take a moment to process what I've just witnessed.

Aïdes has been stealing girls with two Callings because he believes marrying them will form some sort of bridge between hell and earth, allowing him to bring an eternal winter to the surface and free his lost souls. That's why Mama was killed. Uriel knew about Aïdes's plan – he thought Mama was the key, so he got to her first.

I rub my eyes. A strange droning noise falls from my mouth. The information becomes an unwieldy stack of stones, my head a too-small sack, and no matter how hard I try, I simply cannot force what I've just learnt comfortably inside my brain. And I still haven't figured out the most important thing: *How will the mausoleum help me get home?*

'It won't.'

The voice causes me to jump.

I turn in a haze of shock to see the Divine Shadow standing beside me. I never even heard him step inside. Fear claws up my throat and I scramble to my feet.

'What do you mean?' My voice is cracked and dry. *He can hear my thoughts?*

He smiles. 'The mausoleum won't help you get home, Sephie. There is no escape route. There never was. I wanted you to come here so you could meet your predecessors.'

I cover my face so he can't see it crumple. 'Why?'

'Did you honestly think I didn't know that you were refusing my food and drink? I am part of you, Sephie. I run in your veins. I'm in your head. I know *everything* about you. But I need you to stop resisting me now. I need you to say "I do" of your own free will. So I gave you more pain than you could handle. I gave you this.' He gestures to the walls of the mausoleum and everything inside. 'Maybe now you can accept the mercy of oblivion.'

I can't help biting back. It's in my nature. 'If I say "I do" under the influence of devil wing, is it really free will?'

'A minor detail, my lady.'

I begin to laugh. It's unhinged and inhuman and surprises even me. 'Well, you failed,' I say, standing as tall as I can, considering my body is broken. 'I have met your victims and felt their pain, I have grappled with hunger and thirst like I've never known, and I *still* won't eat your bloody food or drink from that stupid chalice. I will *die* before I marry you.'

'Are you sure, Sephie? Because there is more.' He holds out a frosted hand. 'Come, let me show you.'

54

SEPHIE

He leads me through an archway set into the back wall; I haven't noticed the arch before, maybe it's just appeared. The darkness is banished by a wall of candles, their flames bursting into life at our arrival, and we stand inside a small room beside three sarcophagi, all covered with sheets. The nearest sarcophagus sits alone, and the remaining two are grouped together as a pair.

'Who are they?' I ask.

'Take a look.'

My fingers trembling, I lift the sheet from the first grave. Two symbols are carved into the stone: Father Sun and the Divine Shadow. This grave belongs to a Healer and Alchemist. Her name fills my head. *Mama*. My arms take on a life of their own, flipping back the material so the stone figure beneath is revealed.

My reaction surprises me. It's good to see her face again. Oh, how I have missed that face. Her fine features; her kind smile. The wave of her hair, and the tender arc of her fingers, always ready to heal. I run my hands over her cheeks, her nose, her lips, trying to absorb them, feeling like I'm five again and she's my entire world.

'Mama,' I whisper. 'Oh, Mama.'

It doesn't even hurt when I slide back the lid because I'm not in my body any more – I'm back in the oasis, tending to the garden in the courtyard by her side, watching her sniff the roses, sensing the warmth and love emanating from her every pore. And my eyes don't falter as I stare at her corpse.

Except, there is no corpse.

I blink.

Of course there's no corpse. Mama was reduced to ashes in the agora. Nothing remained. Uriel made sure of it.

Aïdes stands behind me and speaks. His breath is a blizzard in my ear. 'I was so sure she was the one. Her Callings were so strong. And when they beat me to her, I thought it was over. I thought my chance to snatch the surface from Father Sun had gone. But then I sensed *you*, Sephie, with shadows like tar in your blood, and a silver light beneath your fingertips. Not only the power to preserve the dead, but to raise them, to read them.' His hands fasten around my waist. 'I *had* to have you.'

I don't even flinch. It's like the fight has finally left me.

'The final two graves,' I whisper. 'Who do they belong to?'

'Why don't you find out?'

I lift the edge of the sheet to reveal the two symbols of the first sarcophagus: Embalmer and Alchemist.

'I don't want to kill you,' Aïdes says, kindly. 'But it's good to be prepared, don't you think?'

I know who this tomb is for. Of course I know.

But I flip the sheet back anyway, confirming my worst fear.

The girl carved into the stone is me.

But this isn't what shocks me. This isn't what rips me in two as if I were the orange rock leading to the Underworld itself.

The stone girl lying on the sarcophagus beside mine is Icari.

55

SEPHIE

'She wasn't where she was supposed to be,' Aïdes says. 'She wasn't at the citadel sanatorium when I sent my demons. My Samael sensed her at the sanatorium near the oasis, but it wasn't the plan. And then the Illios arrived and it was too late.'

I barely hear his words.

Since arriving here, I'd always assumed Icari was safe. I've pictured her going about her duties on the surface. Healing, caring. Missing me, yes, but safe. The thought of her being drawn into this nightmare is simply too much to bear. I think my desiccated body might just explode in a cloud of dust.

'Not Icari,' I whisper. A sob emerges and my eyes itch with the need for tears. 'She's so tender. So soft. She'll never survive.'

A deep chuckle. 'She may not have to.'

'Why?' I manage to gasp. 'Why Icari too?' I study her pretty stone features, the thick, wavy hair I used to weave into a braid, now hard and grey. The pain is a disease eating me from the inside.

He sighs. 'I realized a while ago that the key to my success was finding a mortal with all three Callings. But that is unheard of. So I found a neat solution. Twins, so closely bonded, so connected, that by marrying you both, I was effectively marrying one. *The* one. Because you, my lady, are an Alchemist with a hint of Embalmer, and your sister is a Healer with a hint of Embalmer. Combined, you embody the Celestial Trio. Divine flesh tied to divine shadow. The ultimate union.'

'Icari isn't an Embalmer.'

'Oh, but she is. She didn't discover it as early as you, but mark my words, she is. A quite remarkable one at that.'

I recall trembling in the loculus and hearing the Samael ask Madame if she were an Alchemist or Healer. They weren't just looking for me that day in the catacombs – they were looking for Icari too.

Aïdes smiles. 'Indeed, she's honing her embalming skills on one of my demons as we speak. Her gifts are proving quite useful when it comes to healing the flesh of the half-dead. She will be useful in more ways than one.'

My head wheels. I think I may faint. *Icari's healing a demon?* How in the name of Mother Moon is that even possible? I lurch to the side, or maybe the ground does. I can't tell any more.

'You are weary,' he says.

I shake my head, even though it sets the walls spinning and the candles blurring. The image of the Samael swarming above my sister, swiping her from the citadel whilst she screams and writhes sets my whole body trembling.

'You're going to steal her too?' I ask.

He rests his hands on my shoulders, the exact place his demon grabbed me. The same place they'll pierce Icari.

'No,' he says. 'The Illios are on high alert after the last raid. Another one is quite out of the question. I've had to employ more subtle methods to ensure her delivery.'

'Subtle methods?' My voice is shaking. My breath tastes bitter and my throat burns.

'I can reach you in your dreams, Sephie, because I'm part of you. Because my shadows are in your blood. I can whisper to any of the Alchemists, and to my demons too. You don't even know I'm doing it.' He strokes my face as he speaks. 'But Icari has only light – sunlight, moonlight, yet no shadows. So how do I influence her? How do I *lure* her here?'

I don't reply, but the word fills the room regardless. *How?*

'I have a friend on the surface,' he says. 'They've done the work for me. A rather ingenious solution, if I say so myself.'

'I don't believe you,' I say, although what I mean is, *I don't want to believe you.*

He spins me around so I'm no longer staring upon my sister's beautiful face but looking into the cold blue eyes of the devil himself. I hate those eyes. If I had a spoon, I'd gouge them out and grind them beneath the heel of my shoe.

'Come,' he says. 'It's almost time. Your wedding gown is ready, and so is Icari's. They match, of course.'

'No,' I whisper. 'No, no, no.'

The bronze chalice of pomegranate juice appears in his hands. Devil wing swirls in its red folds like the finest of white sands. The scent is astonishing. Sweet and fruity with a touch of snow.

'Drink,' he says, lifting the goblet towards me. 'Drink and let the pain melt away.'

My tongue grates across the roof of my mouth, my teeth

375

move inside my gums, my throat cramps and my stomach gapes. My eyeballs are two marbles rolling down a dune in the midday sun. Every fibre of my being cries out for the contents of that glass. I take the goblet and stare into its crimson depths. No more thinking about Mama burning on the pyre. No more Talia telling me she's betrothed. No more Underworld. No watching my sister marry the devil.

'Come now,' he whispers. 'It won't be so bad. The lost souls deserve a second chance. They deserve to roam the surface once again.'

'But everything else will die,' I croak.

'It will be cold, yes.'

I pull my eyes from the juice and meet his gaze. 'Why are you doing this?'

'Because I want them to see.'

'Who?'

'Father Sun and Mother Moon. I want them to see that I won.'

'All of this just because she chose him?'

'I never claimed to be perfect.' He places a finger beneath the base of the glass and lifts it higher. 'Come. If you submit, then at least there's a chance that you and your sister will survive. A chance you'll both rule at my side. But if you continue to resist –' he smiles a quick smile – 'well, I already have your graves prepared. And there will be no embalming, Sephie. No afterlife.'

There is nothing left to do. Lifting the chalice to my lips, I drink.

56

ICARI

By the time we reach the Bone desert, the night has grown thick and still. My arms ache, my wings flag and my vision starts to blur from dehydration.

'Shall we stop for a few moments?' I ask.

'Just a few.'

Already, my landing has improved, my wing tips angling forward and slowing my descent so that my toes brush the surface of the desert and I barely feel the impact as I touch down. I release Caszeil, then stretch my back – my feathers shake of their own accord, ridding themselves of the Redland grime and enjoying the rest. They relax down my back like a blanket, covering my spine and the backs of my legs. Their soft glow illuminates the sand around us.

Caszeil watches me and smiles. 'They have a life of their own, yes?'

I nod, spreading them beneath us so we may sit against the rocks without filling our clothes with sand. The sky is strung with stars, Mother Moon no more than a sliver of pearl in the dark. Caszeil leans against me and winces as my head rests upon his shoulder, where the arrows pierced.

'Let me finish healing you,' I say. 'The guards won't

notice, I'm sure.' I gesture to the expanse of pale sand.

He nods. 'Thank you.'

I move behind him, resting my hands on his skin, enjoying the surge of warmth in my body and the sparkle of my palms against him.

As I work, he says, 'Thank you for saving me.'

'I couldn't let them kill you.'

'I told you how to reach Sephie. You didn't need me. You still don't.'

'Need and want are different things.'

His body now gleams like he is made from stars and magic. The shoulder wounds have closed. I've left his face till last, and tenderly, I cup his damaged cheeks.

'What you said back at the citadel . . .' He leaves the sentence half formed, though the meaning is anything but.

'It wasn't true,' I say.

His eyes drop, though he manages a faint smile of resignation.

I can't help but laugh. 'Caszeil, I am more than a little in love with you.'

He raises an eyebrow. 'You know I am a demon?'

'I had noticed, yes.'

He pulls me in for a kiss, and as his lips press against mine, his hands run across my wings and his emotions leak into me. There is love, but there's also something dark I don't recognize. I pull away, surprised.

'Is something wrong?' he asks.

'No. It's just . . . my wings – they tell me what people are feeling.'

He tips his head to the side, his sheen of golden hair

catching in the moonlight. 'You could sense the shadows in my blood?'

I nod, embarrassed.

He strokes my face. 'Were there just shadows?'

'Oh, no. There was tenderness and warmth there too.'

'Good.' He runs his hand around the back of my neck and on to my wing base, where the love and shadows pour into me again. He holds my gaze and blinks, his long eyelashes softening the ridges of his cheekbones so that he looks both strong and gentle at the same time, and I recall his earlier words: *'Good and evil are not night and day. They are a braid.'*

'We should keep going,' he eventually says. 'Or Father Sun will rise and undo all of your hard work.' He gestures to his opalescent skin.

'OK,' I say, my voice trembling at the thought of what comes next.

And then I'm not afraid any more, because Caszeil is kissing me again.

57

ICARI

'There.' Caszeil points to a strip of orange crags. A splash of colour so bright against the white sands, it's almost offensive, like blood on fresh linen. My feathers prickle with anxiety and it suddenly hurts to swallow.

'What do I do?' My voice is so small, it's blown away by my wings.

'Fly directly over it,' Caszeil says. 'Then drop as fast as you can. If the earth senses any hesitation, it will know you don't belong.'

'What if it doesn't work?' I envision hammering into the ground and spreading like paint upon the rocks.

'You have Samael feathers – you just need the attitude to match. It will work, I promise.'

Tentatively, I coast towards the crags. 'I'll leave you on the surface,' I say, my chest pounding. 'If Aïdes catches us and realizes you've helped me, there's no saying what he'll do to you.'

He still faces away from me, but he tightens his grip on my forearms, a protective gesture. 'The Underworld is a labyrinth. You won't find your sister without a guide.'

I'm ashamed of how relieved I feel, for whilst I would

never knowingly put Caszeil in harm's way, I can't bear the thought of going through this alone. Indeed, it's all I can do to stop my wings from carrying me back to the oasis.

'Thank you,' I whisper.

He replies by squeezing my arms again.

Hugging him closer, I climb the pre-dawn sky until we hang over the crags. A breeze caresses my face, holding the scent of sand and earth, and I forbid the horrifying images of twisting tunnels and underground caves from entering my mind. Yet they seep in all the same.

'You might want to hold on for this,' I say.

Turning, he wraps his limbs around me, and I'm so grateful for the coolness of his skin, for the steady beat of his heart against mine, and the weight of his head on my shoulder, I almost forget how scared I am. Almost.

'I don't think I can do this,' I say, fear sweeping through me.

He smiles a gentle smile. 'You're the girl who grew wings, Icari. You can do anything.'

The pull in my stomach intensifies. Sephie is near. So with his words still fresh in my ears, I take a deep breath, grit my teeth, then tip my body so the sky becomes the ground.

Caszeil's arms tighten around my waist as I flatten my wings against my body and aim at the earth like a spear. And suddenly we're plummeting, stone-like, the wind ripping at my hair and feathers, my skin burning, my eyes streaming. Releasing a mighty scream, I will the orange crags beneath us to part, imagining my voice is a hammer and my determination a swinging arm, and just before I dive head first into the rock, delivering myself and Caszeil up to oblivion, a black hole opens beneath us like a dilating pupil and the ground blinks us in.

I don't have time to feel relieved. Down we go. The wind whistles in my ears, the rock blurs around us and the temperature cools. And another sound fills my head: Caszeil is screaming. No. Not screaming. He's whooping with joy. Crying with euphoria. I always knew that for him, returning to hell would be tantamount to returning home, but to experience his elation first-hand is as shocking as the fall.

We burst into a giant cavern and I flip upright, allowing my wings to clack open so I can spin like a maple seed, taking in my surroundings whilst airborne. My feathers tingle with cold and approaching danger. We're inside a monstrous cave painted with ice and mottled with small fires, made angular by giant stalagmites and stalactites. Thankfully, we're alone, but that hook in my stomach tugs a little harder and I know Sephie can't be far now. I land awkwardly, Caszeil and his smile a sudden weight in my arms.

Caszeil jumps to the ground, cat-like, and turns slowly, arms outstretched as though trying to touch the sides of the cave in greeting.

'It hasn't changed a bit,' he says.

His breath emerges in white clouds, yet he seems completely unfazed by the cold. I, on the other hand, am crippled by it; it strips my strength and makes me smaller somehow. My wings automatically wrap around my body, protecting my skin, but my feathers still ache. Even my insides burn, my throat and lungs both lacerated and numb, as if I'm drowning in icy water.

Caszeil rests a hand on my wing arch, and for once, I don't notice how cold he is.

'It isn't just the cold you're feeling,' he whispers, his smile dropping so his face is nothing but concern and familiarity. 'The shadows lie thick down here.'

I rest my hand on his. 'Where now?'

He doesn't need to answer, for at that precise moment, the notes of an instrument drift towards us, mixing with the wood smoke and our breath so the air becomes something dense we might need to wade through.

'Is that a harp?' I ask.

He nods.

It's playing a traditional wedding tune. I recognize it from the day-long celebrations that everyone in the village used to attend when we were younger, cramming the agora with flowers and laughter and the scent of ale. I recall how the bride would dance and swish her white dress, her coronet slightly askew, whilst she tossed posies for the local children to catch. Of course, Sephie would always shove her way to the front of the rabble, not caring who she climbed over so long as she came away with a handful of blooms, whereas I would hang back with Mama and Papa, drinking in the atmosphere and laughing at the drunken relatives as they joined the merriments with wobbling limbs. I'm so glad that Sephie didn't know what lay ahead of her. That there would be no children vying for posies at her wedding, no wobbly-limbed relatives celebrating, and the notes of a harp would echo not around the agora but through the halls of hell.

'Are we too late?' I ask, blinking back a tear.

'No, there's still time.'

'How do you know?'

He replies by pulling my hand. 'This way.'

'Caszeil? How do you know?'

He smiles. 'You need to trust me.'

I study his face, not liking the flavour of suspicion on my tongue. He looks far too excited, too relaxed, and I'm unsure why he's sidestepping my questions, but I let him guide me regardless. *This is Caszeil*, I tell myself. *He loves me.* But another internal voice answers back, *Does he? He's never actually said it, has he? He's never actually said those three little words.*

He leads me through several small caves and narrow tunnels, no narrower than those of the catacombs, yet the walls seem to close in and my wings sense the murderous intentions of the earth itself. I contain my fear by counting my steps, a senseless distraction that stops the voice in my head clanging like a warning bell, a structure that provides a cage for my anxiety, and by the time I get to one hundred and sixty-one, we've reached an opening in the rock.

Caszeil holds out an arm, forcing me to stop.

'Close your eyes,' he says.

'Why?'

'Can't you hear them?'

'The wedding harp?'

'No,' he says. '*Them*. Can't you hear *them*?'

At first, I think he means the Samael, or the Divine Shadow, or maybe even Sephie.

'No. I can only hear music and . . .' I pause. Now that my wings no longer drag behind me, I can also pick out a soft lapping sound that reminds me of the Nubi river. 'Water. I can hear water.'

'It's the river of lost souls.'

'The lost souls?' I don't even attempt to hide my distress; my voice shakes and a heavy tear ribbons down my cheek. I always knew the lost souls were down here, but it's overwhelming to think that they're now so close, I could dip my toe in their misery.

'It's something no mortal should see,' he says, moving behind me and placing one hand over my eyes and the other on my shoulder so he can guide me. The entire length of his body presses against my wings and I feel safe, if only for a fleeting moment. Slowly, he guides me through the blackness. My feet catch on stones, and occasionally, I stumble, but his arms are strong, and I can feel his urge to shelter me as it sinks into my feathers.

'Can you hear them?' I whisper, the question surprising even me.

'Yes.'

'What are they saying?'

'They're telling their stories. Memories, regrets, wishes.'

'And do they know they're forever trapped?'

'It is part of their punishment.'

I swallow, hard, grateful my ears aren't attuned to their murmurings.

Suddenly, Caszeil lifts his hand from my eyes and steps beside me. We're inside another tunnel, and before us is a wooden door with the signs of the Celestial Trio and two interlocking wedding bands carved into the wood. The door is slightly ajar and the music evidently comes from inside; I struggle to breathe with the excitement of seeing Sephie again, the horror that she's about to marry the devil, and the fear that I may not be able to rescue her.

Caszeil peers through the gap and I follow suit. More demons than I could imagine fill a large cave, the stone aglow with the light from their feathers, their skin resembling a sheet of ice that reflects Father Sun. Frozen in terror, only my eyes move, scanning the crowd for my sister, for the Divine Shadow, whatever he may look like. But there's only Samael.

'Where is she?' I manage to hiss.

Caszeil presses a finger to his lips.

The music pauses and the crowd parts to form a perfect silver corridor. My stomach tightens, my skin crawls as I realize it isn't a corridor – it's an aisle. And at the far end of the aisle rests a large mausoleum.

That's when I see her. Sephie steps into view, so close, I can see the individual pearls around her neck, the flush of rouge across both cheeks, her bouquet forged from ice and gleaming with a red liquid I can only assume is blood. So close, I could reach out and grab her. But it isn't her white gown, the blood posy or even just the fact I'm seeing her here – in the Underworld – that shocks me. It's the air of casual confidence with which she walks. She looks . . . *happy*.

She turns away from me, preparing to walk down the aisle towards the mausoleum.

'Sephie,' I whisper, my hand closing around the door handle as I prepare to swoop in and pluck her from the scene, just as the Samael did during the raid.

Yet Caszeil holds my shoulders. 'Icari, wait. There are too many of them. You don't stand a chance.'

'I can't see that changing,' I reply, frustration and fear

386

causing my voice to waver.

He tilts his head, the way he always does when I've both amused and challenged him. 'All right, but before we go, you must promise me one thing.'

'What?'

'If you need to, you must leave me behind. Agreed?'

I wind my fingers through his. 'Absolutely not.'

'You don't need me, remember. Just fly at the ceiling, the same spot we arrived through, and the ground will permit you passage to the surface.'

'I'm not leaving without you.'

'You may have to.'

'What do you mean?'

'How exactly did you think you were going to reach your sister when there are Samael everywhere?'

'I—'

But I don't get to finish, for Caszeil is pressing his lips to mine. I melt into the kiss. And when he pulls away, he whispers, 'You don't need wings to be a bird, my love. You never did. Always remember that.'

Before I can reply, he's moving away from me, stepping into the cave and staggering forward as if injured. He releases a loud groan as he trips down the aisle.

'Brothers,' he calls. 'Brothers, I have returned.'

The Samael close around him, crying his name and reaching out to touch the place where his wings once grew. I'm filled with both hope and horror as I realize he's creating a distraction. Sacrificing himself for my sister and me. It takes a moment to act, for I'm compelled to watch him as he's swallowed by a sea of curious demons. And how I long to fly to him, to catapult myself into the air and lift him from this cold, dead place, but I can no longer make him out. Surrounded by his brothers, he is just another silver-skinned monster. The thought makes me tremble. Then the ripple of white fabric pulls my focus back to Sephie – a snowdrop in a barren land. I'm here for my sister. Not Caszeil. And if we can just sneak from the cave, it will only take a minute to reach the escape point with my wings. I will have to gaze upon the river of lost souls, but I will manage. I will cope because I will have Sephie, and together we are stronger.

Urgency makes me brave. I cross the floor in just a few easy strides and clasp her upper arms. I expect to feel joy, triumph, but I just feel shocked. Shocked that after everything I've been through, the final stretch was this easy. One minute, she was untouchable, lost to me; the next, I'm gazing into her face. It's like I've crossed a huge ravine in a single step.

'Sephie,' I whisper. 'We must hurry.'

Yet she resists, her features morphing into confusion, her eyes devoid of all recognition.

My stomach drops. I'd know that misty look anywhere. She's high on devil wing. Yet it's more than that. The shadows have submerged her.

'Get off me,' she says, batting my hands away, though her movements are laboured. 'Leave me alone.'

'Shhh,' I say, clamping a hand over her mouth and containing her flailing arms as best I can. 'I've come to rescue you.'

She pulls away, anger flashing in her eyes. 'I don't need rescuing. Who *are* you, and why are you ruining my wedding?'

'It's me,' I say, preparing to simply scoop her up against her will, aware that the Samael are starting to turn in spite of Caszeil's theatrics. 'Your sister.'

'Icari.'

But it isn't Sephie who says my name. It's a man. A man with long white robes, a face so beautiful it defies nature, and skin dappled with frost. He seems to have appeared from nowhere, or perhaps he was watching all along, merged into the sparkling rock like a chameleon.

Every vein on my quills rises, like the fur of a cornered cat.

'Aïdes,' Sephie breathes.

She says his name as if he were her lover, not her captor or the source of all shadow, and as he moves towards us, he throws open his arms, anticipating an embrace. Not from Sephie, but from me.

'Icari,' he says. 'My sweet little bird. At last, you've arrived.'

An explosion of adrenaline. My wings tense. I encircle Sephie's waist, fleetingly noticing how thin she's become, and launch into the air. Sephie screams and drops her ice bouquet. It shatters on the ground beneath us, but I only grip her tighter. I have the advantage of being nearer to the exit than the Samael, and Sephie is so light compared to Caszeil, she doesn't hinder me at all. For a moment, I think I might make it. But the Divine Shadow simply swipes his hand to the side, causing the door to slam as if pushed by an invisible arm. Before I can form another plan, the Samael rise, a flock of birds startled by a single shot; white wings fill the air like thistledown. I kick out, but silver fingers are clawing at my ankles, nipping at my thighs, and I'm pulled to the ground with ease.

Sephie stumbles into the open arms of the Divine Shadow, who strokes her hair and whispers soothing noises into her ear. I know she's under the influence of devil wing, but I can't help feeling angry at her for seeking comfort from her jailor.

'Sephie!' I scream.

The Samael surround me and grip my limbs so no matter how hard I beat my wings, the floor remains solid and taunting beneath my feet. I have never craved the sky so.

'Sephie!' I reach for her, but my fingers fall empty through the cold air.

'Who is this Sephie?' my sister says as she nuzzles the Divine Shadow's neck.

'I don't know, my lady, but *this* –' he points to me – 'is Icari, and I know you'll be the best of friends.'

How does the Divine Shadow know my name? As I struggle against my demon restraints, his previous words sound in my head: *'Icari, my sweet little bird. At last, you've arrived.'*

Was the devil expecting me? And the way he referred to me as a bird . . . Why, that's what Caszeil calls me. Dread unfurls in my belly.

'Caszeil,' Aïdes calls over his shoulder. 'Where are you, my child? I believe congratulations are in order. Bringing the Healer here of her own free will was no mean feat.'

My body falls limp. I search the silver demons for the one that I love. I can't believe it, *won't* believe it, until I see the betrayal with my own aching, watery eyes.

And there he is.

Caszeil. Set apart from his brothers only by his lack of

wings, he holds my gaze. Yet they are the eyes of a stranger, the eyes of a traitor.

'Caszeil?' I whisper.

Very slowly, the corner of his dusty-pink lips curls upwards. 'Once a demon, always a demon,' he replies.

58

ICARI

Caszeil saunters towards me. There's an arrogant lilt to his step that I've never noticed before. The muscles on his chest undulate as he moves and his fists are clenched. Surely this can't be the same creature, the same man, who lay broken in the dungeons, or who knelt by my side as we built wings, or who kissed me like I was the only thing in the world that mattered.

The Divine Shadow holds out a hand to him. 'I whispered to you, my child.'

'And I listened, my lord,' Caszeil replies, kneeling before him and cradling the frosted hand as if it were something precious.

'I never abandoned you,' Aïdes says.

'I know.'

'I was always there, in the shadows, in your dreams.'

'You were, my lord,' Caszeil says, planting a kiss on his knuckles.

'I wasn't sure if you could hear me. It's been so long,' Aïdes replies.

Caszeil raises his eyes so he meets the Divine Shadow's gaze. 'An eternity could not erase my love for you, Father.'

Only moments ago, he looked at me like that. The individual bones of my ribcage turn into long, cruel fingers that squeeze and squeeze until my heart explodes and my chest is a vacuum.

Aïdes chuckles. 'I thought, perhaps, you loved the mortal girl.'

'I am Samael,' Caszeil replies. 'I love only shadow. Only you.'

'So you were playing her the whole time?' There's a mischievous cadence to the Divine Shadow's voice, and Caszeil's eyes slide to mine. They are a knife in my very soul.

'Yes, my lord,' he says.

A strange cry fills the cave, halfway between a sob and a scream. It takes a moment to realize it's coming from me.

Aïdes leans forward and kisses Caszeil's forehead, like a father might his child. 'Welcome home, my son.'

The anger arrives quickly, taking up residence in my body like a familiar guest. My muscles harden, my skin feels heat for the first time since I landed in this godforsaken place, and my feathers grow taut and rigid so I imagine my wings are now huge metal plates. I lurch forward, but those strong silver hands hold me back. I'm an animal straining against their chains. I don't even know myself any more.

'I trusted you,' I scream. 'I trusted you, and you brought me here. And for what? So you could get a free trip home?'

Caszeil studies me with detached curiosity. 'You think I did this for me?' He stands and closes the gap between us, his lips pulling into a wolfish smile. 'Haven't you heard a word I've just said? I love only the shadow. I love only my lord. I brought you here for *him*.'

I'm too angry to speak, so I simply shake my head in confusion.

Aïdes stands beside him. 'This wedding isn't just for Sephie. It's for both of you, little bird.'

'What?' My voice is a gasp.

'I'm marrying you both. This very morn.'

'No.' I look to Sephie, who's picking up the shards of her ice bouquet. 'No, no, no. Sephie, my darling, what is he talking about?'

Aïdes laughs. 'You might as well ask the walls, the amount of devil wing she's consumed.'

The rage doesn't dissolve, but it makes room for confusion, for despair, and I look to Caszeil, searching his features for the slightest trace of the man I love. 'Caszeil?' My voice cracks. 'Caszeil, how could you?'

Aïdes claps his hands together with youthful glee. 'You mortals are always so quick to blame my demons. To blame the devil. But sometimes, you simply need to look inwards.'

'What do you mean?' I'm crying now and I don't care. There's no space left for dignity in my body.

'It wasn't just Caszeil,' he replies. 'You had help from a mortal, didn't you, Icari? Help getting here.' He pauses. 'And how do you think I knew about you and your sister in the first place? I've always had my insiders at the citadel.'

I shake my head, an attempt to escape the onslaught of theories that fire in my brain. An insider at the citadel. My first thought is Talia. Of all the mortals, she helped me the most. No. Not courageous, fierce Talia. Surely she knows better than anyone in the citadel the importance of loyalty. And her feelings for Sephie are simply too strong. Uriel, then? After all, it was he who brought me the wings. Was burning Mama and sentencing Caszeil to death the ultimate bluff? And the Illios would never suspect one of their own.

An awful realization hits me: Uriel didn't have filed-down wing stubs because he's Illios, but because he's Samael. That would explain why he is such an accomplished Alchemist. I made it so easy for him, assuming he was a god. All he had to do was agree. A mist of sadness crosses my heart, for I am like my mama in so many ways, yet I never thought we would have loving a demon in common.

'Uriel is a demon?' I say.

A smirk slants across Aïdes's face. 'The High Priest Alchemist? I see why you might think that – he has an alarming amount of darkness in his veins for an Illios. But no. He is a god.' He chuckles. 'Just about.'

'Who then?' I say.

Aïdes sighs as though disappointed in my lack of reasoning.

'You better bring her in,' he calls.

The door opens.

A Samael enters the room, and holding his arm is Madame.

59

ICARI

'Madame Embalmer?' I whisper.

Everything slots together. Of course. Madame told me about the skeleton key because she wanted me to steal the feathers and build the wings. She saved me at my trial because she needed me to survive so I could fly to the Underworld. I bet she even asked to see Xenia on my first day so I was left alone with that vile guard, knowing that Caszeil would come to my rescue.

'You planned this all along,' I say. 'You wanted me to grow wings.'

She laughs freely, without guilt. 'Don't flatter yourself, child. I thought the demon called Caszeil would fly you to the Underworld – I didn't for a moment think that timid little obedient you would be able to grow wings.' She swaggers towards me and runs a finger down my wing arch, leaving a trail of greed and immorality. Her lips brush my ear as she whispers, 'We underestimated each other, it seems.'

'But the Samael tried to kill you.' My eyes land on her chest, the place where a scar forged by demon claws rests beneath her gown. 'Why kill you if you were helping them?'

She laughs. 'Silly girl. If a demon wanted to kill me, he

would have killed me. I needed to avoid suspicion, and sympathy is the best cure for suspicion that I know of.' Her face melts into mock empathy. 'And you have so much sympathy inside you, don't you, Icari? So much love to give.' Her laugh is cruel as her gaze moves to Caszeil.

My wings expand in fury and she backs away, though she doesn't stop smiling. The Samael tighten their grip.

Undeterred by my rage, she pats down her hair, smooths out her dress as if preparing for her sweetheart, then bows to the Divine Shadow. 'My lord.'

He extends a hand, which she kisses gratefully.

'You should be ashamed of yourself,' I hiss.

She doesn't even look at me.

'I trust you acquired your share of the Samael feathers?' Aïdes asks.

'Oh yes, my lord,' she says. 'It was easy enough to steal my cut of the devil wing, especially when Uriel was so distracted.'

The realization is an assault.

'Devil wing?' My voice rises. 'Devil wing? That's what you did this for?' I no longer attempt to escape the grip of the Samael, stronger than iron shackles, but I envision my hands clamping around her frail neck and crushing the life from her. My violent urges don't even surprise me any more. 'You betrayed us so you could mill more Samael feathers?'

Not even a shimmer of remorse tarnishes her delicate features. 'I'm not an Alchemist, Icari. I'm unable to transmute metals into gold. If I want wealth, I must take it.' She grabs at the air. 'I did you all a favour really – supplies were at an all-time low before the raid.'

I look at the Samael restraining me, the many silver bodies herding around their master, and I feel anger on their behalf. My feathers bristle with fury.

'The heads of your brothers now line the corridors of our dungeon,' I shout. 'That is all you are to him. A trade. Will you follow him blindly, even though he struck a deal based on the value of your feathers?'

The Samael nod without feeling. They already knew this. I recall Caszeil explaining that he only learnt to feel whilst on the surface – that everything was numb in the Underworld. They care no more for their brothers than Aïdes does. If I'd hoped to incite a revolution, I was sorely misguided.

Incensed, I turn back to Madame. 'We trusted you. We all did – me, my sister, Zalta, all of the dead students. You betrayed us. For nothing but . . . but pieces of gold.'

The disgust in my voice riles her, and a prim, defensive air settles into her features.

'I didn't just do it for gold,' she says. 'I did it because I believe in the Divine Shadow's cause.'

'What cause?' I ask. 'Forced marriage?'

She laughs. 'No, you silly girl. To bring the Underworld to the surface. To free the lost souls.'

'Sephie?' I look to my sister, but she's too busy straightening her veil to reply.

My eyes flit between the Divine Shadow and Caszeil, desperately searching for answers, my brain unable to process Madame's words.

Aïdes offers me an unnervingly patient smile. 'That is why I am marrying you, Icari. To bridge the gap between hell and earth.'

My knees buckle, no longer able to support the weight of my body, my wings or my horror. And in a final bid for understanding, maybe even help, I look to Madame. For in spite of everything, I still think of her as a figure of authority and justice.

'Madame?'

'We honour the dead, Icari,' she says. 'It is what sets us apart from animals. And what ultimate way to honour the dead than to offer them an equal place at the table. Can't you hear them whispering? Those poor lost souls. Mother Moon abandoned them, but we won't. They don't want to be trapped down here any more. They want to be free.'

A long drape of white silk appears in the Divine Shadow's arms. He offers it to me, his face eager, and I realize the pale fabric slung over his hands like a sleeping ghost is a wedding gown.

'It is identical to your sister's,' he says. 'You will make quite the pair.'

I shake my head, trying to back away, but the wall of Samael remains firm.

'I won't do it,' I say. 'I won't marry you.'

His lips twitch, causing the ice on his skin to glisten. 'Because of your connection, I only need one of you to agree.' He gestures to Sephie. 'And I believe I could convince your sister to marry a gecko right now.'

I turn to her, the despair spilling out of me like something visceral. 'Oh, Sephie, dear-heart, tell him. Tell him you won't marry him.'

She replies by twirling in a circle, watching how her dress oscillates like that of a dancing girl.

Aïdes shakes out my matching gown. 'The problem lies in the fact she no longer remembers you, Icari. If you can get her to remember, if you can convince her to refuse my hand, then there is no wedding. But I can't see that happening, can you?' He holds the dress against me, checking the fit and clicking his tongue against the roof of his mouth.

Wincing, I lean away from him. 'Sephie,' I cry, desperation battling with hope and causing my voice to break. 'It's me. Icari. Your sister.'

She frowns. 'Who is Sephie, my lord? I tire of hearing her name.'

'I feel the same, my lady,' he replies, folding up my dress and throwing me a sly smile.

Tears overwhelm me; waves of salt pulse through my body.

Unperturbed, Aïdes gestures to the dress, a neat parcel in his arms. 'Shall we? You will need to lose your wings, of course. They'll only tear the fabric, and I don't really want you flying away at the first opportunity. Brides should be with their husbands.'

Before I can object, I'm thrown to the floor with such force, my knees crack and the breath leaves my body. My wings attempt to beat, but a thick chain is thrown over me, slicing my feathers and weighing me down. Panic consumes me.

'Help,' I whisper, looking between Sephie and Caszeil. 'Help me, please.'

I'm met by Sephie's confused scowl and Caszeil's empty eyes.

Aïdes moves towards me, no longer carrying a wedding gown, but a scythe. The blade is as long as an arm, as pointed as a beak, and the fingers that grip the handle are strong and cruel and stippled with frost.

I twist and bend, the urge to flee overpowering me, but to no avail.

The Divine Shadow looms over me and raises the scythe. It glints in the firelight like a crescent moon. I anticipate the anguish as my wing bones are cleaved from my spine with a single blow, yet I refuse to close my eyes or look away. I refuse to give Aïdes the satisfaction, instead staring at him with defiance as he swings the blade.

With a sickening swoosh, the scythe drops.

Then everything happens at once. Caszeil leaps forward with an almighty scream, throwing himself over me so he forms a shield. The Samael gasp as I'm torn from their hands and a cold weight pushes me flat against the rock. Then the sound of metal slicing flesh fills my ears, followed by a wail of pain that isn't my own.

Then there's nothing but Aïdes's laughter and the pop of a nearby fire.

'Oh, Caszeil. Caszeil,' Aïdes says.

Caszeil responds with a groan.

'Did you even hear my whispering?' Aïdes asks.

'Maybe,' he replies, his voice a rasp. 'But then the dark is full of whispers, and I was too busy listening to the pure note of a flute.'

'So why did you agree to rescue her sister if it wasn't to assist me?' Aïdes asks.

'Because I love her,' he replies.

A bright, gleaming emotion unfolds inside me, swiftly, like the great sail of a ship meeting the wind. Like wings opening. He really does love me. Everything was real.

His weight lifts from me and I'm able to stand, gazing at Caszeil as he staggers away. The wound from Aïdes's scythe reaches diagonally across his back — it's shallow, skin-deep, disrupted by the nubs of bone that still protrude from his upper spine. What remains of his wings must have protected him from the brunt of the blow. Blood soaks into his loin-cloth and trickles down his legs, but he will survive. The relief is physical.

When he turns towards me, there's a faint smile on his face, and in his hands is the chain that bound my wings.

'Fly, Icari,' he says. 'Take your sister and flee this place.'

My first instinct is to do just that, to grab Sephie and bolt. But something stops me. And it isn't the shock or the grab-bing hands of the Samael. It isn't the seething face of the Divine Shadow or even the sheer joy of knowing Caszeil loves me and always did. It's the sight of his blood as it drib-bles down his ankle.

For it isn't Samael silver. It's mortal red.

'Caszeil,' I whisper, reaching for him. 'You aren't a demon any more.'

Aïdes stares at him, jaw open, eyes wide. 'Your love has made you human.' He shakes his head, disappointed. 'Oh, my child, how could you lose yourself so?'

Caszeil opens his mouth to reply, but it is Sephie's voice that rings out.

'Look. Roses.' She points to the ground on which Caszeil stands.

Where Caszeil's blood has sunk into the stone, the frost has melted and a pink rose uncurls. More blood lands and a fringe of emerald grass erupts around his feet. Somehow, Caszeil's blood, his humanity, is bringing life to the Underworld. Life to death.

Sephie looks at me, her frown intensifying. 'Is that grass?'

'That's right,' I say, scrambling to my feet. 'It's grass, Sephie. Like at the oasis. Do you remember?'

She shakes her head. 'I . . . I . . .'

'My love, look at me,' Aïdes says, his voice deep and commanding.

As Sephie's eyes move to the Divine Shadow, that flicker of recognition, of *Sephie*, sinks beneath an ocean of false love and trickery.

'Sephie, please,' I say. 'Try to remember me. Try.'

But it's like she can't hear me any more.

Desperate, I look to Caszeil. His head swivels between Sephie and the rose. Realization shapes his face into a smile; then he meets my gaze, his grey eyes laden with hope and compassion and humanity.

I love you, he mouths.

He rests his hand upon his throat.

'NO!' I scream, horror dawning fast.

He may have human blood, but he still has demon strength, and he rips out his throat with only a grunt of pain. I lunge for him, my wings carrying me the short distance so I'm able to catch his head as it lolls forward. And as his body slumps to the ground, hot, crimson blood surges from his neck, spilling over my arms and gushing on to the rock, melting the frost wherever it falls. The Calling rises in me like never before and I push my golden hands into his throat, trying desperately to heal him even though I know the wound is too deep.

'Please,' I whisper, pressing harder. 'Please.'

But the golden light flickers and fades like a dying flame – my Calling is aware of what I can't yet admit.

'Look,' Sephie calls.

Lifting my head, I see grass springing up all around us, fresh and bright, peppered with jasmine and delphiniums, tall shoots of larkspur and more roses than I've ever seen. In mere seconds, Caszeil and I are surrounded by a luscious garden, grown from his blood. Pollen catches in my nostrils, and I gasp it in as the light from my palms dies completely.

Which can mean only one thing: he has gone.

Pulling him into me, I imagine that my love is a light that I can somehow pour from my body into his, a light strong enough, pure enough, to bring him back. To make him breathe again. But I have watched enough people die to know that love is no match for death.

My Calling is useless now.

Grief is a fast-growing vine, twisting around my limbs, my neck, my face, forcing its way down my throat and throttling my vital organs. I become the grief, and for a moment, even I forget who I am.

'The courtyard,' Sephie says.

Her voice sounds far away, like she's talking through water or cloth, but I force my eyes to her.

'That's right.' My words sound between sobs. 'The courtyard at the sanatorium, our home.'

She kneels beside me amongst the flowers. Her face is empathic, yet her eyes are alive with fire. 'Why do I recognize you?' she whispers.

'I'm your sister,' I say.

Aïdes strikes, quicker than a viper, grabbing her by the shoulders and hauling her back.

'My lady, she's lying. You can trust only me.'

Sephie gasps and reaches for me.

But I don't fly to her or fight back. I don't even call for her, because it's suddenly clear to me what I must do to make her remember.

'You don't need wings to be a bird, my love. You never did.'

Mama always said that fear divides us into three groups: those who fight, those who take flight, and those who turn to statues. Well, I have learnt to fight. I have even learnt to fly. But right now, I need to do what I do best: be still. Immediately, I shrink with shame, for freezing is what got Mama killed; it's what tied Sephie to the whipping post. But then I push back. I push back as hard as I can. For it was never my fault Mama was killed. It was never my fault Sephie was whipped. I will not accept the sins of others simply because fighting and flying did not come easily to me.

I have always been enough.

I am still enough.

So kissing Caszeil's dusty-pink lips one last time, I lay him amongst the blooms. Then I stand amidst the flowers and grass and try not to sway.

Sephie gazes at me from Aïdes's arms.

'My name is Icari,' I say, my voice surprisingly strong. 'We were formed in the same womb and we are bound by love. By family and by grief, by light and shadows and everything in between. But we will *never* be bound by the devil.'

The urge to act, to fight or fly, to be someone other than

myself, overwhelms me, but I hold it at bay and remain still.

'You don't need wings to be a bird, my love. You never did.'

Sephie studies me, she studies the garden, and then slowly, she begins to smile.

60

SEPHIE

When I first saw her, she was a girl with wings. A stranger. But now I can really look at her, I realize that I know her face. But it's more than that. I recognize her stillness. Her gentle calm. It's as familiar to me as my own skin. And then there's the roses, the larkspur, the jasmine and the delphiniums, speaking of summers in a place I once called home.

Memories push against a thin film of ice. There's a courtyard, an oasis, a citadel and a girl with sunshine in her hair and a constellation of russet stars upon her face.

'My lady, look at me,' Aïdes says.

When he spins me around, the golden chalice is cupped in his hands. The scent of pomegranate juice pulls me from the garden and my mouth immediately wells with saliva.

He gazes at me with those blue eyes. 'You don't want to remember, my lady. The roads behind us lead only back to pain and sorrow. That's why we must move forward.' He holds the chalice towards me. 'That's why you must drink.'

I take the goblet and inhale deeply. The scent of snow leaves me dizzy.

'Sephie, no,' the girl in the garden says.

There's that name again. *Sephie.* Like a finger that won't stop picking at a scab. I look back at the winged girl, and purposefully, she touches her stomach.

A hook snags my belly, and warmth radiates throughout my body. Love. *Her* love. The realization knocks the goblet from my hands. It clatters to the ground, splashing juice as red as the demon's blood across the stone. The girl with wings is family.

Her name rings through my head.

Icari.

Icari, who splashed beside me in the Nubi river and played in the dirt tracks of the oasis. Who held me through the darkest of nights and lifted me from every nightmare. The girl who is always right and irritates the heck out of me, but whose kindness never throws up a closed sign.

Icari. My sister.

Images spool like the brightest of silks, fluttering free in my head. A childhood spent picking fruit with Papa and tending to animals, marvelling at the shadows as they darkened my blood. My mother's death. The stench of smoke upon the desert breeze. But alongside the heartache were lullabies and stories and the image of Mama holding my hand as we strode towards the desert to count the goats beneath Father Sun.

Father Sun!

What I wouldn't give for a minute of his warmth. I am so bloody cold right now. My body issues an involuntary shudder.

'Sephie? Do you remember?' Icari asks, her words tentative, hopeful.

'Yes,' I cry, running to her, a joyous sob catching in my throat. 'Yes, I remember.'

But Aïdes is upon me in a heartbeat, pulling me back, keeping me from the garden and my sister. He manoeuvres me so I face him and presses his hands into my cheeks, delivering a blast of ice that overwhelms me. Devil wing has nothing on this.

Icari screams my name.

At least, I think it's my name.

It all begins to fade. The memories, the emotions, they're sucked from my head by glacial hands.

I sink to my knees.

'Do you accept my hand in marriage?' Aïdes says.

He squeezes harder, and winter pushes summer from my heart.

Yet one image remains.

Mama's face.

The need to succumb to the cold, to lock her image away, overwhelms me. But bricking up the pain also seals away her smile, the scent of roses in her hair, playing games together, cooking side by side, and laughing till we wheezed.

The pain is part of me, and I refuse to lose it.

Aïdes's face is almost upon mine. His blue eyes bore through me and his silvery lips pucker as he comes in for a kiss.

Fuck you, Aïdes. I'll give you a kiss you'll never forget.

Lunging forward, I catch his bottom lip in my teeth and bite with everything I've got. His flesh comes away in my mouth like a piece of lamb liver.

His hands fall from my cheeks and he stumbles backwards.

'My lady?' His words gurgle as blood black as molasses falls down his chin.

I spit the hunk of lip to the ground.

'My name is Sephie, daughter of Daeda.' My voice is proud. 'And I will never marry you.'

61

SEPHIE

Aïdes's expression darkens, matching the blood dripping from his chin. His bottom teeth are visible through the gap in his lip so he becomes part skull. Thank goodness for the devil wing filing down the fear.

'My lord,' Madame says as she dashes to him, but he bats her away as if she were a bug and she skids to the ground.

Stepping over her, he strides towards me, raising his fist to smash my skull like he did all his brides, his bloodied mouth pulled into a snarl. But instead of striking, he leans close. So close, I can smell the blood on his breath.

'You were supposed to be the one,' he says, his spit driving into my skin like icicles. 'You and your sister, you were supposed to be the one. Who knows how long I must wait to find another set of twins.' Turning from me, he clutches his head and mutters, 'There must be another way, a way of salvaging it still.'

'Sephie,' Icari whispers.

The Samael have pinned her to the grass and continue to battle with her monstrous gold-and-white wings. How in the name of Mother Moon did my sister grow wings? She holds my eye and victory lights up her face. And I understand why. Even if we are now to die, we have still won. Because there is no way in this icy hell that Aïdes can salvage this. If I refuse to marry him, he has no bridge.

Suddenly, Aïdes's face eclipses that of my sister. 'Have you forgotten what happens if you deny me, *Sephie*?' He sneers my name and points a wavering finger at the mass tomb at the back of the cave. 'Have you forgotten what lies in the mausoleum?'

'No,' I say, clambering to my feet. 'I have not forgotten the hundreds of women that you drugged and murdered.'

'I was talking about the pair of empty sarcophagi. One for you, and one for your *darling* sister.'

I square up to him. The hundred hooks in my stomach make me strong. I'm carrying not only my own courage, but theirs.

'So do it,' I shout. 'I have already died at your hands a hundred times.' I can still taste his blood like bitter venom on my tongue, and I relish the sensation as I fire a huge globule of black spit into his eye.

He wipes his face with the back of his hand. 'For that, I will kill your sister first.'

My courage unravels like a skein of wool. I can't watch Icari die. I just can't.

'It's OK,' Icari whispers. 'We will be with Mama. We will be together.'

Aïdes laughs. The inside of his mouth is black and lacquered with blood. 'Oh, Icari. There will be no embalming. Tell her, Sephie. Tell her.' He gestures towards the mausoleum. 'I don't embalm my disappointments – I simply let them decompose. You will never rest with Mother Moon.

You won't even make it to my river. Your bodies will rot and you will just cease to be, like your mama. Like all my failed brides.'

His words spark an idea. Because Aïdes is wrong – the women in the mausoleum still have their souls, they must, for I read them, and I still sense them. Which means they can be woken. I'm a necromancer, after all.

Aïdes clicks his fingers. The snap resounds around the stone walls. 'Bring me the bird.'

The Samael with the grey plait and the white eyelashes drags my sister across the rock. Her hair is wild, her tunic ripped and soaked in blood, yet she looks strangely serene.

The demons shove her on to the ground and push her cheek against a smooth protrusion of rock. Then they sweep back her mass of black curls to reveal the fragile column of her neck. Her wings flutter hopelessly behind her, and she reminds me of a pheasant stretched out on a chopping block. No amount of devil wing could stop the horror that envelops me right now, because that scythe is back in Aïdes's grip.

'Don't worry, I'll make it quick,' he says, raising the blade over Icari's neck.

I try to rush to her, but the Samael are everywhere and simply hold me back.

Icari gazes at me and smiles. *We won*, her eyes seem to say. *We still won*. And yet there is also a sadness to her that I don't recall. Her eyes land on the garden and the demon within, and I wonder just how much he meant to her.

As I try to shake the Samael free, the hooks intensify in my stomach, tugging at the skin and the flesh beneath, gathering strength and force until I fear my abdomen may whip across the room. The rage of an entire army of women swells inside me and the shadows gather in my blood like never before. My hands burn with cold, and a silvery-white glow illuminates the cave. It takes a second to realize that the light radiates from my palms. The Embalmer trapped inside me is finally free. Free to join the Alchemist and roar.

The dead in the mausoleum begin to chitter their approval and the Samael whisper amongst themselves, glancing at the building and loosening their grip.

'Silence,' Aïdes roars. 'It is a parlour trick.'

'We'll see,' I say.

Then everything slows down. Everything except my gifts.

See, I've never liked death, especially not since I lost Mama. But it doesn't scare me any more. I've been to hell. I've read a hundred minds in that mausoleum and I've died a hundred times. I've learnt the truth behind Mama's execution. And none of those things have broken me.

Friends, I was offered total numbness and I refused.

So I open myself to the chittering and embrace the hooks in my belly, just as I opened myself to Mama's memory and the pain. My Callings peak, the Embalmer just as strong as the Alchemist. Using my consciousness, I weave my gifts together, creating the thickest of cords. Then I send each cord towards the mausoleum and every battered skull of every wronged woman. And as I connect with them, I sense their bones stirring in their stone boxes. The shadow and light wrap around their remains, like the embalming bandages they never received upon their death. My Callings give their fury shape.

Out I breathe, blowing light and shadows and life into their chests.

The sound of stone scraping against stone fills the cave, and everything speeds up.

The Samael tense like they know something's coming. Aïdes pulls back his blade, an evil grin stretching the wound on his lip so he resembles a carved pumpkin, and Icari takes a deep breath. Yet before the blade drops, a groaning sound exits the mausoleum. It's as if the building itself were awakening.

'My lord?' Madame asks. 'What's happening?'

I can hear rainfall on the surface. Impossible. We're too far below ground. Then I realize it's the pitter-patter of skeletal feet. The door to the mausoleum creaks open, but I never get to see what emerges, because at that exact moment, Aïdes swings the scythe towards Icari's neck.

A rush of icy air. A whoosh of movement. The scythe stops a finger's-breadth from my sister's flesh. I take in the scene with equal amounts of disbelief and pleasure. Gripping the scythe alongside Aïdes's icy fingers is a rotten hand with spindles of creamy bone flashing through the mess.

I smile. The corpse smiles back. Her buck teeth are noticeable even in death.

'Why, thank you, Romi,' I say.

62

ICARI

I open my eyes. A woman wrestles the scythe from Aïdes. No. Not a woman. A corpse.

I don't have time to feel shock or even disgust, for Sephie is pulling me to my feet, away from the blade and the Divine Shadow.

Clinging to her, I survey the cave. It's alive with movement, undulating with skeletons and corpses, all of whom leap and run with alarming speed and agility, and all of whom have substantial injury to their heads. They target the demons by clawing at their faces, climbing on their backs and pulling their wings, yet they ignore my sister and me entirely, flowing around us as if we were stones in a river.

The Samael are strong, but they are far outnumbered by the swarm that continues to flow down the mausoleum steps like the most grotesque of waterfalls.

'Sephie, what's happening?' I say.

She lifts her palms; they emit the whitest of lights. 'I woke them up.'

I knew she was a necromancer, but never did I think she was capable of *this*.

Just then, a demon with a long grey plait and white

eyelashes lunges for me. Before I can react, a skeleton leaps on to his back, scraps of leathery skin trailing behind them like ribbons, and throws him off course. The demon beats his huge wings and breaks free, only for another skeleton to swipe at his legs and a corpse with hair like dried grass to knock him to the ground and skewer him through the neck with what looks like a jagged femur.

'Sephie?' I gasp.

She grips my hand with her ice-cold palm. 'Don't worry, they're our friends.'

The air is heavy with death and vengeance and hatred for the Divine Shadow. A group of skeletons surge past and my wings tingle.

My wings tingle.

In all the chaos, I forgot that I could fly.

Without hesitation, I grab Sephie and power into the air. The novelty of being airborne will never wear off, and even though a battle ensues below, a gasp of delight escapes my mouth.

Circling the cave, I desperately search for an escape route, for the only door remains firmly shut.

Sephie tightens her grip around my arms. 'You are flying,' she breathes.

'And you are commanding an army of skeletons.'

'I guess we have some catching up to do.'

Below, the dead are an ocean, moving like insects over spoilt meat. I sail over Madame. She's been trampled into the rock and her neck is twisted at an unnatural angle. Even though she betrayed us, I feel a flicker of sadness, for the need to nurture life is stitched into my soul.

The cold stings my feathers as I pass over the mausoleum. The Divine Shadow stands near the steps, swinging his scythe, smashing through bones and rotten flesh, his white gowns billowing.

I beat my wings and soar around the rest of the cavern, scouring the stone for an exit.

That's when I pass over the small garden. It's untouched; even the dead know it's a sacred place. Caszeil lies amongst the flowers, peaceful. Love surges through me and my wings falter. Could I carry him too? Carry him away from here and give him the burial he deserves?

Just then, Aïdes's voice slices through my brain. 'You don't actually think you can leave me, do you?'

One moment, he's pointing at us with his scythe; the next, he's melting into darkness, a man built from shadow alone. Then his shape disintegrates and he transforms into thick strands of black snaking towards us, weaving through the skeletons and demons like mist twisting through trees.

'Bollocks,' Sephie grunts.

Dread punctures my resolve and my wings take over. With two strong beats, I'm upon the door. It remains closed, but perhaps if I position myself correctly, lifting Sephie and extending my leg, I'll be able to boot it down. It's the only option. Accelerating, I brace for impact, yet the plane of wood vanishes before me and I travel unhindered, carrying my sister beneath the arch.

'What did you do?' I ask Sephie.

'I transmuted it into air,' she replies.

'You can do that?'

'It would appear so.'

I pull my wings against my body and glide down the tunnel, losing height, unable to extend my plumes due to the cylindrical walls. Sephie clunks against the floor and is forced to run to prevent her legs from dragging against the stone. Her swear words bounce back at me.

I glance behind. First come the Samael, clearly used to travelling in confined spaces. Now that they're no longer hampered by skeletons, they speed after us, part running, part flying. Next comes the Divine Shadow, a mass of dark tendrils spreading down the corridor, blackening the air and extinguishing the torches.

'Can you outfly them?' Sephie calls.

'Just hold on,' I reply.

She digs her fingers into my wrists as the tunnel spits us out, straight into the vast chamber that houses the river of lost souls. I aim high, stretching out my wings and arcing over the waters, refusing to glance downwards. Moisture and regret hang heavy in the air, combining with the cold to make my feathers ache.

'Don't look down,' I call.

'It's OK,' Sephie replies. 'They're my friends too.'

I snatch another backward glance. The sight of the Samael swooping after us like owls hunting a sparrow is enough to make my stomach lurch, but when I see the Divine Shadow curling, frond-like, from the mouth of the tunnel before expanding into a black fog that swallows everything, it feels like my heart may stop. But Mama was right – I do have a hidden core of strength – and I keep moving, keep trying, no matter how futile it seems.

The final stretch of tunnel beckons, so I hold my breath

and plunge. The corridor inhales us, and I jerk my shoulder sharply to the right, tucking in my wings so I begin to spin. Corkscrewing, I maintain my speed. The rock circles past and the torches swirl in my wake. My head rolls, the air rushes through my feathers, and Sephie screams in my arms, but I don't stop. I just spin and spin, imagining my crown as an arrow tip, slowing only when I reach the cave in which I arrived.

The faint scent of sand and open spaces greets us, even though the ceiling remains entirely solid. Huge stalagmites rise in my path and I sweep around them, setting the fires beneath us dancing. I plant my feet in the centre of the chamber. My intention is to use the ground as a springboard so I can hurtle towards the canopy of stone, praying it grants us passage, yet something immobilizes me: the realization that I'm standing in the exact same spot where I landed with Caszeil.

The ghost of him is held in the surrounding air, imprinted into the rock beneath my soles. His cool skin presses against mine, the scent of snow catches in my nose, and his voice echoes in my ears. My hands are still wet with his mortal blood. No core is strong enough to withstand the wave of grief that smashes into me.

'Icari,' Sephie says. 'Icari, look.' She's flapping her hands at the ceiling and cursing in frustration. 'I can't transmute it. Oh, Icari, what will we do?'

Suddenly, the Samael arrive with their blade-like wings and their battle cries, and swirling around them are the shadows, blacker than tar. The fires go out as though caught in a gale and we're plunged into darkness. The temperature plummets and the cold swaddles us. Then the voice of the Divine Shadow comes from every direction, bathing us in its deep, spiteful tone.

'Nobody leaves me. Do you hear me? Nobody gets to leave.'

The frost is marrow-deep. My will begins to crumble. Yet somehow, the grief that dismantles me also makes me immune to the ice and the despair. I have already left my compassionate, wise and beautiful demon in a patch of grass somewhere in the depths of hell. Do your worst, Aïdes.

'Goodbye, my love,' I whisper.

Then I tighten my grip around Sephie's waist and launch straight at the ceiling, letting the glow from my feathers light the way. Before I can change my mind, or even scream, the ceiling parts, and I'm belting towards a plate of blue, my sister in my arms.

63

ICARI

We shoot into the open like water from a geyser. The sky is an endless cornflower blue, and a low-floating Father Sun welcomes us with golden arms. Sephie hollers with delight as I wheel higher and higher towards the dusting of clouds.

'We did it,' she yells. 'We bloody did it.'

Pausing, we look down. The earth is already sealing up like a fast-healing scar. My wings flutter in my peripheral vision and I inhale the blue, letting Father Sun pull every icy needle from my quills.

'Will they follow?' Sephie asks, fear hiding in her voice.

'No. Father Sun is here. Besides —' I gesture to the edge of the orange crag — 'it appears the cavalry has arrived.'

An army of Illios gather beneath us, their golden wings glinting in the morning light. From up high, they look like tiny dolls, but we're able to see them tip their heads skywards and wave.

'Uriel must have sent them,' I say.

'At least he's good for something.'

I laugh and we wave back.

'Now what?' Sephie asks.

'Now we go home.'

Quite the welcoming committee awaits us when we arrive at the citadel that evening. Students crowd the Court of Ash and spill from the dormitory windows, cheering and singing and waving silver-and-gold flags. It seems that an Illios flew ahead to tell our tale. Apparently, defeating the Divine Shadow and preventing hell on earth is enough for everyone to forget I rescued a demon.

I land with a thud against the marble, still clutching Sephie, and a joyous cheer fills the air. I shrink. Sephie, however, soaks it all up, shaking the hands of strangers and letting them slap her on the back, though her eyes are constantly combing the crowds, I imagine for a glimpse of red-streaked hair. Even Ziris offers a reluctant clap, though Sephie is too preoccupied with finding Talia to bother gloating.

Of course, I let people touch my wings and accept their well wishes with grace, but on the inside, I'm empty. Absent. Even though I've grown wings and am physically *more* than before, I feel incomplete, like I'm missing an organ or a major body part. Is this how Papa felt when Mama died? The future unrolls before me like a colourless scroll and I would give the world just to be back in that dungeon again, gazing into those slate-grey eyes.

It isn't until Uriel ushers us into the Sun Temple that I feel something other than numbness or longing. For waiting on a pew, sitting hunched and awkward, is Papa.

'Papa,' I cry.

He stands just in time for Sephie and me to barrel into him and knock him down again. And then we're just a huddle of tears, hot breath and elbows.

'I thought I'd lost you both,' he says, his voice breaking with emotion.

I hold him extra tight. 'You'll always have us, Papa.'

More arms wrap around us, and I realize Leon and Ruari are here too, leaning into the embrace. Then Sephie is hoisting Ruari into her arms and they start to spin.

'Is it true?' he shouts, his voice wavering as he whips around. 'Is it true you beat the devil?'

'It is,' Sephie cries, laughing and setting him down.

'Take that, Aïdes,' he calls, brandishing an invisible sword.

Sephie takes an imaginary blade to the breast and flops to the ground, moaning.

'Tell us everything,' Leon says.

As Sephie recounts the tale in an excited voice, Uriel leads me to the side of the temple where we stand amongst the citrus trees. I'm so grateful to be here, on the surface, in the temple, where a sleepy Father Sun trickles through the glass ceiling and the evening sky is still visible. I never want to be underground again. I just wish Caszeil could be here too. Perhaps . . . perhaps with his human blood he could have tolerated the daylight, perhaps we could have spent our lives together like people in love do. I guess I'll never know. The realization threatens to capsize me.

Uriel fidgets with his eye dressing and lowers his voice. 'I can remove your wings, Icari. It will hurt, but there is devil wing, and the scar is far from unsightly—'

My wings react, opening with an indignant clack. 'My

lord, if you please, I would like to keep them.'

'Pardon?'

'I would like to keep my wings.'

He frowns, but there is something else in his expression aside from disapproval. Admiration? Envy? He wears his regal mask so well, he's difficult to read. My wings bristle with his emotion and I realize it's regret; he misses the sky more than he thought possible.

He rolls his shoulders, his old injury making itself known. 'Are you sure? You will always be different, never fitting in with either the Illios or the Healers.'

'I don't want to fit in. I want to fly.'

'Well, you can always change your mind.'

'I won't.'

He adjusts his eye dressing again, even though it already sits perfectly. I make him nervous now I resemble an Illios, it seems.

'Icari, you and your sister have proved to be quite the asset. The only girls ever to return from the Underworld.'

'I believe we're the only *people* ever to return from the Underworld,' I reply, pointedly.

This does nothing to ease his nerves and he plucks a lime from a nearby branch so he can turn it in his hands. 'You also know things. Things we wouldn't want to become public.'

He's either talking about his own identity, or the fact Aïdes has been stealing and murdering girls for centuries and nobody has done anything about it. Probably both. I glare at him in response, Mama's face filling my head.

'My point is,' he continues, 'we want you to be comfortable. Happy. Please, tell us what we can do so this can be achieved.'

Is he *bribing* us?

'We need to talk about Mama—' I begin.

'Icari, the main reason I removed my wings and became the High Priest was so I could monitor women with dual Callings. I was horrified when Daeda, the woman I loved, revealed she had more than one gift. I begged her to keep it a secret, even though my duty was to . . . to . . . make her disappear. I even ended it with her in the hope that she would seek a simpler life.' He gazes at the sky, his eyes glassy. 'Then she met your papa and her need to heal, well, it seems it was unquenchable. I avoided removing her for years, Icari. *Years.* Then Aïdes snatched several women with dual gifts in quick succession, and I knew she was next.' He holds my eye and his handsome face drops. 'I feared she'd be the one he was looking for. I'm so sorry. If I—'

I stop him with a raised hand. 'I'm not looking for an apology. I'm looking for a solution.'

'A solution?'

'Yes. A way of preventing the Samael from stealing women again.'

He exhales slowly through his nose. 'With respect, we found a solution.'

'A solution that doesn't involve murder.' My voice comes out a little loud, yet I refuse to soften it. 'From now on, instead of banning dual Callings and forcing women to hide their powers, we celebrate them. You publicly request they come forward so the Illios can protect them. Sephie and I will announce our dual gifts at the same time, and this should offer some encouragement after a lifetime of fear.'

Whether or not he likes the idea, he presses his hands

together and nods. 'A more practical solution. Imagine the powers we will harness.'

'A more *compassionate* solution.'

He sniffs the lime, a feeble attempt to hide his embarrassment. 'Yes, yes, of course.'

And whilst I've got him, I quickly add, 'And Papa would like a bigger sanatorium, and all prisoners should receive medical attention and embalming rights, regardless of their crimes.'

After a tense pause, he nods, then he touches his headdress as though reminding himself he's the one in charge.

Hiding a smile, I watch my sister through the leaves. She's waving her arms around in an animated fashion, her eyes wide as she looms over an awestruck Ruari. I imagine she's reached the part when she awoke the brides of Aïdes from their slumber.

'Why didn't you kill Sephie?' I ask. The question surprises even me. 'When you realized she had two Callings at the Illumination Ritual, why didn't you kill her? Surely you were worried Aïdes would use her to conquer the surface.'

He sighs. 'Believe it or not, I don't enjoy killing people, Icari. I'd hoped we could keep her gifts a secret. Everyone knew about your mama, but not about Sephie.' He releases a sad chuckle. 'It was foolish really. Aïdes knows everything about those with shadows in their blood – Sephie. Me. Your demon, Caszeil.'

His name is both a blow to my chest and a breath of joy.

Uriel's face hardens. 'And of course, it turns out he had Madame filling in the gaps.'

My fists clench at the mention of Madame. She wasn't

trying to save Mama from the pyre because it was the right thing to do; she was trying to keep her alive for the devil. When she told me Mama was too special to die, she meant it, but in the worst way possible.

'There's one other thing that's bothering me,' I say.

He raises his brow.

'Why did the Samael steal all of the alchemy students?' I ask. 'If they were looking for me too, why not steal all the Healers or Embalmers?'

'Alchemists can be fearsome opponents in battle – more so than Healers or Embalmers. Aïdes wanted us weak before his conquest. Besides, they thought you'd be easy to find.'

The boughs part and my sister's face is smiling at us. 'Icari, there is someone I must see. Do you mind finishing the tale? I got to the point where the Samael and the Divine Shadow chased us through the Underworld – it's your bit really.'

I know exactly who she wants to see, so I return her grin and nod.

'Just go to her.'

64

SEPHIE

I push through the crowds, dodging the congratulatory hands, and head to the dormitories, where I suspect she'll be. My time in the Underworld must have awoken something in me, and I can hear the dead whispering from the catacombs, but I ignore them. We can become acquainted at a later date. There's only one friend I'm interested in right now.

Talia sits on the edge of her bed, staring into space and wringing her hands. She sees me and her face swings between emotions, but when I smile, it gives her permission to run at me. I sweep her up into an embrace and inhale the scent of her.

'It's you,' she whispers into my neck.

'It's me.'

'I watched you arrive,' she says as I release her.

I'd forgotten the precise colour of her eyes, deep brown and flecked with the leaves that trail into the Nubi river in summer. I get this sudden urge to trace her freckles with my finger.

'Why didn't you come to see me?' I ask.

'I wasn't sure if you'd want me to after –' she bites her lip – 'you know.'

'Don't be silly, I always want to see you.'

She moves like she may hug me again, then changes her mind and settles for taking my hand.

'You're cold,' she says.

'Only my hands.'

She smiles. Her mouth really is a rosebud.

'Icari told me how you helped her build the wings,' I say. 'She said you were a woman possessed – you even knocked Ziris out with a skull.'

She laughs. 'That was just for fun.'

An awkward pause hovers between us; then we both start talking at once.

'I hear you raised an army of the dead,' she says, at the exact same time as I say, 'I missed you.'

We fall silent. The sound of students returning to their lives jars in my ears. Icari and I have been through something so monumental, it's hard to imagine everyone else just carrying on. I've changed so much, yet the world persists.

Talia sighs. 'I missed you too.'

Another pause. I'm suddenly painfully aware I'm wearing a wedding dress splattered with Aïdes's blood.

She must catch my downward glance, because she points at my dress. 'What's all the black stuff?'

'Pfft,' I say, waving my hand dismissively. 'I got into a fight with a jar of treacle.'

She gives me one of her throaty laughs. 'No, seriously. What is it?'

I cringe. 'It's the devil's blood.'

'Really?'

'Really.'

Not an ounce of revulsion emerges on her face and she pulls me in for another embrace. I savour her warmth as it soaks into me. Not long ago, I thought I'd never feel heat again, let alone Talia's heat. But something is missing: that hard little grain of metal hanging from her neck. Her necklace.

'Where's your locket?' I ask, embarrassed by the hope in my voice.

'I went to see Mariam whilst you were away.'

'You did?'

'Yes.' She glances at the floor. 'I returned the necklace.'

I study her face, almost afraid to believe what she's about to say. The evening sun slants through the window and sets the red strands in her dark hair ablaze. Her skin glows, fawn-brown and swathed with freckles. I have never wanted anyone so badly, and the thought of almost getting her, only to have her whipped away at the last moment, is as bad as facing a life in the Underworld.

And then she says the words I long to hear: 'I told her I'd met someone else.'

'You have?' A side-smile creeps up my face.

'Yes.'

'Who?'

She moves a strand of hair from my face. 'I think you know.'

'Does she smell of hell and have bits of bone in her hair?'

'She is sorely in need of a wash, yes.'

We both begin to laugh. Our breath mingles as we close the small distance between us. We kiss. She is soft and warm and tastes of new beginnings.

Suddenly, she pulls away, fear flickering in her green eyes. 'Will he come for you again? The Divine Shadow, I mean. I couldn't bear to lose you—'

I silence her with another kiss and we tumble on to her bed.

'He wouldn't dare,' I whisper into her mouth. 'He wouldn't bloody dare.'

65

ICARI

Several weeks have passed since returning to the citadel. My classmates have accepted my wings, especially since I started flying them over the oasis between classes, and Principal Healer made me a larger workspace to stop me knocking the utensils from the benches with my feathers. And I can now visit Papa with ease – and my new friends Yiannis and Erastus, and the babe I rescued on the day of the raid, whom they adopted. Yet in spite of this, I am mostly sorrow; my blood runs thick with grief and my bones creak with loss. It isn't just that I miss Caszeil, and I miss him with every fibre of my being. It's knowing that he wasn't embalmed.

His soul won't live on.

After evening prayer, I walk back to our bedchamber with Xenia. She's chatting excitedly, telling me about a new potion she's discovered that quells rashes, and I'm nodding along, pretending my mind isn't in a garden in the Underworld.

We find Sephie and Talia lying together on a bed, fully clothed but whispering and giggling as they so often do. Sephie wears the robes of an Alchemist today, though yesterday she chose to be an Embalmer; we've already seen a huge shift in attitudes towards women with dual Callings. Sometimes, I help wrap the dead, and I'm welcomed with smiles as opposed to suspicion. And Talia has an easier life too, for it is now common knowledge that it was never the Farlanders who stole the women of the Sunlands – it was Aïdes. Though she insists she still reserves the right to turn a man to stone with the merest flick of her eye. But she is joking. I think.

'Icari,' Sephie says. 'There's something I want to show you before bedtime.' She holds out her hand. 'You need to fly me there.'

I'm exhausted; bereavement steals most of my energy and I long to crawl into bed, wrap my wings around me, and lose myself to dreams of silver skin and slate-grey eyes. Yet Sephie's face is so full of hope and excitement, I sigh and take her hand, just grateful that her eyes are entirely clear. Indeed, she hasn't taken devil wing or called on her gifts to numb her pain since returning from hell. She even talks of Mama sometimes.

'Be careful,' Talia calls as we balance on the window ledge.

'We'll be back soon,' Sephie replies.

I glide over the oasis and high above the Redlands. I will never tire of feeling the wind in my feathers and the sensation of weightlessness, like the sky is in fact an infinite lake. Sephie guides me over dunes and lizard-studded rocks, over lazy cacti and wild donkeys, and by the time we reach the highest dune in the Redlands, Mother Moon is cut from coral amongst the stars.

Sephie settles on the summit and pats the ground next to her. 'Come. The sand is still warm.'

I sit beside her and gaze upwards. Mama once told me there are more stars in the sky than grains of sand in the desert. I never believed it, until now.

'Why are we here?' I ask.

'Since being in the Underworld, I can tune into the dead whenever I please.'

I must grimace, aware of how she avoids death, because she chuckles and says, 'It's not so bad – I'm never alone, and death has lost its sting now I can hear corpses reciting tavern ditties.'

I laugh. 'Tavern ditties?'

'I add a new one to my collection every day.' Gathering her knees into her chest, she nods towards the stars. 'See that new cluster, right there – so many stars it looks like a smudge of paint?'

'Yes.'

'Well, sometimes, I can hear them whispering.'

'The stars?'

She nods. 'And that smudge of paint is the brides of Aïdes. They finally made it to Mother Moon.'

I think back to the army of skeletons and corpses, not a single one salted or wrapped.

'That makes no sense,' I say. 'Their bodies weren't embalmed.'

'A girl who grew wings does not get to tell me what makes sense.'

A smile spreads across my face, both at her flippant remark and the knowledge that the women Aïdes disposed of so cruelly finally get their happy ending.

'Good for you,' I whisper to the stars.

'And that one.' She slides her finger to the left. 'The one beside Mother Moon – that's Mama.'

I exhale. Hard. Emotions overwhelm me and a tear slips down my cheek. Sephie throws an arm around my shoulders; her skin brushes my feathers, and I feel her love leaching into me like warm water.

'She says that you really are a bird,' Sephie says.

I start to laugh, tears catching in my breath and spraying on to the sands. I saw Mama transmute into butterflies, I saw her dance towards the sky, but only now do I truly believe she made it. My skin can't hold all the joy and it overflows into my wings, causing them to glow all the brighter.

'And that low-hanging one right there.' She moves her finger across the night so she's almost touching the horizon. 'Well, I reckon you can guess who that is.'

I know which star she's pointing to, for it has a silvery hue when compared to the others.

My wings open in greeting.

'How is that possible?' I manage to gasp. 'He was a demon.'

'Not when he died,' Sephie whispers. 'Remember?'

I nod, for I remember every second of every day. 'Can you hear him too?'

'Sometimes.'

'What does he say?'

'Not a lot – he's kind of dull.'

Laughter bursts from my mouth and I nudge her playfully in the ribs.

She sighs and squeezes my hand. 'He says he loves you and he's glad you've kept your wings.' Her eyes settle on my face.

'He hopes you will love again.'

I breathe in the night, letting the tears weave down my face. 'Maybe. One day. But for now, I am enough.'

I fold my wings around us, for even the desert grows cool at night, and my feathers sparkle in the black. Gold and white. The good and the bad braided together so I become a living patchwork of humanity.

After a pause, Sephie asks, 'Do you think they will tell our story for years to come?'

'Yes. I think they will.'

We study the stars in silence, remembering all that has been, and considering all that will come.

Eventually, I stand, shaking out my feathers as if I were a wet dog. 'If we hurry, we can see Papa before he beds down.'

'Promise me you won't do that twisting thing when you fly again,' Sephie says as she dusts down her robes. 'You know how I hate it.'

'Pardon?' I reply, my face feigning innocence, my voice smiling.

'You heard me,' she grumbles.

'I'm not sure that I did.'

'Icari,' she says, a warning note in her voice.

I throw her a grin, wrap her in my arms, and spin towards the stars.

ACKNOWLEDGEMENTS

This book is very special to me. I started writing it in 2018 when I was full of feminist rage, and the idea of a girl growing wings seemed both beautiful and necessary. Since then, I've fallen in love, had another wonderful child and negotiated long Covid, and this book has been a form of therapy for me, exploring the glorious, messy complexity that is life: the light and the dark. I hope you've enjoyed reading it as much – or even a fraction as much – as I've enjoyed writing it. I'm still full of feminist rage. You can probably tell.

My wonderful partner, Simon Rainbow, has been with me through most of the writing, the many drafts and redrafts, so thank you, my love, for always listening to my endless book-speak and for caring about Icari and Sephie as much as I do. And thank you for your constant compassion, your gentle manner and your never-ending humour; you have been both the gravity and the light in my world since we reunited on that serendipitous day at Comic Con.

Thank you to my darling family. Ellie, Charlie and Fern, my gorgeous kids, being your mum is an honour and a privilege and I love you all dearly. To my mum and dad, thank you for always being there with your open door, endless chats, babysitting service, roast dinners and warmth. You are living proof that love is action. And thank you to my dad, who raised me on myths and legends, and made the works of Homer and Ovid as familiar as they are wondrous. To my dear cousin, Lucy Fisher, the strongest person I know. Thank you for lending me your strength when I've needed it the most, I am blessed to have you in my life.

I consider myself very lucky to have so many wonderful friends and women in my life who I'd like to thank for their constant support. There are too many to list here, but a special thanks to Heather Thompson, Jenny Hargreaves, Laura Williams, Catherine Field, Sam Lloyd, Helen Spencer, Jenny Banham, Natali Simmonds and Julia Mackley. Love you guys!

Thank you to Kesia Lupo, my fabulous editor. Your wisdom, guidance and creativity have helped shape this book into what it is today, and helped shape me as a writer. I'm so grateful to have worked with you on this and other books. I will miss you terribly, but wish you all the luck and joy in your new adventure. To everyone at Chicken House: Barry Cunningham, for his ongoing support and wisdom; Olivia Jeggo and Jazz Bartlett Love for their brilliant marketing know-how; to Laura Myers, Laura Smythe, Elinor Bagenal and Rachel Leyshon, and of course, to Rachel Hickman for her work on the cover. I'm so sorry if I've missed anyone out – but thank you to this wonderful publishing house for making my dreams come true, not once, but four times. A big thank-you to the authenticity reader for their insightful and helpful comments, and to Veronica, copy-editor, for her hard work and helpful input. And a whopping thank-you to Andrew Davis for the sublime front cover. One day I may stop looking at it!

I'd also like to thank my lovely agent, Laura Williams at Greene and Heaton, for helping focus my random brain and for guiding and supporting me throughout my writing journey.

To my fabulous readers, thank you so much for your feedback and support: Jenny Hargreaves, Helen Spencer, Alice Yates, Isobel Yates, Lily Gilbert, Gill and Len Waterworth (Mum and Dad), Lucy Fisher, Shanna Alderliesten, and last but certainly not least, my writing Yoda and dear friend, Natali Simmonds. And thank you to all the lovely authors who took the time to read and provide feedback or an endorsement – I'm hugely grateful.

Respect and love to everyone suffering with long Covid and/or ME/CFS, who grow a pair of invisible wings every morning just to get through the day. You are all legends, and one day, even if there isn't a cure, I know that people will come, as I have, to see how much you suffer and how brave you are.

And a shout-out to the Psychologists with long Covid group. I've so valued this safe and validating space to share experiences. Keep on feeling those feelings and holding that hope lightly. Thank you, lovely humans!

And finally, to you, dear reader, who surely deserves a cuppa or a glass of something for getting this far (though I have it on good authority you should steer clear of the pomegranate juice). May you face your demons with compassion, or summon an army of vengeful zombie brides, whatever works!

THE FANDOM by Anna Day

Violet loves *The Gallows Dance* – like every fan, she dreams of being a part of her favourite story.

But the dream becomes a nightmare at Comic-Con, when Violet and her friends are catapulted into the *Gallows Dance* for real. Trapped in a violent, dangerous dystopia, Violet and her friends throw the original plot off course by accidentally killing its hero, Rose.

There's only one way to survive in this world of thorns: Violet must fill Rose's shoes, put the plot back on track, and get out fast.

Compulsive, intricate and genre-busting:
I am most definitely a fan.
KIRAN MILLWOOD HARGRAVE

Paperback, ISBN 978-1-910655-67-2, £7.99 • ebook, ISBN 978-1-911077-43-5, £7.99